Martina Flawd

DANIL RUDOY

ISBN: 9781718066618

Cover design by Ivan Ustinov

Dedicated to my parents because, without them,
I would have never become any of this

Table of Contents

Sex is a subterfuge given to humanity to make it accept the world as the status quo.

UNIFORMITY

I

Abstract Intro

Do you know what it is to be God? To know what no one else knows? To see what's hidden from everyone? To anticipate what others won't feel even post factum?

It's devilishly hilarious. So much so that nothing more hilarious exists.

Planets orbit stars, but they think they only rotate around themselves. We notice only what we want to see, failing to even realize it's possible to want something else. The fact that we want itself justifies our very wanting, and the satisfaction of obtaining it seals the deal.

I used to be just like everyone else. Of course, I thought there was an abyss separating me from the others. Seriously: they were always trying to screw each other over while being nauseatingly polite, and I helped them while cursing cruelly. They had no idea what the abstract was, and I recited poetry to them, trying to explain that our world is but a lopsided replica of something magnificent. They despised and dreamt of destroying those who surpassed them in what they deemed important, and I fell in love with such people, striving to emulate their strengths.

I was absolutely sure I had nothing in common with anyone else except for cellular biology, but I was wrong. The aforementioned trifles, along with a million others, are submerged in a common denominator that levels almost everyone. I unearthed it by accident while reading; the book is still in print and may end up in your hands at some point. If this does happen, however, keep in mind that, to understand it, you'll need not intelligence but unbending intent. I didn't have it either, but I had already grown so disappointed in life that I considered dying. This sounds like a banal verdict, I know; yet some never do what they should until cornered. And when they are, they reveal such strengths that one can't help wondering: where the hell had they been before?

What was I talking about? Oh, right: you are waiting to learn what makes people alike. I'll tell you, gladly, but later: right now, I need to take care of this young lady of about twenty-two in the BA uniform before her pretty face bursts from spite.

"Sir, this is a first-class registration desk," she said in a tone of professional superiority.

"I know," I said with a smile, handing her my ticket.

She looked at it and blushed. I would have felt sorry, but my treacherous memory was already running a twelve-year-old movie: one where I, a tired guy on yet another red-eye BA flight that night, bumped into a stewardess of no more than forty years of age who wore the same perfume as a good half of the female students at my college. It was my fault (I was dreaming about one of those students and walked into her), but before I had a chance to apologize she smiled at me as if she weren't on duty, and I felt sad that this woman had to spend the rest of her life without me in it.

The check-in clerk finally produced my boarding pass, issuing unnecessary directions and avoiding my eyes. Her initial reaction was predictable: my washed-out Canadian tuxedo with its fringe of threads on the worn-out cuffs hardly became a first-class passenger: I looked more like a contractor who hadn't been doing well over the last few years. By the way, have you ever noticed that, the more you think about clothing, the less social inequality bothers you? Frankly, I prefer silk and cashmere, but how could I have dressed in either while anticipating an encounter with a woman who had painstakingly ignored my existence for the last decade?

You know, if you belong to the tribe of sceptics, cynics, and materialists, you won't profit from my tale at all. What I write about here won't even make you laugh, so please: leave before you regret having wasted your time. In order to like my story, you need: one, imagination; two, trust; and, three … but let's take care of the second requirement first. See, unlike the average literary hero, who never existed, I am actually *experiencing* the events I'm describing, so I cannot dismiss them as an accidental opacity in the swollen psyche of a stoned writer. In other words, while you can afford the luxury of an indifferent bystander observing the whole thing out of the corner of his eye while picking his nose, I am doomed to the absolute reality of everything you are reading. For me it's as urgent as for you … well, what's urgent for your right now? So, to dig me, you're gonna have to put yourself in my shoes, whether you like it or not.

Dear ladies, I'm sure you understood that the previous paragraph was meant for men, those strange creatures with the terrible habit of taking a literary hero literally. But we, of course, know that if the title of a novel consists of but one name, it is the bearer of that name who will be the protagonist, even if her story is being told by someone else. Let us sail away, then, and may God save you from all the imperfections of my inimitable Martina.

I did not want to call her name too soon ... But perhaps it's time already, and to think otherwise would only spell vanity and vexation of spirit. Why did I not want to? For me, it's like a joker I can play whenever I want but that loses a bit of its eccentric magic each time it is looked upon by a judgmental eye. See, I have no choice but to take you for good people, regardless of whether you are. By the way, just between you and me: are you?

In informal letters, such questions are followed by emoticons, but since this novel is not epistolary, I'll stick to words, leaving to you the freedom of divining their emotional content. I used to think that the author had to deliver the very sense he intended himself; but eventually I realized it was impossible for me because my fundamental values didn't overlap with those of ordinary people. I have another nasty trait: I can't explain things that are obvious to me and, as if by evil design, these are the matters that strike others as the most abstruse.

But enough of this touchy torture: I already owe you as many seconds as you took to get here from the word "three," unless you aren't after the bare plot and are enjoying my snide tone. In that case, metaphorically speaking, you're in for many an opportunity to pause, close your eyes and smack your lips, savoring the wonderful warmth in your sternum: this is how I react to reading a passage that is so brilliant I wish I wrote it myself. However, if you aren't enjoying yourself this far and, in fact, can't wait for the narrative to get back to the point, whatever that might be, I hate to warn you, but what you've seen thus far is nothing compared to the rest. This novel isn't so much about events as what people feel about them; so, if you don't like what you've read so far, going further is completely pointless. In fact, it could be harmful, so enter at your own risk! And if in the end you feel unfulfilled, remember that I had honestly encouraged you to exit right now.

Martina and I at Atlantic

Anybody still here? You must be waiting to learn about the common denominator, that invisible glue pervading the atmosphere we share on Earth? My advice is: don't think about it and, God forbid, don't try to guess what it is. You won't—not because you can't, but because the correct answer is irrational. Remember that shrewd observation that you can't find the right answer to an improperly formulated question? Well, here, in order to find the answer, you have to take everything that gave your life meaning and toss it into the garbage. Care to hear what you'd be chasing? A ghostly chance to get something that won't give you any advantage in your everyday life. This is nonsense, don't you agree: this is just crap that would make you ridiculous even before your dumb neighbor who somehow qualified for a car loan and bought a rusty piece of junk that he is now riding as smugly as though he were the master of life itself.

I must have been born with that ability, and it must also be responsible for my falling in love with Martina. Such was her essence: she constantly made me re-evaluate things I had taken for granted—and if you think you can get used to that, you are wrong. Although, certainly, the first time does remain the most memorable. A seventeen-year-old virgin who worshipped women and desired nothing more than to be intimate with one of their beautiful number, I had just covered three thousand miles shuffling planes and buses and was arriving at the United World College of the Atlantic, an international boarding school where I was to spend the next two years. Going numb from the imminent need to make myself understood in English, I nevertheless shored up my spirit and declared my name distinctly from the top stair of the bus (as per protocol). The next moment, I was drowning in a tsunami of sound, the assembled crowd roaring and hammering spoons against saucepans (also as per protocol). Little did I know that this tribute was but a prelude.

I don't know what the others were thinking, but I for one was busy as hell. I was done scanning the crowd and now dissolved into it, noting every attractive girl. Of which there were many. I was distracted by my new roommate, one of the three other fellas I was gonna have to share my room with, a caring second-year who had come to pick me up. He reminded me that the bus's belly still held my luggage, something I'd totally forgotten about while greedily breathing in the humid Welsh evening wind. The driver was already diving after the suitcases with an agility remarkable for someone his age, possibly looking to escape the cadent cacophony. He hadn't made it to mine yet, although I could already see its green side looming from behind someone's purple monster, and, celebrating the fact that it had not been lost during the long journey, I took another deep breath and turned back to the door ... only to all but freeze, go dumb and deaf, and liquify into something incredibly, inextricably, and simply sublime.

The half a second that I watched her before she said her name was like a punch in the solar plexus. When I heard the timbre of her voice, it was akin to the slash of a razor to the throat. And when, a second later, I registered that her name was Martina, I could compare it only to having been shot in the heart.

After yet another explosion of saucepans, my roomie delicately enquired whether any of the extracted bags belonged to me, but he might as well have been interrogating a corpse. I was in a parallel universe, staring at her exchanging kisses with a brassy bad gal, a likely equivalent of my own roommate, who merrily grabbed her as soon as her shoes hit the ground. The color of those shoes blew me away, and not because any detail of the image of their owner would: I truly had never seen such a perfect shade of blue anywhere, let alone on someone's feet. But I had no time to think about that because, being led by her brassy companion, my angel was walking toward me, her shoes glowing in the slightly overgrown emerald grass over which her light gray pants were gliding gracefully.

Stumbling, I nevertheless conjured up the strength to produce a friendly smile. Imagine my surprise when this feat slipped by not only unappreciated but entirely unnoticed: she passed by as if a concrete column stood in my place. Stunned, I gaped at her back, her stately shoulder almost touching mine with the edge of her burgundy cardigan while she waited for her two orange suitcases to be set in front of her; each of those guys had an even brighter orange tag bearing a single word—"Heavy"—which looked gorgeous to me. I was almost done formulating a phrase with which I was going to offer to help carry those bags to her house (wherever, goddamn it, it was!) when the brassy girl produced two sprightly, handsome boys, each built noticeably stronger than I. With an authoritative sweep of her finger, the nail extravagantly painted, she pointed at the bags and took off. And when Martina followed, leaving a whiff of her perfume behind, a sudden gust raised a tendril of her hair, and, as if to mock me, brushed it under my nose like a match against the box: subtly, yet insidiously, enough to make me sneeze.

The sneeze woke me up: I was alone in a foreign country and had no idea what to do. So, I grabbed my suitcase and prepared for anything. Alas, the roomie led me in the opposite direction from that taken by my love (yes, it was love: and at first sight, too), leaving me with no hope that we'd be sharing a house. I was trying to persuade myself that it was alright—even advantageous on a tiny campus like this—but something didn't sit well, gnawing at my consciousness, which was already bruised from my inability to understand most of the speech pouring in from every direction. It was only when I reached my new house, a shabby two-story construction named Sunley—which, as I was proudly told on reaching the doorstep, was the newest on campus—I realized that I had spent three and a half hours on the bus with Molly without noticing her once.

While seemingly implausible, this was an implacable fact. Naturally, it wasn't on the campus that I had begun girl-spotting: I had done so as soon as I'd reached Heathrow's Terminal 3, where the first-years like myself were meeting their chaperones. This being my default behavioral program, I was convinced I could not have missed her during the two hours of waiting for the bus itself, which meant she must have hopped on right before departure. But I had deliberately sat on the side of the luggage compartment and looked around later, so I could not fathom how she had managed, one, to slip in unnoticed, and two, to remain so throughout the entire ride.

Perhaps my confusion may seem orchestrated by the fantasy of a naive boy finding himself alone in unusual circumstances, but this story, like a drop of water, is a microcosm of our entire relationship—one in which Molly invariably had me beat, pulling off what I deemed impossible. Crushing my aspirations time after time, she did it as if it were natural, oblivious to how profoundly I was altered as a result. Alas, those changes were hurtful much more often than not.

When, after long, exhausting attempts to orchestrate a meeting with her, a friend of mine who dug the politics of our student society told me that my low social status left her with only a couple of ways to treat me, of which ignoring me was the most humane, I was stunned. First of all, personally, I rank people by their personal qualities; secondly, the college had brainwashed us about tolerance from day one, and I'd completely bought it; thirdly, I thought the others saw me as I saw myself: as a great guy. Lacking a better explanation, I assumed I was not expressing myself clearly enough. I had reason to suspect so: I still lacked confidence when speaking English, so I spent most of my free time in my room with a dictionary. Then, when I thought I was ready, I threw myself into the vortex of campus life, which culminated in weekend nights at the so-called Sosh, a shabby disco bar with perennially mediocre music. The others might have gone there to have fun, but I was working my ass off, studying body language, learning to understand English despite the loud music, and keeping myself entertained during utterly pointless conversations. I won't dwell on what it cost me, but at some point I thought that I'd improved enough, and that the image I was presenting to the world was more or less reflective of the truth. Imagine my surprise when, having serendipitously ended up in the right place at the right time, I caught Molly spitefully parodying all the manners that I'd believed reflected my best qualities.

The more, the worse. After the campus had become fully acquainted with me (during some international cultural symposium I'd recited a poem in my mother tongue, which of course no one had understood), I was given an audience at my paramour's. Despite taking place in the dining hall in view of a multitude of unnecessary witnesses, it culminated in an obnoxiously intellectual discussion of literature and art, eventually extending to her house's day room. But what I had expected to culminate in my triumphant rise to prominence as a connoisseur of fine matters morphed into a cruel battering. With a haughty smile, she heard me out before declaring that the value of a book is determined not by its quality but by the opinions of its readers, and that the most worthy novel, if it doesn't sell, might as well not exist.

I was shocked: so much so, in fact, that I had to spend several nights on the cliffs listening to the waves crashing onto the shore just to offset the storm raging in me. Naturally, I wouldn't have agreed with her even if she had offered to take my virginity, but it was clear that her lickspittle suite weren't trying to win her favor or put more pressure on me, but genuinely agreed with her opinions. This meant that the world I inhabited was even more different from my own than I'd feared, and my prospects were akin to those of the waves being dashed against the cliffs a few yards below.

I don't want to dredge up more examples of her prickly conduct because I don't want to relive that nightmare again. If you only knew how many times she'd struck me dumb by meeting a gesture or a phrase I'd dropped as a paragon of elegance with arctic sarcasm. And closely as I watched her, I saw no artifice. Yet one occasion demands mention: when she kissed me after the graduation ball, a minute before I was to board the bus to leave AC for the next ten years. At that moment, I was in a state best described as catatonic, and I was not looking for her in the crowd, knowing that hers was the morning bus; this is why I was stunned when I saw her nearby, right at the entrance of the bus: fresh, majestic, and absolutely incongruent with the whiny mess we found ourselves in. When our eyes met, she didn't say a word but came up and kissed me, putting more tenderness into that kiss than I had expected her to have for anyone, let alone me, before letting me go and walking away with an impenetrable indifference, as if returning home from the fish store. A minute later, when I ascended the top stair to turn and scan the still-thick crowd, she was gone, and I realized that Martina was a woman so impossible that she simply could not exist.

In the Waiting Lounge

Suddenly the air, smelling like a mixture of still-sanguine hopes, instant gratification, and the exorbitant price paid therefor, was stirred by a vague feeling that brought me back to the present. For the last thirty minutes, I had been submerged in my laptop, typing this novel. In the waiting lounge, I sat right by the window, far from the madding crowd milling around the duty-free shops, so I needed a moment to return to ordinary reality. I hope you aren't too upset by me skipping over how I got here? I sure could tell you that the customs officer was a cyclops or a three-headed monster who had singled me out from all the other passengers for a special inspection, revealing to the appalled public (long since accustomed to monsters and cyclopes) my best collection of fishnets, but why hurry? We'll get to the contents of my valise soon enough; for now, suffice to say that it contained my laptop: a long obsolete model of a long obsolete brand which wouldn't fetch more than two hundred bucks if sold online. Yet the machine possessed three key advantages. First, its keyboard was backlit; second, its battery lasted forever, and third, despite its wide screen, it was as light as the Sunday awakening of a teetotaler. Thus, we never parted: I took the laptop everywhere in case I felt creative; and today, once my gate had been located, I switched my focus to my staunch friend. Yet one paradox of writing was that it sharpened my sixth sense, so when I had the notion that something was up, I didn't doubt that was so.

Pretending to rest my eyes, I cautiously scanned the crowd. It suited the flight and sounded slightly more English than American, owing perhaps to the Britishness of the vessel. Here were uncouth students used to flying over the ocean since early childhood, dignified married couples creased with cared wrinkles and harboring thoughts of retirement, young specialists of all possible professions who thought their best was still ahead. Perhaps Nabokov would have drawn a million unexpected parallels from these folks, noting peculiarities that would make you roll on the floor with laughter, but my mind hadn't yet recovered from the decade-deep dive into memory, so no worthy associations came to it. Besides, I have little interest in appearance: so little, in fact, that even describing Martina is a challenge. I really don't care what kind of opalescent gleam illuminates her wrist when it is lit by the beams of the sun setting into the ocean: I only care about how it makes me feel. Consider this: there must be a type of person, man or woman, whom you find maddeningly attractive; yet every once in a while you meet someone who has nothing to do with that type but still fills your abdomen with a swam of variegated butterflies. So, let's not be distracted by insignificant details like the purple alligator on the brown leather bag of that hopeless vixen of no more than thirty years whose lips practically vanished from her face when our eyes met, and focus on the crux because we have a lot more ...

And then it happened: when I forgot why I had turned away from the laptop and was staring at the next exit's electronic display, which was sheepishly admitting a ten-minute delay in the flight to L.A. On the left-hand side, where floated a whole milky nebula of passengers, my peripheral vision caught a gesture so different from the rest that it took an enormous effort of will not to twitch like an epileptic but rather turn slowly and by only the smallest degree necessary to get a better view without giving myself away.

There are people in this world who are naturally gracious, and they often go through their entire lives without having a clue. Take this lady of about twenty-seven who was responsible for the hand wave that had fortuitously caught my eye. If someone had asked her right now what she was doing, she'd have been puzzled and responded that she was taking a sip of water (her throat supposedly having been dried by the tempting air of the duty-free shops). It would have never occurred to her that that act, full of mundane necessity, carried more charm than the rest of the airport combined.

The irony of life is remarkable: we spend our whole lives with ourselves, and yet we have no idea what we really are. A constant object of male attention (although the male part here is represented by good boys who don't know how to approach a girl but do it anyway), this lady was used to the idea of being attractive, but without those very boys she'd begin losing confidence rather quickly, inflating her real and imaginary flaws to monstrous proportions ... But, to be fair, I couldn't care less about proportions at the moment. No: I was experiencing what I call grounding the ethereal body on the point of power. In other words, Lady 2-7 (as I decided to call her until she offered an alternative) had shaken the reservoir containing the strongest of my emotions, and in the current context this was nothing short of a sweet curse.

Rules of Attraction

Wanna know the main problem of a guy who is too fastidious about women? It is rare that he wants to fuck anyone, even when he wants to fuck a lot, but when he does meet someone he wants to fuck, he loses his mind. All that other women have not received over the years is given to his favored one in a single carte-blanche: all at once, without compromise. But nature cares for nothing more deeply than for equilibrium, so the blank check winds up uncashed. That paradox vexed me for a long time: I was practically running up the wall solving it. Then I did, and couldn't accept the truth. Then I searched for more evidence, and when I'd gathered plenty, I stopped thinking about it. Then I accused myself of cowardice, analyzed everything again, and had to admit that I was right. Alas, none of it didn't make me feel any better.

Should I share? I honestly don't know. See, this is super-personal stuff, like a forbidden sexual practice you can engage in only with those whom you completely trust. The fact that we don't know each other and are unlikely to meet doesn't change anything because shame is what a person feels before him- or herself. But now that I brought it up, leaving the subject would liken me to a scared ostrich sticking his head in the sand. By the way, that's a myth: in reality, ostriches only bend their heads to the ground so that it's easier to run.

Before I begin turning my soul inside out, let's answer a simple question: what do women want? I have heard the best minds of mankind break over it without any success, and I've always been surprised by that, since the answer seems very simple to me: what a woman wants is to be the only woman beloved by the man (or woman) she loves. And this is where my confusion began: my beloved women, copying each other to the letter, invariably neglected me in favor of men for whom they could never be the only ones, even theoretically, while I offered them love in its most unadulterated form. This meant that the cornerstone lay not in *their* desire for singularity but in the fact that these women did not consider *me* desirable.

Well, some did—but I can't think about them without self-irony. Although I'd probably remember Martina in the same way. There is something endlessly vulgar in the realization of love, and I don't mean sex. Sex, if it's good, works as a veil, covering the ugly earthliness. It is only maniac couples that escape the mundane, but I doubted that Molly and I would make one. To keep the flame going, you have to recharge away from each other, and for that to happen the two of you must be on the same wavelength. We were perpetually on different ones, so our best outcome would be to burn out in a series of compulsive explosions, each causing a lot of trouble to everyone involved ... although, in any case, our sex life would still be beyond reproach.

But I got distracted again, didn't I? This crazy sexual thing, always looking for ways to screw with the honest man's head! When I saw that I wasn't desirable to Molly, I had no choice but to become so. To do that, I needed to understand the mechanics of male attractiveness and the female drive. Having analyzed the entire cohort of guys with whom she was in romantic involvements of various degrees, I broke them down into three categories. The first comprised the rich: those whose parents had money, power, and status. I had none of these, but when I learned that the illegal cigarette trade flourished on campus, I made a quick arrangement with my folks back home and was soon receiving a steady flow of parcels. Due to the low cost of such merchandise in my homeland and its surprisingly high quality compared to that being offered by my competition, I made a lot of money and could consequently go all in when it came to chocolate, alcohol, potato chips and other indispensable groceries, all of which I gladly shared with anyone who wanted them. I am positive those goodies, liquid and otherwise, made it to my dear on several occasions, along with rumors of a level of generosity hardly befitting someone on a full scholarship but, much to my relief, this did not change her attitude: I wouldn't have taken it lightly if she'd started liking me for candy, let alone vodka.

The second (and also narrower) category was comprised of those with leading-man looks. Before Atlantic, I thought I had it; then I realized the physique was an indispensable part of the package. I developed some discipline, started going to the gym three times a week, and spent some of my black-market money on protein-rich foods (AC was stingy about feeding us: less was spent on our daily rations than in the average British prison), but I gained only a few pounds. I was incensed: I could win any realistic bet on pull-ups and push-ups, but my muscles remained thin. Then again, my dear would certainly have lost some of her shine if I'd caught her admiring my six-pack instead of my personality.

The third—and the smallest—category was made up of boys with charisma. And that was the most challenging territory for me. I could accept that my socioeconomic background disqualified me for some women. I could even agree that my appearance was less than irresistible. But, goddamn it, I could not believe that I was not the most charismatic guy any of those girls had ever met. It took me years of self-analysis to understand why, but when I finally did, I saw that the kind of treatment I had received from Martina was completely predictable.

My fundamental problem had been that I was a man who gave up his status to make others feel good about themselves. Noble though this may be in intent, it leads to a major misunderstanding of your persona. People (especially women) are unlikely to see the magnanimity of your soul: rather, they will assume you are a wimp and treat you accordingly. This was more than upsetting. Bolstering others at my own expense, I wanted to elevate them to my cognitive level and introduce them to a beautiful reality. Instead, they fed on my energy to get grounded on their own level while I would get exhausted and fall from mine. And as soon as I fell, those whom I had nurtured began to trample me, no one doing it more aggressively than the girls I fancied, and none with more disdain than Martina.

When I realized this, I forced myself to acknowledge that the girls were right. The portrait of weakness, the frailty of my body, my subtle humor, my quest for the unknown ... it made perfect sense that I made no sense to them. But there I faced a dilemma. On the one hand, I did not want to remain on the same trajectory, and on the other I did not want to give up my personality, which I considered superior to any meretricious alternative. Finding a balance was such a long and excruciating process that I could write another novel about it except, much like the AC times themselves, I'd hate to relive that struggle again. I was unsuccessful more often than not, suffering bitter defeats and letting glory slip away when I thought I had it bagged, and if in the end I reaped marvels it was only because I never doubted that I deserved everything I desired, and then some.

Lady-Boyfriend

The first aromorphosis in my personal evolution occurred a couple of years after I graduated from college. That day I had a date with a beautiful young woman I had met on a train a few weeks prior. This was our third date, and we had already slept with each other, so I didn't think I needed to worry; I was wrong, because she showed up with another man.

We were in a downtown Manhattan restaurant that I liked because of its quiet ambiance, convenient location and superb selection of seafood, and the first thought that crossed my mind was that she had double-dated herself. But, acting with enviable confidence, she made her way to my table, her companion trailing behind, and sat in front of me with such resoluteness in her eyes I had no idea what to expect. The man grabbed a chair and sank down next to her, both of them facing me at a slight angle as I slid to the side to comfortably extend my legs without touching either of theirs.

I was silent while she narrated her tumultuous relationship with this man, who had one of those names I always forget despite trying not to. While she talked, I was trying to understand. See, my perfidious date was very attractive, no more than thirty, with naturally blonde hair and such a slim body that I could have carried her in my arms all day. On top of her superior appearance, she also bore that distinct mark of inimitability I invariably fell for. She was almost that magical unicorn who had lost her way in the vicissitudes of Creation and ended up in a world cruelly ill-suited to her fragile nature. The man, on the other hand, was not. At first, I thought he was a convenient friend whom she had temporarily burdened with a more valiant role, but then I noticed an unmistakable look in his eyes, that of a coward who is in over his head while trying to play it cool, and realized that he had already closed on this woman, although I could not imagine how. There was nothing special about him, neither in his appearance nor in his manners; on the contrary, everything about the man was as commonplace as his forgettable name, and he clearly neither knew this nor would have understood what I meant if I had told him. He was just a regular pal in his late twenties, slightly taller than the average, slightly larger too, with short black hair and dull eyes, dressed in blue jeans and a gray coat with a black collar. He looked like a million other men I saw in Manhattan or anywhere else: men who could be great folks or complete bastards without making an iota of difference in the grand scheme of things. But, even though his plain and parochial persona was taking a remarkable woman away from me, I felt no animosity toward him. No, it was the woman's choice that nauseated me beyond endurance, threatening to make me throw up right on the table.

Encouraged by my silence, she kept talking, now going over the futility of our affair which, allegedly, had been clear to her from the very moment I spoke to her on that goddamn train, "goddamn" being the epithet she used herself. Then she apologized for having gotten me into this hopeless nuisance as I seemed to be a nice guy whose feelings she had not meant to hurt, and claimed that it was my empathy that she counted on. Then she began going in circles, as if unsure of whether she was supposed to keep apologizing or switch to an assault.

At that point, all I wanted was for the man to speak, just to hear his voice and find something in it, something that would make him worthwhile. Two minutes later I realized he wouldn't do it on his own. His attitude had changed since he sat down: he had grown less afraid, and his eyes were almost contemptuous, as he must have taken me for the kind of milksop he was himself. I had completely forgotten about the girl and was now staring at him, considering how I'd proceed if we had to go at each other bare-fisted. He weighed at least thirty pounds more than me, his thick bones providing ample space for muscles to grow on, but his pasty wrists suggested that he did no exercise, which was a shame, as he could have taken his image to the next level by spending a mere two hours in the gym every week.

That made me pity him. I interrupted the girl, who was in the middle of another disquisition, and asked him how he was feeling. After a pause, he reluctantly said that he was fine. In a tone of genuine concern, I asked if the conversation was making him uncomfortable. He said it was fine, too. I asked whose idea it was to have this showdown, and he said it was that of his girlfriend, whom he called by her name, providing his first multisyllabic response yet still denying me an audial glimpse into his personality. I asked how they had met, and he said it wasn't relevant. I asked if he knew how I had met her, and he said that wasn't relevant either.

At that point any pity I had felt vanished. He was worse than I had thought, and it was unbearable. In a rush of lurid inspiration, hoping to extract something—anything—respectable from him, I asked him whether he was aware that I had had sex with his girlfriend on our first date, that she came three times that night, and that the next morning she told me she'd just had the best sex of her life. He winced, almost imperceptibly, and repeated that none of it mattered.

And then it hit me. I knew why she had chosen that man: not only over me, but over all the other men available to her: he was reliable. She could do anything she wanted, and as long as they slept together, he'd forgive her. Isn't that the definition of desirability? That "hard and tumultuous nature" she had mentioned was all hers: if it were up to that man, theirs would be the steadiest relationship known to the world. But that would be too boring for her, so she chose to have a foot in each world, leaving her ... well, a little stretched in the middle.

I remembered how I had approached her on the train. I was on a high, having just accomplished something my CEO had deemed impossible. This always gave me a feeling of invincibility, and I carried it into our conversation, so when I asked her to meet me again, nothing else mattered, because no woman could have said "no" to that kind of man. Our first date passed in a similar fashion, me being one of my best selves, so we ended up in my apartment. She was even better than I had suspected, and I had no reason to let her down either, but by the next morning I'd turned into something like a lazy feline, my energy level at a fraction of what she had seen. But then, still high on the night, she'd preferred to ignore the contrast, so it must have been our second date that had made her call it off.

On that day, I had felt perfectly pacific. I was as relaxed as a man in the company of his lover can be, and that must have raised a red flag. My amplitude was too large. It didn't matter that the whole range was positive: she could imagine that a person with such a variety of good moods was also capable of the utmost horror. I simply wasn't reliable like this guy, her longtime favorite, whom she could read like a book she had read a dozen times. And since there was nothing too bad about him, nothing to undermine the convenience of predictability, he was the safest bet for any woman, averaging out all possible risks around one steady zero line.

When I arrived at this conclusion, I got up, left a Jackson on the table for the two glasses of pomegranate juice I had drunk and left the place without looking at or thinking about anyone. I felt sick, so I walked to the World Trade Center to clear my head. What had just happened, along with my thoughts about it, added up to an inescapable denouement, so I urgently needed to acclimate to a new reality: that of having permanently lost the woman who had enabled me to forget about Martina without any hope of meeting another such as her.

Epiphany

When I got home, I made a cup of tea and sat in a leather armchair, leaning as far back as its soft cavity allowed and relaxing every muscle of my body. Then, slowly sipping, I started browsing through the memories of my romantic involvements, starting from the present and going back chronologically: first by month, then, as the memories became more distant, by year. I forbade any indulgence in emotion, no matter how vulnerable this reminiscing left me: the focus was to be on the facts alone. Two hours and three cups of tea later, I had come to a crushing conclusion: I was putting everything into my love life without getting much in return.

With this thought in my head, I approached my mirror, a six-foot-tall beauty in a manually engraved wooden frame that I'd serendipitously stumbled upon and bought on the spot for what I thought was an unbelievably low price. I had not yet changed my clothes, so I saw a tall and elegant young gentleman with an exquisite face wearing an ivory cashmere sweater, a white cotton dress shirt, black wool trousers with ironed straights and a pair of not-so-ostentatious alligator shoes. I looked at him for a while and an involuntary smile broke on my face, which grew as I kept looking. Even if I disregarded everything I knew about this man, his struggles and successes, his thoughts and feelings, his lows and highs, I couldn't help smiling at him because of how friendly he looked.

Returning to the armchair with my fourth cup of tea, a strange indifference engulfed me. It felt like a balloon filled with the poisonous gas of self-pity deflated inside my solar plexus until every vestige of it was gone. I sat still, observing the change with a vague curiosity, and then I stopped thinking. My mind went blank and the internal monologue quieted as I listened to the wind rustling through the nearby trees and throwing an occasional gust at my windows. Soon, my hearing became sharp enough distinguish the rumbling of a distant interstate road, and the roar of the cars driving by my house was suddenly so loud I couldn't fathom how they didn't wake me up at night. The walls seemed to exude a subtle vibration humming in unison with time itself, and I kept listening to it until the room became a vacuum devoid of anything known, the most soothing environment I had ever inhabited.

That night before I fell asleep, enveloped by an inner silence, I made up my mind about three things. First, I forgave all the women who had denied me their affection from the start or preferred other men to me eventually. Second, I decided to never judge any woman for either denying me her affection from the start or preferring other men to me eventually. And third, I allowed myself to pass on any woman I fancied, no matter how strong the attraction, at any point and for whatever reason. This meant, for example, that if I met a woman so stunning she made me forget to breathe, I could ignore her without thinking that I might have lost my opportunity for the best romantic involvement.

The next few days were fine; then my equanimity left me. Panic would overtake me whenever I saw a beautiful woman. MUSE's song "The Small Print" played in my head, with its unforgiving "*You're to blame for all the life that you're losing.*" I felt like I was carrying an ocean of love inside that was doomed to aimlessly evaporate, sometimes feeling so bad that I had to close my eyes, take a deep breath and forget where I was and what I was doing, regardless of where I was and what I was doing. Yet I refused to give in. It was a most stubborn kind of determination, like I would rather die than back down, and the only prop I had was the eerie conviction that I was so right that no rational backup was needed.

After a month or two, the pressure abated, and I began floating in the world like a buoy on the crest of a wave, acquiring an unfamiliar lightness of movement. My posture improved, and I realized I had always slouched. I also stopped looking at people in the street, something I had always done, and developed a new habit of staring over their heads without focusing. And then the best thing happened: I began writing again.

Before coming to the UK, I had written every day, wrapping up three works by the age of seventeen and starting several novels, but the only things I had produced since setting foot on Atlantic's grounds were a smattering of poems and a novella, which I submitted as my senior thesis in college. Other than that, I had been silent, and for no good reason. I never lacked ideas: on the contrary, they roiled in my mind, often dumbfounding in their lush detail, but I simply could not find the motivation to sit down and put pen to paper. In an occasional spurt of inspiration, I'd jot down a few pages of prose; then, a month later, I'd find the discipline to complete a poem I had started years earlier, before slipping back into lethargy. By the time of my epiphany, there were seven major works (five novels, a screenplay, and a narrative poem) that I had started, abandoned, and could not finish had my life depended on it. Do you know what it means for a writer to simultaneously *not* work on seven pieces? It's like living a parody of a bad standup comedy from which all the jokes have been removed.

When I resumed writing, I immediately realized the pause had been created by women. They and literature were the two things I liked best, although I had never had more than four favorite women at a time, let alone seven. But having sex with a beautiful woman is a gratification more immediate than completing a work of literature so, impatient as I was, I pursued the former, much to my own dismay. What amazed me most was that I had taken so long to understand that it was easier to bring my emotions under control by writing. Writing depended only on me, and I had long been aware that I excelled at things that didn't entail relying on others. Team sports had never been my cup of tea, unlike tennis or billiards; dating was also a team sport, and my partners let me down more often than not. But it didn't matter anymore. I enjoyed this new status quo long enough to begin believing in its permanence—until a single incident annulled all my progress in one strike. And the force who hurled it at me, turning my placid existence upside down once again, was that merciless mistress whom I've named more often in the last ten pages than I have in the last decade.

Molly and Self-Importance

Where had she been this entire time, you may ask, having grown tired of waiting for her demonically beautiful face to appear (I bet seeing it would take your breath away). Well, this entire time she was within arm's length yet unreachable. After AC, our education continued in the US: I ended up in the wonderfully primeval Vermont, while she went to Columbia: a university as close to Broadway as an educational institution is allowed to be. Soon after our studies began, I wrote her a letter on Facebook (which was then gradually gaining in popularity), wondering about her situation and her plans for the future. I got no response. Having waited for two and a half weeks, I wrote again, this time sharing my impressions of America: these revelations she also ignored. Undeterred, I waited until Christmas provided cover for another overture but was ignored again.

Then I took a break dictated by a chain of loves toward my own schoolmates, which was interrupted only in the middle of the summer vacation, at this very time of year (tomorrow, to be precise), when I congratulated her on her birthday. That was an immaculately friendly message into which I, beautifully and apropos, wove a sleek poetic eight-liner, no insinuations added. Yet the result was the same.

Having decided that contact had been lost for the foreseeable future, I shifted my full attention to my schoolmates and didn't give Martina another thought until the following summer when, by making a blunder while booking non-refundable plane tickets, I doomed myself to a three-day-long exile in New York City before the beginning of the school year. I had little appetite for the city, but still I told her about my predicament, expecting she'd at least volunteer to give me a tour around her hometown, as I would have done not only for her but for any former classmate of mine. She was silent, and I resented it: so much, in fact, that I didn't reach out again until the end of college. Having congratulated her on her bachelor's degree (and noting that I didn't understand why the degree is not called a "bachelorette's" when appropriate) I refused to open Facebook for an entire week to avoid doing something stupid. At that point I knew that I would be staying in the States and was already devising complicated multistep stratagems, their only goal being a rendezvous with my elusive darling, whose supremacy over other women had never been more clear.

She did not reply to that message either.

Next, there was a break of over two years, during which I was struggling to carve out my place in the competitive American landscape, living in several distant places on the East Coast and working different blue-collar jobs until things turned sour, bringing me to New Jersey—so close to Manhattan that I could go there every day after work, if I could still move. Judging from her occasional Facebook posts, Martina lived on the other side of Treasure Island and hadn't had much luck finding herself as an actress, see-sawing between being a waitress, a personal assistant, and a number of other things that didn't require a degree from Columbia. Every now and then she'd urge her followers to attend an obscure performance with modestly priced tickets, but I never went, continuing the tradition I'd begun back in AC.

Strange as it may sound, I had never seen Martina act, because as soon as I'd learned about her passion for theater I made sure to avoid every occasion that brought her on stage. My reason was fear: the mere thought that she could suck scared the hell out of me, because I'd know it if I saw it. And if she did, it would have spelled a death sentence for my love. After all the pain she'd inflicted, all the humiliation she'd subjected me to, the only excuse I had for loving her, no matter how hurt I was, was that she was supernatural. Merely "special" wouldn't do: to counterbalance her magnitude of arrogance, she had to have something no one else had. And if she had turned out nothing but a self-important soignée brat, there would be no point in even remembering her.

Remember, I promised to tell you what makes people akin? Perhaps you'd forgotten, assuming I wouldn't come back to it. But underestimating the narrator in his own story may cost you some embarrassment—unless, of course, you are entirely unencumbered by self-importance.

Do you know what self-importance is? The most hideous thing in the world. It's when someone is rude to you, and you feel offended. It's when someone is promoted at work ahead of you, and you feel wronged. It's when you get caught in the rain and get angry. It's when you notice a stain on your pants and feel stupid. It's when you buy a house you can't afford; ignore good advice out of spite; defend your point while knowing you're wrong … Put simply, self-importance is what forces you into the ultimate mistake of believing that you matter more than Infinity.

Self-importance paints our weaknesses as strengths, locking us in a trap of illusory grandeur and leading us astray from the true magic we possess as humans. It whispers in our ears that we are the image that we'd created of ourselves, and that unless we live up to that image every moment of our lives, those lives will be bad. Self-importance robs us of our confidence, making us probe for proofs of our value and feel miserable when we can't find any. In short, self-importance is a monster, and the only antidote against it is not taking ourselves seriously.

So, much as I thought I was different, I wasn't. Just like everyone else, I took myself with deadly seriousness, becoming destiny's toy, doomed to be tossed around in a grotesque rigmarole of existence until death plucked me like a blade of grass. The fact that my interests had little to do with those of others didn't matter: the introspective loop of conscious thought, along with the emphasis on my allegedly central role, rendered me as unlikely to attain the sublime as were those who didn't occupy themselves with its pursuits.

Now that you've been briefed on self-importance, I must admit there was one more reason for avoiding my darling; which, naturally, is a corollary of self-importance. Pride. I was loath to give her yet another chance to scorn me. I knew that when I'd approach her with all my amiability and flamboyant solicitousness, she would mock me yet again or simply pretend she didn't know me. I wasn't prepared to take that risk; not without a trump card up my sleeve, anyway.

Then that trump card arrived in the form of a professional jackpot. After a series of ruthless interviews, I was offered a job that shifted me into a different social class. This gave me a new perspective on life, so I thought about it and wrote to Martina one more time, asking her out. There was no fluff in that letter other than the politeness required by a prolonged silence: it was a straightforward invitation to dinner.

After three weeks of waiting (I truly believed that this time she would reply after taking a grand-master pause), I reread our Facebook message history and concluded that I could have done better. What had once seemed like sleek wit now looked stilted, as if I were forcing platitudes instead of telling her what I wanted. And then I wondered *what* I wanted to tell her, and couldn't answer. She remained the only woman I'd ever loved whom I'd never told that I loved, but it wasn't that. There always was something distinctive in the fact that we both knew it yet had never spoken about it; besides, even after years of unilateral silence, I believed she had a right to this uniqueness. The problem was that, for the first time since I'd set eyes on her, I doubted that I still loved her.

I remembered the last time I knew I did. I was in Vermont, wandering through the woods with a voice recorder in my hand and devising a plot to reach one of her friends. For that, I needed a very specific job in a very specific town, so I was creating a cover letter to offset my lack of experience. I was in an excellent state of mind, seemly sentences flowing out of me in a steady stream, and suddenly her image appeared in front of my eyes. She was in a cloud of amber hues exuding such gentle warmth that I instantly forgot about everything except the scene unfolding in my head. We were in a little café, dimmed rectangular lights on the ceiling and scarlet drapes at the windows; she entered on the arm of that friend of hers and was instantly stunned, freezing while the friend introduced us. A soft handshake, burning on her palm and icy on mine, assiduously restrained voices: the ineluctable politeness of two strangers, both of whom are making sure that, at the end of the conversation, the other is left wondering what impression he or she had made. Her friend wouldn't have a clue because Molly would expect me to crack first, and at the end of the night when the imminent parting would allow for a brief moment of intimacy and all the necessary words would have already been said, I'd take a step forward and, hanging over her ear like a lazy bee over a fragrant flower, whisper:

"*Che piacere di rivederti.*"

This, in a nutshell, was the crux of my relationship with Martina: it was based on the assumption that she'd play along, which she never did. Thinking about it had always puzzled me, but now it was clear. I reread the poems I had written for her, the most recent dating back to Vermont, and then realized it had been seven years since I'd last seen her. This made no sense. I could have sworn it was only yesterday that she passed by, blind to my existence as ever, and I could reproduce every feature of her face without closing my eyes. At Atlantic, I used to think her image was etched on my heart with a scalpel; now, an engraved stone would make for a better metaphor, even though no part of me was nearly that petrified. The sculpted memory of Martina, so deeply stored yet so easily retrievable, was the finest masterpiece in my collection, but why did I insist on keeping her at the forefront of my museum when she explicitly refused the role of my muse?

The Cruise

I don't know where this question would have led me had it not been for another absorbing matter. The price chart of the biotech stock I had been watching formed a pattern that indicated a "strong buy," and I made a sizeable bet. A few weeks later, the company announced the discovery of something awesome and its stock price soared, launching an upward trend that continued for over a year. I did not cash out at its peak, but I did well enough to start losing my mind. I had always believed that large sums of money brought tranquility, but in reality, I was frenzied, pacing from room to room at home and walking up and down the stairs at work, trying to decide what to do. Extravagant purchases were out of the question, but I did want to celebrate, and not knowing how was driving me nuts.

No need to tell you who I wanted to share this victory with, but in light of her silence over the years, I was at an impasse. I could not even reach out to her, and attempting an in-person rendezvous was also a bad idea: I was not going to ferret out where she lived to contrive to accidentally bump into her in a drug store hoping I wouldn't catch her purchasing one or more of the many objectionable items that are sold there. I toyed with the idea of sending her a gold ingot engraved with a poem, but then something in me broke. Why did I need to take her into the equation at all? It's a truth universally acknowledged that wasting time on someone who wouldn't care if you were dead is stupid. I must have exceeded the human quota of the pathetic long ago, yet I kept adding to the surplus. But it wasn't masochism or obsession: no, it was merely the readiness to tolerate current inconveniences in exchange for disproportionately greater returns in the end.

In the end, I relented and booked a luxury suite on a Mediterranean cruise liner. I went alone, thinking there'd be plenty of options on board, but merely played out the same scene, fancying women who didn't fancy me and vice versa. I was disappointed, finding little amusement in tourist duties like overeating, trying every Jacuzzi, or playing poker. Fortunately, the breathtaking sunsets did whet my imagination, inspiring me to work on a novel and finish some poems that had been on my to-do list for a very long time.

It was just before returning to Civitavecchia, the port where the voyage had begun, that I met two Italian women in their late thirties who took a keen interest in me. Their English was as terrible as my Italian, so we had to rely on Spanish. The ladies claimed to be sisters and offered to show me around their native Rome. The liner docked in the early morning, and with my return flight departing late in the afternoon, I accepted. Under the pretext of dropping off their luggage, they took me to their apartment, and that's where the sightseeing began.

It was the first time that I had had sex with two women at the same time, and I was amazed at how smoothly it went. Letting instincts take over proved key; as for the ladies, they put out a most praiseworthy performance, which pushed me to the extreme. Which I welcomed, appreciating both their expertise and the chance to flaunt my own. When they were finally sated, I checked the time and could not believe my eyes. There was precisely half an hour left before take-off.

I was livid. And the sisters were delighted, offering me a room at their place for as long as I wanted, but I had to return to work on Monday, so before we resumed, I booked a ticket for the next morning. Yet I couldn't shake the gaffe and wasn't enjoying the sex anymore. I finally fell into a dreamless sleep interrupted only by the shriek of my alarm.

The sisters offered to drive me, but I declined. The cab driver was an opera junkie playing *Aida* on the radio, and, to my utter surprise, I understood several lines of the arias. The airport had not become any cleaner in the nine days since I'd seen it last, and I didn't open my laptop, waiting for the boarding call in a café and drinking cappuccinos that were overpriced yet average in every other respect.

By the time I got on the plane, the stewardesses smiling at me like wax effigies, I was in a sour mood. All of my neighbors were hopelessly prosaic, ranging from a tall dude in a baseball cap worn backwards to an antiquated Italian couple who looked like they had hated each other for the last twenty years but had stuck it out because of property issues. The good news was that I had an aisle seat, although I was sure that the sad forty-year-old woman of obscure ethnicity sitting next to me would go to the bathroom at least once while I was asleep.

As I sat down, wondering if the in-flight entertainment would offer anything worth watching, my wandering eyes were arrested by a slip of paper emerging from the back pocket of the seat in front of mine. The angle at which it jutted out from between the pages of a fashion magazine betrayed utter carelessness and, acting on impulse, I grabbed the thing by the corner and yanked it out. Just as I expected, it was a boarding pass for the reverse route. Indulging my love for numbers, I played with the departure and arrival times, adding, subtracting, multiplying and dividing until the numbers made up a hundred, but when my eyes tracked across to the name printed on the boarding pass, my hair stood on end and an infinite vacuum jolted into being right behind my solar plexus, sucking my soul into a miniature black hole:

MARTINA FLAWD

The Pass

I don't know how long I stared at it before my brain kicked into gear again. By that time the plane was already airborne, the seat belt sign had blinked off, and the cabin was filled with the hum of the engines and usual noises accompanying an international flight. I grabbed—actually grabbed—the wrist of the first stewardess passing by and demanded water. I felt desiccated, my throat turning into parchment. When the water arrived, I gulped the entire bottle in one go; it only served to upset my stomach. All this time, the pass was clenched between my fingers, protruding like a label dutifully detailing the salient features of the corresponding curio, and when I looked at it I quivered as if from an electric charge, feeling ready to throw up. It took an enormous effort to hold down the contents of my stomach, but then my intestines launched a truly unbearable assault. I leaned back, prepared to surrender to the next convulsion, but the spasms ceased as suddenly as they'd begun, giving way to a feeling of complete relaxation, which released the tension and turned my body into a docile, amorphous mass. Though helpless, I liked it better than balancing on the verge of puking, although now I was entertaining the possibility of being possessed by an unknown entity making itself at home inside me.

The thought of it made me shudder. I wanted to fight the implausible intruder despite the apathy that enveloped me, but I didn't know how. A minute or two passed, and nothing changed. I remained in physical torpor, my mind clear, but my body incapable of voluntary movement. Now I believed the condition was my own doing, a ridiculous concomitant of my impressionability. And then I asked perhaps the strangest question I could think of in that setting. I asked it literally, pronouncing the words softly and clearly, and my own voice sounded so melodious I could hardly believe it was mine:

"*Why not?*"

The hum of the engines continued unperturbed, and this detail invigorated me. Moved by a profound appreciation of my fortune, I slid up against the back of my seat, ignoring the fact that I was once again in control of my body, closed my eyes and, abandoning rationality, dove into unchecked contemplation of the lethal weapon still clenched in my left hand.

As courageous thoughts burgeoned in my head, I saw Martina's face, her demonic, deceitful face, framed by curly blonde hair—a detail that always made me view her as innocent. As I kept staring, spellbound by this phantom, the image grew eerie. It took me a moment to figure out what was wrong at first; then I realized that her eyes were no longer hers. In fact, they weren't eyes at all but two pools of radiating light, as captivating as they were blinding. Then the image of her face began to recede, a thin cloud of golden specks shimmering around her. Once she had moved far enough for me to lose the sensation of her body heat, I realized that she was completely naked.

I hate to make this confession but I have to, to at least attempt to steer you away from misunderstandings: I'd never allowed myself to have sexual fantasies about Martina. I had envisioned us together countless times, but none of those involved intercourse or even its prelude. Employing women for imaginary sex was an unusual thing for me to begin with, and Molly had been taken out of that equation completely, though not in tribute to her nonexistent chastity. It was exactly the opposite: I believed she was so superb in bed that a mere fantasy wouldn't do her justice.

She had to be. Promiscuous women come in two types: those who do it out of insecurity, and those who do it out of confidence. The former type is as ubiquitous as the latter is rare, so most men are unaware of this dichotomy. The women of the first kind exude sexual power even if dressed as nuns; the second type exchanges a fraction of sexual power for a profusion of sexual flavor, which elevates them to the venerable position of sexual artists. Theirs is the most exquisite touch imaginable, and all they do is idiosyncratic. Those women are so special that, no matter how unspeakable the sexual practices they engage in, their inimitable magic turns that silly and laughable business into a worthy act. It is only with them that one can have the sex of a lifetime, yet when they leave you they brush off every memory of you, often forgetting that they'd even slept with you—for them, you had already become just another grain of alleged masculinity that was not worth getting wet for.

With this preamble, I want to warn you about what followed on that plane, my fingers clutching the pass like a ticket to another universe. Which is precisely what it turned out to be. But at that moment, while losing every bit of my sanity to a monstrously real vision, I knew only what I saw, although this kind of seeing had nothing to do with the eyes.

It was a dream, but I was wide awake. I heard everything; in fact, my audial perception sharpened to such an extreme I could map out the entire cabin, its animate and inanimate contents, by the noises filtered from beneath the drone of the engines. And yet all that input blanched in comparison with the spectacle unfolding before me, in which I was also a most active participant.

It's hard to describe where we were. We seemed to float in a space pierced by a multitude of incandescent threads issuing from a world-renowned painter's acid trip. Paradoxically, the intensity of the colors was in no way distracting; on the contrary, it felt integral to the moist tangle surrounding my darling and me. I promise to keep my language reasonably discrete, but if you are afraid of your sensibilities being affronted, do skip to the words "When I opened my eyes".

An astute man once said everything in this world is about sex, except sex. Molly and I proved this a lie. What happened between us in that mental projection was nothing but sex for the sake of sex, even though the word "sex" was a euphemism. The two of us fucked like the two insatiable maniacs we were, first fucking until it hurt, then fucking while it hurt, and finally fucking so that it would stop hurting. She lost herself as soon as I pulled her hair, running my knuckles down her neck, and when I reached her chest she went berserk, daring me to tear her to shreds and laughing in my face, implying I would never be able to. I relished the challenge, oscillating between the animalistic and the superhuman, equilibrium evading me. I knew that my only chance was to strike a rhythm in unison with her, an impossible task given how fitful she was. I myself had been notorious for changing rhythm in sex, but she was something out of this world. Perpetually in motion, wriggling and squirming, constantly shifting between fast, faster and fastest, she flowed like quicksilver, enshrouding me and estranging herself in one move, ever a step ahead of my next thought. Then I realized that matching her uncontrolled madness was tantamount to self-destruction and, empowered by this epiphany, grabbed her by the throat, her lower half contorting and undulating, and began setting my own tempo. She fought ferociously, doing her best to disrupt me with uncensored chaos, but it crushed against my intent while I held her in an iron grip. Worn down by my unyielding determination, her convulsive, unpredictable movements slowed until I was flooded by a spectacular sensation. I felt my body dissolve into Martina's, her feelings blending with mine, before I saw that we were no longer two people; in fact, we weren't people at all. We had become a tight knot of energy linked to every incandescent thread, and the mere awareness of that fact filled me with an unimaginable ecstasy that cancelled notions of time and space—I knew nothing other than the uniform bliss I was submerged in, a constant that had always been and would always be.

When I opened my eyes, I was panting. My lugubrious neighbor was solicitously offering me a napkin from beneath her wineglass. While *she* must have thought I was fighting the flu, *I* now knew that I was possessed: I had no other explanation for the phantasmagoria that had played out in my head. I couldn't even call it a hallucination: as far as I was concerned, what had just gone on in my brain was more real than the plane I was on and the universe that surrounded it. The latter seemed a travesty of the incredible realm I had had at my fingertips a moment ago, and the notion of having lost it filled me with such beastly sadness that tears flowed down my cheeks while bitterness clotted inside my throat until there was no more strength in me to regret anything.

II

Boarding

Suddenly, there was a flurry of anxiety around me. A clear voice over the loudspeaker announced that boarding for my flight was continuing, which baffled me: I had no clue it had begun. Lady 2-7 was nowhere in sight, but it didn't matter—I knew what flight she was on.

I closed my laptop, carefully packed it into the valise and headed for the bathroom. Aside from the yellow cones warning about the floor's potential wetness (a seemingly definite condition of public lavatories), it was empty. Knowing this was an abnormality soon to be rectified, I went straight to the mirror.

Good Lord …

Sometimes I wish I were narcissistic: it would spare me such agonizing moments of truth. I had forgotten how I looked in denim, but much to my chagrin, my disappointment had nothing to do with the clothes. It was all me.

I heard voices approaching and, having stolen another glance to etch the image in memory, dove into one of the open cubicles and locked the door, the latch engaging with a prompt, satisfying click.

"*OK*," I thought, leaning the valise against the cabin's flimsy wall and undoing the zipper. "*Let's not belabor the fact that you're dressed in rags. The fact is: you're still not pulling this off!*"

"*OK*," I continued after a pause, ripping off a piece of toilet paper and making sure it touched nothing but my hands and itself. "*The good news is: it's bad enough, no need to make it worse. You have a trump on you.*" I automatically checked for the trump; it was on me. "*So, shoot a little practice round. Be as light as a feather and don't forget: you can't lose if you give it all you've got.*" I wrapped the piece of paper around the lever, flushed the toilet, and tossed the paper into the vortex. "*You have at least six hours between takeoff and boarding, but that's gross because you can't start right off the bat. What if hers is a middle seat? By the way,*" I semi-froze, my body continuing its movements purely by inertia and my mind dissolving into a moment of thoughtless clarity. "*You also need to nap.*"

I immediately ran a reality check: nothing elaborate, just quick check-ups on hands and such. I had a great moment of lucidity, except in reverse: I was keenly aware that I was in common reality. The men who had interrupted my mirror routine had either left or become invisible. As I approached the sinks, slowly dragging the valise, another visitor dropped in, whom I ignored to the point of being unsure of how tall he was. He did not head for a cubicle, but I didn't care. I was staring into my eyes again, a part of me issuing a challenge to the whole. Then I put my hands under the faucet, the sensor immediately reacting with a robust stream of water. Why so cold? "*When was the last time you pulled off something like that?*" I placed my hand under yet another sensor-driven article of bathroom excellence to get some soap. "*And more importantly: have you ever?*"

"*I sure have, fiend.*" I rubbed the foam over my hands, willing the water to get warmer. As soon as I did, it stopped flowing. The usual suspects: devilish trivialities. But I always wash my hands near the women I like. I don't want to accidentally infect their skin when I begin touching it. "*And you'd better remember that one, too.*"

I knew what I meant, but I also had my doubts. Back then, I'd looked the same, but the girl had fancied me before we met. Poor thing: I'd never got a chance to apologize, but this wasn't the time, either.

"*You know what I'm really thinking,*" I asked my reflection as I shook the water off my hands slowly and methodically. "*That you won't manage.*"

"*Really?*"

"*One hundred percent.*"

"*In a decade's showdown? You're messing with me again.*" I was growing impatient, wiping my hands on a paper towel. "*It's simple. If you don't think your life is amazing enough to pluck any woman regardless of what's on you, you'd better stop thinking.*"

"*Does Martina come into these considerations?*"

I cursed: indignantly, dirtily, lengthily.

"*I'm serious. You haven't made up your mind about sex yet.*"

"*And what do you suggest?*"

"*Decide. Before you land.*"

I rolled the used paper towel into a compact ball and tossed it in the bin. Never understood people who let their trash take up unwarranted space. Or why there were so many of them.

I left the bathroom with a heavy heart. By now, the boarding line had grown to its fullest, showing how many passengers were travelling with me. Lady 2-7 was still missing, but I was unworried: on the contrary, the certainty of seeing her soon so invigorated me that I practically flew into the terminal's liquor store—a little gem I'd stumbled upon right after dealing with that three-headed cyclops of a customs officer—and eyed the young, pretty cashier as though it were precisely her I was looking to see.

"Good evening," I said, smiling at her indifferent, absent-minded look. "Do you sell …?" I named the cognac I used to like.

She did.

"How about vodka?"

She asked for the brand. I named four. She had all but the third. I named a fifth. She had it, too. I asked for the first brand of vodka and the cognac. She seemed very confused, but I wasn't through until I'd paid the eighty-eight dollars and thirty-nine cents in eight paper bills and ten coins.

I watched her distribute the money within the register (she clearly lacked experience in that compartment), but the verdict remained unchanged: I was not ready. Waiting for a surge of inspiration, I exited the store and approached one of the windows. I stared at the runway for what seemed a long time but couldn't have been, watching several planes thrusting their cumbersome bodies into the dark, cloudless sky, until the final announcement called my name, threatening to close the gate on me. It was all futile. I couldn't find anything, neither inside myself, nor around. Except, perhaps, the thought that, if a hulking plane could become airborne, even if just for a few hours, then why couldn't I do the same, even if only for a day or two?

"Any chance we'll be late?" I asked the flight attendant, handing him my boarding pass.

"We're right on time, sir," he assured me, returning the stub. BA: "b" for brats, "a" for aristocrats. Now I was walking, all alone, through a predominantly plastic tube, noting the rivets along the seams.

"Can I get a coffee, please?" I asked the pale, youthful stewardess at the entrance a moment before she was to ask for my boarding pass. I meant well, but it sounded rude.

"We aren't serving refreshments yet, sir," she said with a genuine note. Suddenly I felt the urge to confide in her. "May I see …"

"Anything you wish, ma'am!" I assured her. "As soon as you start, please bring me a small cup of strong coffee and seven containers of cream. Seat 7E."

7C and D were occupied by two obnoxious high-schoolers, a bro and sis, both transfixed by their phones, which were broadcasting two different albeit equally horrible things; they both turned their fishlike, suspicious eyes on me when I set the bag of liquor on my seat, the bottles clinking at the necks where the protective wrapping had left them bare. The gesture was spite itself: I wanted them to have no illusions about what having an older brother would have meant. Knowing they'd be a major distraction, I excluded them from my thinking and, having placed my valise into the overhead bin, closed it and began moving down the aisle, now relying on peripheral vision.

Peripheral Vision

I'd forbade myself to look for Molly at the airport, but now all hell broke loose. There were nineteen direct flights from New York to London today, eleven of which were departing from JFK, so meeting her on board was possible. Eight seats per row (four plus two on the left, two on the right) fell comfortably into my field of vision as I set my eyes above the plane's tail, staring through it as far as perhaps a dozen miles. Some passengers were still cluttering the aisle and, while waiting for a thin, nervous lady to find a spot for a bag that looked too big to have passed the carry-on security check, I wondered what my darling would be wearing.

"I'll help you," I said to the struggling woman when it became clear she wouldn't notice the empty space in an open bin a few yards across. Her shoulders dropped in relief, but as she turned to me she grew visibly uneasy. Now it had to be not the denim but my look, which must have resembled that of a blind man. Ironically, I saw more than any three people on this plane combined. Although her bag was very heavy, she didn't thank me when I was done, taking her seat and buckling up with an almost annoyed promptness, but I couldn't care less; so, returning my stare to the tail of the plane, I resumed both my movement and train of thought.

I'm sure you've already guessed that my dear had a royal taste in fine matters, which translated, among other things, into superb sartorial choices. She never wore clothes just because they were expensive: no, she created unique looks that could suit nobody else. Despite not having seen her for years, I was willing to bet that she still dressed so that any male director would offer her a lead role in his play if he accidentally bumped into her on the A-train. She also had the rare gift of looking great in clothing that required charisma and confidence: no other woman I know could pull off a crêpe wool silk dress with puffed sleeves and a deep V-neck in both front and back. And it wasn't even Halloween! Although, to be fair, I also don't know another woman with such an incredible body. The combination of long, slim legs, wide hips and a thin waist is uncommon to begin with, but she also had perfect breasts to top it all off. Strange as it may sound coming from a man, boobs are the last thing I notice in a woman (I don't even know what difference the letters make in bra sizes), but Molly made me pay as much attention to her bosom as to the rest of her.

The rows were moving past slowly but steadily while I gave the passengers in the aisle all the time they needed; yet nothing around me betrayed her unmistakable presence. Could she perhaps have gone for a deep blue dress with long sleeves and a bright belt matching the color of heels: nothing too badass, just the bare minimum to make a suitable impression before changing into the first evening gown? Or would she wear something warmer, cognizant of the plane's potentially frigid air? A pearl cashmere pullover seemed a win, but I couldn't come up with a complementary bottom, as she'd never worn jeans, nor ...

And then I stopped, battling an unbearable urge to dart a glance at the foggy silhouette to my left. This time it was a casual shake of the head with which she adjusted her hair, throwing a strand of hair off her eyebrow with a backward flick, that reeled in my attention like a fish writhing at the end of an invisible line. A dark blue blob resembling a stout middle-aged man loomed next to her, and the cold detachment pervading the space between them made me question his manliness. Taking a slow, deliberate breath through the nose, I brought my head almost to the edge of the luggage bins to catch sight of the row numbers glowing diligently in the dim air; and when I did, I shifted back to direct vision to make sure my eyes weren't playing a trick on me.

Hers was row 27.

The figures didn't change as I kept looking and, having thrown a test glance at my hands (the question is always the same: are these hands mine?), I blurred my focus again and moved on. I continued at the same pace until I reached the end of the cabin, where the stewardesses demanded I take my seat immediately, and returned down the other aisle, this time, with my head slightly turned, being conscious of nothing but Lady 2-7 until the last vestige of her arresting presence disappeared behind the horizon of my peripheral horizon.

By the way, do you know what peripheral vision is? I keep asking you these questions that may seem either dumbfounding or simply dumb, but in my life, peripheral vision, self-importance and lucid dreaming are infinitely more important than driving a car or hitting a bar. Except I've done it again, haven't I? I could pretend that the mention of lucid dreaming was a Freudian slip, but do you really think I would let my narrative run itself without my consent?

Author's Monologue

I know what you must be thinking: these words, they are here just to build a shell, to let you see what is going on, and in what direction. Don't worry: this is not your fault. Over the last decades writers have done a remarkable job of degrading literature to a hybrid of cheap tabloid and lengthy blog, which, ironically, some claim to be an adequate response to popular demand. I have many thoughts on this subject, but the bottom line is: when a modern reader opens a modern book, she has no expectation of finding, instead of a technical manual moving the story from place to place, an intricate design filled with cross-referenced allusions which, when considered together, form a splendid pattern that is as rewarding to discover as it is difficult to craft. No, the modern writer (reluctant to make this stupendous effort that may, in any event, hinder sales) has gladly accepted the notion that the text should be a sterile medium granting the ultimate interpretational flexibility. As a result, the world is drowning in dull writing, bestsellers and unknowns alike; and I am talking not only about formulaic works (like those about young, handsome billionaires falling in love with waitresses). No, literature that positions itself as literary is guilty of the same sin. No Henry James' figures in the carpet to elevate the reader who is either blessed with superb shrewdness or is a born writer himself. Yet the law of equilibrium requires an ocean of undifferentiated texts to be diluted by at least some works that don't betray their divine duty. So, whenever you suspect that my narrative has altered, or anything unusual stands out, or you're compelled to continue after my honest advice to stop reading, ask yourself: what can it mean?

You don't believe me, I bet. You think I'm pulling your leg. It's so strange: sitting in this soft chair, the brother and sister being collected by their stately mother who now seems to be moving them to business class, where she and her putative spouse have taken up residence, I can see you roll your eyes, not taking a word I say the way I mean. What did you think about what you just read? That's it's some sort of a joke I've slapped together in a humble attempt to make you laugh? That I am messing with you? I am not messing with you. I am here to reveal axiomatic truths missed or misunderstood every day, their misapprehension squandering the lives of generations. And if all that's wrapped in an amazing story, it is because such is my nature, and I'd rather die than betray the truth.

The truth, you exclaim, now supplementing the eye roll with a sardonic smile. Is this man holding forth about truth the same who's discovered the woman he had labeled as Lady 2-7 sitting in the twenty-seventh row? But you're forgetting that I'm still the one who must deal with the consequences. It's not enough to throw in a coincidence and then take the back (or first-class) seat: if this is a deliberate move on your part, you'd better take full responsibility for it, either coming up with an explanation for such a conspicuous play, or drawing it out masterfully as it unravels, or both. Taking responsibility is another key concept, but this intermission is already getting longer than my perfectionism will allow, making me a lot of enemies among the writers whose works are forgotten as soon as their publishers cut their marketing budgets in half. The art of writing consists in making a cascade of brilliant points on a journey that is itself splendid, so let's save the deep thinking for a more appropriate setting. Just remember: this text is not written, it's *wrought*, and the only accidental things in it are those channeled through me by Infinity.

This damn self-importance, always finding a way in! I know I got emotional, but, frankly, I am more surprised my performance has been so controlled thus far. If you knew what was running through me as I walked the aisles … The mere thought of seeing Martina was enough to dislodge my assemblage point, and the last few pages show what that leads to. Now that I've started indulging in didacticism, I've begun to lose my touch, which is as clear to me as it may be unclear to you what the assemblage point is. The only way to calm myself is to continue writing, but I want to wait for takeoff first. I always prefer to savor it unadulterated.

I was glad the high-schoolers were gone: I had the whole middle row to myself and would be spared their privileged adolescent nonsense. I moved to the middle seat, buckled up, assumed the pose of a resting emperor and closed my eyes, the engines muffling most other noises. The plane began taxiing, but it wasn't until the turbines roared into life some fifteen minutes later that I turned to the window on my left. Its passenger had the decency not to obstruct the view, yet the microcosm of concrete rushing by in the foreground and the trees and houses sluggishly gliding by at a distance were mere reminders. For me, the takeoff is all about the acceleration. To feel my arms grow leaden as I unglue them from the armrests; to hear the plastic panels squeak under the mounting pressure; to watch the plane's hull reverberate on the runway until a lunge into the air brings an instant release from the jolting earth … All this amounts to the quintessential anticipation of the mystery and success waiting to be retrieved by the ruthless hunter; and even if I'd lacked ruthlessness thus far, the woman in row 27 was a great reason to restore my iron grip.

When the seat belt sign blinked off, I reached for my valise, put the liquor away and extracted my laptop, my Kindle, my cell phone, and a bar of dark chocolate. Then I stripped the Kindle of its case and used the latter to rest my phone against vertically so that its screen reflected enough of the aisle behind to see what was going on in it. Satisfied with my preparations, I continued my mental labors, typing up the thoughts that would later carry the expanded narrative.

"Your coffee, sir!" The stewardess I had spoken with earlier was putting a tray on the only empty table in my vicinity. I glanced at the pots of cream. There were only five.

"I'd like two more creams, and a bottle of still water, please."

"One moment," she blushed before rushing away.

Waiting for the missing dairy, I emptied the available containers into my coffee, stirred the mixture, and took a cautious sip. Still bitter, and the chocolate wouldn't help. Yet the stewardess returned before the beverage had time to cool, proudly setting down the bottle of water alongside four more pots of cream.

I wish I took myself as lightly as they do. If I did, I wouldn't need to go back to AC. At least not physically. Physical travel is so inefficient, it's a joke compared to the other options available to men. Now that I've had to wait, I might as well tell you how I discovered them, but first let me finish the story that brought me to where I was.

Fragolina

For several days after I returned from the Mediterranean, I resembled a somnambulist. I was incapable of solving the simplest tasks at work and barely made it to the weekend, which I spent drinking one and a half bottles of cognac and throwing up. All the way through this episode, I battled a monstrous mental fatigue that had been previously unknown to me. Whenever I started thinking, a gray fog would descend before my eyes and I'd lost my train of thought, as though I were stoned. And, curiously, for the first time in my life, I did not *want* to think, lying in my bed and staring at the ceiling, not worrying for a split second about the passing time.

A few weeks later, however, an unexpected jolt brought me back to life. I got a call from a woman I'd thought I would never see again. She wanted to meet, which we did in a restaurant near Grand Central. She talked about a number of things while I ate an ambrosial salmon stew, eventually asking the waiter to pass a hundred-dollar bill to the chef, a maneuver that yielded a return compliment in the form of a slice of chocolate cake. I parried her provocative questions with succinct civility while refusing to give her what she was really after (whether I was seeing anyone on a regular basis), and when I'd finished the stew, I realized I was fed up with being treated like a fool. I asked when and how she'd split from her lover, a handsome lad who would have been a great sport had it not been for his inferiority complex, which manifested as a need to sleep with every woman who made herself available to him. She put on a good show, approximating something midway between wounded innocence and bewilderment, but the cake made it hard for her to compete for my attention, so she finally bled substance. The story was mundane, and a few leading questions gave me all I needed. He had been cheating on her, and when she lost her job and couldn't pay her part of the rent, he threw her out and took the other girl in. This had happened four months earlier, and all this time she'd been trying to patch things up. By now she must have realized the obvious, so she urgently needed a confidence booster. And what could be of more use to her than an ardent admirer of her feminine virtues who had remained loyal in the past even in the face of her condescension?

I listened to her lie about us in college while I chased the cake with bergamot tea that burned the roof of my mouth but couldn't spoil my enjoyment, and the lower her voice fell, the more certain I became that, no matter the reason for the split, it's in a man's best interest to part with a woman on friendly terms. That is, of course, if he ever wants her back. Most men behave like children when their women tell them they've found other men. "The other man", by the way, is the most sought-after character, and men would be better off asking themselves how to become him, but instead they indulge in anger, undulating between aggression and psychopathic displays of affection: everything that repels a woman best. But, sooner or later, that woman will find herself alone. In this tender state, she'll recycle her memories of those she had been close with, and it is the man who behaved like one at the hour of farewell that will stand out while the rest blend into a pathetic mixture of accusations, insecurities and neediness. I know how hard it is to be calm when your beloved wrongs you, but what hits us so hard in that moment is the fear that we will not find a better woman. And that fear is inexcusable.

When I'd taken the last bite of cake, I leaned backwards and took a long look at her. She hadn't grow younger over the years. The weight she'd gained had softened the formerly irresistible lines of her athletic body, and the pale puffiness of her face reminded me of her drinking habit. She pretended she did not want me to pay for the dinner, but I wouldn't play along. When we left, she asked if I wanted to walk her to Grand Central, from where she was to return to her mother's house—her new home since the breakup. I suggested my place instead, and she agreed.

We'd reached the Hoboken Terminal, which connected the town where I lived with Manhattan, when I remembered the sexual fantasy I often indulged in when taking the late train. To corral the smattering of passengers, the conductors closed off the latter half of the cars with a metal bar, assuming it was enough to prevent access. That joke of an obstacle razzed me each time I saw it, and I only complied with it because I wanted to save the break for the right night. At last, that night had come.

It was only nine o'clock, but the thick August darkness had already set in, and the lamp light, which seemed to hail from the middle of the previous century, was too feeble to cast distinct shadows onto the cracked concrete platform. I led her to the last open car, greedily breathing in the heady air, smelling of hot iron and fresh fodder, ascended the steps, checked our surroundings and jumped over the bar. She understood me immediately and threw a quick glance over her shoulder before following me, her legs performing a pirouette that caused a sweet pressure in my lower abdomen. The train was a double-decker, so no passenger or conductor could see us through the aisle if we went upstairs; we were still visible from the platform, so we hid in the vestibule until departure, kissing fervidly as if trying to make up for the years we had spent apart, and as soon as the train moved I tore myself off her magnetic body and pulled her onward. But as we reached our destination, her face assuming a knowing grin that reminded me of what she used to be, my mind hit a brick wall. There she was, a woman I had desired, at my fingertips, in the midst of a sexual fantasy, but I felt flat. I'd imagined the scene dozens of times: the upper deck, the four front seats of the second car, the grayish light flowing from the ceiling, the dark scenery dragging by behind the glossy window with an occasional line of diamond-eyed cars waiting at a closed crossing. I even recalled the impulses I had thought I would have: to lift the woman's knees to her chest, to run the palm of my hand down the back of her thigh, to whisper some of my favorite words into her ear. But as I watched her grow apprehensive at the sight of my lethargy, none of that translated into action; and when I realized that I wasn't even thinking about sex, I told her that I wanted to remain friends.

We left the barred section like two guilty middle schoolers ashamed of their misdemeanor and spent the rest of the ride in sepulchral silence. She avoided my eyes, but I sat observing both her face and its reflection and realized it had been her grown-up air that I'd fallen for in college, and that by now, looking older than her real age had stopped counting in her favor. When we got to my place, I felt only fatigue; while she was taking a shower, I made a bed for her in the guest bedroom, put a clean glass and the half-full bottle of cognac on the nightstand, and went to sleep. I was afraid she'd come find me in the middle of the night, but she knew better. She finished the cognac and left before I woke up. I haven't heard from her since.

A Metaphor in the Metanarrative

The next morning, I felt revived, my mind regaining its usual sharpness as though having recovered after a viral infection, and I immediately put my mental faculties to work. It was then that the magnitude of what had happened finally hit me. I did not allow myself to look at the pass, leaving it where I had put it the day I returned, but my subconscious must have already reached its conclusions, the most important being my reluctance to regard the event as a coincidence. The mathematical probability of such an occurrence was negligible to begin with, but it was its esoteric segue that moved the matter beyond the odds. I couldn't fathom the meaning of it yet, yet I knew that if I wanted to capitalize on this incredible chance I had to nail it, waiting until I had a plan so thorough it could accommodate the likelihood that things wouldn't go according to it. Betraying the secret in another letter, albeit in line with my naiveté, would be lethal to the power I now possessed, and I'd do anything to avoid relinquishing the advantage it gave me. No, the pass itself was proof that I'd see her again, and instead of rushing, I had to make sure I'd be ready when the time came.

As I indulged in contemplation of our next meeting (which I knew would happen at Atlantic, as no other place could provide the proper continuity), I began to have epiphanies, sporadic yet powerful, and eventually became convinced that, while the effect the pass had produced on me was inexplicable, the fact that it had fallen into my hands in the first place was anything but absurd. My relationship with Martina had been too imbalanced for too long: sooner or later my steady disposition had to find its reward, and the fact that it came in such a grotesque form was but a testimony to our extraordinary nature. What I didn't know back then was that, despite being a dreadfully undisciplined fellow, I was impeccable in my love for her, generating … but of course, impeccability is another concept that may have no meaning to you, and explaining it now would only delay my arrival at the beginning of this story, which I haven't been able to wait for since its first word.

I took my hands off the keyboard and rubbed my fingers, finally feeling the surge. The combination of coffee, cream, and dark chocolate has an invigorating effect on me. At first, it is barely noticeable, except that my pulse increases, but some forty minutes later, a relentless urge to act overwhelms me. My breath comes faster, my eyes water, and I start tapping out rhythms with my feet. Gradually, I grow more restless, anxious to engage people around me or take action, but if I overcome the physicality of this energy and channel it into thought, I become aware of fully-formed metaphors that had not been in my head before. It feels like the lights are suddenly turned on in a dark room, exposing a magnificent interior, and I can almost feel the electricity run through the neurons in my brain. These are the most precious moments: it is relatively easy to imagine an episode, especially if you've lived through it, but imagining a metaphor is much trickier because, unlike an episode, a metaphor cannot be purely descriptive. Perhaps an example will do.

Envision yourself at a club. A bar. A disco. It has to be a large space full of people, music, and colorful laser beams penetrating the otherwise obscure and smoky ambiance. You've been there long enough to start thinking it is going to be the same waste of a night as the dozens of similar ones spent chasing the sublime where it couldn't occur, and then something happens. You don't know what. Nothing has changed. Same clouds of smoke rolling around, same rhythmical noise some call music, same shortage of oxygen and excess of sweat. And then there is a gap in the throng of bodies opening a straight line between you and the other end of the room. You see her. Right there, looking like she could have been there forever or have materialized a second ago, though not out of this humid air that's soaking your lungs even without you breathing. You know everything about her from the first glance. You don't even need to think to know. You're both plugged into the same source: you came from it an eternity ago and have seen the wildest corners of the universe—beyond the reach of any ordinary imagination. None of it matters now. It's a new context, a new time, a new universe. She is oblivious, just as she should be, a reactive element, capable of reciprocation but never of initiation. Whenever she tries, it goes to hell. You've been there many times; you don't want to go there again. Thoughts disappear; no more barriers—neither inside, nor in sight. Next thing you know, you're on your way toward her, bodies surging in on you from every direction: vultures, they sense that something incredible is about to happen and must interfere, not knowing that they had been included in this plan long before they had grown aware of themselves. The distance dwindles to zero, and she raises her eyes, guided by an instinct originating from the stellar knowledge. There is something indescribable in them, something at once farfetched and transcending materiality. The music that was growing louder reaches its apogee, making talking as inconvenient as it can be. It doesn't matter either. Reality is helpless now, its clammy claws serving as a foil to the magic that's about to happen. She eyes you with growing expectancy, fearing you'll be the millionth one she's encountered over the last million years who screws up. It's time: you know it because there is nothing else for you to do except to gently take her by the elbow and, bringing your lips to her ear as close as the lock of her hair permits and, catching the smell of her essence, say:

"*You know …*"

And there it is, the slight shake of her head that takes her far enough to give you an incredulous look, betraying how little she expected your voice to evoke the memories of her best self. Now both her visual and audial perceptions are infiltrated, the first impression making its lethal impact as she takes an involuntary breath, catching the slight trace of your scent which dismantles the olfactory wall as well. The scene is set: all you have to do is be perfect. The space around dissolves, becoming what it was meant to be all along: a conventional framework devoid of meaning outside of the attention one pays to it; and as the last vestige of its predatory power is consumed by your empyrean inspiration, you near her ear once again and say in the exact same tone:

"*You know … you're just my type.*"

Change of Class

The inner voice muttered something unintelligible; I stopped typing in the middle of the sentence, looked at my cellphone's screen and saw that Lady 2-7 was standing by her seat, trying to close the overhead bin. Nobody was in a rush to help her, which seemed strange, though perhaps none of the good Samaritans around had noticed her struggles. Some ten seconds later, the bin's lock finally clicked; Lady perked up and, adjusting the blouse that had slid a little too far up her waist, started toward the restrooms.

When she joined the line, I got up and approached her neighbor. As suspected, he turned out to be short, stout, bold, cleanly shaven, and completely unsuited to adventure, even those taking place in the blockbuster he was watching.

"Hello." I smiled, waiting for him to remove his earphones.

"Can I help you?" he wondered in a Northern English accent.

"You can!" I assured him, leaning toward his ear and switching to a confidential whisper. "The lady sitting next to you is an old classmate of mine, and I was wondering if you'd be so kind as to trade my first-class seat for yours so that I could spend the rest of the flight catching up with her?"

He'd made up his mind before I finished the sentence; the rest was Hollywood.

"You want to trade your first-class seat for mine?" he asked, as if afraid that I was pulling his leg.

"7E, right over there," my finger pointed in the general direction of the pilot's cabin. "They'll be serving oysters later, but if you don't like seafood, you can go for beef or vegetarian instead. I also insist that you try the *Chateau de la Tour*: it'll make you sleep like a newborn."

"Is this even allowed?" he asked in a tone of utmost suspicion.

"As long as the seat is paid for." I held his eyes captive, prepared to continue the theater for as long as needed.

"Are you sure you're going to be all right here? You are quite tall," he said in a tone that carried no concern for my well-being whatsoever.

"I've been making myself comfortable in uncomfortable places my whole life. But you will be able to extend your legs fully."

He looked at the screen in front of him as if wanting to take it with.

"Well, if you don't mind, I sure won't either," he finally declared with a remarkably repulsive smile. "7E, you say?"

"Don't forget your luggage." I stopped smiling. Lady was still waiting, oblivious to my combinatorics, but by now she was next in line.

I returned to the seat I was giving up and quickly collected my belongings. The Englishman wasn't in a hurry, but the occupant of the bathroom was taking even longer, so by the time she entered the lavatory I was already putting my valise next to hers. I knew the model: a hundred bucks, and decent value for money. Hers was somewhat worn out, but I couldn't figure out whether she was a frequent flyer or had simply had the thing for a long time.

The Englishman was right about the seat, but I knew what to do. Having put the laptop on the foldable table in front of me, I straightened my back and relaxed my shoulders, letting the elbows fall, and extended my knees as far to either side as I could. Then I added the little pillow from the sleeping kit for lower back support, slid half an inch forward, and felt almost all right.

When Lady returned, I was already typing up a report of what had just happened, omitting many insignificant details and looking like I'd been sitting there since the plane's previous leg. At first, she thought she'd gotten lost, but a quick check of the row number restored her confidence. She vacillated for a moment, then had no choice but to say:

"Excuse me?"

I like how Americans inflect the midsection of this phrase when something they believe they're entitled to proves tricky. The English do it differently, with the emphasis falling toward the end. I would have gladly obliged her, but nothing in the way she spoke suggested she was addressing me. This was natural: beautiful women are used to everyone paying attention to them, even when counting on that isn't reasonable. But to get mine, she'd have to do better than asking for an excuse when she meant the fault was mine.

"Sir?"

She was now done with excuses, raising her voice and adding a brass note to it, while her body language, which I was scanning out of the corner of my eye, still failed to become adequate. This was disappointing. I commenced a crazy typing streak, hitting no less than three hundred characters per minute, and looked as natural not noticing her as any man not wearing headphones could. If she were a character in my book, I would have made her act already, but I had to wait for as long as it would take her to realize the obvious.

"Hey," she said, as if waving a white flag, and touched my shirt. I had to give her this one: she did it masterfully, disturbing nothing but a fold of denim. First, I stopped typing; then I took my eyes off the screen, and finally I turned my head toward her, displaying a silent look of bemused curiosity, smiling, not saying a word.

"Can I get to my seat?" her voice was half-obnoxious and half-childish, the childish part that of a girl who was being denied her favorite candy.

I took a deep breath through the nose and looked at her as if I had never seen her. She wore just enough perfume to conceal its full bouquet until she was right next to you. I'd already noticed a few more likeable things about her, as well as some things I couldn't stand. The latter were amassing quickly, but I was still willing to forgive all that for the fluttery feeling she was giving me.

"Let's see," I said, sliding from under the table in one motion. She looked at me incredulously, as if measuring my body. She was slimmer than me and should have passed without a hiccup, but she was afraid to appear awkward. I considered intimating that she should raise the armrest first, but in the end she did what I had, except lifting my table slightly with her thin, long thigh, the top edge of my laptop tapping on the back of the seat in front. As soon as she reached her destination, where she fidgeted at length to get comfortable, I returned to where I was.

Where was I? Oh, I remember: the details. Blessed is the writer who intuits the right balance between saying too much and saying too little when it matters the most! For me, the ugliest devil of writing had always been in the detail. When I was younger, I thought that, when describing reality, I had to be exhaustive, the coughs of the passengers three rows behind included, because the shrewd reader may discern in them some greater meaning I myself had missed. Then I realized that, firstly, people did not see greater meanings in anything, let alone books, and secondly, that excessive attention to detail made my writing clumsy, stripping it of the very airiness that makes a dozen pages fly by in one captivating flurry. And I am all about the flight: it allows you to cover tremendous ground before tiring.

Lady was growing progressively more uneasy, waiting for my apology. The entitlement of beauty; how many great women have perished under your insidious touch! The longer she was silent and fidgety, the more tempted I was to ask why she was flying economy if she was as amazing as she considered herself to be. Of course, you should never ask a woman such questions, because they immediately put you in a vulnerable position. A critical thing most men don't know about women is that women are excellent at both putting men in vulnerable positions and exploiting discovered vulnerabilities until men are rendered completely helpless. But, pray, don't blame women for doing so. If they didn't, our lives would lose one of their sweetest victories: that of changing a woman's mind from disliking you to desiring you.

By now Lady had frozen, exuding profound anxiety; I stopped typing and leaned back. Looking away, I considered my options. I had never cast a spell on anyone in this emotional state, but the inner voice told me now was not the time. Besides, I got the notion that her problem wasn't so much with me as with herself. Had she recently been stalked? Had she lost her virginity to a denim-wearing guy? Had her father been abusive? The possibilities were limitless, but all shared a trait in common: they had nothing to do with me. So, I left Lady to her demons and returned to my own, adding the last pivotal point to my fate's line chart that had brought me to this very plane.

The Lucid Dream

It happened three months after the cruise, on a Saturday morning, early in the fall, which was cold and stormy that year. The preceding Friday had been utterly tedious: I'd gone to work, come home, exercised, made dinner, eaten, read a book, browsed the Internet and gone to bed around 1.00 a.m. In the middle of the night I woke up to go to the bathroom, drank some water and fell back asleep.

And then it began.

It started as a regular dream, only slightly more vivid than usual. I was doing random actions in random places with random people, floating through the dream's fabric as I had done thousands of times, until I found myself in a palatial building with white walls and very high ceilings illuminated by golden light. Next, the imagery became noticeably clearer, the ethereal, fog-like colors yielding to sharp contrasts between objects and their shadows. Then I saw three young women, completely naked, performing a seductive dance to a group of well-dressed men sitting in armchairs set very far from one another. Despite the distance, those women looked more real than any woman I have met in life, and yet I knew they were impossible because of their sexual appeal. They weren't just hot, gorgeous, stunning, or ravishing; no, they looked like the only thing they were created for was having sex.

As soon as I had that realization, the woman in the center strode toward to me with as nimble a gait as is permissible under gravity. When she threw her arms around me, her supple yet solid body enveloping my skin with galvanizing heat, I saw that she was even more attractive than I'd believed a moment ago, although a moment ago I would have not believed it possible. The sensation of her body touching mine was hypnotic, and it wasn't the beastly drive that ruled me: on the contrary, I felt an even more rarefied version of my sensuality stretching from the pit of my stomach to the tip of my nose like a gigantic candle flame. Her skin was radiantly white, with a bluish undertone that reminded me of the star Rigel, its ghostly protuberances flickering in the uniform dark ...

And then I realized I was having a dream.

My consciousness wasn't that of a dream character any longer: I thought and perceived exactly as I did during waking hours, except I knew that my body lay infinitely far from where I was. But what struck me most was that the woman did not react in any way to my breakthrough, continuing her manipulations by sliding her fingernails down my stomach, causing a maddeningly sweet feeling that flooded me.

Following a strange impulse, I tore my eyes off her breathtaking curves and looked at my hands. They were greenish, long and very thin, resembling those in a cartoon drawing of an evil sorcerer. First, I saw them as if through a clouded, shaky lens; then the view stabilized. The next moment, I realized the improvement was not merely visual: everything around became augmented and emphasized as if I were in some sort of a super-reality while being fully aware of being asleep.

The woman was now pressing her mouth to the middle of my chest, which was bare under the dark emerald cloak I discovered I was wearing. I felt her hot tongue tickle my skin as it glided south, leaving a trail of coolness. As a gesture of appreciation, I put my hand between her legs. Her belly was as smooth as if no hair had ever grown on it, and the two moist folds of skin at its bottom were softer than rose petals sprinkled with drops of morning dew. She grabbed my wrist, peremptorily forcing several of my fingers inside her, and it felt like they were being wrapped in slippery, wet velvet that shrank and throbbed.

When I realized that having sex with this succubus would bar me from exploring where I was, I instantly withdrew from her. My arousal immediately dwindled to nothing, but a fair portion of perceptual clarity was lost with it. It occurred to me that I might wake up at any moment and shouldn't waste time.

I looked around; a shelf ran along one wall, and as soon as I focused on it I found myself standing by it. I took this completely for granted and examined the variety of tiny figurines arranged on top, which began metamorphosing if I stared at them too long. I glanced at my hands again; they hadn't changed since I saw them last, but now I wore several rings. I flinched at the thought of the woman: I'd hate to have hurt her. I recalled the sensation of my fingers inside her and drew my hand under my nose, catching a trace of her secret, my fingers still moist.

I walked out of the room, entering a hall lined with a profusion of shelves. An eerie sense of familiarity enveloped me as I glided toward a bright arc—the palace's main entrance. When I stepped outside, I was first stunned by the spectacular mountainous scenery, then by an enormous stone staircase leading up to the palace from what seemed the bottom of a deep ravine, and finally by a small procession of well-dressed people effortlessly ascending the stairs.

Next, I experienced a cognitive split between me as I know myself in the everyday world and me as a character in the dream. I remembered that my physical body was in my bedroom, but I also knew that this place was my home. The thought filled me with rapture. Never in my life had I felt more at ease, and the thought of waking up and abandoning this world was excruciating. I raised my eyes to the white sky, wondering if it held any gods, but laughed the next moment, amused by my own foolishness. I almost saw myself from the side: not what I looked like, which was still unknown to me except for the hands, but what I was by nature. The feeling of power engulfed me, but then I realized my relatives, who were among those ascending the stairs, might not appreciate finding the women in the palace.

To spare an awkward scene, I began gliding along a serpentine path, which, a few turns later, had led me to a very different, suburban, area. I met several people on the same path, as well as other humanoid creatures, of which two green giants—a male and a female, each at least eight feet tall—were the most peculiar. Seeing them was delightful: I relished the fact that my home welcomed guests from all over the universe, which made sense as the place emanated prosperity and well-being.

Suddenly I realized a woman was walking next to me. She was different from those in the palace: tall and slim, she carried a gentle rosy glow around her and gave the impression of being local. I felt it was important not to show that I was not taking this world for granted, but before I could act one way or another, she informed me, in a playful voice, that she was looking for a serf for some psychological experiment and that I might qualify for the role. Her words made me laugh. She was clearly a noblewoman, but I knew I was royalty. I continued at the same pace and she followed me, leaning on my shoulder as I put my arm around her waist.

After another turn or two, the road brought us to a large plaza ending in a red brick wall. In its center was what looked like an exhibition of futuristic cars, except I knew that, advanced as they looked to me, in this world they were all retro. I asked the woman what her favorite car was, and she named something I had never heard of. I asked her to show it to me and she laughed; I immediately understood that it was far too expensive to be here. As that thought crossed my mind I felt a warm breeze on my face that blurred my vision, heralding the end of my journey. With the last bit of dissipating attention, I caught a glimpse of the distant mountains, serene and eternal. Then there was nothing but darkness, and I heard the sounds of the world where I'd fallen asleep.

I don't know how long I lay in my bed, fully awake and hanging on to that last image I'd seen, painting it on my shut eyelids as if it could carry me back. It didn't, and eventually I began to cry, overwhelmed by the sense of having lost the only place that mattered. Soon the agony became too acute, and I opened my eyes. There I was: back in my physical body, desperate and distraught, and the rectangular box of my bedroom lit by the cold autumnal morning sun was but a mocking reminder of how imprisoned I was bound to remain.

Sorcery 101

"What would you like to eat, sir?" I heard in the distance. The food trolley was right by me, and there could be no doubt as to whom the question was directed at.

"Everything the lady to my right ordered, plus a glass of apple juice, no ice, please," I said, prepared to defend my thought against any onslaught. Folding my laptop at an almost-forty-five-degree angle, I moved it onto my chest, its base pressing into my belt buckle while the screen rested against the table's edge. Now I was typing with my hands hanging over the keyboard from either side; it was uncomfortable, but I refused to forfeit either the meal or the narrative.

I was not the same after that day. My life lost all its taste, and everything I did seemed a meaningless chore. Suspecting that I was losing my mind, I spent hours forcing myself to write, which had always rescued me in the past. But not this time. One night I was composing a dialogue; an innocuous encounter with a slight sexual subtext. It took me three and a half hours, and when I read the final version (about a page and a half long), I hated it. Not because it was bad: no, it was witty, original and captivating; but it conveyed none of the magic I knew I had.

I still could not explain why it took me so long to get to the crux of it. Perhaps the reason was my pretension to uniqueness. What happened to me seemed so exclusive, so tailored to my innermost self that I didn't want to think I could be dealing with a regular and well-documented phenomenon experienced by countless people. I am talking about lucid dreaming, of course: I'm sure you've already figured it out. But if you don't know what it is: it is when you become aware in the midst of a dream and can control—at least—your own behavior in it, as I did in that mysterious world, although such uniformity and cohesion are difficult to achieve without practice. The fact that I had done so on the first try, however, was not testimony to my talent but rather the result of the boost my energy bodies had gotten from that pass. I'm sure you've already connected the dots, but I learned this much, much later after having infiltrated an incredible realm offering infinite possibilities to those who venture into it.

That realm is called sorcery.

"Excuse me?"

"For what?" I asked automatically, almost trembling with surprise, but still typing.

"Can you let me pass?"

"Haven't you just returned from the bathroom?" I wondered if she was leaving only to get my attention.

"Does that mean I wouldn't go again?"

I finally liked her tone. She was no longer playing a spoiled princess used to men complying with her every caprice at the drop of a hat: she had accepted me as a force beyond her control and was prepared to deal with it. I did what I had done before, sliding from under the table without moving it, except this time it required leaning on the left armrest while holding the laptop in my right hand. Doing so, I glanced at her food tray and saw a glass of apple juice. This made me smile.

She was not afraid to appear awkward anymore and did precisely what she had to, leaning with against her left arm pressed into the headrest of my seat while edging her legs toward the aisle. She wasn't as elegant as I'd have liked her to be, but she did the trick without knocking down my food. And she truly was ready to fight: I knew it both from the tension in her cheekbones and the cold flame in her eyes.

Doesn't it razz you that they interrupt me? Why do I have to get distracted as soon as I touch upon something interesting! But it's better this way: were I to broadcast continuously, you'd get exhausted and miss the main points. This way, you're accumulating annoyance, which raises your overall energy level. And the more energy, the brighter the catharsis. Which reminds me of one of the cornerstone principles of sorcery expressed in a phrase that I'd profaned as soon as I heard it: *the energy is where the attention is*. I won't tell you my phrase, though: it's not in English and translating it will leave only the barren sense deprived of the creative charm. Besides, it rhymes: I bet this alone makes it as valid as the original.

I could get even more ludicrous, but that wouldn't change the simple fact: when most people hear the word "sorcery," their thoughts inexorably turn to fairy tales. Which is great news for sorcerers, because the fewer people know the truth, the thinner their competition. And any kind of competition in ordinary life is nothing compared to what goes on in sorcery, because the stakes there are infinitely higher. Yes, ladies and gentlemen: making a billion bucks, becoming the President, or any other zenith promoted by society as universally awesome is light years away from the maximum a human being can achieve in his or her life. Any human being, that is. Which is why sorcerers who are worth their salt don't even touch earthly goals.

I am in a difficult spot now. On the one hand, I want to show you sorcery instead of talking about it, but on the other, if I don't talk, you may not understand. Remember, I said "cast a spell" before diving into that lucid dream? That was an example of "something catching your eye," as I'd said when I told you that this text is wrought. Did you ignore that phrase? If you didn't, feel free to skip to the words "When I closed my eyes". If you did, read on.

An amazing thing about sorcery is that nowadays most of what you need to learn is available online. The problem is: it's practically impossible to find a teacher. A glut of information creates a shortage of reliability: with so many people looking for mercenary gains in the esoteric niche, it's hard to tell who among them has the knowledge. If anyone. My strategy called for systematic interrogation of the sets of beliefs of a tight circle of potential candidates (those who didn't show hunger for money or manipulation) and trying them one by one. The evaluation criterion was simple: I needed a comprehensive explanation of what the fuck was going on between me and Martina.

I realize that by now I must be coming off as a very unusual type. Not Nabokov's Humbert, but definitely strange. But you have to understand: I was more freaked out about this than anyone. I could accept loving a woman and not being loved back; I didn't even care for that as much already. Yet I still had to deal with that fact, and not on my own terms. My own terms would have been these: I'd keep the right to compose marvelous poetry about her until something good happened, and if it didn't, so what? But the hook sank deep: the way I felt on that plane flying from Rome was superhuman, and to become capable of summoning that experience at will I was ready to invest many a sleepless month of trial and error. And in the end, I hit the gold vein.

Lady 2-7 was coming back any moment, so I didn't begin a new passage, knowing it was time for something else. It was a pity I had to let the food grow cold, but eating right now would draw energy to the stomach while I needed it elsewhere. The hype from the coffee and chocolate had already worn off, which was good, although drowsiness was quickly taking its place. To combat that, I got up and began stretching, sipping my apple juice and looking down the aisle where Lady would come from. She saw me as soon as she left the lavatory but didn't shy away, walking back with long, steadfast strides and holding her head high. I made room for her and she didn't so much as look at me, sliding back to her seat as if that were the very way she'd always done it. I stretched for another minute until the warmth in my thighs reached the lower back and the calves; then I threw my laptop into the overhead bin and sat back down, ready for the first meditation of power.

The Ethereal Body

When I closed my eyes, it came instantly: the hot spot at the bottom of my stomach that resembled a freshly boiled potato. Yet I made myself do the whole preparatory routine, first focusing on my breathing, then adding the heartbeat, and finally including the spinal wave. After two or three minutes, I began filling my body parts with awareness, moving from my toes to my head. Soon, I began perceiving myself as a single unit, my attention being sucked into that potato-like feeling which had grown to the size of a soccer ball.

This is known as moving the assemblage point onto the ethereal body: a maneuver that, among other things, sharply increases one's sexual appeal. Put simply, the ethereal body is an invisible entity that enshrouds your physical body and is responsible for your sensations, sensuality being one of them; as for the assemblage point, you'd better research that one yourself, because it is quite a personal matter. Mine, for instance, is where my cell phone is: meaning that if it is in the bedroom, the priorities of my life are linked to the activities that normally take place there. If my phone is in the living room, my priorities shift, and God forbid I ever forget it in my drug dealer's car again.

That was a joke, though I feel I still need to persuade you that attention is key to everything. But here is what was going on right now. By focusing on that hot spot that had already grown wider than my physical body, I was creating something like a two-way magnet that communicated with the people around me in ways that are incomprehensible to the mind. The closer those people were, the greater was the impact, although this doesn't have to be so: the ethereal body can instantly reach someone on the other side of the Earth if you target that person specifically. Yet my current tactic was different: I wanted Lady to react to me of her own accord. This is similar to fishing: I was offering such a tasty bait that she was compelled to take it. Why? See, the habitual position of my assemblage point is on a much higher spot than the ethereal body, and when I move it down, a great deal of power comes along. So, it doesn't matter who I'm dealing with: a Hollywood star, a supermodel, or a princess. After the preparatory routine that tunes the energy up, a woman can ignore my bait without being a sorceress herself only if she has her assemblage point higher than where I usually keep mine. In my whole life, I have met only a handful of ladies who could accomplish that feat even temporarily, and you already know the name of my favorite among them.

My eyes still shut, I grew the spot to a yard in diameter; now it resembled an amber bubble, and I sensed Lady's ethereal body, reading her feelings as if they were running over my own skin. She knew that I'd changed seats because of her, but not why I'd ignored her since. She wasn't afraid but concerned that I would impede her somehow. And, most importantly, it hadn't occurred to her to view me in sexual terms. That is, until about five minutes ago.

A contact between ethereal bodies is similar to that of flames: they can merge to exchange energy, and the stronger one has the upper hand. Her assemblage point was lodged on the mental body: it is a respectably high position, but she still had no chance. Yet I was unsure of how to proceed, because I actually enjoy the Mental. It's that borderline twilight zone that links the subconscious and the supernatural; a most fragile and unstable area prone to making grave mistakes about both those realms. And yet it is capable of inimitable magic in its own right: most of classical literature is written on that level, as is this chapter.

I opened my eyes and the environment, harsh even in the dimmed light, intruded into my head. An eyelash got into my right eye and I rubbed it until the tears flushed it. Lady was watching a comedy show, most likely attributing the changes in her mood to that; I kept looking at her screen, the characters performing the usual routines that gave clumsy clues about the script, and then a simple solution crossed my mind. I turned my head to face her, not even pretending I was after the window, which would have been lame anyway as there was nothing but darkness outside.

She had very fine facial features and wore minimal makeup to hide the rough edges that merciless age begins leaving on women soon after they attain majority. Her eyes were blue and pellucid; her eyelashes left an almost visible trail to seduction as they hovered in the air; but when it comes to the female face, I am a strange fellow, going for the nose. Hers was long and thin, marked by a slight upward curl at the tip that pierced my bubble from the inside with a demand for a kiss. But its proud owner was still engrossed in the show, failing to acknowledge my undivided attention. I wasn't rushing her, playing with the bubble, which shrank but became denser; my arousal was just around the corner, but I wouldn't take the last step yet, collecting as much behind the dam as I could before letting it out on both her and myself.

When she did notice, it was like her mind became aware of what her body had known all along. First, she stopped blinking, then she stopped watching, and finally she turned her head, meeting my eyes askance, but clearly ready. I changed nothing of what I was doing, except now that her face practically glowed before me in all its unstoppable beauty, it took everything I had in me to hold back the flood and hide the struggle within.

Lady 2-7

"Wanna tell me something?" she demanded, extracting her headphones from her ears.

"Pick one thing," I said coarsely, clearing my throat with an almost inaudible cough.

A look of disbelief crossed her face. Then she chose to play it straight.

"We both know that you weren't here before."

"Define 'here'".

"There was another man in this seat. Where is he?"

Another man, I thought. *Not again.*

"Still on this plane. Why, did you think he hopped off?"

She took a moment; then she frowned.

"Is this a joke?"

"I'm not amused. What about you?"

"Definitely not."

"By the way." Here I took a pause. "When was the last time you were?"

"Excuse me?"

"When was the last time you were?" This phrase was a perfect replica of the previous one, every intonation and inflection mirrored.

"I heard you. What do you mean?"

"The meaning of this question does not go beyond the customary semantics of the words that make it up. But I can reconstruct the sequence ..." She was eyeing me like a bird of prey. "It began by you supposing my previous question …"

"I get it that you asked when the last time I was amused was, English is my mother tongue, thank you." I was glad she caught the insinuation: I hoped it would make her up her game. "And I don't see how that is relevant."

"The truth escapes the eye more often than many people would have liked. But I have to confess something." I smiled, taking another calculated pause. "I lied to you."

"Gonna elaborate?" she asked a few seconds later with a sideways shake of her head that I think women of her age pick up from modern TV shows like the one she was watching.

"I *am* being amused," I revealed in a most amiable tone.

"Good for you." Now the head shake was vertical, yet it wasn't a nod. "And I'm still not."

"By the way." Now I had to remember just how long that first pause was. "When was the last time you were?" I said and sent a jolt into her.

This surprised me more than her: she twitched and rubbed her thigh against the seat. Not that she minded the feeling: she just couldn't figure out why on earth she'd think of sex *now*. She probably also had a vivid sexual image flash before her eyes. As for me, while I displayed none of these reactions, I relived them on the inside.

"Why do you keep asking?" She was trying to buy time, and I was happy to oblige her.

"I'm curious." Now I was talking along the energy line flowing between the pits of our stomachs, increasing its intensity by low and deliberate breathing. "You strike me as fun, and I want to get to know you better." I delivered another jolt, a much softer and longer one, and its sweetness lingered between my legs just as it must have stuck between hers. "In college, I used to cross the Atlantic up to four times a year. And during all that time I only had a fun seatmate once. Now every time I take a long flight I get a first-class seat to trade with a person sitting next to someone I like."

I paused, waiting for my words to sink in. She was not thinking mentally anymore but wasn't aware of it. The flow became steadier with every breath she took, and her cheeks finally turned rosy.

"And how do they react?" she said finally, as if unsure herself whether she was asking about those to whom I offered my seat or their lucky neighbors.

"Exactly as you did. A break in continuity baffles the reason." I stumbled upon a strong personal emotion and immediately threw it into the flow. "Once upon a time, I was flying to New York from Florence." She responded by leaning toward me, and I immediately cast another thread of energy through our chests. "I was about to board when I saw this incredible young man who looked like he'd stepped from a Balzac's novel and made a trip to ..." I named my favorite luxury fashion house, "before buying his ticket. He was an aristocrat to the bone, if you know what I mean." I gave her a searching look. An aristocrat to the bone herself, she had no idea what that meant, but her lips parted, revealing a moist gap. "It means that you don't belong to the world surrounding you. And I don't mean being incongruous. It is true that a bona fide aristocrat looks best in a palace, but ... you're not getting it at all, are you?"

"I do—why?" she said defensively, reinforcing both the flow and the thread with her genuine emotions.

"Okay, let's give it one more try before we call it a flop." I sighed, wondering if it would be better if she thought I was joking. "Have you ever played the game where you try to figure out what animal someone looks like?"

"Sure," she lied.

"It doesn't matter if you haven't. You just look at someone and try to figure out what animal that person reminds you of." I paused, reveling in the amber effervescence inside my pants. It felt like I was being assaulted by a bunch of diaphanous-winged fairies, and all I wanted was for them to continue their siege.

"And?"

"Well, a true aristocrat is someone for whom you can't come up with an animal."

She smiled. *Finally*, I thought. But I wasn't complaining: the longer the initial resistance, the more complete the eventual surrender.

"Now that you put it that way, it makes sense," she said.

"No, it doesn't," I shook my head in mock despair, aroused to the point of sensing heatwaves radiating from my intestines. The bubble had grown so large that it had completely engulfed her again; she'd picked up some of the charge, but not enough. "If you're good at this game, you'll come up with an animal for whoever. For a true aristocrat, it's usually a bird. Although I worked with a woman who looked like a lizard. And her sidekick was a veritable toad, warts included."

"What do you do for work?" she asked hastily, the stomach flow quivering like a swirl of smoke in a beam of light.

"Forex trading. Crosses. A cross is a currency pair that doesn't include the dollar," I reported, watching her clench her thighs together in a movement that had to be involuntary.

"That's as far from me as it gets," she said, shaking her head slightly and missing the beat again, clearly absorbed by what was going on between her legs.

"That's what most people think. Which is a shame, because few things affect them more than forex."

"How come?"

"Because, depending on the price of your currency, the goods and services you buy are either relatively cheap, or relatively expensive. And the range can be very wide."

"But how can a currency have a price when it's already money?"

I smiled: I had heard that question before.

I spent the next ten minutes explaining equity trading, major macroeconomic factors, and other nonsense. I even mentioned some of the technical indicators. She paid no attention to my words, daydreaming and riding the wave of attraction. Naturally, I didn't mind. I was busy anyway, blending the flow and the thread into a circuit, its charge growing whenever either of us fed an emotion into it. When I stopped talking, she was silent for a while, breathing slowly and deeply. Then she gave me a long look which I would have struggled to interpret had I not orchestrated it, and said:

"So, you're only a crazy trader who gave up his first-class seat to sit next to the girl he liked?"

"If I were only that, I would have never boarded this plane."

"What brings you to England?"

"It's the closest place to my destination."

"Scotland?"

"Not quite."

She gave me a long, searching look, as if she wanted to say something but chose not to in the end; then she turned back to her screen and started a new show.

Lunch Break

After a minute of thinking, I decided to eat, assuming she was processing the roller-coaster ride we'd just been on. I liked that she was neither nervous nor talking: I also needed a break. This ethereal business is very taxing energetically, and I hadn't eaten for so long I couldn't remember what I'd last ate.

As expected, the food was cold, but getting upset about that would mean not taking responsibility. Fortunately, she was vegetarian, going for tofu with pasta; the rest was a medley as commonplace as it gets in economy class. A cup of hot tea would have been handy, especially for the bread and the muffin—both equally stale—but I'd missed the boat and didn't want to bother the stewardesses, who were taking a break, so I contented myself with the water and the rest of my apple juice.

She hadn't paused the episode she was watching, which ended at some point during my financial revelations, the screen switching to the flight map. We were near Greenland. The cabin was lulled into dark quietude, most of the passengers either snatching a few minutes of uncomfortable sleep or catching up on shows and movies. I listened to the turbines as if trying to hear a false note, but nothing betrayed a slightest deviation from the planned course. That should have made me feel good but didn't. I knew something was up but didn't know what.

Lady remained silent, avoidant. It made sense: the ethereal trip was ruthless because I threw in all I had; most of the time it ends up as overkill, but the couple of times I'd taken it easy and failed taught me to not slack off; so, although I stopped maintaining the circuit consciously, it kept running in the background. Suddenly, I felt exhausted. The cumulative tiredness of the last few days spent in escalating anticipation hit me again, melting behind my eyes and sinking deep into my forehead. Unwilling to resist the assault and assuming it was better not to anyway, I let my eyelids fall, propping the back of my neck against another one of those plane pillows that must have been designed with the best of intentions but seldom, if ever, worked.

I was almost dreaming when I heard:

"Hey?"

I still hadn't learned to see with my eyes closed but I felt her with every pore of my skin, the circuit's charge picking up immediately. It was also a good kind of "hey."

"Need to pass?"

"Not if you're asleep."

"I could use the bathroom myself," I said, returning to reality as if by the flick of a switch. It was roughly the same. "Besides, we need to take care of these tables, don't you think?"

"Like you're finally gonna fold yours? God, you were really getting under my skin with that! Do you always give the women you like a hard time?"

"Only when I know they will benefit from it. Besides, the skill will remain with you forever."

"In case I end up in a situation like this again?"

"You'll never end up in a situation like this again," I said. "Not even a pale shadow of it. So enjoy it while it lasts."

I got up, picked up the tray and folded my table, fixing the clip securely and watching her legs: they were lean, and supple, and elegant, and a dozen other adjectives that neither did them justice nor had ever evoked this rush of fire in me when I'd read them off a page. The lustrous fabric of her plum-purple pants creased into soft, velvet-like furrows, and as she passed by, her scent teasing me once again (this time not so much with its elusive bouquet as with the tones of arousal woven into it), my entire ethereal body momentarily touched hers, producing the feeling of a slight electric charge hitting all of my skin at once.

I waited for her to choose a direction and went in the opposite one, tray in hand, observing the cabin, which was engulfed in that blissful serenity that sometimes marks doomed places before the hammer of judgment is brought down. No stewardess was in the alcove separating first class from economy, so I left the tray by the sink. The first lavatory I tried was taken, but its counterpart on the other side of the aisle was free, and as I slid in I wondered whether my moves had been seen by anyone.

Despite the constricting space, this close to a large mirror, I could see myself almost from head to toe. I hesitated for a coy moment before meeting my own eyes, and when I did I did not mind. My eyes shone like two razor blades; the angles of my face sharpened; and even my clothes somehow didn't seem bad anymore, as if this augmented portrait of mine extracted an extra layer of dimensional depth from the denim, saturating its blue with a shade of mystery. I cautiously unzipped my fly, probing the area underneath intently with the tips of my fingers. The verdict was unambiguous: I was ready, and the potato inside, now baked to a golden crust, was set to break with a crackle when the thing started growing in size again.

The cells of my body reverberated in unison, and when I stopped the sense of satisfaction was complete. This time, I sanitized my hands after having washed them, and when the last drops of that smelly liquid evaporated from my palms I tore off a piece of toilet paper, opened the door with it and threw it into the nearest bin, noting that my tray was still untouched.

When I returned to my seat, she was already there.

"Easier with the tables folded, *n'est pas*?" I asked her legs, smitten.

"Almost feels like a real flight again."

"You mean that boring sequence of events required to get from one airport to another while your body slowly grows numb in a series of awkward positions? That won't be for long. By the way, I still want to learn more about you."

"What exactly?"

"Everything but, given the zeitnot, let's be efficient. Tell me about the most exciting thing you've ever done."

She frowned.

"What do you mean?"

"Have you ever done anything exciting?" I patiently asked. "Rope-jumping in Nepal? Scuba diving in the White Sea? Meeting an alien on a Sunday stroll in Springfield, Ohio? Something that doesn't happen to everyone and is awesome?"

"I lived in Guam for a year, if that's awesome."

I smiled. I knew she'd have something up her sleeve.

"You tell me."

"All?"

"Start by telling me how you wound up there and let's see where it takes us."

She took a few more moments to get ready, and then started talking.

In Guam. Part I.

"It was my first year out of college, and things weren't going my way. I got a job I didn't like because my parents refused to make the payments on my student loans unless I accepted it. I shared a tiny apartment in lower Midtown with two girls I'd never be friends with—living, I guess, the kind of life that's out there for young people who come to Manhattan. Except I didn't care for Manhattan. I just wanted a life."

"You weren't getting any at all?"

"Time was always an issue: I never had enough of it. I put up with it for a while, but then a friend told me about this Guam work-and-travel gig that would pay just what I needed for the loans while everything else would be taken care of. I had never travelled outside the US; it seemed worth a shot, so I gave it one. As my dad says, never turn down a good job offer."

No, he wasn't abusive, I thought. *He just had no clue about his daughter*.

"What was the job?"

"Hotel associate. Which meant doing whatever was needed from the front desk to the kitchen. No room service, though."

"Did you know much about Guam?"

"Not really. I'd heard about it, but I couldn't find it on a map, if that's what you're asking. It seemed nice in the pictures, and I love the ocean. But one thing I didn't realize was that the ocean also means hurricanes ..."

She proceeded with the logistics of getting to Guam and her early days there. I kept my eyes closed, letting her words paint a picture; it required no effort at all. She was an honest storyteller, omitting much but keeping the essentials intact: meeting her best friend, hitting the beach for the first time, buying an aquamarine ring. I wished she'd worn it: from the way her voice quivered when she mentioned it, I knew it suited her. And what kind of aquamarine wouldn't suit these ocean-blue eyes?

So far it was a pure vacation at an exotic resort, although the necessity of work cast a pall over her days. But evidently, none of the heaviness had stuck like the image of the white-throated doves in the lush foliage. She kept talking, and her emotions became yet another layer of the movie concocted and played by my imagination. It was a beautiful sight, although perhaps the plot was too sunny at the core as I instinctively gravitated towards the phantasy of being in a paradise with a dear lover of mine: a role she fit perfectly. There it was: the hoarse whisper of the ocean rolling slowly on the beach and carrying the rhythm of eternity on its foamy edge, its irregular white bands lingering on the damp sand before being lifted by another wave, and the thick woody smell of an open fire nearby. The most eager have already picked their skewers, but will they roast the marshmallows to a nut-brown crust without burning them? Seagull-like birds inhabiting this edge of Oikumene flew solemnly in the air, which shook in the fire's heat; scavengers of time, they were looking for edible bits to collect for later. It was a wonderful story, but alas, it couldn't take us anywhere.

Next, I brought my shoulder closer to hers while casting a surreptitious look back through the gap between the seats. The people behind, an attractive elderly couple, were both asleep. I checked out the rest of our row. Most of the passengers were watching their screens, but none had any reason to look our way, let alone notice anything. People walking the aisle from behind us were the only threat, but I had an idea of how to take care of that if needed.

"It's getting cold here," I said. "Why don't we use a blanket?"

I ripped the plastic sleeve off mine. It was large and thin, and great under the circumstances. I spread it over both of us; she was surprised for no more than a second, likely recognizing that achieving the same result on her own required too much effort. I held my edge of the blanket under my arm, stretching it tightly; she let hers lie loosely, only adjusting it to smooth the wrinkles.

"I liked what you told me about Guam," I said in a low voice, leaning away. "Now I want to hear about the worst storm you survived in that place."

"I was just gonna tell you," she said eagerly. "It fits what you described earlier: awesome and all. But don't get your hopes up: there's nothing like people getting washed off the shore and never coming back."

"Although if they'd been stupid enough to walk the shore, that's precisely what would have happened?" I asked, suppressing a smile.

"They'd still have been found, I think."

"And I think you are describing the perfect crime. Bring a person to Guam on a stormy day and the rest will be taken care of."

"You have to bring them a day in advance at least: a storm like that doesn't come out of the blue, so they close the airport way before. But even then, how'd you explain why the person ended up on the shore?"

"Would psychological trauma count as an excuse? But we got derailed. You were saying that yours was a pacific story."

"I never said pacific. I said no one got killed."

"I want to hear everything, then. You gave a catchy preamble and promised that the ending wouldn't be tragic. I'm ready to go; just keep reminding me of the counts of people when you guys start ending up in isolated groups."

"Sounds like you know how it works," she chuckled. "Been caught in a hurricane yourself?"

"Those usually hit me from the inside. But why should I complain? At least I'm always in a good company."

She continued, and so did I. We were now in late summer: the air temperature hadn't changed, but the humidity was absolute. On a small island, the dark and clouded sky merges with the ocean; the rain seamlessly completes the transition, and there is only a tiny speck of land to counterbalance all that: the piece that is being scour by the hurricane. *Where would you hide?* I wondered, now looking for clues about her hotel. Was it at least made of brick? No chance: in this place, everything is plain wood except for the US ships. But those leave the harbor before the storm to avoid landing a few hundred yards inshore in all their imperial glory. The basement, then; which was constructed of concrete. Judging by the thickness of the walls, it must have been a former military building put to civilian use. There was nothing to be afraid of here, even if the wind tore off the rest of the building: the concrete went all the way to the ceiling, enclosing the space. *You are practically in a bunker, and you're the kind of girl who understands what that means; but why are you still afraid? Is it because you are indulging in a childhood fear? Or do you think one of the scoundrels you're locked up with is going to make a pass at you when the fatuous exhilaration of survival fades and the sober realization follows: that the weather will not change for at least twenty-four hours?* A brief mention of the cast of characters allowed for the exclusion from the potential creeps only the few women present in the basement. The men held the power, though, as the hotel's general manager was among the stranded. Or was I getting it wrong this whole time? Was it not a pass she was afraid of but the lack thereof? One of those scoundrels seemed cute to my angel, and she hoped he wouldn't be stupid enough to miss the opportunity.

The cacophonous anarchy outside is a nice background for a ride of introspection, but when would you want him to move? Sure enough, when the others would be resting, but who could sleep through this hell? The locals, but that's less than half of those present. The others are all an inexperienced breed, mostly Americans, with an accidental Brit, so at least some of them will fret and wander around instead of staying tightly packed on the mattresses. It must have been the Brit you fell for; not because he was special, but because he sounded so.

"... and suddenly thunder roared ..."

It was completely instinctive: my conscious mind had no part in it. If we'd been in a more permissive setting, it would have made sense to put my arm around her, but the current context demanded a different course of action. Having sex was out of the question due to space constraints, which left but one option, so as I heard the roaring thunder in my head, my right palm moved under the blanket until it found the inner side of her left thigh.

"You were saying," I broke the silence a few moments later.

"What's that?" she asked cautiously, looking for me to take responsibility.

"My hand."

"Why is it there?"

"You were scared. I wanted to support you."

She took a pause.

"I was."

"I saw this terrible lightning before my eyes, and I felt just as you must have because I don't recall having ever felt that way."

"So, you weren't actually asleep this whole time?"

"I haven't missed a word."

She paused again.

"And how did you feel?"

"Like I've just seen the bolt and am expecting the thunder, but there is none. I wait, and wait, and wait, and the more it doesn't arrive, the more scared I become. And then I tell myself that the lightning must have struck very far away and by the time the thunder comes it will be muffled. And then it finally comes, exploding like God's final wrath, and I tremble helplessly, thinking how dreadful it must have sounded where it struck. It was so horrible that I wanted to give you my full support—emotional, above all."

"Is that so?"

It was my turn to pause.

"No." I said finally. "You caught me again. I lied."
"When was the first time?"
"The first time I lied? Or the first time you caught me?"
"Tell me about this one."
"It wasn't emotional support that I wanted to give you the most."
"And what was it?"
I leaned closer and whispered into her majestic ear:
"Head."

She inhaled sharply, her back arching, which reminded me of a song I liked. Then she gave me a look that said it all. My hand, which had remained on her thigh, felt heavy, and I moved it slightly to get more sensory input; she reacted with a barely audible groan and it required all of my discipline to remain on the surface of her clothes instead of jumping straight to her skin.

Few people realize how much sex originates from gentlemanly motives.

In Guam. Part II.

At this point I was ready to pass out. She … well, how do I say this? She was more than attractive to me: she felt right. Even if only for the time being. And that "being" could take a long time. I could see myself marrying this woman and spending at least ten years in a committed marriage without having sex with others, unless she was also involved. Yes, I liked her that much. And the problem was that, now that I'd moved my assemblage point so low, my perceptions were channeled predominantly through my basic instincts. Consequently, I struggled with vivid sexual imagery fueled by what my hand sensed.

Gentlemen, if, when putting a hand on the inner thigh of a woman, you encounter heat, it's a great sign, so use it wisely. I, in the meantime, was figuring out what "wisely" meant in this context. My own arousal was overwhelming, and the hot spot was no longer a sphere, losing its immaculate geometric shape to resemble the ragged edges of a burning flame, akin to that which radiated from her center of womanhood. It was scalding on the tips of my fingers, baking at my nails, and promising that underneath the pants and, possibly, underwear, lay an equatorial swamp dying to welcome a daring pioneer. Although the first pioneer must have trodden the landscape at least a decade ago. I suddenly felt like a dinosaur from two hundred million years ago and wondered how they'd felt about being alive. Like reptiles, I bet.

Still caressing her encased thigh, I brought my fingers closer to the epicenter but didn't touch it, hovering just above and straining to detect a change in humidity. She suddenly tensed; she knew what was going on as soon as I threw on the blanket, but there was still a chance that I wouldn't go all the way. Now she knew the truth, so she had to give it her final consideration. I paused, waiting for her to catch up. Why do women make it hard for men to do things that women want from men anyway?

Even with my hand on it, I still didn't know what fabric her pants were made of, but, much like the looks of things, it was secondary. The whole area adjoining the bottom of her stomach was hot and damp, and each second there were fewer and fewer reasons for me to remain on the surface. Yet I did, mostly to regain control over the madness that reigned in me. Now it was almost a malady but, curiously, I knew that somewhere nearby lay the safety valve. For the emotional constituent, that is, because as far as the physical one was concerned, I had already gone beyond the point of no return. But nor did I want to retreat.

I made a few extremely cautious adjustments to my position. To anyone walking the aisle, I had to appear like a man sleeping diagonally in his seat with his head tilted to the left. The fact that my eyes weren't fully shut should have been an enigma to everyone, Lady included. I didn't leave much of a gap between my eyelids, yet enough to make sure no one would unexpectedly rise up behind my shoulder to ascertain what objectionable activities we were engaged in. Although, personally, I found nothing objectionable in anything I'd done this far, or in what was to follow.

With these preparations taken care of, my arm stretched out comfortably, allowing me to perform at least at ninety percent of capacity. We had about two and a half hours before landing, which left at least an hour of quietude. She seemed relaxed and was getting impatient, but the time was finally coming: we were safe, as anyone coming from behind would be caught by my peripheral vision in time.

I squeezed her slightly and let go, waiting for her to catch up. After a moment's hesitation, she did. Then my little finger slowly slid under the hem of her blouse, curving up and then gripping her waistband. This simple move caused an eruption of emotions inside her, which she expressed with one deep, slow sigh. First time on the plane? Perhaps the pioneer simile wasn't that far off.

It was time, and every part of me knew it as well as my little finger. I slid it in all the way, passing her underwear's lacy edge and getting under the ribbon. I wondered what color it was. Now several slow lateral movements around her belly; her hair was present but reduced to a minimum, and her petals were large, soft and very pronounced. I adjusted my hand inside her underwear before entering; and when I did the image of a warm knife going through butter came to mind, except the melted butter had nowhere to go, rather mixing with the honey that filled the chamber.

I know I am opening myself up to most undeserved misunderstandings, but I am fully of the opinion that the best way of communicating with a woman is when she is sexually aroused. This state grants her access to instant knowledge, and sorcery isn't even the greatest feat she can accomplish in it. I wouldn't be surprised if I could teach Lady 2-7 all I knew in less than an hour, spending the rest of the flight on the questions I couldn't solve, and I bet she'd feed me at least one good idea before landing. But alas, magic was not at stake, and all I could do was to go on with my fingers.

I would much rather have done her orally; in fact, I could almost taste her lips on my tongue, but the current arrangement also had its perks, one of them being that I could lean to the left to extend my right arm fully and to give my hand the freedom it needed for this fine work. Some think it's easy to do a woman with the fingers; others say it's an art worth a king's ransom. I think the method is viable as long as you don't get unduly fancy, but it shouldn't be abused; and if there are no better alternatives it can be prescribed with all the usual cautions.

I lingered on her pants for so long partly because I wanted the temperature of my hand to catch up. I was cautiously feeling for all the usual spots; she reacted gently but calmly, and I suspected that she could be ultimately turned on by stimulation around an obscure area on her lower back or somewhere else equally inaccessible at the moment. But soon the heat inside her reached a new degree, and another explosion of slippery wetness made its way down the area I was exploring.

The next round was more fruitful: she began responding to my strokes with micromovements, giving me further clues as to what to do. It was nothing startling: a few maneuvers everyone interested in women should know, but a few minutes in I realized that one of her erogenous zones was right there: the spot between the tendons near the place where the leg starts. Accidentally stroking it once, I noticed a positive response, and a sustained effort moved her to the next stage within a minute. I stopped fiddling with the spot then but grew even more aware of what my fingers were doing inside. Care, love and, above all, softness were the passwords. I was glad I'd filed my nails last light: I was perfectly groomed for the job. So, when my middle finger had gathered enough slipperiness, I went in all the way with the ring finger as well, alternating between stimulating her front with the palm of my hand and bringing the thumb for help. I was lucky she was to my right: doing the same with my left hand would have been torturous. But hell, what did I stop at when it came to women?

By now her hand had passed the belts of both my seat and my jeans and crossed the waistband of my briefs, although she still hesitated to grab the culprit, as if considering whether she should do it at all. I slid my fingers deeper and added a slight twisting move; after the third twist she continued. Not stopping, I put my left hand over hers and showed her the most efficient gestures. This proved handy as she wasn't a leftie. Her palm reinforced my fleeting thoughts of what being married to her would have been like; but now that her orgasm was right around the corner, all my attention was on getting her there.

Two minutes later, she was ready to fly, squeezing my wrist under the blanket and fine-tuning my movements to the exact rhythm she needed. I was now working on one of the non-g-spots with swift circular strokes until a short involuntary exhalation told me she had taken off. Now it was up to her: if she thought it was worth it, she could scream. Electrified throughout, she rolled her closed eyes up and shook, coming deep on my fingers, shaking more, coming again, and not wanting to stop, and not caring if anyone noticed, but not screaming, as if knowing, sensing, solving in her beautiful head that the affairs of those-who-are-aristocrats-to-the-bone are, above all, no one else's business.

"It's weird," she said into my ear later, long after I'd withdrawn, keeping my hand on her thigh. "I am not like that at all, I swear. But I feel like I've known you forever."

"You have," I assured her, watching golden specks shimmer around her. "You can know a person for years and he'll still be a stranger. But when you find your energy match, you are drawn: instantly and irresistibly."

"Do you believe in energy matches?"

"Matches, my dear, are something I truly believe in." I smiled. "As for energy, believing isn't the right word." I buried my nose in her hair to inhale more of its sweetness. "I work with it."

"And how does it work?"

"Like a charm."

She brought her lips close to my ear, and the rest took place in a low whisper.

"I would finish you off," she said. "But I'm afraid people will notice."

"The thought of you doing it here makes me rock-hard," I observed nonchalantly.

"I really want to. And I'm good at it."

"Seems like I'll never know now."

She hesitated. I could feel she was having a bout with herself. Then she waved the white flag.

"I can do it with my hand."

My look was designed to convey utter despondency.

"It's fine, don't worry," I said when the look was noticed.

"Hey." She pinched a fold of my skin under the blanket: tightly enough to let me know she was serious. "I *want* you to come, and I *want* to blow you. And I would have done it already, if we were in a different place."

"You were just saying you're not like that, no? Listen, I believe you. This is what life's all about: you want to do something, but everyone around tells you it's a bad idea, so you either agree, or you don't."

"Wanna try the lavatory? It's pretty small, but at least no one will see."

"I don't have sex in public bathrooms. Makes me feel like I'm stealing."

"I'm sorry."

"Don't worry. Besides, I didn't give you head either. I would have loved to, though. I can see myself do it with no effort. In fact, that's what I'm picturing right now."

"You're something else. By the way," she said in a different tone. "What animal do I look like?"

"Gazelle," I replied instantly, as if giving an answer I'd had all along.

"Wanna know what you look like?"

"Dying to."

"Cheetah."

"I can see us sharing a beautiful valley, close enough to the ocean to catch its salty breeze in the air every once in a while. Ethiopia could do." I wanted to give her a kiss but took a slow, deliberate breath instead. "I thought you'd pick giraffe."

"Don't be silly," she said slowly. I was right: a kiss would have disturbed this peaceful triumph of beauty. "Giraffes are herbivores."

The Parting

The rest of the flight took less than two hours, and I spent it acting as if we were married. While we relaxed, drifting in and out of weary drowsiness, I held her hand under the blanket, caressing it gently. At some point I saw the man whose seat I'd taken. He glanced at us indifferently, not showing the slightest wish to be in my place. Perhaps he knew something about himself that I didn't. The final meal served was a breakfast, but I was hungry and didn't mind. I consumed the food quickly, chasing it with multiple cups of tea with cream and helping Lady finish hers, as she was in no mood for croissants and raspberry jam on this transatlantic flight.

"Well, why not?" I said when the screen map showed we had twenty minutes left before touchdown.

"What?" she said, shaking off the torpor.

"You took me on a journey, I wanna repay you in kind," I said, opening my phone's music library and selecting a song. "Play it and tell me what you think."

I set the volume just high enough for me to know where in the song she was. While she listened, I filled out the landing card and prepared a slip of paper on which, making sure she wouldn't see, I wrote the number 27: this was going to become part of the game later, along with two notes from a bulky roll of fifty-pound notes in the back pocket of my jeans. The roll contained five grand and could have appeared monstrous, so I hurried to conceal it.

"What do you think?" I asked her when she removed her headphones.

"I like it."

"Caught any of the lyrics?"

"I wasn't paying any special attention, but I think I heard everything."

"Sometimes the lyrics of songs move me. Like this one's, for example. How did you like English classes in school?"

"Literature used to be my favorite subject."

"Let's revive the ecstasy, then. The beauty begins with the opening line: *I got green and I got blues*. The best play on *blues* I know is in *Sweet Virginia*, in *Drop your reds, drop your greens and blues*. Here it's not so much a juxtaposition as the lack of one, as the next line confirms: *little less difference*. The third seems a miss as we don't yet know it will be summoned again, but then you get a gem in the fourth: *I ain't really drowning 'cause I see the beach from here*. Try telling that to someone who can't swim, yet you know the lyrical hero is right. The fifth and sixth lines are averagely melodramatic, but the seventh and eighth are the distilled essence of the song: *take two of what you're having*, a simple yet powerful allusion to drinking, and *take all of what you got*, consequently, to perform the required act ..."

It wasn't working. She trailed along after the shadows of my words but couldn't fly up to what cast them. And I wanted her to partake. It was as if I felt guilty for not having given her what we both wanted.

"*Don't be ashamed of things that hide behind your dress*," I was saying in the meantime. "How do you like that for paternal advice?"

"It's a strange one."

"It's brilliant. And I totally disregard any dubious connotations made possible by the "sister-daddy" vehicle. Even if you take the line literally, it remains one of the best pieces of advice a dad can give to his daughter. He absolves her of anything that could be viewed as a sin in the future. *Belly-up and arch your back*. Imagine a woman in this pose: what do you think she's doing? But then," I looked at her closely; she was all ears. "Then the climax comes. People often think it's in the end, but it's not. In *Romeo and Juliet*, the culmination is not the death of Romeo and Juliet. It is at the core, in the middle of the middle, so in a three-part piece it falls in the second act. Now, each act has eight lines, but the last two form a refrain that aims not at being unorthodox but at solidifying the leitmotif—the main idea, that blend of mood and thought that captures the essence of the piece. With only six lines, the climax falls on the third and fourth lines of the second act. *Belly-up* is the third; do you remember the fourth?"

"Something about not coming back?"

"*Belly-up and arch your back.*" I whispered, my eyes tearing up with elation. "*Well, I ain't really falling asleep; I'm fading to black.*"

She didn't say anything, and it was perfect.

"Do you know what the hero is imagining here?" I asked at the peak of the pause. "Death."

"How do you know?"

"I was that guy. Can I ask you a personal question?"

"Why not, after all?"

"Have you ever loved?"

"Of course."

"How did it end?"

She didn't reply.

We spoke more before landing, but nothing we said meant much. I felt tired, sleepy and sad: sad to part with Lady, but I still wouldn't prefer to skip my reunion to marry her instead. In fact, the only thing that could make me deviate on her behalf ran along the lines of a fictional spy story: something about her CIA cover having been compromised, her life being endangered, and me finding out about it and doing everything to save her. I would have taken her to the reunion, I realized with glee. What place in the UK could be safer, save for the Queen's bathroom? And if henchmen began showing up, wouldn't we fight valiantly? We sure would—it would be a great fight, and natural selection would prevail. I estimated my own chances of survival: very slim, especially if I protected her myself—a task I couldn't relegate to anyone.

The landing was quick and uneventful, and the picturesque views of London were gone from behind the window before I could begin paying attention to them. The cabin didn't clap when the plane's wheels clutched the ground, except for a few disjointed attempts ignored by the majority. The crew quickly opened the doors, and soon the passengers were on their way out.

I waited for her at the exit; without a word, we went down the windy path involving multiple corridors and escalators on the way to border control, each rolling our valise behind, our reflections a pleasure to the eye. I didn't want to indulge in untimely sentimentality, but the two of us did make a beautiful couple. We cut in front of the passengers issuing from a plane from Paris, which had landed at the same time as ours, saving us a lot of time I'd rather have lost. The border officer asked me a few probing questions while both of us knew everything was alright. What confused him was the floating date on my return ticket: I could hop on any of the planes flying back to JFK in the next three days. This cost me a few extra bonus miles, but I had to be ready for anything.

She had an American passport, which raised no questions at all.

It was only when we walked into the general waiting area that I felt I was in England. Good Lord, it'd been a while! And the occasion was already stained by an impending loss. There was nothing else for us to do together, but how do you part with a woman you love? I had done it enough times to have grown inured, yet part of me demanded retaliation. I looked at her again; she was tired and beautiful, somber and sexual, pensive and in a rush. And while she was all that, I felt deeply responsible for what would happen to her from now on.

"I have an idea," I spoke a moment before she would when we reached a corner where no passerby could overhear us. "Let's meet for a drink when we both get back to the States."

"I can't," she said in a determined voice. "I have a boyfriend."

"That's something I absolutely can't believe." I shook my head, smiling. That smile could have fooled anyone, but it cost me a tremendous effort.

"Why is that?"

"Because you just flew to England alone."

"He has work."

"Don't you guys go on vacay together?"

"It was a last-minute thing; I had to go alone."

"Tickets on sale?"

"Yeah; I got mine really cheap," she said, relieved. "Like, ridiculously."

"How long have you known him for?"

"About a year." She exhaled and shifted her weight from one foot to the other. I noticed that she wore white tennis shoes.

"You look striking like this," I remarked, taking a step away and squinting my eyes as if watching bright light.

"Like what?"

"The way you're standing. Has your boyfriend ever told you that the mere act of you standing somewhere is a superb source of beauty?"

"No, he hasn't."

"He should have," I said, stepping toward her. "Because that's a fact. Looks like I already know more about you than he does," I concluded, summoning the smile again. It was even harder this time.

"I don't think so." She was impatient, but worse was the anxiety that was covering her skin with chilly goose bumps. Somehow, I had her in a corner, without wanting to, and the end had already been determined, so all I had to do was execute.

"You choose to relinquish? Why, because of the responsibility? But this way you accept it all."

"I just don't want to give you false hope," she said, and it sounded stale, like a quote from a book I'd never want to read.

"Nothing is false while one hopes for it. But how do you know what my hopes are?"

"I don't," she admitted with a transient look of sheepishness that did not suit her.

"I'm not blaming you." I said, feeling hollow. "You may fall in love with me and hate yourself for that. But I need to ask you something before you go. It doesn't matter if you tell the truth, so you may as well do that. I want to know how old you are. If what you say matches the number I have here," I showed her the slip, "you win a hundred pounds." I showed her the money. "If it doesn't, nothing happens."

"You want me to guess what you think my age is?"

"Yes." I nodded, appreciating her quick thinking. "If I remember anything about England, this should buy you a leather belt or a silk scarf, which I can't give you myself anymore."

"Listen, I'd have played it with you for a hundred pounds." She looked deep into my eyes, down to the very bottom. "But I have to go. I'm twenty-six."

And then it was: a step forward, her chest against mine, and a kiss on the lips. She started walking away, and I was in a coma. The feeling was so powerful that my physical body was frozen while my ethereal one fluttered about, chargeless. As for the Emotional one, it turned into a whirlpool, threatening to sink into the abyss but equally capable of taking flight, leaving it up to me to decide. And somehow, despite all this mess, I was thinking, so before she could get too far, I figured it out and yelled:

"No, you're not!"

She stopped immediately but took an extra moment turning around, worried and confused.

"You're a Leo." I neither lowered my voice, nor moved. "It's the end of July. You're either soon-to-be twenty-seven, or you're still twenty-five."

"Today's my birthday," I read on her lips. Then she smiled. "Goodbye."

I watched her until she reached the corner and regretted it as soon as she disappeared. She reminded me of Florence. Few women did. I knew it was a man she'd flown to see, but somehow the sexuality wasn't there. The scenarios ran the gamut of possibilities, but one by one I dismissed them as implausible. Single traveler, small carry-on, didn't check her phone after landing ... how many women fit that profile? Or had I really hijacked an agent on a mission? I closed my eyes, reconstructing the moment I first saw her and searching for the initial vibe she gave me, that basic scent that had been veneered by my instant attraction. The picture of the JFK Terminal 5 boarding area crystallized, but she was almost not there, blending into the flaxen specks on the white wall behind her back. Why was I worried she'd notice? Did I think she would? But who could? Never fall in love with a stranger: that should be the first thing they teach in spy schools.

It was only a photograph in my mind; without the feeling, it was worthless, and after a minute I stopped. The simplest course of action was to assume that I was wrong about everything, but the inability to verify that was galling. She even had that guacamole… I mean, Guam background! Should I start giving the women I love little transmitters telling me where I could bump into them again? But then again, how would I feel if Lady 2-7 started emitting a permanent signal from the middle of the Thames?

Bus to the Railroad

Unsure of the answer, I turned around and walked toward the nearest info board: I had no idea where to go from here. Yet I recognized Heathrow, its busy hum reverberating through the air dominated by English accents. I listened to everything I caught, slowing down near particularly melodious flows. It was just around one o'clock, but the morning sluggishness hadn't yet cleared from the air, lingering and procrastinating on a sunbeam's bounce from the coffee shop to the cab booth. I liked the duty-free area better, despite how sterile it was underneath the smell.

The screen didn't reveal much, and I looked for another, beginning to feel a slight urgency. England was only a stopover on my way to Wales where, on the shore of the Bristol Channel, United World College of the Atlantic lay, and the combination of airplane schedules and the whereabouts of my own shenanigans presented me with a conundrum. I was at least three hours ahead of schedule, and I did not want to spend all that time on campus, which meant I had to lose the time before I got that far.

The trip as I remembered it was simple: I needed to take a bus to the railway station and hop on the train to Swansea; from there it was only a cab ride away. *Rock me mama like the wind and the rain, Rock me mama like a southbound train*, I sang in my head while staring at another screen displaying a map of the premises. For a moment it smelled like a waft of cheap cigarette smoke, but I recognized the absurdity of such an inference. But despite the surplus of time, everything else pointed to the need to hurry: while the buses left at relatively short intervals, missing the nearest train could mean spending the extra time at the station. I did not want to be forced to find an alternative route, so I rushed in the direction my gut told me was right.

I was proved right.

"Good afternoon," I greeted a stern woman in a booth, who sold tickets but looked like that wasn't the main thing about her. "How do I get to this station?" my finger indicated the desired stop on a map nailed to the wall of the booth.

"Number seventy-one," she said in a disgruntled tone. I wondered what she'd have said had she known what had just happened on the plane that brought me here. "Go all the way to the penultimate stop."

"Are you quite sure?"

"Are you going to Wales? Nineteen pounds."

Could have been worse.

The bus wouldn't depart for another quarter of an hour, so I decided to eat. The store nearby had what I didn't even hope for: gluten-free protein bars. Pricey per se, they cost even more here, but I had plenty of change from the fifty I broke to pay for the bus; it stretched to cover a bottle of water as well. Drinking was crucial: after the plane breakfast, I was thirsty rather than hungry. I wouldn't even have worried about food, but I had no clue when my next meal would be, or what it would include. The bars were great: I could have finished all three in five minutes, but I chewed slowly, extracting every bit of taste before taking the next bite. I drank equally responsibly, holding the water in my mouth before swallowing it, and when I'd finished the bars I still had half the bottle left. I felt great; so I bought three more bars and another bottle of water, spending nearly all that was left from the fifty.

Rumor has it, England is expensive.

As soon as the bus arrived, I got inside and took the front seat: the one before the windshield, to the left of the driver. The bars and the water went into the same side compartment of my valise and I congratulated myself again on having gotten the thing. It had been priced at a point that had led me to question whether I'd extract an equivalent amount of value from it, so in the end I'd based my decision on the fact that its particular shade of orange reminded me of a tiger's camouflage, but the value was all there, and then some.

"*Why did you do it?*" I thought when the bus pulled off, staring through the window behind which some industrial scenery was gradually unspooling. "*You gave her one-in-a-lifetime experience all right, but it cost you. Think of what you had to go through. You were nothing to her to begin with.*"

"*Maybe I'm getting ready for Molly,*" I supposed in a feeble attempt to justify myself. Yet I knew my stand was weak: I was more tired than I'd expected to be at this stage. "*I was nothing to her to begin with, too.*"

"*It shouldn't matter. Also, have you made up your mind about sex?*"

"*Yes.*"

"*And?*"

"*Inevitability itself. I am already stained; stopping now is pointless.*"

"*You're only using that as an excuse.*"

"*It shouldn't matter.*"

"*If you can keep your cool about it.*"

"*There's only one firing squad ahead, and I sure shouldn't be missing it if we meet.*"

"*You're so confident, it's remarkable; it's as if you hadn't just lost your head.*"

"*Mine's on me. And the only way I'm hearing from her again is if my CIA theory is right, which would be a thing in itself. Otherwise, she's gone.*" I paused, savoring the feeling. "*Anyway, what exactly is your problem?*"

We argued all the way to the penultimate stop, my alter ego claiming that I wasn't duly prepared and me telling him to go to hell in words that were growing progressively fouler. I knew he may be right, but if I were to face whatever was coming, it had to happen on my terms lest I betray something fundamental to me. The blow could come in whatever form or not come at all; to try to figure out which was better was as tempting as it was pointless, but the mantra prevailed: none of it should have mattered at all.

When we arrived, I left the bus slowly and carefully, checking out everyone who exited with me and stayed behind. That trick Molly had pulled obliged me to be on my toes whenever I dealt with buses in her context. Sharing a bus was less likely than sharing a plane, but now the odds improved dramatically: if she was on the same route, she'd have to end up at this railway station no matter what.

This railway station—what a mundane place for a meeting of such ineffability! I'm sure it was an old, noble building with its intricate bas-reliefs, respectable history and proud general manager, but its present condition offered nothing to the eye. Even the usual Friday afternoon anticipation of a miracle generated by the hopes of workers who had toiled all week failed to lighten the air, although at least some of the people waiting for the same train had to be coming home for the weekend.

When I saw the schedule, I had a decision to make. The train I needed departed in twenty-three minutes; the next one after that wouldn't come for another three and a half hours. A lovely arrangement on a Friday night, but then again: I was travelling to another country. The earlier train would get me to campus by five-thirty. Yet the answer was clear: I had to get to Swansea, and if I felt like waiting, I could do it there.

I gave the station another look and thought that the only two things that changed since I'd come here last were the temperature and the lighting: the previous visit had been on a January night. One pilgrimage still had to be made, though: to the men's bathroom. Eleven years ago, it had been surreal: the dimmest possible shade of club-blue light, cracked white tiles that looked too large on the walls and too small on the floor, and black burned spots on the low ceiling that, even in this shadow of a space, looked gray … boy, I could almost see a heroin addict keeled over in one of its corners, a crimsoned syringe dangling from his vein. But first I had to get a ticket. Nostalgia is only good when you have nothing to do.

The woman at the register eyed me with suspicion, but the roll of fifty-pound notes was just what was needed to persuade her. The price was astronomical; nevertheless, I left with a round-trip ticket with an open-ended date. As always, being prepared for anything took extra energy: ninety-six pounds in total.

"*Three hours to Swansea and a fifteen-minute cab ride,*" I thought and settled on an uncomfortable bench in the waiting area by the tracks, putting my feet on top of the valise and hoping it would look quixotic even to those who didn't know what that word meant. I may have just lost all my wits in a conflagration of love, but my math was with me, confirming that I was close. *Will it storm at me all at once*? I thought, smiling. No, subtlety is deadly: perennially so. Reality seemed to have suddenly thickened, but it was only the pressure inside. Now it suffused my whole body: genitals, stomach, chest, lower and upper back. But pressure I could handle; besides, it helped me to feel my ethereal body as one compact and alert entity.

Reality Check

I was about to reach for my laptop and spend the rest of the battery on my initial impressions of what had just happened when I realized I hadn't performed a reality check since boarding. Cursing, I looked at my hands, recalling where I'd woken up last, when it had happened, and whether it had made sense. So far, so good: the hands were mine, they hadn't changed, and the details of my most recent awakening raised no red flags. Thursday morning, 11.30 a.m., my bedroom, the first conscious look upward. *Do you always wake up late on Thursdays?* No: it was my day off and I'd given in to utter self-indulgence knowing that my sleeping routines would be soon interrupted. *Why would they be interrupted?* I am attending a high school reunion in Wales: a couple of one-pound coins provided tangible proof. *Did it seem strange?* I searched around for a clue and saw a banner bearing prominent text; the text remained unchanged for a full minute, throughout all five glances I gave it. To answer your question: no, it does not, but please check back in half an hour.

For a while, I'd thought the best reality checks were digital clock–based. In dreams, such clocks' digits are all messed up: not only do they not show the right time (if there is such a thing as the right time in a dream), they show things like invitations to parties. Then the hack failed me when lucidity would have been of immeasurable benefit: it was a real-time jump to my office, with some of my colleagues already there. My desktop was suspiciously large, but glancing at the time (I use Windows at work) quieted me: it was 9.15 at the first glance and the second, 9.16 at the third. Although, to be fair, Windows' digits have rounded sides: perhaps a clock with the numbers made up of straight dashes is foolproof.

After a roughly ten minute-long scavenger hunt for further proofs, it was time to go. The train had not yet arrived (it was coming from London, running across the latitude), but the bathroom begged for my attention. The station was convenience itself: all the trains were channeled into but two tracks, and I was already on the right side of the platform. The day had reached its full glory: summer in England often feels like a joke, but today the sunshine filled the air with a pleasant heat. It was still far from being Guam, but if I were King, I would have ordered all the train stations to be made of limestone and surrounded by green lawns.

My valise clattered over the threshold of the bathroom, whose wide-open door revealed nothing suspicious. In broad daylight the place looked simply empty. I hesitated for a moment as to whether to bring the valise but nothing signaled any menace. I wished that walking in had felt like entering a bubble that calmly pops, but it was more like visiting the set of a movie that was shot a long time ago and never became a hit. Not that I cared for this memory, but something could have been left here, ideally in the form of pure understanding. Or was it the kind of understanding that comes only when you already know?

Back on the platform, a train was making its way toward the station. A crowd was waiting to board. I was now slowly making my way from the head of the train to its end, looking for a suitable target. It turned out to be an old gentleman whose valise was adorned with the same silly airline tags I still hadn't removed from mine. For some reason I'd supposed that the old man was returning from Zurich, but instead he'd been somewhere in Italy. His accent was undeniably English but lacked certain phonetic peculiarities; he confirmed that the train was mine, though.

I walked on, eyeing the passengers, paying attention only to women. I was finally beginning to feel like myself. This brought, among other joys, the ability to perceive everyone on the platform at once. This was not the ethereal body: for this, you need to be at least on the Mental one. Perhaps you've read about such folks: those with flawless memories and the ability to restore any past moment at will. It begins with concentration, which becomes discriminatory as needed when you zoom in on a particular detail.

The train arrived making the appropriate noises but with an air of being fed up with it all. I hadn't found anyone attractive in the crowd boasting no more than forty women and men. At least a third of the women were in my target age group, so I didn't hurry to board, waiting for the latecomers to slip through the platform's doors. I liked trains: I always did things on them that were worth doing. I also had multiple strategies for various scenarios, but now I was curious to see how they'd work in my outlandish English. The conductor gave me a stern look, certain I'd be his customer and disapproving of me taking so long. A special breed, these folks; I've met some amazing people among train conductors, but alas, this wasn't the time for courtesies. I had to know for a fact whether Molly would board the train, and the first step consisted of this very check.

The train's sojourn was over: I knew it by the yell of the conductor who was now standing with his back toward me. In America, it meant something like: "*Okay, everyone is on board on my end, let's lock this baby up and move it, shall we?*" He had to be the only person in England aware of me, but he was so aware he'd grab me if I tried to board his train on the move. I knew he would help and not push, cursing profusely and enjoying another aspect of his job, but there was no need for that. I wasn't evading a chase: I was the one chasing. Once the platform had cleared and anyone rushing to make the final boarding call would be conspicuous, I ascended the stairs behind the conductor. I considered showing him my ticket but changed my mind when he turned to operate the buttons and keys on a dashboard by the exit. The next moment, the doors clanged shut and I started toward the first car. By the way, if you *are* trying to lose a tail, hop on the train like I did, at its very last exit, but only a moment before the doors close. This way, you'll have the entire train in front of you and see if anyone is trying to board it as recklessly as you did, and how successful they are. And by walking all the way to the first car you'll make sure there are no move unwelcome visitors.

Girl on the Train

The cars were the same as those on American long-distance trains: they had seats, tables, and windows. The latter promised a lovely view, but I was busy switching between peripheral and direct vision to notice a glance from someone who'd recognize me. Yet the only noteworthy thing was the absence of free seats: while there were plenty of open seats per se, each required sharing a table with at least one stranger. This did not change as I advanced, but catching a glimpse of a woman I thought I knew reminded me there could be other alumni on this train who wouldn't know that we were going to the same place. To simplify things, reunions of ten, twenty, thirty and so on years all happened on the same weekend, so this lean gentleman with the flower in the lapel of his brown jacket could be reminiscing about the assembly hall, and that rosy matron with the gold bracelets could be breathlessly waiting to hug an old enemy and confidant of hers on the plush cushions of Hearst Room. But all of this was immaterial as long as I stayed out of sight of my own classmates. So far, I hadn't seen any, but there was one car left.

And there they were, in the first car, occupying a whole table at the front. For a moment I thought the route I'd chosen from Heathrow had not been optimal, but then realized they were probably coming from London. Four were clearly visible, the presence of the fifth was conjecturable, and the corner had to hold one more. I knew them mostly by reputation: not obnoxiously rich, but offensive enough to be permanently annoying, often acting excessively to impress their enemies. If they saw me, the alumni etiquette would oblige me to join them, but unless Molly was there I never would. She wouldn't be sitting with these people nine out of ten times either, but how could I know for sure and stay incognito? My gut was telling me to get out at the next stop and re-enter from the front … but that was already dangerous. I'd see the fifth one from that vestibule, but to catch a glimpse of the sixth, I had to step inside the car—no matter what. Not to mention that, having seen the fifth and still being unsure about the sixth, I faced the prospect of getting stranded in the vestibule for nearly two hours until the next stop.

And then there she was: a little angel that was too perfect to disregard in favor of any murky alternatives. Toward me, phone in hand, a girl of no more than seventeen was moving, although *moving* was already too crude. From how she stared past me I knew she was meeting someone, so I stepped closer to the exit door to give her way. Shortly after, she stormed past, barely noticing me and not slowing down at all. I waited for five seconds after the door closed; then I took a deep breath and went after her.

My taste in women is strange: I seldom fancy those who are younger than me. This disqualifies a healthy chunk of the population—a state of affairs that will only worsen with time—but now I was more interested in who she was meeting. I hoped it was her parents: I was dying to see them, even briefly and if only to remember them for a novel in which they'd appear as fugitive characters. As it turned out, two cars later, she met up not with both of her parents, but with one of them—the right one.

You may consider me whatever you like, but I adore women in their late thirties. That almost-forty mark is unmistakable; it's purely imaginary, but it works each time: women feel it's the last battle of beauty in which they can prevail, so most do their best. And I really don't mind the age gap, because these women often look gorgeous: you wouldn't mistake them for twenty-year-olds, but that's fine because, one, had they looked like this at twenty, it would have been weird, and two, this is just what they need to look like now.

I studied them out of the corner of my eye while pretending to read a map representing what seemed like the entire public transit system of Great Britain. There was a distant possibility of the woman being the girl's sister, or cousin, or aunt, but I didn't put much stock in that. It would be easier with an aunt, but the extra layer of piquancy made it worth the trouble. Yet I didn't know how to get rid of the girl. It would become necessary at some point, so I was already comparing various possible futures while we were headed toward the same one on this train.

Girl on the train … isn't there a movie with that title? I wonder what happens in it. Perhaps two lovers meet unexpectedly on a train and have to dispose of a girl who is in the way? I hope the girl gets away with her share of the fortune, but the train remains the perfect crime scene. Which is why it's so sad that writers who aspire to tackle the subject invariably fail to meet expectations. They will conjure up a trick to salvage the ending, and their lopsided story will understandably be worse than *Murder on the Orient Express*—problem being, *Orient Express* is an average read at best. So, if you need to get rid of someone, instead of Guam, take him on a long-distance train; ideally, for a long distance. Let him get used to it, calm his nerves and feed his confidence, and when he thinks he's got everything under control, wait for the first sign of weakness and deliver the deadly blow.

I am fortunate my mission doesn't involve any such horrors. I am too good-natured a man: crime stories sadden me. I prefer virtuous plots like this one—I'm not talking about what I had in mind for the girl; I mean this entire novel. I hope it's running before you like a favorite movie, but if it doesn't get visual enough, pray tell me. Tell me in a gentle whisper, and my soul may hear, wherever it is, and wherever you are; and the next time I touch upon what you'd rather see unfold in front of your eyes I will pass on every vividness of color and every evidence of love in these dry, hollow black and white lines until you feel the warmth, and the heat, and the fire, and the blaze.

It was time to consider my options. The girl and her presumed mother were in the middle of the car, which was full but not to the point of enabling me to land at their table without an excuse. I already had one, as they'd made a rookie lovers' mistake, sitting on the same bench and leaving the other one up for grabs. True, few people would dare to interrupt such beauty and charm, but some will. I needed a few lines to restore their confidence once I joined them; I could be a lost foreigner, but that didn't appeal, and pretending that I thought the woman knew an imaginary third party was silly. No, from every angle, it looked best to tell the truth straight off the bat.

The conductor appeared at the door of the opposite vestibule and I instantly made up my mind; the rest was a matter of timing. I paused for a few more seconds and then began walking: slowly and as if unsure of something, tiredly dragging my valise behind. A few steps later I stopped, extracted my ticket from the back pocket of my jeans (the *other* pocket, of course) and began perusing it as if in search of crucial information. But help was near: the conductor stood by their table. And as soon as he was done, I was next to him. He checked my ticket and I landed on the bench in a most natural fashion, as if only to let him pass. Then I smiled at the ladies. Creatures of magic themselves, they both sensed I was up to something, even though neither betrayed herself yet.

I wanted to demonstrate my intentions immediately, so I threw my valise on to the baggage racks above the window. A large dark-blue suitcase shared the rack, and it must have belonged to the mother: the girl carried only a backpack. Then I sat back, relaxed, and waited for them to get used to me while they continued to discuss white wine, which had been their topic before my appearance. I waited for a fitting pause and then began.

"Good afternoon," I said to the mother, as if I'd known her forever.

"Good afternoon," she returned with such perfect neutrality that it could only have been a masquerade.

"I overheard the conversation you were having with your sister and it made me think she might be the person I'm looking for. I need assistance in a delicate affair and I would gladly pay her for the trouble."

I knew the smile that dawned on her lips well: it was that of a woman who thinks she has me.

"Emmanuelle!" She shot her daughter a triumphant look. "Do you hear? You are being hired without an interview!"

"Emmanuelle, yours is one of the most beautiful names there are," I said, hoping she wouldn't take it for a cliché.

"Will you be so kind as to tell more about what you have in mind?" the mother asked before the girl could speak, and I realized that she was masking agitation.

"Gladly." I took a brief pause. "There is a party of six in the first car of this train. I need to know if someone I am looking for is among them. But I can't check myself. Emmanuelle, if you walk over there, remember their faces, return and describe them to me well, I'll pay you fifty pounds."

I took out the roll of notes, making the bills flap in the air like the pages of a book, peeled off one and put it on the table in front of her and, with deliberately slowness, returned the roll back to my pocket.

"Emmanuelle, this is how you know a gentleman!" The mother was still teasing, but she was happy I hadn't meant mowing my lawn. "He'll match his words with action without delay. But I'm afraid, sir, that as the mother of this underage lady I have to intervene and respectfully refuse this offer."

"I could never imagine the lady was underage. But that tells me her mother is even younger than I had thought," I replied, wondering if I'd chosen the right grammar for my feelings.

She was flattered.

"On what grounds are you refusing?" I demanded further.

She looked at me in disbelief; then she leaned forward, moving the weight of her upper body onto her arms, and said in a low whisper:

"Do you think there is a better candidate for your job than my daughter on this entire train?"

I quickly considered the inventory of realistic possibilities.

"Most likely, not," I admitted.

"Then why are you offering her a measly fifty pounds?"

"Because the whole thing should take less than five minutes: going, remembering, returning, and describing. Fifty pounds for five minutes is six hundred pounds per hour. That sounds like a good wage, even for a country with England's prices."

"True, but that doesn't take into consideration that no one on this train would be better. You yourself concurred. So, double your offer, and she'll do it."

"Will you, Emmanuelle?" I asked.

"If my mother doesn't object," the girl said meekly.

"Well, we've already taken care of that, but talk about proper upbringing," I said, repeating the whole process of extracting a fifty but skipping the dramatic irony. "I'll pay a hundred, but I'd like more security. Do you ladies have a pen and a piece of paper handy?"

They did: an entire notepad with a clean front and only half the pages missing, and an orange marker.

"Perfect," I said, inviting Emmanuelle to sit next to me with a nod. She changed seats with excited readiness, eyeing my work intently as I reminded myself of an ice hockey coach scribbling on a portable whiteboard in a rushed attempt to explain something that might never happen after the faceoff throw. "The arrangement is simple." I drew six circles, three on each side of a rectangle representing the table. "But you have to remember so well that when I point to a circle at random—like this," I demonstrated, "you'll be able to describe that person in detail. Can you do that?"

"Sure. Do you want me to sketch them?"

"You draw?"

"A little." She blushed.

"Then you do have all it takes for this job. No, sketching would be overkill. Just photograph them in memory."

"Yes, sir!" She hopped on her feet, eager to go. "I'll be right back!"

Her mother sat silent as she left. Neither of us spoke for a while. Then she gave in.

"What if my daughter had refused?" she asked, waiting for something.

"You mean, if *you* had? I'd have done it myself, risking exposure."

"Was it that important to you?"

"It still is."

"Okay," she smiled, as if hiding a regret after a minor defeat. "Let's say the person you are looking for is there. What will you do?"

"I'll pay your daughter, walk over there and pretend I'm breathtakingly excited to see all five of those other people."

"You always plan ahead?"

"Things tend to go better when I do. Even when they don't go as planned."

She was still unsure about something.

"What if she is not there?"

"I'll pay your daughter, plan what to do next, and act accordingly."

Something in her face changed, and I knew Emmanuelle was behind me. Now I was evaluating the success of her operation by how her appearance made her mother feel. I don't know if she counted on the girl's help, but she seemed like she could use some.

"Six, like you said," Emmanuelle reported, appearing in front of me with a very strange look: almost of trust, though a strangely blind species thereof. "They are quite a bunch. Who are these people?"

"Some called them scoundrels; others wanted to be like them. I never found out for myself. Show me where the men sat."

They were right where I'd seen them. *Information on this train travels slower than the speed of light*, I thought. *And it's only three cars!*

"Wonderful. Now, forget that you've ever seen them. Describe this lady," I said, pointing out the one I was sure about.

She confirmed it quickly by mentioning the sweater, not knowing clothes wouldn't help her anymore.

"Forget her, too. Hold on a minute," I said, pausing for my own sake. "Do this one." I pointed the marker at the one whose hair I'd seen. Emmanuelle gave an excellent description, but I needed the kill shot.

"Eye color?"

"Definitely brown."

"Ten points to Griffindorf." I exhaled. "Do the last one."

"It's Gryffindor, if you're making a Harry Potter reference," she said coyly. I was surprised she knew: she was probably not even ten when that movie came out. It must have felt like a ticket to magic to her, but what a sham one it was.

"*Dorf* means *village* in German," I explained patiently. "I like German. Griffin's what it is. I like it, too. So, it wasn't a reference but an allusion made by drawing a mimicking analogy with its own semantic twist."

Silence followed. She was very smart, bouncing between the Mental and the Emotional bodies, but she couldn't figure that I was waiting. Her mother knew, but with all her wisdom she wouldn't help. There could be several reasons for that; I hoped she was guided by the noblest.

"I still think you should say Gryffindor," Emmanuelle finally asserted. "The last girl is about thirty; pale skin, big blue eyes, thin nose, sharp cheekbones, but they don't look too bad ..."

She could be describing Molly from the standpoint of a competitor, I thought.

"Is she attractive?" I quickly asked.

"Quite." She didn't even entertain the possibility of being considered less beautiful than that girl. "I'm sure men like her."

"Enough," I said with a smile. It had to be Esther. "You've told me all I needed. The money is rightfully yours; be so kind as to accept it."

She did. Her mother was very proud; Emmanuelle, in turn, looked like the notion of what a hundred pounds really meant hadn't sunk in yet. As such she'd make the perfect AC student: I hoped she was going there the next year, anyway.

Real Estate Matters

Emmanuelle was telling her mother something about school, re-channeling the high emotions she was feeling, and they were so powerful that I caught myself reacting to her story with cadent nods as if she were talking to me. The rest of my attention was trained on her mother. She assumed the stately pose of a beauty who didn't work for money and didn't take it for granted. Such women make the best partners in business, in crime, and in love. Although, with them, all of those things often merged into one.

"Have you made up your mind?" I heard her say. She was talking to me.

"About what?"

"You said that if the person you were looking for wasn't there you'd have to decide about what to do next."

"Yes, I have. It seems the best course of action is to stay here. Do you mind?"

"No," she smiled benevolently. "Not if you shed some light on the whole story."

"You were so right, you know," I said, as if agreeing. "Emmanuelle totally deserved the hundred." The girl smiled. "But there is something I'd like to discuss with you first. Do you know anyone in this country who owns property?"

"I suppose I qualify."

"Is that so?" The joy sparkling out from under my raised eyebrows was genuine. "In that case, you could also be the person I need. I am a foreigner, but I have a tremendous interest in some countries' real estate markets—the UK being one."

"Forgive my curiosity: what other countries are those?"

"Mostly island nations like the Bahamas or the Caymans. Anything with zero tax has my interest."

"Well, you're definitely not getting any of that on this island."

"True, but with careful planning even this island can serve a good purpose. Where is your property located?"

"In Swansea, if you've ever heard of it."

"I have," I smirked. "A lovely town with a chess team. How long have you owned the property for?"

"Over seven years." For the first time, she gave me a glimpse into her. There was sadness inside.

"A lot can happen even in a shorter time," I said, as if to keep the conversation going. "Is it a house on a lot of land?"

"No, it is an apartment."

"I see. And during this time, have you had any reason to complain about the property taxes; for example, how large they were to begin with, or by how much they increased annually?"

"The taxes can always be lower, but no complaints in particular."

"Now, one last question. Would you say you can sell this property now for more than you bought it for seven years ago, and if so, by how much more?"

"That's a tricky one." She thought for a moment. "The prices have gone up by fifteen to twenty percent over the last five years. But I'd say I could squeeze out twenty-five, provided I had patience, and as much as thirty if I got lucky."

"Why wouldn't you?" I said with a smile, and I meant it. "The English have never been anything but that. Where I come from, you can't invest in real estate until you're rich. But here you can do it like that," I snapped my fingers, producing a pleasantly sharp sound. "And with as little as fifty pounds."

"Where do you come from, by the way?" Emmanuelle asked.

"From a place where fifty pounds is a lot of money," I said didactically, letting her know she was precocious. "Naturally, fifty is but the beginning. The dividends are paid quarterly, so you'll see an ROI in no more than three months, at which point you'd figure out that a bigger investment would also mean bigger returns."

"Do you mean to say you can invest in real estate with only fifty pounds?" the mother said skeptically.

"Precisely. Ever heard of …?" I named a UK company specializing in crowdfunding for real estate projects. "They make income-generating properties into publicly traded companies where anyone can buy a share. Let's say an eight-flat apartment building in London sold for two and a half million. That price is broken into a hundred thousand shares that are sold for twenty-five pounds each. The number of shares remains fixed, and if the price of the building increases, so does the price of each share. And, since it's a rental property, it generates net income, so if you combine the cash flow with appreciation you are looking at a double-digit annual ROI. ROI is *return on investment*," I explained to Emmanuelle, who raised her beautiful eyes to look at me.

"I know," she said indifferently before returning to her phone.

"I've heard of this, but you have to factor in the fees, which are often significant and not transparent at all. Besides, properties can lose value, too," her mother observed. "Especially if you buy at the top of the market."

"A friend of mine made that mistake." I was talking to Emmanuelle, who abandoned her phone in my favor again. "He got himself a million-dollar house in Miami in 2007. A million-dollar house in Miami is more like a three-million-dollar house near Manhattan. So, everything was good until the recession hit and the house lost half of its value. Then the teaser mortgage rate expired, making his monthly payments shoot through the roof. He kept his job, but he wasn't going to spend the rest of his life paying for that house. So, he thought of something else."

"Did he declare bankruptcy?" the mother asked.

"No, he didn't even think about it," I smiled slyly, waiting for

Emmanuelle to look at me again. "He burned down the house."

"What?"

"As far as his insurance was concerned, it was worth enough to cover the mortgage balance and then some. Although I think the bank rats bagged all of it, including the paid-off portion."

"That's a very peculiar story." This was the mother's way of saying she didn't believe a word of it. "Did the insurance company not investigate?"

"It sure did, but to no avail. He told everyone that, the day before the fire, he'd gotten into a heated argument with some people after barely avoiding a car accident and they'd threatened to kill him."

"That's a nice story, but I'm not convinced. A simple check will tell the truth: did a neighbor not see the guy moving his valuables out of the house before the fire?"

"You know your stuff." I smiled, noting a healthy rosiness in her cheeks. "But my friend isn't a simple kind of guy. He left everything inside, save for a few items that were irreplaceable to him. But as far as three-piece silk suits, or seventy-five-inch plasma TV, or even his passport go … all that went to hell. He told me later that when he confronted the pile of ashes and realized that he'd just lost all his belongings, he actually fainted. So, when he was interrogated later, he never needed to fake his reaction."

"Are all of your friends this resourceful?"

"I can't stand people without imagination."

"What's your friend doing now?" Emmanuelle asked.

"He is a windsurfing coach in San Diego. He says it's the best place on Earth. Have you ever been?"

"No, but I've always wanted to go! Of all my friends, I'm the only one who hasn't been there!" she added, talking to her mother.

"Make sure you go asap," I said before she could respond. "People who visit San Diego for the first time tend to regret not having done it sooner."

"What do *you* like about it?" the mother asked.

"The climate. This planet lacks places with conditions truly benign for humans. Take Greece: one of the cradles of humanity, and yet … ever been to Athens in January? Italy is no better. North Africa, on the other hand, is unbearable in July. Now, San Diego is great all year long. Some people say that Bali is ahead on a number of points—the cost of living being one—but ironically everyone I know who's immigrated to Bali spends a lot of time in the States."

"Do you know many people who've immigrated to Bali?" Emmanuelle asked.

"Disturbingly many. Where I come from, it is one of the most desirable destinations."

"You still haven't told us where that is," the mother prompted.

"Bali is about halfway between Australia and Malaysia. Imagine you are flying from London to Sydney …" I talked incessantly for two minutes, drawing shapes in the air, until she seemed to have moved on. "So, in short, even from San Diego, Bali is almost three times as far as Hawaii, but in the end it's worth it because you get a unique equatorial experience cheaply."

"We have to go—either to Bali or to San Diego!" Emmanuelle declared, jumping to her feet. The next thing I felt was the sleeve of her jacket brush my elbow as she rushed down the aisle.

"Sounds like I'll have to pay for an expensive vacation soon, all thanks to you," the mother said pensively, watching Emmanuelle over my shoulder. "But if you really are looking to invest in real estate here, you should know that the growth rates have recently stalled. If you consider a five-year time horizon, the rate of appreciation was ahead of inflation in most places, but only because of the bounce from the recession lows."

"How do you know?" I asked suspiciously.

"I'm a real estate agent," she said, looking me in the eyes. Listen," she continued in a tone that I can best describe as "strange": it was neither something that suited her, nor something I'd expected. "When my daughter comes back, I'd like you to go to the vestibule: I'll meet you there in five minutes. I need to talk to you in private."

"Meet me in two," I said calmly. "There ain't nothing there for me to fiddle with for that long."

Teen Mom

We did as planned: when Emmanuelle returned, I asked her to watch my valise and headed for the vestibule. Five minutes later I was still waiting, curiosity tickling my innards with its taut tentacles. She showed up shortly thereafter with an expression that was impossible to read, but I wasn't looking for simple answers.

"I needed to talk to you in a quieter setting …" she began as a piercing shrill of metal scratching against metal ensued from underneath the car.

"Sounds like you found just the place."

"I hope this won't baffle you," she continued, brazening it out. "Or make you feel awkward. But I couldn't help noticing how you were looking at me."

"And how was that?" I was genuinely interested.

"Like … you felt a certain way."

My eyebrows curved upward all by themselves, inviting her to elaborate.

"Like you ..." she paused. "Wanted to have sex with me."

"I say!" I exhaled.

"I was right, wasn't I?"

"Not quite, because what you're saying is a gross underestimation. I don't want to have sex with you. I desire you vehemently." She was concentrating intently on me. I like it when women do that. "But are you telling me this to figure out if you want to sleep with me, or is this your way of letting me know that you can't wait for me to go ahead?"

"You're certainly straightforward! If you were only looking, I wanted to say that I don't mind that. But if you'd actually like to have sex with me ..." She was shyly staring at her feet. "We can do that too. For seven hundred and fifty pounds."

I didn't know whether to be more surprised by the offer, or by the figure.

"Why not seven hundred flat?" I blurted out to gain a few seconds.

"According to my phone, that's how much a thousand dollars will buy you today. You're coming from the US, aren't you?"

Rip off your luggage tags as soon as you get a chance, I thought.

"A thousand bucks?" I looked at her, playing the American. "For that much, I'll have to know that you'd 've done it with me anyway."

"You're a handsome lad—why?" She kept looking away.

"I bet I'm older than you think. But still—why?"

"I have my reasons, and let's leave it at that. What do you say?"

"I'm thinking. What would you do for that much?"

"I'm an honest woman, but I have my kinks. You'll like it."

"You're not married, are you?"

"No."

"How old is your daughter?"

"Almost seventeen."

"How about I pay a thousand and she joins in?"

"How dare you! I knew you were a rogue!" she cried before biting her lower lip and looking down again.

"She actually *is* underage?" Now I was completely confused. "So, you must be even younger than I thought!"

I looked out the window: a field of sunflowers was passing in luminous yellow streaks. A few more seconds revealed cows, their backs dark, heavy blotches in the bright sun. I always wondered why cows came in so many different colors while all being just what they are.

"So?" she finally demanded, interrupting a distant Buddhism-related thought.

"I need a moment," I said, as if waiting to say it all along. "Where I come from, there are people who live on less than a thousand bucks per year."

I focused on the scenery again. There was nothing particularly notable about it other than the usual summery pastoral charm, but it seemed so much better than everything going on inside me. The train suddenly rolled from side to side; the trees along the tracks shook their foliage and branches, refusing to give in at the trunks. That could be a rookie metaphor for resilience, but to what extent was it applicable to my dilemma?

There was only one way to find out, so I grabbed her by the waist and pressed her body into mine. She reacted just as I was afraid she would, being completely obedient and nothing more. I knew this behavior from the woman she reminded me of: that one never had any feelings for me. This one wouldn't have considered me as a romantic partner without the money either. The problem was: that other woman was the best lay I'd ever had.

"Where'd we do it?" I asked at last, letting her go.

She dithered, as if considering calling the whole thing off. Then she developed the look of someone who's bringing herself to a hard decision, stepped back, and faced me.

"In the bathroom."

"No," I peremptorily declared. "The place is disgusting."

"It's the best one we have in the circumstances. Will you do it?"

I thought again, this time taking but a few moments. The hazard was already there, so I was compelled to go all the way.

"Yes, but not on this train."

"Where, then?"

"At your place in Swansea."

"That's not a good idea at all!"

"The best we have in the circumstances."

"There are hotels in Swansea. You can look for a …"

"I'm not looking for anything in Swansea," I said. "For that much money, this is how I see it. You take me to your place, send your daughter away, and we do it. How far from the station do you live?"

"Close by."

"Do you hear the train whistles?"

"Not really."

"Good for you. I still have months on my owner-occupied property before I can move out."

"You actually *are* a real estate investor?"

"Let's do this." I drew the roll from the pocket. "I'll give you two-fifty now, we do as I say, and you'll get the rest." I counted out five bills and handed them to her. She hesitated; then she took the money and hid it in her shoe.

"I'll tell my daughter I closed on you," she said. "That you were looking for a good investment and I had just what you needed."

"An excellent way of putting it." Suddenly I had an overwhelming impulse to press her up against the wall, draw my right hand around her belly underneath her blouse, slide it down to her loins and, making a languid semicircle along her waist, put all she had within her underwear into my palm. "Do you actually have anything worth looking at?"

"What's your price range?"

"Let's talk about it in the car. I go first."

We discussed property for the next hour. Emmanuelle was bored; I, on the other hand, was bewitched. The dive of the pound after the Brexit vote offered an opportunity to buy and hold until the recovery, which couldn't take longer than seven years and was likely to end sooner. The annual rate of return promised to be in double digits throughout the wait, but, no matter how handsome, it wasn't the ROI that I was attracted to at that moment. The encounter in the vestibule hadn't yet let go of me, and the sweet anticipation of intimacy with this dreamlike woman ignited the best parts of my soul, so when she headed for the bathroom I could barely stop myself from turning to watch her bottom shake to the beat of her walk.

"So, Mister …" Emmanuelle's voice brought me the needed clarity.

"Courage."

She chuckled.

"Is that your real name?"

"That's what my name translates into in English."

"It must have been rough for you growing up."

"On the contrary: it was invigorating."

"Weren't you mocked?"

"Only by a few people. The rest adored me."

"A perfect childhood," she said with a note of regret that I caught because I had been waiting.

"Listen, Emmanuelle," I began in a serious tone. "Your mother is one treasure of a smart woman and she has just offered me a deal I can't pass on. But we need to act immediately, which is problematic due to the limits your country puts on deals like this one. I'm not a UK citizen," I added cautiously. "The deal is such that no witness should be involved, especially relatives. You probably have the same law in your constitution; in America, it's called 'pleading the fifth' …"

"Are you guys gonna break the law?" She looked at me with admiration.

"Of course not!" I exclaimed indignantly. "How could you think this of your own mother! But I need to know something," I continued in a quieter voice. "How long has she been in the real estate business?"

"For about seven years. Ever since dad left us." She sighed.

"How far did he go?"

"To another woman."

"I bet she's worse than your mom."

"Of course." There was a spark of spite in her eyes.

"Why did he leave, then?"

"Because he doesn't understand. He's a man, you know. His new wife is younger than mom. But she sucks. Compared to mom she's just … ordinary."

"I'm ready to agree without ever seeing her."

She gave me a long, searching look.

"You know, sir, I don't know what mom told you, but frankly, you're not her type. She prefers strong, broad-shouldered brunettes," she added in response to my inquisitive look.

"That's the marine type," I said absentmindedly. "Is your dad an admiral?"

"No, but my great-grandfather was an officer in the Navy in the Second World War!" she said proudly.

"Pity." It was my turn to sigh.

"Why? Are you actually German?"

"Is that bad?"

"No, but your accent is different. And you never did tell us where you were from."

"You've never heard anything good about my country. England hates it more than anywhere else in the universe."

"Is there a reason?"

"None, much to my chagrin. Unless you take the billions my compatriots have invested here for one. By the way, has your mom done a lot of deals recently?"

"Why do you ask?"

"I want to know how protected my interest is. Your mom is a charming lady and, between you and I, she is gorgeous, but I've just met the two of you and have no idea what risks I'm exposing myself to."

"Well, isn't the whole point of removing the witness that she doesn't know anything?"

I paused. She had me: any way she wanted. Although I knew the way she'd want me the most.

"Emmanuelle, I adore your brilliant, witty mind," I said at last. "If more people were like you, this planet would be a tolerable place. You are completely right. If anyone ever asks you about this conversation, say it never happened. I'll do the same."

"Will you?"

"Yes. I'd hate to hurt you or your mom. Besides, where I come from, we all exhibit one supernatural quality: caring for others as if they were ourselves," I revealed with a candid smile.

"You're sweet-talking," she said with a scoff that had more arrogance in it than it was possible to expect from a princess of her age. "That never happens."

Definitely not in England, I thought.

"That's why it's supernatural," I reminded her. She was a lovely child.

"What did I miss?" I heard coming from over my shoulder. I'd known it could happen for the last minute or so, yet it still did when I least expected it.

"Your client claims he cares for others like he does himself," Emmanuelle declared without skipping a beat. "My turn," she added, getting up. "Behave, you two!"

"How did you land on that subject?" the mother asked when the girl was out of earshot.

"I began prying into your private life, needed to feed the little thing some confidence and divulged a great secret about myself."

"Don't call her that. I told you, she's almost seventeen."

"She understands more than that. But I'm still in the dark. How often do you do it?"

"You won't catch anything, if that's what you worried about."

"Not to sound supercilious, but you wouldn't know whether you had something I wouldn't want to catch."

"Are you telling me you don't want to do it?" she enquired sharply.

"I'm thinking the thing through," I clarified patiently. "There's a slight chance that I'll change my mind, but if I do, you'll get to keep what you already have. Would you still want me to come? Two-fifty for nothing, or five hundred on top for …"

She gave me an annihilating look. I smiled. She had to know there was no way I'd back out.

"I told Emmanuelle we needed her out," I said.

"How?"

"Gently. You are selling me a property; I'm not a UK citizen; there ought to be no witnesses. What are her options?"

"Her best friend is in town; I'm sure they are dying to see each other. Don't improvise like that in future."

"Never ask that of an honest real estate investor," I said in mock reproach.

"You're anything but honest." She exhaled thinly through her puckered lips, moving a strand of hair hanging over her forehead.

"Prove it," I said, looking her squarely in the eyes.

She could not.

The Oral Exam

The rest of the ride passed in an animated phone conversation between Emmanuelle and her friend, who was indeed in town; it was eventually settled that the friend's dad would pick her up. Not a word more was said between me and her mother, and she also avoided my eyes, allowing me to probe her with my ethereal body. I knew she was free from venereal disease; it was her energetic well-being that I questioned. A stunning long-time divorcée in her mid-thirties who doesn't mind offering herself for money can boast a most eclectic array of sexual partners, and women are highly vulnerable to picking up damage from the men they sleep with. Intercourse profoundly agitates one's energy fields and establishes a permanent channel through which one's vitality can be stolen. The more sexual partners an ordinary male has had, the more dangerous he is to females; for a virgin, the danger increases exponentially. If a woman loses her virginity to a promiscuous man, having mistaken his popularity for a token of his high value, she is practically guaranteed to suffer major energetic breach through which she loses her power and strength even if she never sees the man again. Power here means the ability to influence events around you in a desirable way; the energy is what helps you, say, wake up in the morning without wishing to die. Unfair? Well, why do you think such men appear attractive to begin with? By the time you meet them, they've already sucked a lot of life from a lot of women. But they are usually as clueless about it as you were until a minute ago: all they're after is adding another notch to their belt, which helps mitigate the boyish insecurity hiding under the stubble, tattoos, leather, and whatever other macho paraphernalia is currently being promoted by the media as the definitive characteristics of the alpha male. I used to be perplexed as to why society not only doesn't teach the concept of sexual vulnerability but dismisses it with the finality of a bigot; then I realized that energetically crippled people are the easiest to control and take advantage of. Fortunately, there is a simple procedure that allows for closing—if not the gap left by the loss of virginity—then at least the other sexual ruptures, but now that the train had begun slowing down for Swansea, I had no more time to talk.

I took the suitcase down from the rack, tempted to ask who'd put it there but maintaining the silence, and soon the three of us were on the platform. I saw my classmates from a distance; they were in such a hurry they wouldn't have noticed me even if I'd walked by. It was warmer here than it had been in England, the slight wind carrying humid traces of the ocean's smell that reminded me of Lady 2-7. I searched for her imprint on my ethereal body but couldn't find the slightest trace; I was Emotionally saddened, but Mentally jubilant: sad because it meant we were as separate as if we'd never met; joyful because I'd remained immune to whatever disasters she carried within herself.

The first cab Emmanuelle hailed brought us to her mother's place. The whole ride took about four minutes, one and a half of which were spent in the Welsh version of a traffic jam. The mom had a fiver ready, and the driver was so obliging he didn't let me touch the luggage, taking the bags with the grace of a professional porter while I wondered what kind of a trio he was taking us for. I bet he wanted to be in my place anyway; but would he change his mind if he knew how much he'd have to pay for the honor?

The apartment being under the roof of the three-story building, I gave myself an excellent workout counterbalancing her suitcase with my valise. My gallantry didn't go unnoticed: she gave me a brisk look while searching for her keys in her purse as I stretched my back.

"I apologize for the mess," she said as we entered the apartment. It was dominated by shades of white and pale green; the walls were covered with framed pictures, paintings and photographs, and every door had a little semicircular stained glass transom window at the top. Naturally, the space was in an exemplary state of tidiness. "Can I get you anything?"

"A cup of tea would do. Tea puts me in a businesslike state of mind," I said, removing my sneakers.

"You don't have to do that." I gave her a puzzled look. "The shoes. I don't have a pair of slippers for you."

"Now I know what to send you for Christmas," I chuckled. "But I can't afford to bring dirt into this cozy place of yours."

"The floor hasn't been mopped in over a week, it's probably as dirty as ... You can't go without showering!" she cried as Emmanuelle put the phone to her ear.

"Mom," the girl said tiredly. "I've already showered today. Hey Patty, I'm home; when will you guys pick me up?"

I thought she'd give Emmanuelle a hard time, and the girl seemed ready for it, but she let it go. I followed her into the spacious kitchen, where everything seemed to be made of plastic but nothing looked cheap. I asked if she had Welsh Breakfast; she scoffed and poured me a cup of Earl Grey. I drank it in the study, the smallest room of the apartment, where the shades of green grew darker, reaching their apogee in the emerald felt on the old oak table. It would have been perfect for writing, but I looked forward to putting it to an even better use.

Emmanuelle left—eventually. Her mother sneaked down the stairs, evidently to make sure that the girl had indeed gone. When she returned she froze in the study's doorway with her right hand on the jamb and the left arm akimbo, looking at me as if it were only now that she remembered why I was here.

"Do you … want to take a shower?" she asked cautiously.

"I don't sweat all that easily," I said, watching her silhouette etched against the hallway lights. I hadn't paid much attention to her clothes but, suddenly being brought into such close proximity to removing them, I thought of my own and realized what a dire contrast my denim made to the surrounding scene. "Or are you suggesting we shower together?"

"I wasn't thinking about that," she admitted, blinking fast. "How about a drink? Other than … tea."

"I don't like mixing sex with liquor. But you can go ahead." Suddenly I was reminiscing. "The drink I like best on a woman's lips is whiskey. And, please: no vodka. Ladies who want to be attractive should never touch it."

"I was thinking of cognac." She named the brand that I'd bought in the duty-free shop. "Have a problem with that?"

"There have been lips on which I liked it better than anything else." I slowly got up and approached her. "And I already know how it will taste on yours."

Some women hate it when you go straight for their skin, but she didn't, closing her eyes and taking a long breath as I squeezed her waist. Her fragrance smelled stronger now; I inhaled it and saw the pheromones dance in the air. It was an illusion, but it was working its magic as my palms glided up to her shoulder blades, which were traversed by a tight bra strap. I brought my face to her neck, not kissing it but stroking in search of a place that would make her gasp, almost imperceptibly yet distinctly enough to mark the first link in the chain of erogenous zones to be ignited under the impact of my considerate love.

She twitched and opened her eyes, swallowing audibly. Then she placed her right hand on my chest, not pressing but only indicating a barrier.

"I need a drink," she said, as if unsure of what was going on.

"You're doing fine …" I eased my grasp without letting her go.

"I'm very nervous," she murmured.

"… you're just a little nervous." I relaxed my hands completely, drawing on her ear with the tip of my nose. "Because you've never met someone who made you feel so good simply by coasting over your neck."

A surge of tension rushed through her body, and I mitigated it with a move of my fingers along her spine, striving for that perfect balance where mere ticklishness becomes excitement. She twitched again, instinctively bringing herself closer to me, and as soon as we touched I grabbed her fully. She gave up instantly, falling into my arms; and, riding the bliss of the moment, I picked her up and left the study, the felted table disappearing from my thoughts as an excessively clumsy figment of my imagination.

"Careful, careful," she kept muttering as I carried her to the bedroom. I used to be amused that women didn't expect me to handle them; now I used their surprise to augment their emotions. I brought her to the bed, cautiously put her down on top of the duvet, and took off my shirt.

This roused her from her languor: she studied me with remarkable sobriety as I relieved myself of my jeans. The boner in my briefs was getting uncomfortable and I pointed it upward: it wasn't time to take it out yet.

"On the train," she said, unbuttoning her blouse as I lay down next to her. "You pretended you stumbled upon us, but I knew it was an act."

"How?"

"I'd seen you dally by the exit." She threw her blouse onto the chair in the corner and began working on her pants. I assisted her, marveling at her legs. "You were definitely up to something."

"Up to dallying with you, of course," I sighed. The pants flew in the same direction, and I stopped her as she touched her bra. "Not so fast. I'm just beginning to get warm. And you are anything but that."

She vacillated, as if considering saying something that could hurt my feelings.

"Just relax for a minute." I said in my best timbre.

"Well, that's exactly what I can't do!" she declared resolutely. "Not without a drink anyway."

"Is it because of Emmanuelle?"

"Because of her, too."

"What else?"

She paused.

"Do you think I do this every day?"

"That's another reason to take it slow. Listen. I will do everything myself, until you want to take over. And if you don't want to take over, don't feel obliged."

I drew my fingertips along her cheek and neck, waiting for a familiar reaction: that of a deep breath broken by slight spasms. When she showed it, I kissed her so gently most women would not be sure if I'd done it at all. She let out a warm sigh that lingered on my mouth before vanishing into the air on either side of my face; I heard a barely audible moan and sank my lips into hers as if I were dying and she were the last thing that could keep me alive.

After a few minutes of kissing, the tension in her body subsided and she began moving freely beneath me. Her breasts were small, but her entire chest seemed erogenous as she successively froze, twitched and moaned in response to the touch of my lips and tongue. I was playing with the ridge of her rib cage and the sneaky circle of her belly button, gradually making my way to the frontier of her panties. But when I crossed it, it was only to discover that she was dry as the Sahara. This left me but one course of action—coincidentally, it was the very course I wanted to follow.

Some men never give women head due to personal beliefs, but if you're a man reading these lines, don't worry: I don't expect you to know anything about it anyway because the number of men who do is negligible. The good news is that you are about to get a key which, combined with a modicum of imagination, will make you into a highly revered man. Ready? But you're not! Your slighted self-importance made you recoil, so now you are willing to forego this knowledge for the mere opportunity to tell me to go to hell. We men are so childish. It wouldn't be so bad, but it leaves women, like this accidental lover of mine, on the outskirts of sexual pleasure instead of taking them straight to the core. With my cheek on her inner thigh, I was growing progressively more impatient to give her what she should have received from every man who had managed to trick her into sleeping with him; and since you didn't give her that either, you'll have to be on the receiving end as well.

It's simple: to be good at giving head, you must enjoy it. Did you hear? You must enjoy it. Because if you do, you will know what to do. And there is no reason why you shouldn't enjoy it. The view of the area, the texture of the skin, the smell of the moisture: all this was created to attract men. So, if you don't find it attractive, ask yourself: are you pursuing the right sex? Because the nagging urge at the end of the rod doesn't yet make one a man: it's giving to women what's theirs that does.

I was already working, mapping out the fairway to determine the optimal route. You have to be especially attentive to the woman at this stage because, while some strokes bring her closer, others will make her stall or even lose the ground already captured. She was being one magic treasure, forgetting herself in a cascade of turbulent twists, unchecked sighs and other manifestations of female cuteness; but while she was ascending, a part of me was grappling with profound frustration because the fact that I was the first man taking this stunning beauty up the stairway to heaven meant two decades of wasted potential. This woman wasn't just good in bed: she could use sex to move her assemblage point to positions coveted by most reasonable sorcerers. And all the unreasonable ones, of course.

I thought I'd finish her in ten minutes, but she plateaued about three quarters of the way in, and it required painstaking effort to carry her over the peak. Her first orgasm was quick and bashful, with minimal contortions and sounds: one of those forgotten within minutes of happening. But its mediocrity only whetted my enthusiasm: I was dying to find out how high I'd bring her from such a low start.

"That was very nice of you," she said as I played with a strand of her hair.

"Just normal." I smiled, restraining myself from lecturing her on the variety of sexual experience. "Feeling warmer?"

"I am," she agreed meekly. "Are you?"

"Definitely. But you know what would help me further? Getting under this blanket …"

There it started, within five minutes. I wasn't in a hurry: she simply forced me in. Her hand was exquisite and dexterous, and on the inside she was wet enough to slip through the initial adjustment before the growing momentum would slip ahead on its own. I was in a mild mood, unwilling to try anything crazy yet, so when she climbed on top and discovered an angle that gave her goosebumps I aligned my moves with her feelings, and soon she came again. I watched a dozen of introspective expressions wash over her face in as many seconds, her mouth opening and teeth chattering, all one show of blithe ecstasy.

"Will you come, please?" she whispered at the end of it, falling onto me.

"Not even for a million pounds," I said, suppressing a laugh she would have misunderstood. She was completely betwixt. Did she believe me? "Why, are you getting tired?"

"Not yet, but I'm not what I used to be."

"You're fishing for a compliment." I began moving again. "Besides, this is why you're having this experience in the first place. Think of your poor daughter: she'll have to live without it."

"She's turning eighteen soon," she said, suppressing a groan. She should have gone for it. "By your next reunion, she'll be ready."

I looked at her in amazement: as I could, given the angle.

"How did you know?"

"You AC brats have something about you around this time of year. Plus, your ambiguous accent."

"I'm glad yours is anything but that," I whispered, submerging my face in the cloud of her hair. "The English accent is heavily underrated for its sexual allure."

"I bet you say that about every accent."

"Bet half a grand, and I'll walk out of here for free."

"Is that what you want to do?"

"No. I want to keep going."

This time, she was off to the races instantly, her insecurity and alleged tiredness vanishing as I took control. I wasn't gentle anymore but rough and commanding, manipulating her as I deemed necessary. She liked it better: not because she was naturally submissive, but because the earlier preparations had warmed her so well that even a painful movement had a pleasant charm. I locked my ethereal and mental bodies on her, intending to feel her orgasm as mine, but I must have lacked the proper concentration. I gazed through her face as she was coming under me, maintaining a powerful grasp on her neck, and when she was done I didn't move, letting my erection subside little by little as she lay with her eyes closed, breathing deeply and irregularly.

"I want to tell you this tale, even though I feel I shouldn't." I contracted my muscles inside her; she flinched. "It's about this honest librarian with a beautiful nose …"

"How do you do it?" she said lethargically, stretching herself as if she had just woken up.

"… and a perfect English accent to go along with it. She wasn't attractive per se, but she spoke like a duchess. She taught me *splendid*; not the meaning, but the contextual usage, and she wasn't even talking to me. Once upon a time I was in the library hitting on a girl. Nothing serious, just a silly fruit game. She could never guess which fruit I would bring, apple or orange, because once I showed up with a pear."

"The librarian, or the young lady?" Suddenly she opened her eyes and looked at me with alarm. "When are you due? For the reunion?"

"Whenever I want."

"Aren't you missing the welcome dinner?"

"I hope I am. Why?"

"It's getting late." She sounded legitimately worried. "My daughter could be back any moment now. Can you please leave soon?"

"How soon?"

"Now."

That hurt.

"It's a close cab ride from here."

I was silent.

"Is everything alright?"

"I need a moment." I struggled to speak.

She remained still like a scared mammal pretending to be dead.

"Is it really because of your daughter?"

She nodded.

"Call her."

After some deliberation, she left my arms and fetched her phone, landing on the edge of the bed edge and wrapping the duvet around her shoulders. Its puffy folds gathered around her lower back and I felt her waist through them, stretching my hands where I lay without moving my body. She was superlatively gorgeous.

"Hello, dear." Her voice was faultlessly normal, as if she hadn't come in weeks. "Is everything alright? Tell Mrs. Austen she will absolutely have to come over for the chocolate brownies. Great. How long do you think you'll be staying?" She glanced at me. "No, if Mrs. Smith doesn't mind your sleeping over, I don't either. Splendid. Yes, but call me before going to bed."

"I never told you it was during a phone conversation that she did it," I said wistfully when she'd hung up.

"Who did what?"

"The librarian. You said *splendid* the exact same way. Must be a local thing. And you just gave me a brilliant idea. When you got out of bed you moved your thigh like this ..."

Another hour or so passed, and this time was the best. She was relaxed, and supple, and had finally accepted that she'd met a real man. She came two more times, the last one being so powerful that she screamed, unconcerned about Emmanuelle, or the neighbors, or me, or anything except for the all-consuming sensations flaring up through her core. She shook, and trembled, and gasped, and laughed, and epitomized all I sought in a woman. And I was the happiest I'd been in a very long time.

I hugged her for some twenty minutes after she was done. I knew this time was the last; it had nothing to do with her age, but she'd come to her limit. If I spent a month with her this would be just the starting ground, the level she'd get to within half an hour before venturing into truly amazing heights, but all I had left were a few minutes of warmth and the sorrow that she would not get beyond this. I was pressing her into me and myself into her as she stroked my arms, but I couldn't get enough of her, suffering like a virgin about to part from the beloved whom he's failed to touch yet again.

"I'll call you a cab," she said when the room's blue twilight was pierced by the orange glow of the street lamps.

"If that's the best thing you can call me." I sighed, not letting her go. But I didn't have to: she'd left the phone by the bed.

"Five minutes," she said, putting the phone back on the floor. "They start the meter one minute after they arrive."

"Their time can't be more expensive than yours," I remarked, bracing myself for the final moment.

I stretched it for four minutes, not thinking verbally and floating in her energy fields, which were magnificent.

She was perfectly calm the entire time, except for her breathing ...

"Was it really because of your daughter that you couldn't relax at first?" I asked when we were dressed: in the denim and a white bathrobe, respectively.

"Yes." She made sure not to show too much of her breasts. "We are very connected. I was afraid she'd know."

"That connected? Do you know when she lost her virginity?"

"Of course. I knew it a month in advance."

"You're a good mother." I reached for the roll. "You understand that this," I shook the bills in the air, "is for her, and any penny you take for yourself will have to be repaid with a hefty interest?"

"Why do you think I need the money? College," she added as I wouldn't guess.

"Fine. Keep the advance, and let's make it seven fifty on top." Driven by spontaneous inspiration, I counted out five more bills. "Knowledge is one of the three things I value most. Besides, I cost you an extra effort. You hated every second of it, especially the last time, didn't you?" I neared her. "I took forever getting you there, and when you got there I dropped the ball so quickly. You thought you couldn't come back. But then again: the money. Remember von Trier's *Nymphomaniac*? That moment when the hot girl on the train says: *If you're about to puke, think about the chocolate candy …"*

She covered my mouth with her palm, looking me squarely in the eyes. I thought she'd say something, but she didn't, and I put my hand over hers, drawing her closer.

"You don't give yourself enough credit for what you do," I said as our hands slid to my neck. "Your daughter may be too young to appreciate it, but at some point, she will."

"I hope she'll never have to," she said with a sadness that brought salt to my eyes.

"She may or may not. But you are still beautiful," I said, dissolving in lips that tasted like the honeyed curse of my life.

Nostalgie

She didn't see me to the cab, and who would blame her? The area must have brimmed with nosy neighbors, although all I noticed were middle-aged people who seemed to have no suspicions about anything, except an open bottle of hard liquor toward which they were making their way. "*Hello Mr. Jones, hello Mrs. Smith. Do you know the lady from apartment thirty-two? Yes, the one with the lovely daughter. I just paid her a thousand pounds for a few hours of love while Emmanuelle was at a friend's place, but I still haven't learned her name. Eleanor, you say? That can't be right: I had already paid that woman all she deserved …"*

The cab was a pitiful sight: a black hunchback resembling a hearse. The driver was short, hairy and reticent, of which I welcomed only the last part. I let him deal with my valise and plunged into the back, stretching diagonally across the seat and looking through the side window as if expecting to see a reflection there. There was none, but when we took off I felt more in unison with the vibrations around. England made me strangely comfortable: when I arrived in London for the first time twelve years ago I didn't realize that the bus was driving on the wrong side of the road. Wales gave me a different feeling: one of indifference. It allowed me to stay, but that was the extent of its hospitality: the rest was up to me to provide.

I sure did, the story just ended being one of the better ones. The suburban scenery of Swansea hastening past my eyes, I couldn't help but wish I lived in a world where such incidents were commonplace. Ever heard the phrase *life is the best playwright*? It's puffery, because for each true story that's worth including in a novel there are entire lives spent in quotidian haze. So if you want your life to count beyond the ordinary, start taking risks that are worth taking, else you'll never end up in a real adventure; not with an English woman, anyway.

English women … so hard to draw appreciation from. Much like their American counterparts. Sometimes I almost saw threads connecting English and American women, separated by the Atlantic Ocean, yet sharing startling similarities. What do I like them for? The language? The accents? The pride? And why did I just pay a thousand pounds to one of them? The inescapable answer was: *because you thought it was worth it*. Did I still think the same? Calculators in my head illumed their faces and began crunching numbers, but I turned mine away. Superb as she was, she did it just for the money, so if I hadn't had any, she would have squandered her chance. I smiled sardonically. To pay a woman to give her the sex of her lifetime: wasn't that one hell of an unappreciated overkill?

I kept staring out of the window on the way to Marcross, the local bar that was the default haunt of the ACers. Now that I was so close, a different mood began to take hold; I would have called it nostalgia, but the French *nostalgie* fit better. Its meaning precisely the same, it differed only by carrying its hefty load down to the last syllable, adding a further sense of hopelessness. Which is apt, because nostalgia that isn't hopeless is only a waste of time.

In a lazy shuffling of sporadic thoughts, I recalled the game we'd played in the first-year camp, a grueling three days outdoors that involved endless hikes and jumps into the ocean. This particular activity consisted of standing in a circle and singing songs full of allusions to masturbation, and when I figured out what we were singing I shook with fury and made off. One of the chaperones, a nice second-year girl, rushed after me; I told her a long, convoluted story that had nothing to do with what was going on, but by the end of it she agreed to let me retire to the tent to which I was ascribed. And when I got inside that tent, a huge construction intended to host at least a dozen of us, I crawled inside my sleeping bag and cried like I hadn't in years. The tears streaming down my temples were scorching on my skin, still cold after the ocean in which I had just swum for the first time, and as they gathered in my ears my mind went numb. I felt complete, impersonal loneliness, and the only force I could oppose it with was a resolute refusal to give up even the slightest fraction of what I considered to be my true self in exchange for any advantages society promised.

Freedom carries the highest price because nothing else is worth paying for: twelve years ago, it was a subconscious thought erupting through the crust of naivete in a seizure of pain; now it became a palpable proposition. I recalled sleepless nights spent persuading myself that I had no right to complain, even when I'd come to the cliffs to howl into the storm like a dying wolf. But the most amazing thing was that, despite being a seventeen-year-old boy without the faintest idea of how to live properly, I somehow sensed that the social riches being dangled before me weren't worth deviating from my path. In all honesty, we were nothing but an eclectic bunch of young brats who'd gotten away from their parents for the first time and wanted to make the best of it. For some people, that involved getting wasted and throwing up on the lover they were losing their virginity to; for me, it meant coming back from the study room at three in the morning without needing to justify myself. And frankly, if it weren't for my infantile infatuations, there'd have been no happier person in that whole goddamn place.

There was another crucial commonality among all of us, which nobody figured out before it was too late: we all missed a lot more in AC than we hadn't. Those two years were a cruel carnival of errors, and it didn't matter what others thought about you because in the end the luckiest one of all was but a notch above the most miserable. I was far from that notch, which is why I learned so much; and if I could have gone back I'd have changed a great deal, but then again: I did not want to go back, so I didn't even mind the impossibility.

"Stop right here, please," I asked the driver when there was only one turn left. "I'd like to walk."

He tried to object, but I took but a twenty in exchange for the fifty I handed him, and he yielded. He extracted my valise as carefully as if it were made of glass, thanked me profusely, and left. I waited for his hearse to go out of sight; then I took a deep breath, allowing myself a moment of truth.

I had no cigarettes, but I pretended to have one, striking a match I took from my valise before taking off.

Soon I approached the front gate.

I saw people in the distance, but they could not see me.

I heard noises, some of which weren't identifiable.

I let it all pass.

And then, jerking my hand as if flicking the imaginary cigarette away, I took a deep breath and entered the United World College of the Atlantic.

III

Arrival

Am I tripping, or does the air smell like turpentine? I must be: I don't even know what turpentine smells like. The green lawns prevailed, patching the ground with enviable consistency; and, observing this lopsided chessboard as if for the first time, I sensed that the grass served as a perennial incitement to the depravity flourishing here. I needlessly checked whether I was hot. *What time is it*, I thought and, much to my satisfaction, I couldn't answer the question.

Oh, right: you ain't alone! I veered to the left, the valise's wheels squealing in protest, and took cover behind the corner of Tice, one of the newer dorms on campus: coming at me from a dangerous angle was a dangerous trio, and I could almost imagine Martina as its centerpiece. Luckily, it was only Diane with her retinue, and I'd noticed them a second before they would have returned the favor. Their voices rang in the darkness with comfortable drunkenness; from the way they leaned on one another I could tell they couldn't wait to start leaning on something more masculine, and I had a bodily knowledge that at least one of them wasn't wearing any underwear.

When they'd moved far enough I left my hideout and stared at Sunley: the house where I'd lived as a student; coincidentally, it was hosting our famous ten-year reunion. I could infiltrate the building in several ways, two of which involved the roof, but nothing seemed better than using the main entrance, even though it increased the likelihood that I'd meet some of my old classmates. I wanted to postpone that hassle until after I'd hit my room, but getting in through the window seemed inappropriate because, firstly, I had no clue who would be staying in it, and secondly, getting to it would make me visible from the dayroom: the center of every dorm. In Sunley's case, the room boasted a panoramic view of the back yard through a wall of glass. I looked at the sky, locating the moon: it was full and bright. *Front door it is*, I resolved.

I descended the stairs to the front porch (the house was built in a little ravine), valise in hand to minimize noise. A cigarette smell hovered in the air: someone had to be smoking nearby. The second-floor hallway window was brightly lit, and voices were coming from above. The door was wide open and hooked to the wall at a ninety-degree angle. No welcoming vibe hit me as I carried the valise over the threshold, but I'd have been surprised if it had.

I wonder if, with all the aforementioned having been mentioned the way it was, you are now taking me for a sentimental fellow: a rosy dreamer hopelessly in love, a feeble soul making its way through the valley of darkness … Well, if that's the case, let me make myself clear. Having set foot on this campus, and having just entered the building where I had lived and suffered for two years, I felt nothing. The possibility of stumbling upon Martina herself did not alarm me as the wheels of my valise rolled on the floor tiles. I was in a state of complete detachment, although I must admit I wouldn't have attained it without Emmanuelle's mom. Sex elates me; sex with a beautiful woman adds inspiration; sex with someone like her takes me beyond the human. So, what I was now, having come to terms with the fact that I never became as attractive to her as she had been to me all along, was pure cognition—when the desires that normally plague you (say, those of love) can't reach you with their petty claws. It was unfortunate that I had to spend this precious state in public instead of entering into meditation in a secluded spot, but at least I can show you its workings. I promise to tell when I snap out of it, but if you've been tuning your wavelength to mine (which I hope you have done anyway, because otherwise the rest of my story will be even more painful than the beginning) you should feel it yourself, which will mean that you partook in this act of sorcery in your own right.

I flung open the first door on my right, entering a small square space, three blue cushion seats to my immediate right and the dayroom's open door a few steps ahead on the left. The sounds coming from the room blended into a jarring mélange, but I recognized several of the voices. There were four more doors: one to the storage room, one to the telephone room, one to the drying room (all three of which were used for sex), and the last to the corridor leading to my room. It was mine de facto as I'd been assigned to a different one located at the other end of the building, in an area I had hated for its unbearable smell of dirty laundry. The idea of staying on that side of Sunley was abhorrent, so I refused to entertain it at all.

I went ahead and, a moment before I passed the dayroom's field of vision, I threw the arm with the valise forward, allowing myself to be carried forward by the momentum and quickly escaping the firing line. Next, I ascended a miniature staircase counterbalancing the campus' uneven landscape, and when I reached the last stretch of corridor, I was still alone. I went all the way, and the next thing I knew was me standing in my old room.

It was empty.

I had never seen it like this: no mess on the floor, no books on the shelves, no posters on the walls. The wardrobes exposed their intestines, thin wires bent into ugly hangers hung in uneven rows, and the shoe compartments at the bottom hung agape. The window seemed even smaller than it was in reality, and the lazy summer draft had nothing to pick from the abandoned chests of drawers. Had it not been for two suitcases standing by the beds on the right, I might even have felt something.

I realized that I needed to pick up the keys to my wardrobe from wherever they were taking attendance—most likely in the castle. I wouldn't have bothered, as the bedsheets were already on the bed, but the ACers were known for stealing; a habit like that doesn't change without an outside influence and, knowing what kinds of lives my classmates had lived in the interim, I had no faith in their reformation. On the other hand, few of them, if any, would have the guts to purloin the entire valise, so if I left mine behind like my unknown neighbors had, I'd probably find it waiting on my return. I considered whether there was anything inside other than my laptop that I'd really miss if it went missing. A few items came to mind, but lamenting their loss would reek of philistinism. The risk appeared worth taking, so I moved my valise next to the bed I'd occupied in my second year, made sure the lock was on and, dismissing the thought of checking the labels on the other two bags, left for the dayroom.

Man in the Room

The dayroom is where it all happens, if by *all* you mean the socially sanctioned aspect of socializing. Which, of course, amounts to only the visible tip of the political iceberg drifting in the icy waters of college life. One of the things I didn't understand about this world was why the people inhabiting it would compulsively lie to one another: about themselves, about others and, above all, about how they felt about the others. Something had to provide grounds for elevating hypocrisy to a universal law in this odd universe, and an elite club like ours acted as the perfect fish tank allowing for the observation of its convoluted workings—as long as one didn't mind getting stained by the occasional billow of blood.

I never played the political game in AC, and for good reason: I didn't know it existed. It just wouldn't fit into my sentimental mind that the very people smiling at each other, at everything and at nothing, would form cabals and pursue popularity with a singlemindedness more appropriate to the highest political office. Don't get me wrong: I never shied away from popularity, believing myself to have far less than I deserved, but paying for adoration with dignity always seemed like a raw deal. My neighbors regarded the matter differently, so if betrayal could move them up the food chain, they sacrificed their allies without a second thought, only to keep smiling at them, cognizant of the fact that their double-crossed victims would have to return their smiles as if nothing had happened. This is an art in itself: to be polite to the archnemesis who had been the bosom friend. Although I doubted any of these people had friends, here or elsewhere, much like England herself, who never had anything but her own interests.

My heart began racing as I approached the dayroom, and I quieted it with a silent order. I didn't bother with the internal dialogue: it died out by itself as my hearing dissolved in the cacophony rushing headlong from around the corner. I envisioned what the space would look like before plunging into it: only to discover that it was as hopeless as I had envisaged, and then some.

They were standing and sitting, talking and laughing, hugging and kissing, and they had no clue. So absorbed in the trifles, so exempt from responsibility, so bound to cease unnoticed, they were one moving tableau representing the fallacies of the idle mind. The air was obscure, but what could suit this masquerade better? The women, habitually domineering, looked like they'd stepped from the ads of top fashion houses; the men, habitually subdued, were all horny and covered in sweat. The words that were said were meaningless, and the only sure guess was that all of them wanted more than they already had.

I advanced by two more steps, putting the entire room within my field of vision, and my thoughtless perception became knowledge, as if a computer file with pristine information was uploaded directly into my brain. It was no longer room and people but a dynamic snapshot of Infinity filling me with her unfathomable reach. And while I was stripping those stray beings of their calculated fictions, mapping their physical bodies as blurry energetic conglomerates that dulled whenever they lied and would have brightened had they ever told the truth, none of them had the faintest idea that I was there.

Do you know what it feels like: to enter a room full of people and not be noticed? It's … inexpressible. It's invisibility at its finest: the very kind that terrifies. I had them all by the innermost secrets they wouldn't admit to unless threatened with annihilation, and they kept rolling on with their dreamlike fantasies, cocksure that their idea of reality was the only feasible one. I drew a breath through my nose, smelling the power evaporate off their heated bodies into the air where it was to be plucked by voracious forces to whom humans were but obedient livestock eager to procreate whenever the basic imperative would ring the bell. And the force did make sure the bell never stopped ringing.

Esther with her hips burning toward Carter, Aurora picturing Edward inside her, Matilda itching between the legs for a stroke of Coco's tongue ... If they knew what I knew about them, they would murder me on the spot. Not only because they'd feel exposed, but because exposure would come from such an unlikely source. They'd never considered me human: to them, I was a reminder that, sooner or later, we all had to face God. The prospect was so inadmissible to them that they erased me from memory as soon as I was out of sight, which is why, failing to face me now, they couldn't be anything but honest in their visceral attitude.

I and they, God and human ... this terminology I am promulgating is just so massively flawed! Why? Because it implies division—and not mere division but stratification into elements of fundamentally different properties. If you did get this impression, know that it's also wrong. I am not separating myself: firstly, it will happen naturally, both without my needing to try and regardless of any deliberate effort, and secondly, of all the groups possible under the Sun, this one boasted one of the highest net values. Which is why I loved these people: with both my heart and my mind. I bet you know how to love with the heart; loving with the mind means acknowledging the object's worth regardless of whether you like him or her. In other words, you may hate the bastard, turning inside out in his presence, but only until it comes to his objective merit as a person. At that point, the emotional reaction is to roll up into a tight knot, giving the mind space for unrestrained admiration.

I would have given an example, but I'm sure you've already figured it out. By the way, do you know what I mean by a group's *net value*? It's the sum of everything its members are capable of. A billionaire and a beggar, a warrior and a weakling, a mastermind and a mediocrity: in the theater of life, every role counts. And we, the cream of the lucky, had it all. Yes, goddamnit: absolutely all, from paradigmatic aristocrats to refugees who hadn't made their first acquaintance with sewerage until after they'd obtained majority. We had our villains and geniuses, whores and priests, traitors and heroes, and—shiver my timbers—we had Martina and myself! The born playwright and the born actress: these two always go hand in hand, even when falling from each other's sight for a decade. Perhaps I'd never have embarked on this voyage if I'd known it would take so long, but if by the end of it I get what I want, time itself won't matter.

I leaned on the edge of the low wall separating the kitchen area from the dayroom proper. The room buzzing about me maintained its star-like, filamentous quality, but the memory of Martina hit me like a sledgehammer. She wasn't here, and yet I sensed several of her mnemonic images twirling in the epicenters of social gravity. If she were, she would have noticed me: by inadvertently turning her head in my direction, or in a well-played act intended to leave an imprint on her audience. She would have known that I'd had her, then: naked to the marrow of her bones, reduced to the primal element of our true selves, and elevated beyond the treacherous reach of subjective reality. And, bringing the silent force into sharp focus, I would have pierced her subtle bodies all at once, rebooting her hibernating essence and returning the spike of the thrust back to myself: to ignite my own being and to defy the taxing laws of this cumbersome universe built around the flimsy principle of mutual attraction. But alas, it was all a dream, as there was no Martina to hook to the fleeting power dissipating from my perceptual grip, and when it was gone there was nothing left but a bunch of physical bodies standing and sitting, talking and laughing, hugging and kissing, and having no clue.

I twitched, as if waking up from a nap.

I felt despondent and desultory, as I so often had in the past.

The act of sorcery was over, so I turned around and left the room.

Seven Seconds

I found my quarters as I'd left them, my valise sleek against the gloomy background of the cold white brick walls; the other bags hadn't budged either. I opened the lock, extracted the duty-free bag and was ready to go when I remembered that it would take no more than a pair of pliers to bite through to my laptop. I toyed with the idea of copying the new excerpts onto a thumb drive I could add to the things I carried on myself. I'm a picky editor, and usually a quarter of my novel doesn't make it to the final cut, but what I'd typed in the airport and on the plane, inspired by the benevolent proximity of Lady 2-7, were passages of a pre-eminent sort. Yet, with so much more at stake than my literary perfectionism, I was ready to gamble. AC had already robbed my trusting self of many treasures, and, under the circumstances, losing a few thousand words of majestic prose seemed a sacrifice worth making just for the ridiculousness of the effort required to collect it. Besides, I hoped the cognac would mitigate the kleptomania in another billionaire's child, or at least deflect it from my valise, so I put the shiny box on the chest of drawers before departing for another attempt at jumpstarting my dayroom mingling. This time, at least, I had all the necessary equipment.

The surest way to get noticed in AC, besides being an attractive girl, is to have alcohol; it was to that end that I'd brought the vodka. It was a very good brand, one of those considered pure: meaning that if you have any problems the next morning it's your own fault. There was no nostalgia to it either: as far as I could remember, no adventure of mine linked to this kind in any obvious way. Which shouldn't be surprising since my adventures here usually took place on what was procurable from the local off-license, and to call that stuff even *decent* required a leap of imagination.

There was a catch, however: I didn't drink. A blessing I'd grown accustomed to over the years, it now seemed problematic as it put me at odds with most people here who were either drunk or on their way there. *Well, isn't life full of challenges,* I thought, pouring a good tenth of the bottle down the hallway sink: for the game I intended to play, it was imperative that at least some of the vodka was gone.

The game is simplicity itself. It's called Seven Seconds. Ever heard of it? I bet you haven't, because I invented it. I suggested Seven Seconds as an idea to my roommate Vince in in our first year, and he was never the same since. Don't get me wrong: he had been a badass drinker since before we'd met, but I think I messed with him in too subtle a way. I told him something he hadn't heard of but deemed impossible, proved it was possible, and let him do the same, all within five minutes. Not even five—it was more like two.

That night, he had a bottle of horrible vodka that was but seventy-five proof (a genius chemist—the same one who discovered the Periodic Table of Elements in a dream—had proven that vodka should contain exactly forty percent alcohol). Two more guys were to join us, so I decided to hit the Languages. We got settled in one of the rooms and, as Vince broke the seal, I nonchalantly mentioned Seven Seconds. He challenged me to it and, much to his surprise, I won. The rogue repeated the feat immediately, and it wasn't seven seconds but more like ten. For the rest of the night he drank straight from the bottle, and when the other guys came he practically attacked them, threatening to perform acts of macabre vileness unless they played. Knowing Vince, they both did, and when they won their amazement was incomparable.

Brushing the memories off, I walked into the dayroom like a loafer without a worry, and immediately scanned the premises for Martina. She was still absent, and I broke that chain of thought before it could drag me off to some dingy dungeon. The crowd didn't number even half the attendees I'd I expected, but the trio I'd spotted outside suggested that the rest were in Sosh, a place better suited to my darling as it allowed for greater freedom of sexual self-expression.

I don't know if it was because of the vodka gurgling in the bottle, but I heard my name almost instantly: Trisha, who screamed it across the room, was sufficiently wasted to forget that the only connection we'd shared was a class on Geography. I paid my respects to her and a group of low-profile individuals, most of whom I couldn't name. One thing led to another, and soon a group babbling nearby recognized me as well. They all made snarky comments about my outfit, with one of them venturing to ask if it was the same one I'd worn ten years ago; I assured them it was. Their interest in me immediately waned, and then both groups dissipated under the pretext of needing to talk with this or that person situated at the other end of the room. By doing so, they left me in a very comfortable spot: alone on the sofa facing the middle of the room, two more groups to my left. With my experience and purpose, it amounted to the position of a spider in a web, and the vodka I placed on the coffee table in front of me guaranteed that, sooner or later, someone would take the bait.

It took less than five minutes of waiting before one of the female shapes traversing the room vacillated in the lower left-hand corner of my field of vision. After a few seconds of dithering, her body language reflected a change in thinking, and the shape moved toward me. It turned out to be Bridgette; she was very drunk.

"What is it?" she demanded in a tone that carried nothing positive yet denied me the knowledge of whether she realized that these were the first words she'd said to me in ten years.

"Vodka," I said.

"Bram is the head chaperone tonight," she hissed like a serpent. "If he sees it, he'll kick your ass."

"How much would you bet on that?"

She paused for a second longer than her usual three-and-a-half, as if unsure of how I dared.

"You clearly don't know what he did to the reunion party last year," she blurted.

"Provided a gallon of pure alcohol?" I hoped she was telling the truth.

"Just be careful, Courage," she maliciously advised, her lips curving into a spiteful crease. "You have been warned."

She left, wiggling her thighs and likely thinking she'd done something grand. I didn't like Bridgette: she was consciously rude. Worse yet, I wasn't attracted to her. A third of the guys at this college were openly mad about her; another third was hiding the fact; the rest were gay. But I was immune to her inexplicable charm: she couldn't have aroused me even if she'd danced naked in front of me for an hour. In fact, by the end of the hour I'd probably have been asleep.

I was about to return to waiting when a stentorian voice sounded in the hall. There could be no mistake as to whom it belonged to, so I braced myself. A moment later, Vince appeared. A tropical storm of a human being, he was already drunk and looking to get more so quickly. He wore black jeans and a white shirt that was unbuttoned down to the middle of his broad chest and bore the distinct marks of lipstick. As soon as he entered, he emitted the cry of a Mowgli in his own jungle and began searching the crowd for someone, but when our eyes met he produced the priceless expression of a baby caught unawares.

"You fucking arsehole!" he yelled, causing most of the room to turn quiet for a second; then everyone realized he was talking to me and returned to their own engrossing conversations.

"Glad to see you too," I said with a broad smile, getting up as he neared me.

"You never visited me in DC again, did you, motherfucker?" he fired.

"Must've never gotten a chance. Besides, what's with your language, *motherfuckers*?"

We hugged.

"I see what you've got here. Russian vodka!" he declared in one of those inimitable imitations of my accent that so endeared his phonetic capacities to me. "Mind if I give it a shot?"

"This one doesn't come in shots. This bottle is for an arcane drinking game called Seven Seconds. Ever heard of it?"

"I might have," he said, doing a mediocre job of suppressing the wry smile on his lips. "'Tis quite a challenge you're throwing down. Do you think …" he paused, looking at me almost pleadingly. "Do you think I can try, maybe?"

"Anybody is welcome to. But you'd better be sure you can handle this." I was speaking to him, but we both knew the exchange was intended for a wider audience. "Just a couple of weeks ago I watched a guy not make it and puke all the vodka right back up."

"Poor fellah!" Vince exclaimed, grinning. "How long did he last?"

"Five seconds, and about as many gulps."

"All right, then. You'd better take a step back." He grabbed the bottle and twisted the lid off with a casual movement that must have cost him a great many bottles of practice. "Have a watch handy?"

"The one on my wrist should be close enough." I raised the cuff; it was half past five in New York. "Three, two, one …" I looked at him and murmured: "Go, motherfuckers."

When he threw back his head and started to gulp, I began counting the seconds out loud while watching the room. The only two groups ignoring us were the housewives on the sofa by the door to the backyard and the two lesbians on the kitchen table: the rest paid the scene at least some heed while pretending to have better things to do. I felt disappointed in everyone for failing to acknowledge that Vince's performance was, in fact, awesome.

"Seven!" I roared at last. He tossed his head forward, the vodka in the bottle making a loud splash. Some violent growling followed, which was solely for the benefit of the public: Vince could finish half of the bottle that very moment and not feel too bad. Someone clapped, someone laughed, someone said something. He couldn't care less.

"How much did you drink so far?" he demanded, coming back to himself.

"I don't drink," I confessed in a tone of utter resentment.

"Who was the first to play it, then?" He seemed confused, and I made a crestfallen face. "No one? That'll keeps in sum goot shep," he said, mimicking yet another accent. "If these people keep having at it at this pace you may well save the rest till the next reunion," he laughed, his rosy cheeks starting to grow red. "Now, where are you staying?"

"Room one."

"No shit! I got it, too. Must have been deliberate."

"Possibly not." I shook my head. "I was given a different one."

He gave me a long, silent look. He understood me perfectly.

"We're keeping that room to ourselves," he said with ultimate finality. "By the way, do you have any food? I haven't eaten since yesterday."

"I've got granola bars." I was worried for him. "Come on."

"Hell, I'm so proud of myself," he said on the way out. "I haven't played Seven Second in a while. I didn't even know if I still could!"

"You?" I chuckled. "I once saw a guy gulp three full bottles of vodka in one go. Most people can win Seven Seconds, but they've never tried so they doubt themselves. It's like sex. The difference is: most people will give sex a go."

Mirror for a Hero

The first thing I noticed when we entered the room was a man next to my bed. The second was that the cognac had disappeared. I was certain that the man hadn't taken it, so I decided to deal with him first.

"Good evening, Oggi," I declared in a voice that shook him. He looked at me like a rat from a hole, his nauseating, meticulously trimmed

Spanish beard gleaming in the lamplight. "You haven't changed one bit. Feel free to pull my valise aside, if it stands in your way."

"Oh, so it's you who took this corner?" he began, not meeting my eyes.

"I'd be damned if it wasn't," I confessed. "Ain't it the best one?"

"Looks the same as any other," he said, and I knew he'd never had the corner by the door. "Ah, I think there is some sort of a mistake in your booklet."

My attentive silence invited him to elaborate.

"Mine says that I have corner 1A in Sunley, which …" He studied the brochure. "Is here."

Vince made a growling sound and I remembered that he was hungry.

"Life seldom conforms to our expectations, leaving us scrounging," I revealed, approaching my valise. Oggi took a step back, and I saw that his entire luggage consisted of a single fat leather weekender; judging by its look, it cost a few thousand. "Swapping places is but one example. Imagine you are on a plane, and you suddenly see a beautiful woman who makes you feel alive." I located the granola bars and handed them to Vince; he began eating at once. "Oggi, have you ever seen beautiful women on planes?"

"Of course, I have," he said almost spitefully. "I just don't see …"

"Marvelous!" I exclaimed. "A beautiful woman on a plane, what can be better? By the way, what class did you fly to England this time?"

"Well, business—why, I don't really see how that's …"

"Oggi," I said into his forehead with all the seriousness I could muster. "We have a problem." His neck muscles tensed. "Even if the plane is small, your chances of sitting next to her are less than one percent, and on a large plane they are essentially zero. So, what do you do?"

"Well, I don't …" He paused and stared at me with something more than a lack of consideration for anything but himself. "What do you mean?"

"This is really simple." I stared into him, and he shivered; now it was only a matter of talking. "It's a situation in which you have to prove that you are a real man. A real man, as opposed to *another man*, is someone who can rectify the odds when they are against him," I clarified in a confidential whisper as Vince tore the wrapper off another bar. "So, in this particular scenario, you need to swap seats with whomever is sitting next to her. The thing is, you must be completely, absolutely, perennially unobtrusive. You are crossing an important boundary, and while she'll reward you for your courage if she likes you, she may also not appreciate your valor, in which case you must treat her as if she were your sister … until she does. Now, Oggi." I was staring into him again. "Next time you see a beautiful woman on a plane, will you swap your business class seat with the person sitting next to her?"

"What?" He looked at me in disbelief. "Of course not," he added a few seconds later as I looked at him with an amiable smile. "That's preposterous!"

"That's called *living*," I revealed, giving him a friendly pat on the shoulder. "As opposed to being a lemming without imagination. But you are no lemming, Oggi, are you?" My voice was full of crisp honesty. "You are capable of imagination, isn't that right?"

"I sure am," he said solemnly after a pause that should have been shorter. "But I still want ..."

The third granola bar cracked open behind me: I was running out of time.

"Then tell me something," I said. "Of the people assigned to this room, are there any particular friends of yours? People with whom you'd especially like to spend time during your stay?"

"I don't even know who's staying here besides me," he said in the voice of a prima donna who's just learned that she must get to her show in a cab. "But I have good relationships with everyone ..."

"It would be unjust to suspect otherwise," I assured him. "But would you say that it is this very Vince whom you came here to see?"

"Well, I came here because I wanted to see everyone ..." he said, a worried look crossing his face as he stared at Vince.

"I expected nothing less!" I said with the same honesty. "And you will have copious opportunities to do precisely that in the castle, dayroom, or in this very room if you choose so, all while lodging in a corner of this house that is a mirror image of this one." I felt my stare become icy. "In Room 6."

Next, I heard the noise of multiple plastic wrappers being crushed into a ball. A thump in the garbage bin followed. Then Vince cleared his throat with a hearty cough.

"Hey Oggi," he said, "what time do you go to bed?"

"Well, I'm definitely a morning person, so ..."

"And you like getting a good night's sleep, without being woken by various intrusive noises in the middle of the night?" Vince continued, something changing in his accent, which now felt like a whip. "Like, for instance, that of a very drunk man kicking open the door and marching in singing a foul tune?"

There was a long pause.

"Of course not!" Oggi said at last.

"Then take him up on his offer, cause otherwise you won't sleep tonight."

Oggi looked at me helplessly. I gave him an encouraging smile. I think it helped.

"You know what your problem is?" Vince asked me when Oggi had left. "You fuck with people too much."

"Never!" I protested. "I only encourage them to unlock their potential."

"Speaking of which." His eyes bulged as if from the pressure of a good idea. "How about some musicality?"

"That would be lovely," I said, suddenly knowing precisely what to do. "Can you play *Blue Jeans*?"

"Even *Jean Blues*." He opened his laptop; it was as huge as any of his other ones. "Who is it by?"

I told him.

"Are you kidding me?" he cried.

"Let's call it repayment for my not letting you starve to death," I proposed.

"Okay," he acquiesced. "But don't you dare sing."

"How about a pantomime?" I asked innocently, taking off my sneakers.

Vince struggled to navigate his way through the interface, hitting the wrong buttons and cursing, but eventually, the song began. He stared into the music video blankly, miles away from appreciation. When the guitar stepped in, I thought he was going to throw up.

But I didn't care.

"*Blue jeans. White shirt*," I sang, taking a dance step toward him at each emphasized syllable.

"*Walked into the room you know you made my eyes burn*."

A sharp turnaround, my arm stretched out, index finger pointing at Vince.

"*It was like*."

A loud finger snap.

"*James Dean*."

The languid look of a woman trying to seduce a man, eyelashes batting.

"*For sure*."

Vince begun contemplating what to throw at me.

"*You so fresh to death and sick as ca-cancer*."

Me retreating to the valise in a series of jumps, knees bending low, letting the singer talk until:

"*You fit me better than my favorite sweater, and I know*."

A look over the shoulder, my hand inside the valise, another pause.

"*And love hurts*."

A sideways move of my hips.

"*I still remember that day we met in December …*"

I let most of the refrain speak for itself and focused on locating the items I needed until the coruscating "*Say you'll remember, oh baby, say you'll remember oh baby ooh …*" which the singer herself didn't get right; and just as Vince thought the worst was over I sashayed over to him again, unbuttoning my shirt.

"*Big dreams*."

A different word starting with a d would suit better.

"*Gang Star*."

Another blinder on the poet's part.

"*Said you had to leave to start your life over.*"

I finished undoing my shirt.

"*I was like.*"

My moves becoming those of a hooker who'd failed a hundred auditions but wouldn't give up.

"*No, please!*"

Me throwing my shirt on the floor and unzipping my fly.

"*Stay here!*"

The next two lines skipped as paragons of the trite and the superfluous, respectively.

"*I stayed up waiting, anticipating and pacing …*"

Vince saying he'd murder me.

"*But he was …*"

The hooker giving her best show in the dramatic pause before the:

"*Caught up in the game, it was the last I heard.*"

My pants joined the shirt. That was the last straw. Vince killed the song.

"Pass me the vodka, will you," he said blandly, looking away.

I did.

"Who's … James Dean?" he asked a few gulps later.

"The Elvis Presley of the fifties." I returned to the valise. "Died much younger."

Vince didn't reply, busily selecting a different song, something by *The Doors*. I watched him from across the room but, apparently, he'd decided to ignore me until I got dressed. Given the summertime sadness of Welsh nocturnal temperatures, it was opportune.

I'm sure you've figured out by now why I arrived in working class clothing, and up to a few moments ago I was going to stick with the initial plan, ensuring that my classmates enjoyed the continuation of their unflattering image of me: it made them less likely to interfere. But when I caught a glimpse of myself in the mirror, the urge to change had made me itch all over. I checked my reflection once again and realized how incongruous with the disguise were my boxer briefs and the cobalt socks, all of a brand that, along with the money, should have given Emmanuelle's mom at least some comfort as to my controversial self.

I smiled and pulled on the blue jeans: the *other* blue jeans, of course. Sixty seven percent cotton, thirty three percent silk: you'd strangle me if you knew how little they'd cost me. Frankly, I hadn't expected the seller to accept my offer and was prepared to add two hundred on top (I wouldn't leave without them) but then I'd realized he'd never find another customer that would fit into them. God knows what devil had possessed their designer, but they were so perfect that a belt added nothing but weight.

The white shirt was next. A cashmere long-sleeved polo is hard to find, but it also turned out to be a superb deal because the sleeves were long enough for me to take a Small. I am not a fan of tight tops on men, but my figure benefits from them a lot: at least as far as onlookers are concerned.

Shoes were the finishing touch, and I had settled on the white leather sneakers. The purple ones were out of the question due to their color, and I was reluctant to put on the brown suede moccasins as they would not do well outside. I knew I'd get out at some point, if only to burn my rags in a healthy ritualistic pyre.

The shoelaces tightly knotted, I stretched up, kicked the old denim under my bed and studied my reflection again. Did I look better than I just had? It went without saying that I did, but were the homely clothes a good reason to pass on the riches of my inner world? It's difficult not to judge a book by its cover, but after you've spent two years reading it, shouldn't you start noticing its content? Especially when the writer himself does everything to draw your attention that way, despite the brutality of honesty?

Here I had a definite advantage. The good thing about attending boarding school for two years is that by the end you will know beyond a shadow of a doubt what kind of person you are. What you'll do with that knowledge is another story, but suppose for a moment that you did not sweep the revelations under the rug. Suppose that, instead, you looked at yourself in the mirror and acknowledged the bad in you: at least, the portion you knew was there. Sounds impossible, does it not? To acknowledge the bad in you … doesn't that already reek of a scam concocted by a televangelist aimed at your pocket and your vulnerable sense of self-worth? But wait: acknowledging the bad in you only goes halfway: the other half is about forgiving all the bad around you. And I mean: all of it.

Which brought me back to my classmates. Did I not care for them because they did not care for me? But would *I* have cared had *they* cared? The longer I thought about it, the muddier it became. But, for them to care, I had to be a different person, and that was something I would not choose for all the care in the world. Now, for me to care … I paused, coming up with a pose that looked great: not because I cared, but because, since I was here anyway, I might as well show some class. So, for me to care I'd have to disregard their bad … which put me on the wrong track as it created a dependency on them. Their caring or not caring couldn't be a factor determining my own attitude: otherwise, I'd be reactive, which is not permissible in a creator. To transcend the trap of self-reflection I had to be exemplary in letting go of their bad …

I felt dizzy and gave my forehead a rub. Going in circles like that infuriated me, but it only served to emphasize the same point: I had to forgive all the bad, except for the portion existing inside of me. I sighed, checking the reflection in the mirror for the last time. Still slim, still silvery.

Pity I hadn't had these jeans ten years ago.

"Someone's looking sleek!" Vince announced, assessing me from head to toe. "If you'd dressed like that before you wouldn't have had to complain about women so much."

"I never complained about women: I whined. But I had no money. Which reminds me." I returned to the valise. "I have a present for you."

"Tell me it's a deck of cards, and we'll play Durak!"

"How did you know?" I stared at him, truly puzzled.

"I thought you'd get at least a little nostalgic," he smiled, catching the deck on the fly.

Suddenly my eyes fell on his chest of drawers.

"It's not *that* clock, is it?" I said, already knowing the answer.

"No, it isn't." He shook his head. "I shot *that* one a long time ago."

I could almost see him standing with a Colt in his hand, unsteady as though he wasn't even sure if he had the gun, let alone where the target was; then raising his hand in one motion and burying a bullet right in the middle of the clock's face, the plastic cover shattering with a penetrating crack.

"Did the plastic screen shatter with a penetrating crack?" I demanded, gulping thirstily.

"Like a motherfucker," Vince assured. "And the ping of the ejected spring hung in the air for at least ..." He gave me a long look. "Seven seconds."

"Good shot." I blinked involuntarily. "I wish I was there." Then I realized the clock hadn't been there when I'd come to the room last. "Hey, do you remember seeing a box on my chest of drawers?"

"I don't know," Vince said indifferently. "What kinda box?"

"One with a bottle of cognac."

"Definitely not." His indifference was gone. "You think that asshole Oggi took it?"

"Definitely not. But I also bet it didn't grow legs to run away by itself."

"I'll keep an eye out for it." He nodded, studying the cards. "You know, I feel a strong urge to play Durak right now ..."

"We can do that." I nodded. "In the dayroom. Also: the cognac was for you, so now that it's gone, feel free to take the vodka."

He snorted.

"I have two bottles of vodka in my suitcase. But I won't pass. I'm gonna Seven Second the motherfuckers with it." He grabbed the bottle by the neck and took a sharp swing toward the door. Then he froze. "Eureka," he said triumphantly. "Seven Seconds should be the punishment for whoever loses a round!"

"The inventor must be exempt: otherwise I can't play," I reminded.

"You mean you can't lose?" His eyes momentarily grew foggy. "Wait. Motherfuckers?" He was all doubt. "Did you invent Durak?"

Appulse

Teaching Durak to foreigners is very entertaining. Ever seen those grotesque comedy shows where they vulgarly exaggerate a blatant truth, usually with paroxysms of canned laughter in the background? It's just like that, except the laughter is genuine and securely confined within. I've heard people ask questions that I thought were impossible. But once they learned the rules, their game was actually decent.

Vince was uncannily good at Durak, and he loved it: so much so that he'd wake me up at half past two in the morning to play. We'd both have classes at eight, but he'd refuse to accept this disheartening reality. Angry as I was, I usually wasn't asleep either, analyzing yet another failed encounter with Molly. Durak provided a catharsis: Vince gave me the satisfaction of winning against a worthy opponent, and I didn't mind losing to him, marveling at his natural grasp of the game.

It didn't take more than a minute after we returned to the dayroom to get the ball rolling: as soon as we were seated on the sofas (comfortably far from the DJ station, which one of the more gifted alumni had set up on the kitchen table) we were stumbled upon by Selene and Sulamith.

"Are you guys playing poker?" Sulamith inquired, her lustful voice implying she was ready to gamble on every garment she wore.

"No, we're playing *Du Hast*!" Vince said friskily, giving the deck in his hands a few extra twists. "I mean, *Durak*!"

"*Durak*?" she repeated, butchering the word charmingly.

"Means *Fool* in English." Vince sliced the deck into halves and began shuffling like a veritable croupier.

"I know a game called pool. Never heard about Fool," Selene declared.

"Why is it called Fool?" Sulamith insisted.

"It's so simple you'd have to be one to lose," I explained casually. "Care to learn the rules?"

She did, and I let Vince talk. The girls were eager to learn, which bespoke the tediousness of their other options, and soon the game commenced: first with cards exposed, then properly. I stayed for a few rounds, but when three more people with a bottle of whiskey joined us, I left the circle. I was thirsty; besides, it was time to reconnoiter.

When contemplating this reunion, I had deliberately restrained myself from sexual exaggerations, but I'd clearly been too reactionary. Sex was in the air, everywhere, penetrating my lungs with every breath. And it wasn't the guys who were setting the tone: they never do, since their attraction is a constant: the girls were the true mistresses of the escalating titillation. I refused to try to guess how much thought and preparation they'd put into this, but most of them looked the prettiest I'd ever seen them. They twittered, and laughed, and shone, feeding off each other's energy in a merry roundelay; and I wondered if any of them knew that all they did was just for their favorite guys who flocked around clumsily, pretending that seeing an old buddy mattered more than a candid chat with a bygone love. But something was still missing from this performance, as if a secret ingredient was being held back by a savant cook who didn't want the broth to thicken before the tantalizing smell crazed his guests out of their twisted wits.

I had already poured myself a glass of water and taken cover in the shadows by the bookcase when they arrived. They came together, a risky pack drenched in lechery and high on heat, magnetic pheromones dancing in the air around them in giddy strings, and the DJ station itself seemed to subserviently lower its voice before theirs. No one knew where they'd come from, and they'd have laughed spitefully if we'd asked, but be it Sosh, the lifeguard quarters or a French brothel, they were now the undisputed trendsetters.

Chloe and Nicolette entered first, the amount of bare skin they flashed in the first second mesmeric. The former wore a blue summer dress on two thin straps, her breasts teetering on the verge of falling out; the latter was all rosy pleated shell over azure shorts. Then came Fury in badass gray jeans and a charcoal shirt embroidered in white and yellow along the neckline. Diane was next, scarlet up top, in ultramarine capris with amber sandals and more sex-appeal overall than was advisable given my impressionable nature. In her wake trailed Gina in a white shirt under a red blazer, her platinum pants shining along the subdued but visible straights. Evangeline, wrapped in black leather except for pink velvet stilettos, concluded the procession; yet so much of its arresting course remained mere speculation.

The public parted before them like the Red Sea; they took it for granted, looking around with a mixture of scorn and anticipated pleasure. Some still failed to notice them—mostly losers caught up in catching up with their like—but the rest had but two options: to accept their second-tier status or to fight for a spot in the elite, knowing they wouldn't make it. And as they lingered in the middle, pulsating in concentric circles of exclusivity and repelling the other groups further into the periphery of the night, I sipped my water and watched their studied, deliberate movements but remained deep in my mind, on the outskirts of a memorable dream, wondering how different this night would feel had it been lit by Molly.

Her absence was idiocy: it couldn't be a fact, yet it was. I took so long in getting here because I wanted her to have already arrived. And she hadn't. The watch I hadn't yet adjusted read half past six; now the chances of her arriving in five minutes or at five in the morning were equivalent. The problem was that the chance of her not showing up at all was about the same.

All right, I thought, closing my eyes and stretching. Several of my joints cracked. *You've played well so far. It's time to get to work.*

Next, I experienced such a strong unwillingness to move that I would have stumbled had I been standing. Up until now I had been taking a passive position, so I was in part responsible for the mess surrounding me. You know how social dynamics work, right? The only way a female group can take over is when the alpha males let them. Frankly, I'd had high hopes for Moses, one of the more prominent silverbacks in our cohort, but he'd already absconded with Beatrice. The two had had an affair that was as torrid as it was fleeting and, knowing the temper of that hot Southern beauty, I didn't expect either of them to resurface before dawn. I felt a bite of regret: Beatrice was my type inside and out.

I finished the water and headed for the kitchen, scrutinizing the battlefield. Diane's clique played the classic game of "come if you dare", and so far everyone who did was turned down. Which was their own fault, because none of them struck at the center. I put the glass into the sink, filled it up and made sure all my attention was focused on myself. Then I waited for Diane to begin speaking and took off.

I made a careful semicircle, dodging accidental bodies and smiling at everyone, and approached her from the blind side. She was drunk, relating a story she found captivating, and her self-assuredness propagated to the entire clique. I was right behind her, and everyone saw me—everyone except for Diane. Her perfume was strong and heady; it would likely have smelled kitsch on a less powerful person, but she made it seem like she'd designed it herself. I watched her dark bob swing on her shoulders as she moved her head for emphasis, the amplitude growing as she neared the focal "… his hand tight on my elbow; and then I finally turned around and said: *excuse me, Ambassador Rein, but tonight I'm going to have to let you go.*"

The clique expressed admiration; it was a predictably pedestrian show.

"Hey Diane," I said with all the seriousness I could muster, squeezing her elbow. "Do you even realize that you're not a real princess?"

Silence followed, shutting off the rest of the room from our little circle of vacuum. I felt the clique's eyes on me, but looked into Diane's as she faced me. She waited for the pause to culminate, stifling a smile yet already sure of her next line.

"Ambassador Courage," she said when the time came, the clique freezing in anticipation of a deadly thrust. "You are one of the funniest men I have ever met."

"That won't do," I said, observing her eyebrows breaking at an impossible angle. "I can't afford to be anything but the only."

I extended my hand, and she gave me hers; it was vibrant. The clique must have thought it was awkward, but Diane enjoyed every move—as did I. Diane wasn't just hot or attractive: she was the living definition of a sultry woman. As such, she would have made a great movie star, although I doubted she'd have the discipline to get to the level of a Audrey Hepburn. Rather, having enjoyed the initial success, she would have lost interest. Her attention constantly needed to be whetted, in every respect: so much so that I had no idea how she managed to be the brilliant student she was. She must have scored higher than I on her final exams, and I wasn't sure how I felt about that. Not that I ever was a paragon of academic excellence, but I certainly spent more time in the trenches.

We chatted for a minute, going over a handful of trivialities. It was vital for Diane to seem like this was the first time in ten years that she'd thought about me, and I was willing to play along. The balance of power between us was that no one else knew anything important about us, and we left it at that. But the clique, sensing danger, began distracting Diane's attention by expounding on her comments while ignoring me altogether, and within another minute she was sucked into an artificial discussion of people I'd never known. I smiled, remembering when this tactic had sufficed to neutralize me: it works only so long as one took oneself seriously.

I was about to introduce a topic ushered in by a slip of Evangeline's tongue when I sensed I was being watched. Leaning back in an imitation of a laugh, I scanned the dayroom until I met Abigail's eyes. She didn't look away, and it took me more than a moment of clever acting before she realized that all I did was an act.

Abigail was a natural blonde, the roots of her hair of the same shade as the ends each time I'd checked in the past: which was many. She'd always liked me, but I liked her only enough to forgive her peccadillos. And who wouldn't, for this look of well-rehearsed coyness? Her stand was safe: not only did she not have to turn to see me, she was also engaged in a conversation with three of her friends, predominantly nice girls who ran no chance of getting laid tonight. That explained their friendships with Abigail, who could drive some worthy company their way yet was too insecure to realize she'd do better without these nuisances—although Abigail would have had no qualms about ditching them for a man she liked, if he was willing to take the flack.

"Hey," I said to Diane, touching her elbow again and interrupting another unnecessary story. She shook slightly, instantly turning her attention to me. "It was lovely chatting with you, sweetheart, but for now I'm gonna have to let you go."

The next thing she saw was my back moving away.

Abigail and Friends

Abigail saw me as soon as I took off and pretended that she hadn't. That was fine: she had to be ignored until after she rushed into the convention herself. I considered her friends; Haley was uncouth, and Janet could like me, so without further ado I fell upon Clementine.

"Hello dear!" I shouted like a schoolboy celebrating an old friend. "Look at you, aren't you gorgeous! Well, they say time flies, except with you it must be flying in reverse! Are you married by now?"

"Why, no," she blabbed with a silly, self-conscious simper while the others stared at me.

"That reminds me of an old friend of mine," I was now talking to Haley. "That guy always looked at least five years younger than his real age. No, I'm serious!" I added emphatically, sensing distrust from every direction. "Once he was even carded in a Canadian bar, years after college. Anyway, he marries this beautiful girl ..." Haley began blinking, and I turned to Janet. "Blonde hair, green eyes, slim as a deer. I mean, most people would consider her hot. I certainly did, although in my opinion she lacked character: too inert, never took initiative, just floated wherever the flow would take her, not even bothering to jump into the right flow first." I returned to Haley. "Now, she doesn't love the guy for a split second, but she's thirty-one and dismayed about it, and he has money. So, they get married, and the strangest thing happens to the guy: his real age starts catching up to him!" Keeping all attention on myself, I shifted to peripheral vision and conversed with the whole group, excluding Abigail. "A year goes by, then another, and all of a sudden he's thirty—and looks like it! He gets promoted at work, his mother is so proud that her son finally looks like a man; even his wife grows fonder of him. So, everyone seems happy, except for the guy. Day by day, week by week, he grows more and more sullen until, one day, he gets a divorce. No one saw it coming, especially his ex-wife, and the guy doesn't falter under the pressure—thank god they didn't have kids. A few months later I run into him in the gym and I can't believe my eyes: he looks five years younger again and bench presses more than his own body weight. We end up in a diner afterwards ..."

"Excuse me," Clementine said. "I need to go to the bathroom."

"I'll join you," Janet agreed.

"... and he reveals the secret of his youth," I continued. "He says a relationship with a woman invariably taxes a man's energetic well-being because of the need to bestow, which men are evolutionary conditioned to exhibit, and the more seriously the man takes his role as a caregiver, the greater the drain. So, the best way for a man to remain young is to remain single!"

"Judging by your look, you must have been single your whole life," Haley hissed.

"You hit the nail on the head!" I exclaimed, laughing. For a couple of seconds, they both thought I'd continue talking. But they were both wrong.

"It's actually quite remarkable how little you've changed," Abigail spoke finally, her ring finger running over the rim of the glass she held in her hand. "It's a pity the same doesn't work for women."

"You wouldn't want that." I shook my head, talking to Haley. "Besides, women don't need to look as young as men do."

"What?" Haley stared at me in drunken blankness. "That's the dumbest thing I've ever heard!"

"What do you mean?" Abigail asked seriously.

"A young woman attracts the lowest kind of attention," I explained to Haley. "It is only when she grows old that she begins to get noticed for her personality. And isn't that what women want? To be considered as persons?"

"Did you hear what Courage said?" Haley addressed someone behind my back. "That women should be old."

Someone behind my back laughed.

"Courage, this is stupid," Haley declared, taking a sideways step to maintain her balance. "You don't know shit, and you talk shit. Do you want some more wine?" she asked Abigail.

"Thank you, dear, I'm fine," Abigail assured her.

"Are you positive?"

"Yes. But Clementine wanted some, I think."

"I'll get the whole bottle," Haley said moving straight ahead before realizing she wouldn't be able to walk through me. "Excuse me," she said begrudgingly, squeezing between me and someone behind my back as I let her pass.

"So," Abigail declared, tossing back her head and giving me the submissive look of a cat looking to induce a tender caress on her soft fur. "How's life?"

I considered how much of the truth I could tell her. By all accounts, "not much" seemed the correct answer. But before I could inhale enough air to speak, another man rose up between us.

"I have been looking for you guys!" he said with tipsy elation. "I was telling myself: I have to catch up with them sooner rather than later!"

"Hello, Fidelio," I exhaled. "Great sweater."

The thing was a definite improvement on the T-shirts he used to wear in the past.

"Thanks," he replied conceitedly. Abigail gave him a warm hug: a

Buddhist, Fidelio was completely safe and probably still a virgin. "So, how's everything?" he asked me, as if looking for support. "How's life?"

"You know, there's something I have to tell you," I said, waving my hand for emphasis. "For some reason, every time you ask me "*how's life*" I hear "*how are your women*"? Why is that, do you think?"

"I really don't know," he said, pretending to be baffled but failing to conceal his joy. "Perhaps you're just that kind of a person—maybe everything makes you think of women."

"You may be right!" I exclaimed. "In fact, the more I think about it, the more sense it makes. I never can wait for the conversation to get through the small talk and reach the topic that was the reason for the start of the conversation in the first place. But therein lies a contradiction. Just before you joined us, I was having a chat with Abigail, and she, too, asked me the same question. Funnily enough, *her* question did not make me think of people at all. But when *you* did, my mind went blank except for thoughts of women that it would make at least some sense to talk about in your presence."

"Perhaps that's because Abigail is a woman?" he supposed, unfazed.

"This is most certainly an accurate observation," I admitted. "But shouldn't a woman's presence be even more of a catalyst for such a segue? Especially when she's as beautiful as Abigail!"

"A lot of men would disagree with you," she scoffed, turning red.

"But would they be right? I think—and please, Fidelio, correct me if you think I'm wrong!—that Abigail is one of the finest ladies who's ever walked this campus."

"You're exaggerating," she said, attempting to hide both the pride and the sadness behind a display of nervousness.

"Of course not!" I said emphatically. "It's true that I'm biased because, as you both know, I've fancied Abigail ever since I first set eyes on her. But, my feelings aside, her beauty is an objective fact."

"I didn't know that," Fidelio said seriously. "That you fancied her, I mean," he hastily added.

"That's because Abigail is too much of a lady to put a man in an awkward situation by revealing his interest in her to her male friends," I explained. "If you were a girl, however, you would have known. I bet there wasn't one among Abigail's girlfriends whom she didn't tell about my wooing her."

"That's not true!" Abigail interrupted, growing red in the face.

"She may have caught me there!" I winked at Fidelio. "She's too clever for that. Of course, she told only one of her girlfriends: the most talkative one." I turned to face Abigail. "It wasn't until long after AC that I realized why quiet girls chose blabbermouths for their best friends. But what is a more efficient way of spreading information than telling a friend like that something labeled as a secret?"

"You make me seem evil," she reproached.

"Real," I corrected. "And convivial. Men do it too. Don't they, Fidelio?"

"I have no opinion on the subject," he said authoritatively. "You lost me a while ago. Somehow you always manage to turn a decent conversation into an argument."

"Who's arguing? But I am glad you're on Abigail's side. Besides." I looked at her again. "I'm not angry with you. First of all, you did what every fair young lady ought to do, and quite elegantly, too. Secondly, by telling others, you did me a favor, as you presented me in a romantic light to a group of your friends who could try me on as a romantic partner in their imagination if they had any such interest in me, becoming my romantic partners in real life if they liked what they imagined." I wasn't sure when Fidelio had lost me, but I knew Abigail never had. "Finally, and most importantly: since most men here failed to acknowledge your beauty in action, I'm proud to have somewhat compensated for the injustice—which, personally, I don't even understand. I just wish the story were more exciting!" I concluded with sadness.

"What kind of story would you prefer?" Abigail asked daringly.

"Something inappropriate enough for neither of us to tell it to others," I said like someone who's nailed something well. "Our bond was too risk-averse: the gains would have been astronomical, but you never played more than you could afford to lose."

"I'm not the most playful person," she said.

"I'm no gambler either. But I saw you at a party once." I focused my mind's eye on my forehead, instantly falling into memories. "I don't know who your favorite man was, but your eyes shone brighter than I'd ever seen them. You wore a dark-blue dress that sat tight on you, softening every curve of your body without adding any volume to it; but the most amazing thing was how you moved." I paused, ready to wait for as long as it'd take to elicit a response. "Like a panther," I continued after one followed. "A slight gait, a slow shoulder, a languid moment to watch the floor. Dated, but graceful no end: like Hollywood in the thirties. I was bedazzled, and I didn't even tell you it was the most beautiful you I'd ever seen. But now I am. I want you to know: that night, you were stunning."

"I wish I recalled the night, but I really don't," she said quietly: and truly, for all I knew. I waited for a second or two, and then I realized why she didn't: she didn't know which one it was.

"I may have only imagined it." I sighed. "In one of those brutal endurance contests of creativity when you have to find a way to combine a bunch of familiar words to paint a previously unfamiliar feeling."

"I wouldn't be surprised if you imagined it!" Fidelio scoffed, and a pause followed.

"Do you guys ..." Abigail said finally before cutting herself and looking at Fidelio with a plea.

"Yes?" he said a couple of seconds later.

"Do you guys ever think about anything other than girls?" she fired.

"Sorry, no slacking on this one," I felt like I was conveying fate's will. "There truly is nothing else."

Abigail blushed: barely noticeably, but finally, in appreciation.

"You definitely haven't changed," she said, suppressing a joy that would have been greater if she'd showed it.

"It's my trump card." I took a deep breath, finally catching her perfume in the air. "People thinking that I'm the same."

"And you surely aren't!" Fidelio exclaimed, and I remembered that he was the one who'd taught me the first lesson in social politics. He knew them well: he believed he needed to, to be able to condemn them as rotten.

"I'm sorry, but I have to go," Abigail said, feeling anything but sorrow for leaving us. "My friends are all scattered; I want to make sure they're all right."

"When our commitments take the best of us, we should at least remember our personal freedom." I chuckled. "Nice talking with you," I said, giving her a hug. She took it readily, her heart fluttering like a caged bird. "Looking forward to doing it again."

"I'd better get going, too," Fidelio said, looking around for company he could attach himself to. A gang from the social service seemed his best bet. "I'm sure we'll talk soon."

They left, and I sank into the nearest empty couch, assuming the resting position with my eyes closed and facial muscles relaxed. So far, everything was fine: neither would approach me again without a good reason. Do you know how bad it is when an acquaintance interrupts intimacy that starts between you and someone else, especially if you had such a tough time establishing it? I wasn't afraid of Abigail, but Fidelio was a deal breaker: his mere presence could be sufficient to prevent Martina from appearing in the room. No, he wasn't a bad guy at all: he was just unbearably anticlimactic.

Invitation to a Beheading

After a few minutes of relaxation, I realized that I had no reason to remain in the dayroom. It was where I would most likely meet Martina, true, but mingling was as tiresome as not mingling was suspicious.

Besides, I had some important business to attend to, so without further ado I gathered my body from the couch and left.

After the dayroom's hellish music, the corridor felt like a sanctuary, and when I reached the room the noise level dropped so much that I could hear the ringing in my ears. I took off my shoes and fell on the bed diagonally, stretching and growling in carefree satisfaction. It was only now that I felt how taxing the recent interactions had been, and I would have fallen asleep despite the bright lights had it not been for the restless urge twisting inside me like a drill. I had to keep going, despite the dull pain in the body and the dull pain in the soul, all while being unsure of what direction to take when I ran out of moves.

Accepting the inevitable was hard, but eventually I got up and opened the valise. The idea of burning the denim had occurred to me months earlier, so I had brought all I needed: a medium-sized backpack, a box of matches, a bunch of old drafts, a sharp penknife, and a small plastic soft-drink bottle half full of pure ethyl alcohol. A liquid fire starter would have been simpler to procure, but would it have any poetic significance? Not to mention the foul smell. The bottle fit into the backpack's outer pocket perfectly, and the main compartment was large enough to accommodate the rest.

Next, I sat on the bed and considered what to change into. The white golf pants seemed a decadent choice, but I wanted to save the crème trousers for future use. It was also getting cooler, so a T-shirt wouldn't do without a warm top; in the end, I went for a charcoal dress shirt, viscose with a hint of nylon for durability, reasoning that the fire would give me enough warmth anyway, and that there was no point in hanging out there in the cold without it. The tennis shoes were to remain unchanged.

The pass itself was the last item to take care of, and when I did I had a clear sensation that I had done everything right.

As I left the room, I was in a state of perfect mental readiness, but just as I passed the dayroom (pleasantly indifferent to how its contents had changed in the meantime) and entered the main lobby, I stumbled upon Gina.

"Hey Courage," she said, a look of surprise crossing her face. "I was just looking for you ..."

"For the first time in your life," I said facetiously, and then I remembered that it was the second.

"I don't know, maybe," she said as if we were talking about something trivial. "Where are you headed?"

"Outside. Is that what you were looking to ask me?"

"No," she vacillated. "I wanted to ask if you'd like to join us on the cliffs."

The objective reality around me jerked and I rewound the last minute.

Gina was coming from upstairs, where all the girls were lodging, and I had heard some chatter that now, in retrospect, appeared to have had her voice ringing in it; but who had she been talking to? Alas, there was but one name I could safely exclude from the possibilities.

"Not even telling me who falls under the profound pronoun *us*?" I asked in the tone of a lady to whom an idle loafer had offered sex without bothering to introduce himself. "Who else is coming?" I added, seeing confusion in her eyes. Had to be the language barrier.

"Most of the Cliff Girls."

"Are you inviting me in your name, or in the name of everyone going?"

"I'm inviting you in everyone's name," she said, staring straight into my eyes, clearly unaware of how drunk that made her look. "We all want you there."

"So, who else is in *we*?"

"Are you looking for someone in particular?" she asked. I had always liked her better when she was on the offence: she was the Amazonian type, someone who'd have led a group of female archers in the War of the Roses.

"I've been doing that recently," I admitted. "But she won't be joining us, I'm afraid. When are you guys leaving?"

"Right now. We're all waiting for you," she lied.

"Waiting for me is a thankless business," I warned her. "What if I had already left?"

"We'd have thought of something," Gina chuckled. "So, are you coming?"

"Going," I corrected her. She was confused again. "Yes."

She instructed me to remain in the lobby until the troops arrived, and disappeared. Unwilling to remain standing for an indeterminate period, I retired to the adjacent hall and sat on one of the blue-cushioned seats, listening to the noises issuing from the dayroom and simultaneously trying to discern the sounds of the sexual intercourse that had to be occurring in at least one of the rooms. Yet nothing but the dreadful music reverberated through the walls, and everything else I discerned was just as unrelievedly dull.

It occurred to me that I should have been feeling something special. I had never been invited to the Cliff Girls' bashes before, and I had every reason to believe that it wasn't my clothes that had tipped the scales this time; yet instead of trying to deduce their covert motives, I was simply happy. Happy for an opportunity to be distracted from Martina, even if by condemning myself to a society of her kin. I smiled, wondering if there was one among those girls who didn't think that I was not in the same league as she. They were correct, of course: except that their league wasn't superior.

I caught a movement in the lobby through a narrow strip of glass running along the door; it was Chloe. She was leaning against the wall by the entrance with the air of someone waiting. The designer leather bag hanging from her shoulder bulged promisingly and, driven by some unusual curiosity, I left my hideout in her favor.

"I heard the girls are going to the cliffs," I began. "Are you coming?"

"I am." She looked at me inquisitively. "Who told you?"

"Gina. Should she not have?"

"Diane is the one who comes up with the guest list, so if I were you I'd check with her."

"Do you guys really have no say in it?" I arched my eyebrows in affected surprise. "But I have a strong feeling that she wants to see me more than anyone else."

"I wouldn't be so sure."

"You mean, you want to see me more?" I innocently inquired.

She rolled her eyes, abruptly annulling my affable attitude. I was about to return to my seat when Bridgette and Nicolette showed up. The former also had a handbag with clattering contents; the latter carried a rolled blanket.

"Have you heard the news?" Chloe asked them. "Apparently, Courage is coming."

"Instead of Rohatyn?" Bridgette made a wry face. "What about Moses?"

"Gone MIA," Chloe said. "So's Luke."

"Luke's no surprise," Nicolette giggled, eyeing my backpack. "Someone's ready to go!"

"It wasn't for this outing that I prepared," I assured.

"Really?" Chloe studied me with interest; she must have thought I'd dressed for them. "Where were you headed?"

"The cliffs."

"What for?"

"To make a pyre."

The girls exchanged a series of meaningful looks.

"Isn't that prohibited?" Bridgette asked. "To make a fire around here?"

"You bet it is. In fact, if this weren't, I would have thought I'm dreaming right now." I rubbed my hands together before checking them out; they were invariably mine.

"A fire would be nice," Chloe noted casually.

"How are you even gonna make it?" Nicolette asked.

"By combusting flammable materials," I revealed. "Paper, wood and alcohol are particularly useful."

"And where are you gonna get wood?"

"In a place that's about five minutes away."

"Awesome, get back to us when you have that fire going," Bridgette said.

"I'll ping you before that, because I'm not carrying a pile of wood to the cliffs all by myself."

Nicolette looked at me hesitantly.

"Are you actually serious?"

"Deadly. I'm making a pyre no matter what; the only question is whether you gals want to be part of it. Because if so, I'll need you to lend me a few of your exquisite hands."

"Why don't we use branches?" Nicolette ventured.

"Because there aren't that many on the cliffs," I explained calmly.

"I think it's a bad idea. We're going to be very visible," Bridgette said as I listened to a series of stately steps descending the staircase.

"Why are you bitches still here?" rang out from behind my back next.

You are getting drunk, dear, I thought.

"Have you heard the news?" Nicolette rushed to ask. "Courage wants to make a bonfire."

"Where's Moses?" Diane clearly had an agenda. "And Rohatyn?"

Bridgette and Nicolette launched into apologetic explanations, none of which were satisfactory even to me; the disquisition was halted by Fury's arrival; she also carried a blanket.

"Evangeline's out," Fury informed Diane. "I think she's gone with Luke."

"Too soon for her own good," Chloe remarked. There was an unexpected multidimensional intonation to her voice that made me wonder. "Do you want a fire, or not?"

"What?" Diane walked around and stood next to my left shoulder. "What would we feed it with?"

She was asking everyone except for me, so I remained silent.

"He wants to get wood somewhere," Nicolette said.

"Where, exactly? The Estate shacks?"

"Those are too far." I shook my head. "The sheep farm should do. If you guys help me, we can have a large bonfire. If not, I'm gonna have a little one to myself."

"Of course we want a bonfire, you twat," Diane said, finally facing me. There was a mischievous smile in the corners of her mouth, as if she had just allowed herself to feel happy that everything was developing according to plan.

"But what if they see us?" Bridgette insisted in a worried voice. "A fire is easy to spot."

"Not if you know where to make it." Diane's lips curved in a slightly arrogant fashion. "I hope the shore hasn't changed so much around here as to eliminate my little cavern."

"I don't think that's gonna fly," I said, and everyone looked at me. "I know what you're talking about," I continued, talking to Diane. "The cavern with a tire stuck between two rocks?"

"Courage, you have no idea what I'm talking about," Diane said in a peremptory voice, and both Bridgette and Nicolette giggled. "When I'm old and decrepit, I may crawl there to curl up in a ball and die, but for now I'm going to stay out of that hole."

"All right," I said, curious as to what cavern she meant. "Are we ready?"

"Gina's coming in a minute," Fury said. "Are we waiting for ..."

"No," Diane said firmly. "Looks like Courage will have to be the champion of masculinity tonight." She looked at me. "Think you can handle that?"

I stared right back, suppressing my self-importance with a hearty dose of self-irony.

"What makes you think there is even a theoretical possibility of me giving a negative response to that question?"

No one knew what to say, and we left it at that.

The Sheep Farm

Soon we left Sunley: a drunk, reckless bunch accustomed to attracting attention even when it wasn't wise. Diane thought she'd lead, but I joined her at the head of our procession with such nonchalance that Bridgette herself didn't think to nag. I wouldn't have minded playing second fiddle, but the sheep farm was my territory. I did the lamb watch here two years in a row, saving a great number of the animals as part of my estate service, and I was betting that the pile of wood hewed for the heating furnace remained under the same piece of tarp. Yet walking this road now, minutes before midnight, was drastically different from walking it at half past three in the morning back then. Few things in this world were a better embodiment of the desolation reigning inside me than that nocturnal quietude sprinkled with orange blobs of lamplight, the frigid wind susurrating in the trees, and the thick smell of wet hay suffused with plenty of other odors one would expect in a rustic setting.

"It stinks like crazy," Bridgette announced, and I imagined her rosy, pampered body lying asleep in a warm bed while my rubber boots slushed through the mud on the way to the lambs. I used to imagine what the insides of the dorms would look to an eye capable of seeing through the walls at night. I found it grotesque that the same campus that was so soothing and almost benign to me after dark turned into a taxing test of my inner strength when daylight compelled the students leave their rooms.

"Have you guys ever been to the sheep farm?" I suddenly asked. I said it sternly, as if I'd been meaning to say it all along but had only now accumulated enough urgency to do so.

"Why the hell would we ever need to?" Bridgette fired readily.

"To explore the tiny place you spent two years of your life," I suggested, reminding myself to take it easy.

"I've been there," Fury said. "With the social service."

"Have you?" I asked Diane.

"Not that I recall," she said calmly, and I knew she was lying. Perhaps it was a sexual affair that had brought her here when every other secluded spot in a three-mile radius had already been taken for the same purpose, or maybe she was on an introspective streak, analyzing those she'd slept with and those she'd sleep with soon. I wondered if Molly had ever come to this temple of contemplation, but alas, as for her reasons, she'd have been in the same boat as Diane.

I shivered, sensing an almost palpable barrier between me and the girls. Every step felt strenuous and contrived, and the echo bouncing between the road and the trees lagged eerily. Why had I agreed to come? What shards of my bygone soul was I looking for in these soiled, overgrown asphalt cracks? And if it must be true that some parts of ourselves are best buried, shouldn't it be up to us to decide whether or not to attend the wake?

I was sick to my stomach, but I wouldn't dream of showing it. The girls were chatting carelessly, as oblivious to my inner turmoil as ever, and I had never been more grateful for their lack of consideration. I'd made a mistake in treating the matter with levity: instead of being a walk in the park, it was rapidly turning into a battle, and I needed my old friends to prevail.

Do you like sheep? I hope you do, because I love them, for two main reasons. The first is wool. The other is their strength. Ever tried moving a sheep where it doesn't want to go? You can't: it is easier to carry one than to make it budge. So much for that universal symbol of docile obedience. Then again, is there any better metaphor for mankind?

Is that what they really are to me, I thought, glancing at the girls and smiling at the notion of how amazed they'd be if they knew I considered them in these terms. Priggish philosophical postulates prescribe seeing the humanity in every human, but what if each time you looked you found nothing but an empty space that reels you in by the hooks of your instincts? I could come up with a long list of reasons why I shouldn't sleep with anyone present, yet I agreed it would be much more fun if I did: with all of them.

Am I really as bad a person as I appear? Or am I simply living proof of the universal law that compels the higher level to take from the lower one everything that's needed: to give everything that's needed to a higher level still? I watched a pebble shoot away from under my shoe before clattering to a rest on the road in a seemingly chaotic move, and an owl celebrated this instant of eternity with a prolonged hoot. I would have apologized to the Cliff Girls for their lives having been temporarily reduced to a fleeting imprint on my exacting nature, but alas, there are things that you can tell a woman only after you have slept with her.

We were now under the barn's roof, the pens to our left and right, the small service shack straight ahead. I automatically checked whether the animals had fresh hay; they didn't, and the straw mats hadn't been cleaned in a while. I approached one of the pens, and the sheep inside eyed me with unease. Lifting the steel bolt had always been one of the most satisfying feelings on this campus: it felt like unleashing a secret power and capping its inhibitors in a single motion.

"What the hell are you doing?" Chloe asked.

"Saying *hi* to my old friends."

The sheep were growing more worried, getting up and backing into the far corner. I tried imagining what I looked like to them, but nothing definite came to mind. They weren't afraid of me per se; rather, they were afraid out of habit: just like the Cliff Girls, and just like most people I've met in life. People are peculiar creatures. You can wish them nothing but the best, you can save their souls, but in the end they'll still sell you out.

You ain't a shepherd, you fuck, I thought then, a prickly heaviness gathering behind my sinuses. *You say you can't see the humanity in them because there ain't none? Well, how about seeing the good? One of the most fortunate men who ever lived in this dead-end world, you are wasting yourself on indulgence in contemptible superiority, all the while ignoring the fact that each of these women can bring happiness to more men than you'll ever be friends with. Besides, this posture of a jaded bastard you're assuming aside, whom among these girls would you have rejected ten years ago? And, if they had been good enough for you to desire, why all this patina of condescendence, all this snot of a seasoned breeder who takes only the best and therefore doesn't take anyone? What if the light of your life went out at this very moment: would you then think about what they aren't, or about what they are?*

The sheep stared at me blankly, and the girls began fussing and grumbling. I didn't blame either of the herds, but I wondered if I could make happy everyone. The sheep ... well, those were easy: all it took was for us to leave. But the girls? How much would they appreciate a secular conversation by the fire if they had to have it with a man who could understand them all?

"That's the wood I was talking about," I said to interrupt the unrelenting monotony of my inner voice, which kept at it, dredging up more examples that I wished nobody in the world knew. He was completely right, and I wasn't in the mood to argue; I just wanted to understand what I had to do to avoid falling into that pit of self-importance again.

Midnight descended on my shoulders like plasma, the orange halos of the lights swimming in liquid blobs that effortlessly separated and merged. *Why is it that you can never put things in their proper perspective before you feel the breath of death on your neck, if only as an apparition conjured up by your own hypochondriac fear? Look at them, these charming, peerless ladies prepared to give their best as soon as they can escape from each other's judgmental eyes? Have you paid any heed to their lovely attire, or elegant movements, or breathtaking scents? Here, on the rural, hard-working ground of the sheep farm, don't they look like at least one of the triumphs evolution has reached while operating with but a measly arsenal of physical elements? And if you truly do have the secret key that imbues matter with purpose, shouldn't you have already dissolved in the divine euphoria you yourself would have never achieved had it not been for these girls' exquisite, dainty touch?*

Against the pile of wood, the Cliff Girls resembled a painting capturing the proximity of the prosaic to the supernatural, and it made perfect sense that all six of them stood with their backs to the viewer.

"Grab one quarter-log each; that should suffice," I said in a voice that almost cracked but didn't despite the pressure behind the sinuses reaching its zenith. "Take the smallest ones: all the axes are locked inside."

And then it finally hit me and, blinking my eyes quickly, deliberately, I bent my head low, squeezing out the tears to make sure there would be no wet trails on my burning cheeks. A careful observer would still have noticed the glistening halfmoons in my lower eyelids, but who would have looked that closely at a ghostly shadow that blended with the cool air, which carried all of the memories but none of the weight of the past? There was a sudden silence that hit my ears like a grenade, but when Chloe spoke, shyly and hurriedly, the sinister setting was instantly transformed into a scene so serene that the sheep themselves would have fallen asleep had they not been so irremediably curious.

I bolted the gate, moved to the pile and found a few perfect quarters; I handed some of them to the girls, then grabbed two pieces myself and drew the tarp back over the pile. It felt like I had walked through a pitch-black tunnel and came out into a flood of heavenly light. The Welsh night often brought me treasures, although I invariably had to battle for those. *Don't get hung up on the battles*, I reminded myself. *You haven't got a conversion from this place yet.*

Logs in hand, we resumed our journey, and this time I not only didn't rush to lead but waited for the girls to form a column before bringing up the rear. Some folks advise that you never look back when leaving, but I couldn't depart without a sentimental visual embrace. The sheep were still anxious, but they simply indulged us as there wasn't one among them that didn't know we were done here. I bid them and the place a silent goodnight, and the moon protruding from the milky clouds was the only witness of the tears that squalled out of my burning eyes.

You are a wicked animal completely devoid of any sense of gratitude, I thought when the last lamp of the sheep farm had disappeared behind the trees of the grove we were to traverse. *You are a travesty. You are a fiend. Be honest: what is it that you enjoy the most, spreading happiness, or spreading confusion and consternation? Because if it's the former, you'd better look straight ahead. What a procession of character! What a parade of luck! If they must abuse you, let them try: to impregnate their dubious tendencies with your immortal, impeccable glee. And if they want to relish life in your candid company, let them: to allow them an opportunity to see your love for themselves.*

I became aware of a warm, pleasant tickling in the top of my stomach, and I realized that I'd been smiling ever since we'd left the farm.

I looked ahead, marveling at the prepossessing party I was a part of.

I was finally feeling the Cliff Girls as if I were one of them.

The Cliff Girls

The Cliff Girls was the most prestigious club on campus. I won't say "ever," because the heirs and heiresses of various monarchies had attended AC in the past, but it was surely at the apex of the contemporary hierarchy. At first, the club was conceived as a girls-only one (hence the name), but soon the founding members discovered that something crucial was missing from their gatherings, and men gained access to supply the crucial something. Malicious tongues said that the Cliff Girls were so depraved they indulged in Caligula-style orgies, but, of course, that was nonsense. The Cliff Girls were but a bunch of snobs in search of yet another proof of their elite status, who spared no alcohol to fuel it—and those who condemned their orgasmic pursuits must themselves have been sexually frustrated.

We were approaching the shore at a sharp angle, and unless a turn happened soon, Diane had me beat: I would never have suspected there was a cavern nearby, let alone one that would fit us all. The rumbling of waves was already audible, and the fresh breeze blew softly but steadily, playing with the loose parts of my companions' garments' and cooling off my aroused fancy. Knowing I couldn't do anything about it, I surrendered to the attraction, letting it take me to the abstruse corners of myself where the heat and the pressure had had enough time to consolidate into intricate labyrinths that were as easy to enter as they were impossible to escape.

The night, and the breeze, and the moon, and the salty smell of the ocean, and the heady wafts of the Cliff Girls' scents soon got the best of me, so when Diane brought us to a stop I was caught off guard and had to looked around to reorient myself. We were to the east of the campus, halfway between Sunley and the soccer field, some fifty yards from the cliffs' edge, and right by the ruins of an old limestone fence. What Diane had meant by "cavern" was a spacious cavity in the little hill that began on the other side of the fence, the latter serving as a solid wall protecting adventurers from curious eyes yet leaving the view of the skies over the ocean unobstructed. I recalled having been here once when Vince had thrown a party for his girlfriend, but the only reliable conclusion I could remember drawing from that night was the resolution to never again mix vodka with bourbon.

"Is this the cavern you were talking about?" I asked Diane.

"Are you complaining?" She squinted her eyes.

"No. This should work for a bivouac."

Gina giggled.

"Courage, if it wasn't for your accent, you would've passed for a native speaker of English," she said.

"*If it weren't,*" I corrected her.

"What?"

"*If it weren't,* because you are implying an impossibility, much like when you say *if I were you*. But I know *bivouac* only because it's French."

"You speak French?" Diane demanded. She seemed annoyed at me for giving Gina a hard time: she'd rather reserve the privilege to herself.

"No," I said, throwing the logs on the ground and taking off my backpack.

I let the girls take care of the space and commenced with the fire. Even the smallest log was too large to incinerate instantly, so I began by tearing off the bark and whittling thin strips of wood with my pen knife, assembling the shavings into a heap on a piece of paper. It was a series of observations made on a given evening, mostly rhymed couplets with an occasional aphorism. Yet as soon as I struck the first match, an unexpected gust killed the flame. Surprised, I inserted the dead match into the heap and struck another, this time sheltering the flame with my cupped palms before setting it to the paper. It burned quickly, its edges curling and turning into weightless flakes of ash, but the heap stubbornly refused to join the party, so soon only a thin tower of smoke remained.

"Do you think you can actually do it?" Fury asked with audible concern. The girls had already spread out the blankets and finished the first bottle of wine.

"It's like anything else in life," I said. "You keep trying until you succeed."

"It'll be a bummer, to have brought the wood, only to find out we can't have a fire," Bridgette complained.

Unfazed, I collected the wooden pieces again, this time while rerunning a piece of dialogue from a novel still unfinished after several years of struggle. The moon provided plenty of light; so much, in fact, that one could easily have read, but the fire was nevertheless a superior source of romance. I covered the heap with a cupped hand and held the burning match within it. This was looking much better. The shavings caught up quickly, and within a minute the larger slivers I was adding to the top of the heap began carrying the fire along their edges as well.

"Do you want a glass of wine?" Diane asked me as I assembled two large logs over the growing fire.

"You guys brought glasses, too?" I asked in amazement, seeing two in her hands. "Thank you, but I don't drink."

When the fire was safe, I turned away to evaluate the configuration. The girls had made themselves comfortable on the blankets and were drinking leisurely, their faces glowing with beauty and anticipation. Their body language still excluded me, but now it seemed an invitation to capture their attention if I could. I sighed. I hated to fight for what I considered mine, but there was no point in being a silent guest at this party.

I gave them a few more minutes of chatting and toasting, making myself at home on my backpack and relaxing my entire body, and when another pause occurred I began.

"This reminds me of this one time when my friends and I had a midnight party at a sand quarry," I said, the rhythm of my voice undulating smoothly. "We were all wasted before sunset, and then the host remembered that his auntie's old car was parked in the shed, and that no one would mind if we crushed it," I explained to Chloe, who was avoiding my eyes. "It only took us forty minutes to start the engine, and off we went, to the quarry. Have you guys ever been to a sand quarry?"

"I ride past one every time I take the train to London," Gina said reluctantly when no one else spoke.

"Doesn't count. You have to step inside to appreciate it. It feels like being on the moon. And have you ever seen quarry trucks? They're so large their wheels stand taller than a basketball player."

"Trucks? You are becoming Americanized," Diane remarked.

"*Old man lying by the side of the road with the lorries rolling by*," I sang, watching Bridgette suppress a laugh with a sip from the bottle, her long brown hair dangling dangerously near the flames which danced like the twisted tongues of a magic animal and licked my skin with their benevolent heat. The fire was now well established, and the two logs at the top looked like they could go up any minute. Or were they already burning?

"So, Courage, how come you don't drink?" I heard through the orange haze.

"I don't like alcohol—neither the taste, nor the effect."

"The taste I can accept, but the effect?"

"Why, it's worse than the taste. Besides, some of the most ridiculous situations I've ended up in were induced by alcohol. One time, for instance, I got so drunk I forgot that I'd just moved into a new apartment and tried getting into my old one. The key wouldn't fit, but I knew how to get inside through the landlady's kitchen, which she never locked. The apartment was on the second floor," I told Nicolette who seemed to be listening to anything but me. "To get to the kitchen, I had to climb over a wrought iron fence topped with arrow finials. There was barely enough space between each pair to set a foot, but I had done it before, so I thought I'd be dandy. And sure enough, I climbed to the top without a hiccup; but then a gust of wind flung a branch in my face, and the next thing I knew, I was upside down, the cuffs of my pants hung up on the spikes. And the pants wouldn't tear, no matter how hard I pulled …"

"I hope it wasn't his only pair," Nicolette said to Gina.

"If you only knew what a sore spot you're rubbing salt into," I sighed. "America often makes me feel like I need to gain fifty pounds to find the right clothes, but those pants fit me like a second skin."

"Why do you live in America?" Fury asked.

"If you'd asked me that a few years ago, I'd have said it's because I'm used to it. But now I know better."

"So, why?"

"It's embarrassing," I said shyly.

"Oh, c'mon!" Diane exclaimed. "Is that what you call being a champion of masculinity?"

I looked at her.

She had me cornered, and the Cliff Girls knew it.

I didn't mind.

"The reason why I live in America," I said plangently, reluctant to hide a mischievous smile, "is …" Their indifference was gone: they were all listening, as if intuiting that something bizarre was to follow. "American girls."

"Wait, are you saying you like American girls?" Gina said after a brief pause, as if she'd just woken up.

"It's not that simple." My smile grew wider, and in the fire's pallid light I must have resembled a frisky imp. "I like them, sure. But the key is that they are the hardest for me to love."

"And there are no Americans here!" Bridgette exclaimed.

"Too bad Miss Flawd failed to honor us with her presence," Chloe remarked.

"She wouldn't have joined," Fury reminded her.

"Much to his chagrin," Nicolette scoffed.

"But then Evangeline would have," Gina whispered.

"You can't be serious," Diane declared.

I took a deep breath and looked at all of them. In the fire's trembling, indefinite light, they looked like their beauty had just reached its peak.

"I cunt be," I admitted. "But I am. Speaking of which, a funny thing happened to a friend of mine recently. So, he's dating this girl from London, and her accent is a symphony …"

"Courage," Diane continued where she'd left off, annoyance plain in her comfortably drunk voice. "Forget about your friend. What is it you like about American chicks?"

A loud crack ensued, the log structure collapsing onto itself, and a cloud of sparks shot upward. It was a mesmerizing sight that did not last long, but the logs kept burning as if the flames had soaked into them.

"The question stands," Diane reminded as I placed two more pieces on top.

"What question?"

"Are you kidding?" Diane exhaled exasperatedly, emptying another bottle of wine into her glass. "What kind of man are you?"

"I'm not a man: I'm a walking stress test."

"Diane asked you what you like about American chicks," Nicolette elucidated.

"Oh, that?" I returned to my backpack, shaking it before sitting down. "I don't know. I simply like them, that's all."

"Because … they're the hardest?"

"Unquestionably so."

"So, what do you do with them?"

"I court them, in my own peculiar ways."

"Like?"

"Do you really expect me to tell?"

"Sounds like he's afraid of us!" Bridgette exclaimed.

"Courage courting someone; that's something!" Nicolette agreed.

"You courted Gretchen!" Diane was implacable. "That's a fact."

"Never." I shook my head vehemently. "I just told her I loved her, and then repeated myself in writing."

"How did she respond?"

"She said I could always count on her as a friend."

"Yeah, that's one way to dump a guy," Nicolette sneered.

"What are the others?" I asked innocently.

"So," Diane continued in the voice of someone solving a math quiz. "How many girls did you love in AC?"

"Counting only those I actually loved, or also adding those I only fancied?"

"Do the loved ones first."

"I didn't say I'd do both, but you've already called it. Between one and six; I can't quite recall."

"That's one hell of a range. Are any of them here?

"Now you're making me regret leaving Gretchen behind!" I laughed. "That would be an easy "yes" instead of a hard "no"!"

"Courage, you gotta be kidding!" Gina said threateningly. "You're surrounded by a score of the hottest girls in your class, and you have the audacity to say that you were never in love with *any* of them?!"

"*He had white horses and ladies by the score,*" I sang. "That line brings to mind a female choir singing from a single sheet of music. By the way, a few months ago I finally hit the Metropolitan Opera with a friend of mine ..."

"I'm pretty sure he's lying," Bridgette declared.

"He's gotta be!" Chloe agreed.

"So, I'm standing in the lobby waiting for her because she has the tickets, and I see this couple, a man and a woman, both in their mid-forties, dressed like they've just stepped out of *Eyes Wide Shut*, that early scene where Nicole Kidman is left alone at the ball ..."

The only thing saving me was that no one present knew that a beautiful woman speaking with a proper English accent was enough to put me on tilt, so for the last hour I'd felt like I was balancing on the edge of a precipice. It was true that I'd never loved any of these girls, but not because I didn't fancy them. Quite the contrary; I fancied them all, but if they knew it, I'd be done. One of the many things that loving Molly taught me was that the worst thing I could do to myself in the company of an attractive woman was show her that I found her attractive, so all I could afford was the very playful politeness I had so generously displayed thus far.

"... I mean, Freud himself would have never happened had it not been for the sexual frustration of the time!" I concluded. "And I wouldn't have had a clue, had it not been for Arthur Schnitzler. He wrote the play that Kubrick turned into *Eyes Wide Shut*," I explained to Gina, who was staring at me, two tiny reflections of fire quivering in her green eyes.

"All right," Diane said sternly. "Since you've already insulted us poor English girls, I want to know: what's your ideal woman?"

"How about I just give her sexual characteristics?"

"This is gonna be so-o-o inappropriate," Bridgette declared.

"That's pretty shallow," Chloe scoffed.

"You never impressed me as someone to whom sex mattered a lot," Diane said.

"Then you must have always had the wrong impression of me."

"Then it's about time you gave the right one."

I leaned back, looking into the stars as if they were a mirror. Infinity was all around us, hiding in the fresh breeze, in the chirping of insects, and in the bashful shadows trembling on the limestone wall. I wanted a moment alone, to appreciate this depth from a place of internal silence, but when all the wrong women are asking you all the right questions, you have no choice but to man up and speak.

"She," I drew a long breath through my nose and closed my eyes, "is out of this world. She is fluid, daring and unpredictable. She is never afraid to express herself, without second-guessing whether this is the right thing to do or what others will think. She constantly experiments, not settling even for the diamond crown, and habitually pushes herself to the extreme. She is ruthless but never cruel, cordial but never mawkish, proud but never vain. In short, she is creativity personified."

"Very few women fit that profile," Diane said in the tone of a judge reading a verdict. "If any."

"Some do," I said. "But that's what every woman should be. Granted, sex is hard for women. It is easily available to them, often at scale, but its quality is so low that a woman who's slept with a hundred men may still not have met one who has awakened her magic. Yet that doesn't mean she should give up on herself. After all, what better pursuit does life hold than self-discovery?"

One of the girls said something, but seemingly not to me; I wasn't sure, as my attention was distracted by Nicolette's suave and deliberate pose. With her back perfectly straight and her hips slightly turned, she was offering the best view of her clothed body that was possible after midnight. Kissing her on the lips suddenly became a consideration, and even Diane shimmering in the background wasn't a distraction anymore.

I looked at Nicolette, smiling. The smile could have seemed foolish, but when a woman fancies you, she doesn't mind. If you only knew how much a woman can forgive a man for the butterflies he sets loose in her stomach! We locked eyes, and I held her stare with boundless affection. By now Bridgette and Gina were practically asleep, lying in each other's arms and whispering giddily; Fury stared into the fire with the expression of a sentinel prepared to stay awake until dawn and club to death any wild animal or human that would dare to disturb the calm of her camp; and Diane and Chloe were discussing their plans for tomorrow. At first, they were different, but then Chloe adjusted.

"It's getting late," Bridgett announced, yawning. "Do you guys wanna go?"

"Good idea," I agreed. "You guys should get some rest."

"What about you?" Fury asked.

"I'll stay."

"What for?"

"I wanted to come here to be alone for a while. I haven't had a chance to do that yet."

"Are you having a secret meeting here?" Chloe quizzed.

"I bet he's waiting for Molly," Bridgette taunted, and I felt a chill on my back.

"Was that really your plan?" Gina asked incredulously. I looked at her, a question in my eyes. "To make a fire just for yourself?"

"Not for myself," I shook my head slightly. "For the past."

"Courage, find yourself a girlfriend," Diane sneered.

There were so many things I could have told her, and they'd all have been a waste of words.

"Good night, ladies," I said softly when they had all collected themselves, and their blankets, and their bottles, and their bags. "I wish you all marvelous dreams tonight."

I heard their muffled voices echo in the air for a little while, and then they drowned in the distant rumbling of the waves.

Fire from the Past

Finally, I thought, stretching. *A score of the hottest girls in your class!* I rubbed my eyes gently, trying to recall when and where I'd woken up last. This was easy, and I focused on a more pressing question: what had facilitated the energy surge on the sheep farm. I played devil's advocate at first, but the only verisimilar explanation was Death. I sensed its proximity there, and even though it was no further from me now, I didn't feel its presence so intimately.

A few minutes later I decided I'd indulged enough and began to work. The fire was burning aggressively, and it could consume the denim even without the alcohol, but I still poured some on the shirt before feeding it to the flames. They instantly changed in color, a swamp-green shade erupting alongside the yellows and oranges, and when a slight gust of wind carried the overwhelming smell of combustion toward me, I felt nauseated. I hated that smell: this wasn't the first time I'd dealt with it, although the former occasions weren't quite as noble. I coughed a few times, turning aside; then

I poured more alcohol over the pants and threw them in as well.

It was tempting to consider this act a ritual, but it was only a trope. The actual clothes I'd worn here had been disposed of years ago, and these were mere imitations, sufficient to satisfy my indifferent classmates, but not the Spirit. And yet I had to do it, if only to pretend. The delinquent elements of my consciousness inextricably linked to this external masquerade, I had to pull every lever there was to rid myself of the hooks still lurking inside. After all, the next chance wouldn't come along for a while, and who was to say I'd live that long?

Suddenly struck by melancholy, I was shuffling through the relevant recollections, driven by the propitious influence of the place. My life here had seemed like walking through a brick wall, and every episode I remembered was replete with impressions of weakness and defeat. All but one, that is, because the universal laws of equilibrium prevailed in my case, too, granting me the magic of a single episode where I did everything right.

It was on a bright September morning, the ultramarine sky seeming close and rock-solid, when I first spoke with Martina. I had intended to do it for weeks, but couldn't find a moment with her alone. So when I finally did, spotting her on the front lawn, sitting on one of the benches facing the ocean, I proceeded in a single motion, somehow knowing it would play out right. None of the fear that had plagued me persisted as I was devoid of any sensation other than an infinitely passionate drive for eternal bliss. And, looking into her eyes—which were saying to me *Oh, really?*—I knew there was no one else who could honestly answer *Yes*.

"Hello. Are you Molly? An actress, right? I heard the guys talking about you," I said, smiling. "I thought to myself, boy, if even a third of what they say is true, I better make sure she knows who I am."

"What guys?" she inquired, clearly curious.

"Theater class, or dancers. They are all the same to me."

"What were they saying?"

"A bunch of stuff. Apparently, you're talented." I scrutinized her. "Is that so?"

"I do my best," she said in sham modesty, clearly flattered.

"Is that so?" My eyebrows arched upward. "Do you think you're gonna make it big one day?"

"That's the plan," she said, giving me a long, searching look. She couldn't wait to ask about the guys. "So ..."

"What's your locale of choice, then? Broadway or L.A?"

"If you're serious about acting, it will always be a combination of the two."

"If I were serious about acting, I wouldn't go near New York," I said.

"I've spent my whole life there," she said accusingly.

"You mean, you can't wait to finally move to a better place?"

"Name one place that's better."

"Close your eyes and poke at a map of the world: there's your answer. Besides, being a star where you come from feels like an easy way out."

"Is that so?"

"Unquestionably. I'd tell you more about it, but I have to run. Let's grab a coffee after class tomorrow and continue. Meet me in the dining hall at one thirty; I'll take you to the best bench on the lawns."

"I'm busy tomorrow."

"Friday, then."

"Can't promise that either."

"Don't promise. Just come."

"You have to tell me who the guys were."

"Ask them yourself."

"By the way." She looked at me like she were the only one who knew. "You never told me your name."

"You don't know it?" I look at her in sincere amazement. "You may be the only one on this campus who doesn't."

And so I left, and she never showed up, contrary to the logic of the cinema where an exchange like that is the prelude to a love affair. I think she waited for me to make a pass at Sosh, but I just couldn't endure the clamor and the foul squandering of the adolescent spirit the place was associated with in exchange for a fleeting moment of overdue luck—which shouldn't have been luck to begin with, but somehow the world coerces us into accepting its ridiculously rigged standards as the status quo.

By now, most of the denim had burned through, but the shape of the pile of fabric hadn't yet disintegrated. I almost forgot about the sneakers but then recalled them and filled them with most of the remaining the alcohol. This time, green flames rose unchecked, stretching almost as high as to lick my face, and the suffocating smell nearly made me faint. I took a few steps back but kept looking, the pile imploding and crumbling, and the sneakers' rubber soles melting and bubbling before turning into black smoke. A part of the sleeve, or perhaps the leg, jutted out of the flames and was only smoldering; I moved it further into the flames with an unused log and then sat on it.

What else would you toss in, now that you're all out of the physical stuff? I thought, rocking back and forth lightly. *What specters of your disappointed past are you looking to add to this pile tonight?* Painful memories rushed in to proffer their tortured remains, but I repulsed them in anger, having no pity for myself. Then, remnants of Molly prevailed, arranged in concentric circles vibrating in tune with my sorrow. But could I take them for a reliable measure if the only consistency in our relationship existed in my own mind?

You are losing it, I thought, watching the undulating flames. This thought, where did it come from? From ten minutes, or ten years ago? And if it ever was mine, why did I feel like a thief groping for a wallet in a commuter's bag? Why was I still carrying this clumsy, cumbersome load of the past, as if expecting time to rewind to the point where space becomes a dot? Let it burn instead, let it burn in short spurts, let everything about this act of cleansing be short and definite, because in a dimension where you are what you want to be, none of this had even happened, as you had never been so foolish as to keep going down the wrong alley once you saw that the first step was a mistake. *Let it be short*, I repeated. *Short, like the introduction to a new chapter in your long existence, in which you have learned enough of the gimmicks and enough of the words to project yourself not as the static figment of an overweening imagination, but a fluid and supple power that has acquired a multidimensional form.*

I sat silently for what seemed a very long time, staring into the fire as if there were nothing besides its light. When I heard steps behind the fence, I was neither surprised nor concerned, taking the noise as a herald of the imminent phase. Deep in my heart there rolled a distant, profound longing, and quenching it one way or another was only partially up to me.

I tore my eyes from the flames, prepared to face the unknown.

But it was Chloe, wrapped in a blanket from head to toe.

Chloe

"Courage, what the hell are you doing here?" she demanded, seemingly legitimately surprised. Was I supposed to believe her?

"Do you realize that *I* should be asking you that question?" I inquired readily, studying her for clues.

"Well, I asked you first," she chuckled, although to me it sounded more like a gulp of something liquid. She was definitely drunk, but not wasted.

"I'm burning some old clothes." I said, as if it were the most natural thing in the world.

"Old clothes? Whose?"

Like I said: drunk, but not wasted.

"Mine," I admitted. "I brought some old clothes with me from across the Atlantic: clothes I've wanted to burn for a long time. What about you, did you forget something here?"

"Forget? Yeah, I think I might be missing something," she agreed after a brief moment of thought, blinking profusely.

"Take a look over there." I pointed at the spot where she'd been sitting. "That's where you sat."

"I know where I sat." She moved right to where I showed. There was nothing there.

"What are you missing?" I reminded her a few seconds later.

"Missing?" Hers was a very inquisitive look. Then she remembered. "A chain."

"Not a necklace?" It could have been anything. "Didn't you use to wear cameos back in the day?"

"Cameos? Me? I suppose you can call them that," she acquiesced. "Have you already burned it?"

"Your cameos?" I asked, just in case.

"You silly boy!" she giggled, folding the blanket and dropping it next to the fire, across from me. "Will you help me look?"

"What's my finder's fee?" I asked, not budging.

"I'll think of something. It's a beautiful thing, and it's worth a lot."

"Sure," I said, still motionless.

She eyed me with surprise, eventually making a series of confused and impatient gestures. I got up and approached her. Acting as unaffected as if I were buying soap at a grocery store, I adjusted the blanket and sat on it, extending my knees toward the flames and leaning on my left elbow.

"You are warm," I remarked, sliding my right hand behind her back without touching it.

"That's why I sat here."

"I meant that your body's already warm," I explained, adjusting.

We spent some time in silence, watching the fire and listening to its crackle. I didn't know what Chloe was thinking, but I was asking myself whether I wanted to have sex with her. Soon the answer came: *yes*. I did. Chloe was bad in many of the ways that bad manifests itself, as I saw it, but I was still willing to forgive it all for the formidable urge she raised in me every time my eyes fell on her hips from the right angle. Hers was a curious appeal: that of a bad girl who'd be a good girl all the way to the bedroom, but who'd show whoever got her there what a treasure of a bad girl she really was.

"By the way," I began in a voice that was heavily reminiscing. "Why did you always used to hate me?"

I knew exactly what I was doing, and it was making me fucking sick. The previous sentence is a poetic two-liner. But you know that otherwise I'm innocent: I hadn't used any tricks during the outing, not even the fishing game. Although I probably should have, so that you could see how it works. Chloe came back because my average chance of being attractive to a girl I was attracted to hit one hundred percent with her. Pure math, nothing else … except sex.

She was still silent. It meant she knew.

"Don't worry. I know why. I just wish you'd done it better. Because why wouldn't you, after all?"

She gulped and then inhaled sharply through her nose.

"I have to make a confession," I said in a lower voice. "Whatever happens between us tonight: I cannot take my pants off."

"What?"

I was silent for a few seconds, and then she dissolved into laughter. While amusing, that was also worrying.

"Where's that coming from?" she said, having gotten over it.

I shrugged.

"I had to warn you, that's all. And don't get me wrong: I wish I didn't need to keep them on. But I have to, if only to take care of a distant probability."

"What are you talking about?"

"It's a secret. I can't tell."

"Wait." She made a quick gesture with her head, as if fixing it in a position from which it would be easier to see me. "The reason why you have to keep your pants on is a secret?"

"Not exactly. The reason per se is not a secret, but the reason I'm doing all this would take half a novel to explain."

"So … what's the reason?"

"I have something on me that I can't risk losing, even to the unlikeliest possibility, because fate can catch my negligence just at that."

You should remember this phrase, you forgetful swine, I thought. *Wait. What was the one about the chains? You swine!*

"Wait, I …" she began, losing the rest in mirth. "I don't understand …"

"It doesn't matter." Now I was so entuned to her I could separate the smell of her body from the smell of her scent. "Because." My right hand began aching, and I let it envelop Chloe's back. "If we think about it logically." She straightened her back and pulled her shoulders behind, creating an immaculate silhouette along her high breasts. "What would be a reason for me to end up with my pants down tonight?"

She put her arms on me as soon as I began moving my lips closer, and then we kissed as if neither of us wanted this night to end. Her breathing came in irregular intervals, sometimes so unexpectedly that I would forget to breathe myself. This time, it was everything it wasn't with Emmanuelle's mother. Chloe was greedy for me and couldn't have enough, giving me more passion in five minutes than I had gotten since dawn. And I was not in a rush to extrapolate the trajectory, but it quickly became too much to withstand.

When I took her panties off, she was already wet, so I proceeded without further ado. She must have taken several gulps of hard liquor before returning because she had grown much drunker since we began. It took at least twenty minutes of hard, uninterrupted action before she began showing the signs of an approaching orgasm, but each time she was about to enter the level where it was inevitable her muscles contracted involuntarily, making her lose focus and letting the magic slip. I considered finishing her off orally, but then a serendipitous brush of my hand over her thigh revealed an erogenous zone that worked well with the position we were in, and within a few more minutes she was ready. I was surprised at the longevity of her orgasm, her legs clenching behind my back, but it seemed neither particularly strong nor particularly bright. I gave her a minute or two of gentle pushes and tugs after she was done before bringing us to a complete halt, and by then she was as relaxed as if she had just woken up from a nine-hour-long sleep.

"I had no idea you were so good," she said in a slow, deep voice a few minutes later.

"Many women don't," I said. Then I remembered *just at that*. "The difference is: some never find out."

"I wasn't going to return. But then you said something." Her face wore a mask of peace. "Something about the stars."

"It probably wasn't me," I said, gliding my fingers over her cheek.

"Ticklish!" She laughed, not opening her eyes, and I realized that the fire didn't have much left in it. "Can I ask you something?"

"Only if it's worth it."

"Is it true what you said earlier?" She looked at me with her quick, immoral eyes. "That you never loved anyone here?"

I sighed: deeply and melancholically.

"I just think it's strange," she continued. "To use Molly as cover, sure. But to really never have loved any of us?"

"Why do my deepest feelings always remain unknown even when I turn them inside out?"

"I know more about you than you think," she said cuttingly, and I believed her.

"It's all about the peak, which you can reach only through love," I whispered confidentially. "Think of yourself. You feel that charge accumulate between your legs, the one that will eventually paralyze your body while contorting it in sweet seizures. But can you really consider that explosion outside of the context of who facilitated it? The role of the man is not mechanical. He is also crucial as the emotional trigger. That's why sex in the bathroom of a nightclub with a desirable stranger who doesn't know what to do may be better than a night with a sex guru who doesn't mean anything to you."

"Are you a sex guru?"

I grabbed my hair in mock despair. Then I realized she actually wanted me to reply. I hugged her tightly, clenching my hands over her butt. I suddenly felt very happy. I couldn't understand why I'd never fallen for her in the past: she fulfilled just about every requirement of a smoking hot chick. We spent a few minutes in a lip lock while my fingers were working on her. One of the beauties of not coming is that the woman becomes more desirable to you after sex than she was before, so you can pick it up right where you left. Suddenly she became much wetter; I increased the amplitude of the pull and prolonged the deep phase of every push until she found her rhythm …

I made her come once more, and when she came to herself again she took a long, warm look at me, collected the blanket, and ran off into the night.

Abigail Again

I stayed put for about ten minutes after Chloe was gone. She disappeared like a gazelle into the tall savannah grass, and it was perfect. I made sure the fire had consumed my entire offering, and that nothing but ashes remained. I poured the rest of the alcohol over them. There was only hissing.

My return was quiet and uneventful. I half expected a hellish beast to jump out at me from the bushes as they are wont to do in sagas featuring comparable scenery, yet the night held nothing but moonlight and the incessant chirping of insects. Not that I normally indulge in such fantasies, but at least it'd mean that I was asleep: so far, every reality check pointed to the contrary. This time I didn't bother with my hands: I was jumping up in the air every so many steps. Aspiring lucid dreamers often think the first thing they'll do is fly; but to consciously control flight you either need to have a knack for it or train like a pilot.

My attempts at flight were interrupted by the sight of a couple making out near the fence around Dickenson's house. The girl had surrendered herself completely, and the man was either too timid or too stupid to recognize it and take control. When I got closer, I saw that the man was Rohatyn, so the riddle was solved in favor of stupidity. The girl wouldn't have been so obvious had it not been for her metallic light-purple and fuchsia leather plissé skirt. It did a perfect job of attracting attention, but Marylin, who was wearing it, didn't have the personality to pull it off, so it turned her into a target that was as easy to spot as it was pointless to hit.

I neither disturbed them nor slowed down, soon sneaking back into Sunley through the front door. The dayroom was much darker now and had lost most of its populace, yet at least a dozen bodies remained, sitting motionlessly or moving with hectic luster like molecules pinned to a two-dimensional plane. No flame of heavenly color erupted as I looked around, confirming the suspicion that Martina ... well, at this point you should be familiar enough with my style to deduce the truth without needing me to spell it out.

When I got back to my room, which was familiarly empty but dark this time, I felt a surge of creative energy. I imagined a conversation I would have been having with Chloe had she been here and, noticing that my thoughts were growing more golden around their edges, I grabbed my laptop and began to work. Sentences were flowing out with the ease of a mountain creek, but after a few pages of uninterrupted bliss I wondered whether these newly discovered heights were sufficiently verisimilar. Luckily, there was a foolproof way to anchor even the most ethereal literary work without grounding it, and to that end, laptop in hand, I returned to the dayroom to capture the authentic signatures of my old classmates.

There, everything changed. My attention was arrested by the social practices unfolding around me, causing me to wince at most of the things these people were doing. Take Tara, for instance. Her tremulous movements in the chair where she sat with her legs crossed, facing Uls, betrayed her desire to please that cold giant. He, in turn, surveyed the effect he was producing, but remained both unperturbed and unamused. And how about Feodor acting like a brave fellow while covering a fresh, greasy stain on his tight white pants? Did Mia realize the orange shawl on her shoulders was but a confession of despair under the self-conscious simper on her overly red lips? And was Gerald aware of the nervous tic that made him pivot his left wrist as if releasing a watch that had stuck too low? But then again, those were their own choices, and I didn't judge them at all. I was just oh so sad at being the only man who could look at this carnival of sadness with my kind of eyes.

I was so engrossed in work that, when a gracious body took its place on the cushions next to me, I'd be lying if I said that I saw it coming. The craze of my typing streak must have reached an apogee then, unchecked brilliance finding its verbal manifestations in ways I wouldn't have considered possible before Chloe, and only a darn fool like myself would agree to forego such magic in favor of something that couldn't be better than sex. I finished the paragraph, knowing the only thing I'd have to change in it was punctuation. Then I slowly took my eyes off the screen and turned them toward my guest.

It was Abigail.

"Hi," she said with veiled curiosity, her ring finger running around the brim of her wine glass, which was filled with something stronger than wine. "What are you doing?"

"Hi." I pointed at the drink with a slight nod, not letting her eyes go. "What are you drinking?"

"Cognac," she confessed, the tip of her tongue touching her lips before she spoke and her mouth remaining slightly open after.

"Cognac by the wine glass?"

"That's the best I could find." She was almost apologetic.

"What is it?"

She named the brand: it was mine.

"Is that your drink of choice?"

"Someone had a bottle. I gave it a shot. Would you like some?"

"Thank you; I don't drink."

"That's a pity. I thought we'd have a drink together."

"We still can. Would you be so kind as to get me a glass of water?"

I paused, eyeing her. The dim bluish light of my computer did not do justice to the rosiness of her cheeks, but it made her hair glow.

"Sure."

She rose to her feet, the deliberateness of her movements suggesting that she was drunker than I'd suspected. I watched her make the necessary preparations at the kitchen sink and realized that I did, in fact, want to have sex with Abigail. I'd let her be as rough as she liked. It's remarkable what treasures often lurk behind the façade of coyness. Some men will skip over her out of fear, others because they think she's too nice to not be a lousy lay, so whenever she meets a man who goes all the way she is compelled to give her best, which is worth its weight in gold as solid and pure as the color of Abigail's hair.

She was back in less than a minute. She had at least two opportunities to prolong her absence by talking to acquaintances, and she passed on both. The whole time I was thinking about how Abigail did it: dropping her friends when she needed to. This time she sat to my left, in a nook where the back of the sofa and my own body—close enough for me to feel her heat through her dark-blue dress—protected her from the dayroom at large. There wasn't enough light to give that dress the thorough examination it warranted, but I did anyway. She caught my eyes and blushed; I didn't so much as blink.

"So, what are you typing?" she said, putting the glass in front of me.

"A novel," I said absentmindedly, typing.

"What's it about?"

"Never ask a writer that question."

"Why?"

"He doesn't know until the novel is finished, and I crossed the equator less than two hours ago."

"How can he write about something he doesn't know?"

"He lets Infinity do that for him."

She looked into her glass, as if regretting there was so little left.

"Can you at least tell me what happens in it?"

"Read it yourself," I said, gently sliding the computer onto her lap.

She adjusted it to have a better look at the screen; then she squinted and began reading. Her vision was poor; she had to wear contacts. She was equally hot with and without glasses, but this time I wished she'd had them on. I also wished someone would tell women like Abigail that they can make a man fall for them just by choosing the right frame.

"When did you start writing this?" she said hoarsely a few minutes later, clearing her throat with a quiet cough.

"Seven years ago."

I turned my head to face her; her eyes looked like those of an anxious bird.

"I was afraid you were writing about what was going on in this room," she finally said, putting the laptop on the table. Its screen dimmed as soon as she did.

"I was. It's two pages above from where you began."

"Am I part of your novel?" she said daringly.

"An inescapable one," I admitted.

"How come?"

"You are beautiful: that's all it takes to get in."

"Oh, please!" she exclaimed. I kept silent for a moment; then I reached for my computer, very slowly, and closed it, both of us instantly blending in with the surrounding dusk. Then I picked up my glass; it was very cold.

"Abigail," I said, looking at her. "I have a toast. May you never doubt that you are gorgeous."

Not waiting for a response, I clinked my glass against hers, simultaneously putting my left hand on her thigh. It was a slight touch, but I left my hand where it landed as nonchalantly as if it had landed on the sofa's cushion. Then I slowly brought the glass to my lips and took a sip.

Call me childish, but I derive immense pleasure from this stage of flirting—when the intention has been made clear but no reaction has yet followed. To me, it feels like I'm living through a magnifying glass, sharply aware of every detail that makes up the episode. Abigail froze, waiting for my next move; but why would I hurry, as if the situation were anything out of the ordinary? So, I simply continued drinking, tilting my head back and observing the elongated silhouettes of our classmates reflected on the glossy glass wall around the corner we so classily occupied.

"If only men agreed with you," she said bitterly.

"Men are silly," I assured her, feeling her thigh grow hotter under my palm. "And I'm suffocating."

She was silent as she finished her cognac, puckering her lips. There could be no doubt about it: I desired Abigail more than Chloe.

"I need some fresh air," I continued when she placed her empty glass on the table, moving her legs but not shaking my hand off. "And I have a plan. Ever been to the roof of the Sciences?"

"Yes," she said in a low voice.

"Ever looked at Bristol from there at night?"

"Yes."

"Then come along, and we'll do it together."

She took a deep, slow breath through her nose: very calmly. Another waft of light drunkenness erupted in the slight sideways tilt of her head. *She'll do it*, I thought, watching her raise her eyebrows, as if in response to her own internal inquiry.

"Why?" she asked finally.

"I want to take a few pictures. I have none from this place." I smiled, confident that she wouldn't believe me.

"I promised Marilyn I'd watch a movie with her," she said in a tone that rang with decade-long familiarity. Nine out of ten times I would have been silent in response, but this one was the tenth.

"I saw her half an hour ago, near Dickenson's fence. With Rohatyn." My fingers slid along her thigh. "Watching movies is anything but a priority for her right now."

Her breathing deepened, and I saw the lower part of her belly rise and fall to its cadence. Her exhalations were far longer, and she held her breath at the end of each before letting the air out in a quick, almost spasmodic push. Then she gulped, as if suffering from an unquenchable thirst, and looked me in the eyes.

"It's not true, is it?" she whispered.

I leaned back to give her space while my hand kept sliding. My fingers had almost reached her knee when she drew her palm over my hand in a masterfully executed movement that would have been hard to spot even for someone watching us closely. I stopped, waiting for her to continue, and she took my hand off her leg.

"Thank you for the invitation," she said firmly. "I hope you catch some beautiful views."

Then she got up and left.

Campus Keys

I waited for a few minutes, watching the dayroom; through the glass wall, it resembled a zombie dancefloor. I felt sad—Abigail was a story I'd never write again. Well, as they say in poker: you win some, you lose some. No reason to change the strategy.

When my feelings had settled, I made my way to the exit, laptop in hand, dodging no more than a couple of bodies who were too drunk to notice. I was about to grab the door handle when I felt someone's hand on my shoulder. Alas, it was only Fidelio.

"Calling it a night?" He was tipsy and adventurous.

"Before it's too late."

"Abigail said you wanted to go to the Sciences, to take photos or something?"

I didn't blame her: she must have felt sorry—for herself.

"You won't get much if you do," he continued. "I've tried that before. You'll either end up with a blur, or everything will be so tiny you won't know what's what."

"Any way to help that?" I asked, genuinely interested in his opinion: when it came to visual matters, his expertise was nothing to sneeze at.

"Not without a professional camera with a zoom lens." He sneezed. "Damn, is it getting cold here?"

"Like one of those they'd have in the Visual Rescue department?" I asked carefully.

"I'm sure they have some good cameras there." He performed a series of operations with his nose and a charming handkerchief. "But I'm sure the building is locked. They have a lot of expensive equipment in there; if any of it goes missing, they won't be replacing it for a while."

"Sounds like an easy one," I smirked. "All it takes is finding the keys."

"Well, good luck with that," Fidelio laughed.

"Where in the room would that camera be?" I asked, sensing a familiar excitement that made me disregard everything else.

"In the editing room's locker, maybe" he said, somewhat deflated. "Which also requires a key. So, if I were you, I'd think twice before trying to break in."

"I've already thought thrice. What vulnerabilities does that room have? A window that used to be broken, for instance? Chances are it was never repaired. What about the roof? Is there a way to get in through the ceiling?"

"Not that I'm aware of. Wait, you *are* thinking of doing this?" he asked in a tone of dubiety, as if deciding on something at the same time.

"Not even thinking," I gave him a pat on the shoulder. It felt stout. "I would have invited you, but there are way too many beautiful ladies in this room: some of them need you here."

"I doubt that," he scoffed. "Nor would I necessarily want to offer that kind of help."

"Really? Even to Abigail?"

"I would have given her a respectful "no"," he said solemnly, and I left him to his congenial opinion of his high moral standards.

I had already dropped off my laptop and was about to exit the building when I realized I needed the kind of reinforcement that only a lady could provide. Acting nonchalant but going from sweat to snow on the inside, I passed the front door and ascended the stairs to the second floor where the girls were lodged. The air smelled of a host of cleaning agents, and yet I caught a trace of the death-proof bouquet of hundreds of different aromas, fragrances, scents and perfumes that had been saturating this space for decades as the women who inhabited it did their best to unveil and emphasize their every laudable feature. No one met me in the eerily quiet corridor where I had to choose which wing to enter and, after a moment's contemplation, I pulled open the door closest to me. Behind it, the bouquet intensified, and, unwilling to play the guessing game with three more doors, I knocked on the nearest one.

No response.

I moved to the next door and knocked again.

Nothing.

The occupants of the last room were clearly awake: I heard noises and music there; and as soon as I knocked, someone invited me in.

It was strange to see a girls' room wanting, but in the few hours that had passed since the beginning of the reunion, Fury, Thalia and Rosette had not turned theirs into a cozy space, the only pieces of decoration being three or four empty bottles of wine on the floor next to Fury's locker, a half-full one on the table next to Rosette, and two open boxes of chocolate on Thalia's bed. They also had a fourth member, but I had no interest in finding out who she was—it was enough to know it wasn't Molly by the size of the jeans lying on the blanket.

"Good evening, guys," I said, grateful that I didn't need to introduce myself. "How are you doing?"

"Pretty good," Fury said as Thalia and Rosette eyed me suspiciously, the former resembling a ground squirrel and the latter a water rat. "What's up?"

"I need a pin," I said, leaning on the door jamb and wondering why I was the only man in this room. "Does anybody have one?"

"A pin?" Rosette asked in a very confused voice. "You mean, a PIN number?"

"Precisely." I nodded. "Ideally, for your bank account, but I also take credit cards."

"What do you need a pin for?" Fury inquired leisurely. She was considerably drunker than she'd been by the fire.

"I wanna break in somewhere."

"Like … where?"

"Like some place that has locks," I revealed.

"Why would I give you my PIN number?" Rosette insisted, and I realized that she was even drunker than Fury.

"You can open a lock with a pin?" Thalia chimed in.

I smiled.

"I think I've got one," Fury said, reaching into her purse. "Let me see …"

"You're not … not seriously gonna give him your PIN?" Rosette worried.

"Why not?" Fury looked at her with surprise and coughed loudly, hand in purse. "I have a spare, I think."

"But …" Rosette stared at her pleadingly.

"What's the matter, baby?" Fury asked, pausing.

"I don't think you should do that." Rosette shook her head. "You know Courage. He's a bastard." Now she was shaking her index finger as well.

"It's all right," Fury reassured them. "I've got plenty of pins; I can afford to lose one."

"It's not about the pin, really," Thalia reminded. "It's about what he'll do with it. What *will* you do with it?" she asked me.

"Found anything?" I asked Fury.

"Here we go," she said, extracting precisely what I needed.

"Thanks a lot!" I said, snatching the pin from her hand.

"Wait, you mean a hairpin?" Rosette exclaimed in disbelief as I retreated.

"No, Rosette. This whole time I was talking about your bank account's PIN number," I said, grabbing the door handle. "Have a good night, gals."

It was only in the corridor that I remembered Rosette was one of the richest of them all. *You should keep better track of them*, I thought. On the other hand, her eyes, round with wonder, were worth everything she could have in that bank account of hers.

I was finally outside again, breathing the fresh air of the British seaside and walking toward the castle along the narrow road that I used to take several times a day. It cut through a cow field, chest-high barbed-wire fences on either side, and was as full of sharp pebbles as ever. The left half offered an unobstructed view of the Bristol channel, and I turned my head to enjoy the nebula of lights on the English bank. Shortly after, I encountered a trio of middle-aged people, two men and a woman, the latter looking eerily familiar. We greeted each other politely, and as soon as they'd passed I recalled seeing the woman on the train, in the very car where I'd met Emmanuelle's mother. I was uncertain whether the omen was good or bad, but made sure to avoid running into anyone else.

I was about to ascend the last flight of stone stairs before the Visual Rescue department when a curious thought crossed my mind. Since I was breaking in anyway, I might as well check the place where the campus keys were dropped off during normal college hours: the library's pigeonholes. It'd be ridiculous to suspect to find the keys there during a reunion weekend, yet there had to be some sort of watch duty going on campus, which usually required an exchange between the curfew makers and the night sentinels. It was only a short walk from where I was; besides, it seemed like a good excuse to finally visit the castle.

St. Donat's Castle, the nucleus of AC and the source of its deserved pride, remained as good a thing now as it was back in the twelfth century when it was built. And it hadn't been modernized much since then. The sewage was surely better, and so was the heating, but the walls and the ambiance bore that authentic, fairytale quality that marked it as a suitable set for a Harry Potter film. I felt nothing for the place but unadulterated respect, and if there was one thing I regretted with respect to it, it would be not having played the Presto movement of Beethoven's *Moonlight Sonata* on the assembly hall's grand piano on the night after that unfortunate St. Valentine's Day ... But then again, nor did I play the piano, and regretting not having had sex with Molly here wouldn't be any less pathetic than lamenting not having done it in any other place in the physical world.

Distant memories popping up from isolated compartments of my mind, I entered the castle through the inner court, the massive wooden door reluctantly yielding to my pull. It was pitch black inside, and no dubious sound reached my ears as I waited for my eyes to adjust. I followed the corridor, as devoid of sinister echoes as the basement of an American cottage built during the Great Depression, and after a few turns I found myself before the gates of the library, my favorite part of the castle. The gates were locked and barred, as expected, but the pigeonholes were affixed to the wall outside the gates. Calm and collected, I slid my hand into the main compartment, prepared to encounter emptiness and continue with the original plan ... but my fingers grabbed hold of something jagged and cool, and when I yanked it out my hand held a set of campus keys chained to a large block of rough, unlacquered wood.

I rubbed my eyes with the other hand; then I bit my thumb, but nothing changed. I could have sworn it was the same block of wood I remembered from ten years ago. Most of the keys must have changed, though. But it didn't matter, because I had them all. This one keychain gave access to the vast majority of the academic buildings, as well as some inviting regions of the castle to which access was restricted. The fact that it lay there was miraculous, and I immediately checked the time.

It was 8.20 on the East Coast.

I threw the keys up in the air and caught them on the fly, weighing them alongside the facts. Whoever handled the lockup had to have brought the set here very, very recently, possibly within the last quarter of an hour. But why had the sentinels not collected the keys? Every single alumnus on campus had done curfew duty at least once, so with the keys lying in their usual place, it was only a matter of time before someone like me traversed the flimsy barrier between a calm night and an array of exciting possibilities. Or was the college looking to get in trouble?

The more I thought about it, the faster my heart raced. Was it a coincidence that this small act of negligence had taken place on Friday? Because, with the news hitting the airwaves on Saturday, many of the hungover alumni would feel indignant and more willing to donate, compensating generously for all the losses that may or may not have been incurred. In this scenario, everybody won, and even if the reckless burglar got away with ten grand worth of, say, camera equipment, no one would try too hard to apprehend the thief. It'd be like the standard English agreement where the party who does the job gets mere ten percent, except in this case the ten percent would be less than one.

I tossed and caught the keys again, considering the metaphorical level of the hypothesis. I wasn't going to steal or damage anything, but, if I were correct, I'd still become a tool in someone else's hands. Although, granted, it'd be better if something did get stolen or destroyed: putting a precise numeric value on the loss made it easier to quantify the response it would elicit. I wondered if the AC officials would agree to sustain the damage from a Category 5 hurricane to inspire a prodigious donation. But, of course, the prudent founders of UWC had known where to plant the institution's flagship: the worst storm that had ever happened around here had taken place in my own heart.

I threw the keys in the air once more, this time all the way to the twenty-foot-high ceiling, and when they fell back into my palm I decided that I didn't care anymore. I had my own agenda, and even if the keys had been left behind deliberately, freedom of will was still mine, so I turned around and walked out. I had no doubt as to where to go. Visual Rescue had never been my domain, unlike the Languages: not because the building also housed literature classes, but because no other structure on the AC campus was better suited to late-night sex.

Staying in the shadows and stepping carefully, I approached the Languages. The front door was locked, but I was looking for something else. I circled the building; the initial check revealed no open windows, but

I didn't believe this. The members of our class could still afford to fall headlong into impetuous teenage lust, but the folks from the twentieth, as well as the cream of the thirtieth, had much more to lose when indulging their sexual drives. What they didn't have, though, was a bad motherfucker in their class who'd predict their trivial attempts at infidelity and bust their asses without hesitation or remorse.

I chose the right key on the first try—an excellent sign. I wasn't sure how many rooms I had to check; I only knew the two best had code locks on the inside, which made them perfect for those who knew the codes. I did, and the notion of never being able to put that knowledge to sexual use suddenly became painful. I rushed into the first room to my left: no one would be having sex on the first floor of this two-story building, but no smart person would leave a single window open on the entire first floor once having gotten inside.

I checked all eleven classrooms on the first floor, except for the teachers' room, being too lazy to look for the right key. Every single one of the windows was locked—a giveaway in itself. So, when I stepped on the stairs and heard rhythmical noises descending from above, I was not so much surprised as curious as to what room those scoundrels had chosen for their love nest. Much to my dismay, it turned out to be where my German class used to be given—something I couldn't forgive in people with a choice of ten other options.

I fleetingly gave my attention to the groans, but it was immediately obvious that they betrayed nothing more interesting than a prosaic instance of intercourse laced with inebriation. I was disappointed, sensing the need to restore the glory of my old linguistic feats. The classroom's door was closed but had no lock. I could easily have walked in for a dramatic effect; but of course, that was the furthest thing from my mind.

"How are you guys doing?" I yelled, banging on the door with my fist. Noises signifying fright and confusion resulted. "I was just wondering: did you happen to see an old friend of mine here?"

The sounds of consternation ceased entirely, leaving only a taut, strained silence.

"She is tall, blonde, and very beautiful," I continued. "I would tell you her name, but I doubt it'll ring a bell."

I cupped my hands around my ear and put it to the seam between the door and the jamb, listening motionlessly. It was quiet at first, but then a man whispered in a trembling voice:

"*He's drunk … He'll go away.*"

I chuckled and cupped my hands around my mouth.

"One thing you gotta know about her," I shouted into the seam. "Is that she is really good in bed. Can you say the same about yourselves?"

They couldn't, unfortunately.

Smiling to myself, I quietly walked away, wondering how long it would take them to leave the room. Locking every window on the first floor was clever, but when had cleverness ever been a sign of courage? I noiselessly descended the stairs, exited the building, and locked it. I could have hung around in any of the covert places offering a first-class view of the Languages to check whether they'd be clever enough not to use the front door, but why would I care? Especially now that the glee had evaporated, and the dagger of self-pity was sinking slowly into the naked flesh of my soul.

The past pursued me like a black panther; I saw her sharp ivory fangs wherever I looked. Orange circles danced before my eyes, making it difficult to see in the dark, and my head spun, as if after a triple somersault. I walked on autopilot, grossly indifferent to the direction I was taking and slowly growing enraged, oscillating between regret at not catching the Language lovers with their pants down and self-ridicule for performing such a crude lobotomy on their basic instincts. And, fixed between those disposable extremes, was a ruthless, impersonal imperative to keep going until the end I sought was mine. The stars and the moon looked like they understood me, and I was so hot that I thought I'd combust.

Gina

This was becoming unbearable. I felt caged on the entire territory of the campus, and boy, did the cage feel small. The place had changed a lot: it wasn't even the same Sunley, and the locks grew worse. Mighty crickets. They always made me feel like something momentous was about to transpire.

Suddenly, I felt the purely animalistic sensation of a human presence nearby and pulled myself together. I looked around and eventually discerned a slender silhouette next to the shadowy wall of Powys, the dorm I was then passing. I couldn't see who it was, yet it was clearly a young woman; I found that strange because Powys had been assigned to an older class, the members of which had already gone to bed, judging by the building's darkened windows. She leaned on the wall as if she'd just gotten in trouble and had no clue what to do next; but was it really an octogenarian alumnus who had gotten her there?

I shifted to peripheral vision, nearing her at an angle and interpreting her body language. Did someone just dump her in favor of another woman? Was she waiting for a late-night date? Was she just drunk off her face? I could safely ignore the last guess: she stood perfectly straight, as if supported by an internal axis. I took a few more silent steps, and the second hypothesis was also refuted: she was being nothing but introverted. Three steps later, I finally recognized her by the red blazer and the platinum pants.

It was Gina.

I didn't mean to scare her but still did; yet she pretended I hadn't. Her pupils grew large, and when she'd recovered she showed a fleeting expression of indifference to herself that I had very seldom seen in women but had learned to appreciate. I wasn't going to take advantage of it, but there was only one sure way to help her.

"Hiding from someone?" I asked, as if we were best friends who had bumped into each other in the street.

"No, just chilling," she said and waited for me to continue. I didn't. "Do you have a cigarette on you?"

"No. Do you?"

"No. But I want one."

"I want you to have one, too."

"Why?"

"I like the smell of tobacco on a lady when it blends with expensive perfume. Yours is." She was surprised I knew. "Dostoyevsky said that nothing is uglier than a woman smoking a cigar," I continued, giving her a slow, evaluating look. "But he never went to AC."

"I wonder what he'd say about a woman smoking …" She named a popular cigarette brand. "Isn't that what you sold, back in the day?"

"No, I sold …" I named their competitor. "Much better stuff."

"I'd take either right now." She shifted from one foot to the other. "What are you doing here, anyways? I thought you wanted to stay by the fire."

"I did that. Now I'm getting into various places. Those that open with this magical set of keys."

I dangled the bunch in the air.

"What's so magical about it?" she asked, pretending not to be curious.

"It was available when it could easily not have been." I was suddenly empowered by a realization. "By the way, weren't you part of the Visual Rescue service?"

"Never. Why?"

"I'm looking for something that's inside that building. The locker with those sensitive cameras. Can you help me find it?"

She eyed me in silence, blinking incredulously.

"You gonna break into the Visual Rescue?"

"No." I shook my head. "I'm gonna walk through the front door."

"Is that … allowed?"

"I wouldn't be doing it if it was."

"I don't know." She was all doubt. "It's kinda dangerous."

"What are you risking?" I said, knowing she meant me.

"Well, what if we get busted?"

"I'll tell them the truth. That we were both looking for cigarettes."

"Well, I'm sure they don't have any in the VR," she said, suppressing a chuckle.

"We'll never know unless we check."

She paused, as if considering the plan. As for me, I felt thorough indifference. I couldn't care less if Gina came with me, and her eyes told me that she knew it. She wasn't even vacillating: she made up her mind and waited for me to say something that would make her change it. But I was silent, leaning on my right leg, away from her, relaxing my body from head to toe and enjoying the beautiful night that covered us with it velvet wings.

"All right," Gina said finally, separating herself from the wall. "But if we get caught, I'll tell everybody it was your idea."

I didn't object.

We covered the distance between Powys and the Visual Rescue quickly, and no sirens sounded as I opened the door. The chain held a lot of keys, and one of them could have granted access to that very locker, but once we got inside, it was clear that neither of us cared for photography. The first couch we found was old, dusty and squeaky, yet much more comfortable than a blanket on the grass. I considered turning on one of the table lamps to have a better view of Gina's body but thought better of it. It wasn't the authorities I feared but the other alumni: at this hour, there had to be many couples and groups looking for a secluded spot, and the dimmest light in a window would lure them like moths.

This time, something different possessed me. I can't say I liked Gina better than any other attractive girl on this campus, yet I acted as if she were Molly herself. Her underwear was very tight, clearly a calculated decision, and I kept it on as my right hand took its place within it. She danced on my fingers for a while, offering me the other parts of her body that wanted attention, and I gave it willingly, sending her into convulsions when a glide of my tongue hit something special in the middle of her rib cage. My underwear hand was inundated, and I replaced it with a superior substitute, proceeding with hunger, gusto and class.

At first, she tried to prove herself a leader, but she soon realized she'd be better off following. I must have tried ten different positions in the next ten minutes, finding something rewarding in each but being evaded by a sensation to match the scorching lust that flourished in me. It was as if this time, instead of holding a flame inside, my body had turned into one itself. Ravenous, I slid my middle finger all the way in along what was already there, and as I began massaging her petals with my thumb, she uttered a series of loud groans that provided everyone scurrying around in the dark with an example to emulate. She came within a minute, bursting into a cascade of quivers and almost screaming until I withdrew my finger and put it over her lips, where she bit it with her sharp teeth and enveloped it with her hot tongue while I searched for her other erogenous zones, staying deep and continuing my careful spiraling movements.

"Are you a Taoist?" she asked later when she'd caught her breath.

"Never have been. Why?"

"Every man comes after having sex with me," she declared in a slighted tone.

"That's probably not good news," I chuckled. "I bet they all did it first."

"Isn't that what all men do?" There was a note of naivete in her voice that could have come only from a good soul, but—dear me—how many layers of social conformism it was buried under! "At least the first time," she hastily added.

"I don't think your men knew how to deal with your beauty," I said seriously. "It's very easy for a man to lose his head to begin with."

"Don't you like me?" she asked after a brief pause.

"I do," I assured her, reminding myself not to tell her that I would not have had sex with her otherwise. "Why?"

"I want you to come," she said with determination, the barren beams of a distant street lantern shining onto her stunning face. It was as if the thoughts in her head had found a focal point, a hole at the bottom of a reservoir through which all the pressure could be released. She neared me and pulled up her skirt; I felt the hot, wet touch of her flesh at the base of my stomach, and I saw no reason not to advance.

I let her pull all the levers she could reach, helping without interfering. First, she worked so hard she wasn't enjoying herself, but as she grew tired the spasmodic moves of her pelvis subsided in both their frequency and amplitude, and I was able to surreptitiously take charge. The known erogenous zones of her body had not changed, and now she responded to my caresses with even greater abandon. She was also wetter, allowing me to easily adjust the moving parts of my skin as I pulled myself out of her up to the tip before thrusting back in. After a minute or two of this I felt dangerously close to the precipice and dove full depth, switching to slow sideways shifts and searching for other spots that could ignite her. I thought I was doing everything right, but then I noticed a change in her breathing and realized that I had forgotten about caressing her. I resumed, finding another rewarding area above her tailbone. There, she hit the home run. Soon before coming, she grabbed me violently below the right shoulder blade, making me twitch in pain, but that very twitch revealed an angle that she welcomed with such an splendid groan that I matched it, dissolving in her heavy breath and savoring every millimeter of our accidental intimacy. Her second orgasm peaked no sooner than a few minutes after inception, her teeth chattering the entire time, and at the end of it she was panting like a gazelle that had just outrun a leopard and was too exhausted to even pay attention to the fact of her own survival.

"You never give an inch, do you?" she said eventually as I was sliding into slumber.

"I do, each time: between six and seven of them."

She laughed.

"Now I definitely need a cigarette."

"And I don't," I said, inhaling her.

"I thought you liked smoking women."

"Smoking hot."

"You still want to get into that locker?"

I opened my eyes and realized that I didn't. This graveyard shift had been fun, but it had failed to subdue my urge. I enclosed Gina in my arms again, stroking her well-built legs, which were neither too thin nor too muscular, and pausing on her inner thighs. I could have gone on with her, feeling more attraction than when we'd begun, but the iron whisper of my discipline told me to continue the search for whatever I had to find within me on this campus. So, we kissed like old lovers for a little longer, then got up off the couch and fled the scene.

The Buddhial Body

She waited patiently while I shuffled through the keys to lock the door, as if afraid to stay in the dark alone, but she didn't return to the castle with me, instead taking the road to Sunley as we approached the fork. I met and saw no one on my way to the library, which was hardly surprising, given the late hour. When I reached the pigeonholes, I listened intently at the dark quietude, but it was as good as dead—and no ghost emerged to share its heartbreaking story. I held the keychain at arm's length and let it drop, the wooden block hitting the bottom of the pigeonhole with a thump and the keys adding a brass note. I expected to encounter company as I turned around and noted a dart of disappointment on seeing none.

The castle, the VR, and the rest of the campus behind my back, I now walked yet another road to the cliffs. This one ran downhill, cutting through the lifeguard quarters, another popular destination for those pursuing illicit pleasures. I would give you detailed accounts of a few swimming pool parties that had occurred here, but I was just thinking: perhaps there's too much sex in this novel? I read somewhere that, apparently, there are only fourteen kisses in the complete works of Jane Austen: most of those are women kissing other women and children, only three are between a man and a woman, and one is bestowed on a disembodied lock of hair. Was I trying to counterbalance her outdated chastity with my personal opinion on universally acknowledged truths? But then again, why would I feel the need? And why, whenever it came to sex, did I begin by considering potential damage? Was it because I'd seen the ship of love run aground too many times? Take Gina, for one. Was that not an affair worth having? The surprise, the suspense, the coincidence … What woman would not wish to have such an inadvertent adventure? And did I not wish her well? So, why was my heart skipping a beat as if, instead of gifting a beautiful woman a one-of-a-kind experience, I had done something wrong? Was it because I did not want to be misunderstood?

From the viewpoint of conventional morality, I'm highly controversial, so reading me requires taking a moral stand. Since you haven't quit, by now you know how explicit the matters I expose here are. So, given the naughtily introspective bend of my narrative: why are you still reading? You don't have to tell, but whatever the reason, I hope it's not because of the sex. I write about it because it can serve as a springboard to the liberation of the spirit, and it is always the latter that is at the crux of this work. Or any other, for that matter, written from outside the buddhial body's insatiable reach.

The buddhial body has nothing to do with the Buddha, although even he had to have been on that level at some point. Instead, it's the ideological framework that explains and validates the acts and thoughts we generate as byproducts of being alive. When a suicide bomber detonates an explosive at the center of a crowd; when a math teacher spends forty years at the same high school; when a young woman marries an old man she can't stand … all of these evidence the buddhial body at work. It's that quiet question "why?" behind everything we do: everything— but, above all, the things we take for granted.

Why do you live the way you do? Why do you do this but not that? Why is being alive a good idea? The answers you give are that of your buddhial body. And it would all be fine, were it not for one little spoiler: the values we are accustomed to taking for our own, including our most intimate convictions, are hardly ever ours.

Remember *The Matrix*? It's true, except for the silly machinery.

Almost every one of us does have an invisible jack in the nape through which information is loaded into the brain. It can be the crude propaganda of a totalitarian state, or the subtle adverts of a democratic one. The former is labeled brainwashing, the latter is called marketing, but the result is the same: manipulated people living in accordance with imposed standards created by the select and possessive few.

I could bore you to death by regurgitating tales about the buddhial body, but I'd be talking about something I don't even have. Hence, everything that seems strange about me: the jocular and the shocking, the powerful and the impotent, the carnal and the sublime. It's the rarest ticket one can pull from fate's lottery, but it's also the only one that is worthless unless you cash it out.

I was walking the path along the cliff's edge, the lifeguards' quarters behind my back and the dark blocks of the academic buildings far to the left, when all this flashed as a preamble to a vision that filled my head like liquid nitrogen seeping in through the top of my skull. I saw a guy who looked just like me at the age of seventeen and a half, sitting in the Sunley dayroom. The gloaming was at hand, and the final beams of the setting sun were breaking onto the ceiling through the trimmed crowns of the nearby oaks. His skin was of a peculiar shade that blended seamlessly into the group around him, laughing as though they were plotting mischief. He was one of them, part of a plan woven on the fly, and he had already slept with enough of the girls to know that the rest would come to him on their own.

I stopped, dismissing the pictures and focusing on the feelings alone; they were considerable, and I fast-forwarded them by a few months. There were two fleeting relationships in that span, and a third, the longest of all, was about to begin. I studied the guy, who had grown noticeably older, and then I dove into his perception. I felt him on a train with his girlfriend, headed to her parents' house for a long weekend; I heard the solicitous chatter of her mother over the clinking of cutlery against a porcelain dinner set; I saw the London Eye in the distance, and a reserved sunset erupting through the clouded sky. Those were excerpts, disjointed and incoherent, but, like early threads in a fabric, they formed a structure that would be replicated by the new threads, no matter how many would follow. Soon they did, and they were all the same. Repetitive landscapes, predictable dialogue, unexceptional sex ... But the guy didn't know it, having nothing to compare it to except for the gnawing feeling inside that left him puzzled as to why his seemingly fulfilling life had the distinct taste of not being worth living.

The joints in my left ankle cracked and, wincing in pain, I bent down to give the spot a rub. The pain persisted, and I impulsively took off my sneakers and sat on the ground. As I did, I felt happy, overpowered by the notion that I had no right to complain about what had happened to me here. Folding an origami rose for Gretchen the night before she lost her virginity to a first-year student; climbing the watchtower at three in the morning after the St. Valentine's Day ball; seeing Rohatyn carry Abigail to the second floor of the Medical Center, thinking that no one would know ... all those were crucial milestones in my personal evolution, and regretting them spelled nothing but foolishness. Then I grew sharply cognizant of the eternal friction of the tide on the cliffs while all my visions, memories and opinions blended into a uniformly solid sensation of menthol coolness behind my eyes; and, yielding to its mounting pressure, I shut my eyes, which had already filled with rapturous tears, and brought all my attention into the center of my forehead. Having taking a breath so deep that it made a vertebra in my lower back crack, I exhaled:

"A-a-a-a-a-a-a-a-a-a-a-h-u-u-u-u-u-u-u-u-u-u-u-h-m-m-m-m-m-m-m-m-m-m-m-m-h."

Next, there was a high-pitched ping in my ears, as if from a silver triangle struck by a fairy, and when the last trace of its dulcet tone dissolved in the darkness behind my eyelids, I took another impossibly deep breath and repeated:

"A-a-a-a-a-a-a-a-a-a-a-h-u-u-u-u-u-u-u-u-u-u-u-h-m-m-m-m-m-m-m-m-m-m-m-m-h."

When the pitch followed, I knew I was not worth my salt as a sorcerer, because I had had to come here physically. Anyone good would have set this up without moving a foot from the paths they usually trod, let alone crossing an ocean. I focused on my breathing, then on my heartbeat. The spinal wave had always been the trickiest. But as my chest expanded to what seemed the size of a hot air balloon, and as I confirmed my commitment in another

"A-a-a-a-a-a-a-a-a-a-a-h-u-u-u-u-u-u-u-u-u-u-u-h-m-m-m-m-m-m-m-m-m-m-m-m-h,"

I felt its rhythm as if it had never been hidden. There were no more pitches, only a four-dimensional panoramic view of what this shore used to look like millions of years ago. It was dark, save for the moon shining sheepishly through the crenulated clouds, and no fauna was visible, yet I still saw more with my eyes closed than I had seen in both of my years at AC. I witnessed the battles of power that had taken place here and sensed the longing of all the forces who'd ever trodden these grounds; a longing so loud and powerful that I could hear its stentorian roar erupt from below. Victory, death, and everything in between became available to me at once. I felt immeasurably distant from my known self, thrown into the endless loneliness of a primeval frontier, condemned to an eternal vigil on this arbitrary cheekbone of the earth. All of my pursuits, including those involving inhuman ambitions, diminished to molecular proportions, but, as I watched them dwindle and dissipate, a part of my soul stoically clung on, refusing to surrender of its own accord and laughing hysterically, as if someone had whispered in my ear whether I'd like to give up my human form for an antidote to love, and all I'd uttered in return was a contemptuous *No*.

The Climbing

I woke up to the sensation of cold water on top of my head. It sent an electric chill throughout my entire body that was anything but pleasant. I groped around me like a helpless child and scratched at the roots of my hair, trying to get rid of that sickly sensation. Wait, what? Seaweed? How had it ended up here?

Avoiding any brisk movements, I sat up, small pebbles penetrating the seat of my pants. I wasn't sure what was going on, but that wasn't my main problem. Because, as I immediately discovered, instead of being at the top of the cliffs, I was down on the shore, stuck in a tidal lagoon, and the tide had already cut me off on both sides.

Or had it? I jumped up and ran to the ridge on my left, but when I got there I saw that, to get out, I'd have to wade through knee-high water, all the while not knowing what was behind the next turn. And I wanted to stay dry for whatever else I had to face tonight.

I shivered again and again. The motion came straight from the head, as I already knew where I was headed: straight up the twenty-five yards of nearly vertical wall. There was no other option. I had less than thirty feet of ground before the ocean, and the combination of the flat shore and the strong tide meant that those feet would be consumed in no time at all. I had a mere minute to think, and by the end of it the water had gotten so close that a wavelet splashed my jeans.

Which made me notice that I was barefoot.

I cursed in my mother tongue and approached the cliff. I would much rather have marveled at the fact that I'd miraculously landed in this place, but I hardly had time to even perform a reality check. Which I nevertheless did—very thoroughly. I decided that if it proved a dream I'd walk straight into the ocean. But in the end, I had to admit defeat.

I was awake and barefoot.

In the light of the challenge I faced, the fact that my only sensible clothing choice had been stripped away by my own effort seemed as ironic as it was annoying. Well, at least I hadn't taken off my socks. I studied the cliff again. The only helpful thing was the rock's porous quality: I could get a decent grip, even if my hands got wet. Which I hoped they wouldn't. Yet I had no idea where I was. While these cliffs could have seemed all the same to an idle observer, some of them were amenable to climbing, while others were deadly. I knew that because, practicing the dexterous badass in myself, I used to climb around here when in a bad mood: without anyone watching, of course, because it was a reckless thing to do. And it was all good until one hazy afternoon I found myself hanging some twenty yards above the shore in a spot where the very top of the rock was completely covered with earth. At first, I didn't even blink at it, seeing the end only a few yards away from my hands. But two steps later, I faced a paralyzing sensation: that of my body sliding down despite me grabbing onto everything in reach.

It'd been over a decade, but I recalled that episode as well as if it had to do with Molly. I think what saved me in the end was my single-minded resolve to live. I knew that falling could be lethal, but I also knew that right beneath me lay the solid rock that had got me this high in the first place. So I clung to the curve, minding nothing but my balance and waiting for my feet to feel something. When they did, I'd learned some new things about myself, the most important being my habit to put my life in jeopardy to prove that I was worth more than the women I loved considered me to be.

Later, I learned that most of the cliffs to the east of the campus were precisely that: a silent trap topped with soil. Was this one of them? I looked up, trying to see. The crest definitely held some vegetation, shrubs or bushes, but that didn't mean much. I glanced at the ocean; it was now only a few feet away. Then I muted the internal dialogue and began climbing.

It took me under a minute to cover the first twenty yards. I was never a professional or even a dedicated climber: climbing simply made intuitive sense to me. Near the top, the sound of the waves softened, and even the moon seemed closer. But as I raised my hand for what appeared to be one of the last times, my fingers sank into treacherous soil, little clumps of earth crumbling off and raining down on me in a simulacrum of an avalanche.

There I was again, ten years later and just as puzzled and paralyzed. The situation was so ridiculous I still doubted whether it wasn't a dream, except now that my hands were busy, fewer reality checks were available. Had I not done a good job learning from that first time? But those discoveries, they'd felt legit. I kept thinking, hanging on and struggling to bring my thoughts under control.

After some time, I decided not to rush. My situation was a stalemate: I was actually quite comfortable, exerting myself not much more than I would have if standing on flat ground, and the water wouldn't rise high enough to wash me off, though it might surge up at my feet, showering them. Such was the good news. The bad news was that, one, the tide would remain high until after dawn, and two, my only active option for that entire time was moving horizontally along the cliff until I found a place where I could climb straight up.

There was a third possibility, but I wanted to save it as a last resort. If I went far from campus, I could spend a very long time looking for the right spot. And, not finding it, I could attempt to force the climb. I'd risk falling, but by that time the tide would be so high it'd be like falling into the deep end of a pool. Of course, I'd be soaked, but I'd get unlimited tries—at least for a few hours. Which could even be fun.

Yet I still went with the dry option, feeling my way parallel to the shore step by step and constantly checking what was at the top. After a minute or two, I reached the ridge that had stopped me below. It had another surprise for me: its fragile, sharp edge.

I gingery touched it. I had no explanation as to its origins because, if taking a geography quiz, I'd have guessed that any such sharpness should have been weathered by the wind. Was the rapture recent? That would explain the brittleness. I looked down, trying to see the water. Then I broke off a piece from the ridge and threw it down. I heard no splash, but there was no smash either.

It must be so strange, to be a stone, I thought, holding another in my hand and hanging on with the rest of me. I had a nagging sensation of losing time, as if I were at home, having just finished a TV episode and being about to start another. As if I had infinite possibilities at my fingertips but had willingly chosen to be stranded on this notorious cliff. Was this really a blast from the past? I closed my eyes, trying to remember all I could about that first time.

Molly had brought me there, I bet. Or had she? Perhaps I only used her as an excuse. I opened my eyes; it didn't make much difference. Was that really it? Was I using Molly as an excuse? I paused, listening to the palpitations of my heart. An excuse for weakness? For indulgence? I felt I was on the right track. I closed my eyes again, trying to see through to the middle of my head. How did I only manage …

It wasn't that! It was my reckless creative self! A muse embellished with the power of life and death: is that not a muse worth having? And that's what I made her into, despite her desire. *What if you had died that day? Remember the anguish as you slid the first inch? But you still thought your name would be emblazoned on her heart in golden letters. You thought she'd understand, and you were willing to pay for her understanding with your life. Do you still feel the same?* I whispered, looking hundreds of miles beyond the invisible black wall in front of me. *Do you still feel the same?*

And then I knew where I was, the location of the lagoon emerging in my memory like a picture from a book I never finished. At the top of this cliff lay the football field, and right next to it the sheep farm. I was no more than a mile from where I'd lost continuity, and I had an excellent chance of retrieving my shoes before they were discovered by a worse match. All it took was to circumvent the ridge: once I did, I'd be able to see the lighthouse, too. But, as if guided by a swift force that worked its way around my better judgement, I stretched my right arm and grabbed the earth above me, a prickly weed biting the palm of my hand and coming unstuck with all its roots.

More than anything else, I wanted to give it a try. Why had I not forced it back then? Had I really thought I'd fall? Or had I not wanted to risk something precious for something ephemeral? But how do you make a haughty muse consider you if not by showing her the real status quo? And it was such that, even caught barefoot in the middle of an Atlantic cliff, I remained the one who brought this and a thousand of other dry, categorical descriptions of reality to a state where they transcended their conventional meanings and became what they were intended to be all along: magic.

That's it, you fool! I cursed. *It was in front of your nose all along, and you didn't see? Why do you let women cloud the significant! The only detail that mattered was what you felt when you thought you would die. You can't get a better look at yourself.*

The next thing I knew, my fingers were sinking into the soil. Then I began sliding, except this time I was ready for it, so when my body came to a stop, I moved my right leg up. It suddenly felt like I was going to fall off, but that was only an animal fear not dissimilar to that which captures you when you approach a woman you fancy. It took me a few seconds to reach an equilibrium, and when I knew I couldn't fly backwards, I shifted my weight to my feet and moved my hands further along the crest of the cliff. The first step, as always, was the hardest: as I passed the bulge underlying the soil layer, the angles turned in my favor. Two steps later I was convinced I had made it, but I didn't weaken my focus until I'd reached the top.

There I was, standing up, watching the lighthouse glow in the distance and listening to the chirping insects. It was a fine summer night in the British Isles, and the faint smell of hay in the air made me nostalgic for a time when I had fewer memories to look back on. Then I took off, consumed by the languid serenity reigning around and ignoring all my thoughts in favor of how my feet felt. I had never walked outside in socks, and the first few steps were a bit rough, but once I learned how to properly curve my soles, the sensation was so pleasurable that I could not understand why I hadn't tried it before.

Ten minutes later I was near the place I'd departed from, and the emotions running through me felt like sameness in reverse. Can one really change in an hour? In a month? In a decade? I smiled to myself, knowing it wasn't a matter of changing but of emphasizing those elements that did change. When I saw my shoes, I wasn't even surprised, but before I put them back on I first strode across the lush grass to reinforce the levity and acuteness of perception I was enjoying, and then meticulously cleaned my socks of the blades that had stuck to them.

Wash your hands, I thought, yawning, when I was finished. *You may need them before you fall asleep.*

Lady Di

Unwilling to gamble any further, I returned to the house. It was at last too late for the others, so Sunley belonged to nobody but me. I walked through the corridors with the gait of an emperor, and spent at least five minutes in the bathroom, rubbing, scrubbing and scraping my hands under a stream of hot water. They turned completely red, and yet I had never been surer of being awake. Which was not to say that I wasn't dying to fall asleep.

The dayroom was everything I liked about it: obscure, spacious, and quiet. I took off my shoes, lay down on one of the sofas that must have been recently moved, and tried to relax. My body screamed in pain: the tiredness, the insomnia, the jetlag had all caught up with me at once. My eyelids grew leaden, and my consciousness began drifting away from the realization that all the efforts of the last hours, despite being dazzling, mind-blowing and supernatural, had not, in fact, brought me an inch closer to my only goal.

All right, I thought sternly. *You'd better stop whining. Her absence may be annoying, but it's no reason to drop the ball. Come on; it's so boring! It's something anyone could do in your place.*

I looked at my watch, which I still hadn't adjusted; it read half past eleven. *I wish*, I thought, stretching my hands above my head. A pleasant itching hummed in my neck, concentrated around the muscles of my collar bone. I closed my eyes, trying to think of where I'd go the next time I became lucid, but soon slipped into recalling the times when I'd flee to the dayroom during sleepless nights. I wouldn't even be studying but ruminating over eternally unimportant topics which invariably took their toll, urging me to arrange myself on the cushions in a doomed attempt to find a perfectly static pose. Strangely, no particular night stood out as they all blended into a long stretch of sketches unified by the same yellow shadows and the metallic buzz of the kitchen light.

I was considering killing the light and falling asleep right there when someone moved in the corridor. I was so immersed in the dayroom's stagnant air that I sensed a waft rush through it before any sound reached me. When it finally did, my heart jumped, wiping out most of my unwarranted sleepiness; but I could immediately tell that it wasn't my darling by the unapologetic heaviness of the steps. Another semi-transparent shadow fell on the wall next to the entrance, and two seconds later I saw that it was being cast by Diane. She made it as far as the turn into the kitchen area, and then her reflective eyes stumbled upon me.

"Courage?" she asked, as if checking whether she was mistaken. "What are you doing here?"

"*And all of the ghouls come out to play,*" I sang, assessing how drunk she was. So far everything pointed to "very". "Dear, I demand satisfaction."

"You are preposterous." She walked into the kitchen and began looking for something, ferreting through each cupboard in turn. Then she put her arms akimbo, puckered her lips and emitted a violent sigh of exasperation before announcing into the sink brimming with dirty dishes:

"There is not a single clean cup in this entire bloody place!"

I watched her rinse a wine glass extracted, after some struggle, from the bottom of the pile, which imploded with a menacing clash. I believed I could catch its foul smell in the air, but at this point that could have been anything. Diane filled her glass with tap water and drank greedily, her throat reverberating with each swallow, making me realize I had never seen her like this before. She looked commendably carnal, even though sex couldn't have been among even the top ten things she was thinking about. When she was done, she refilled the glass and headed straight for my sofa.

I gave her all the time she needed to get settled: the cushions didn't sink under her the way she wanted. Firmness and gentleness: what more to wish from a woman? Especially from one that is hot as hell?

"Courage, you're a bastard, you know that?" she began at last.

"Never been called that before," I retorted.

"You fucked Bridgette, didn't you? Don't pretend; I saw her," she continued, despite me showing no sign of objecting.

"What makes you think it was me?"

I could have spared the phrase: she was absorbed in drinking again. The process was a complete replica of what I saw before, except that this time she was sitting. When she'd taken the last slow, deliberate gulp, she bent forward, put the glass on the table and returned her attention to me.

"There's something I could never understand about you," she said.

"I will never believe there was only one such thing."

"That's true," she agreed in an almost didactic tone that sounded funny coming through her inebriation. "But, honestly: what do you like about Martina so fucking much?"

The question hit me when I wasn't watching, and it required more than a fair amount of self-control to pretend that nothing had happened. But just as I thought I was ready to speak, something inside me wobbled again.

"I mean, is it because of your thing for American chicks?" Diane continued, oblivious to my dismay. "Do you seriously think they're best? Don't answer that question!" she added threateningly. "I mean, sure, I like French men, but not to the point of preferring them over everyone else. And of all the American girls, have you really not met anyone better?"

I finally got a grip. It was nothing but a drunken fluke, and if Diane knew she'd just stabbed me in the heart with a bottle opener, she'd add a few twists before yanking it out. But she knew nothing. She was just a sad girl who hadn't gotten laid tonight despite her best intentions, as the two men she was after had both gone ahead with someone else.

"Why do you hate her so much?" I asked cautiously. "She isn't even here."

"Well, I hope it won't hurt your feelings too much if I call her an overbearing cunt?" she said, leaning back on the cushion. "And I'm disappointed she hasn't come. I would have ripped her head off."

"*And every demon wants his pound of flesh*," I sang, feeling it was time but not knowing for what. "Dear, I would have thought you're serious, but I know you too well to allow any such hope."

"I *am* serious," she declared gravely.

"No, you are not," I said, sliding my toes under her right thigh. She gave me a look of surprise, but I kept quiet. A few seconds later she shifted her weight to her left loin, as if inviting me to dig deeper, which I did. "It's the same trap for every princess: all bitter irony and no real action."

"Did you just call me a coward?"

"No, I just called you a lady."

Now my entire right foot was under her thigh, and the left foot followed. Her eyes were growing more incredulous, but I couldn't care less. Nothing damages majestic women more than being courted by submissive men, and I considered it my solemn duty to show her a viable alternative, all without a second thought about what I was doing and intending to go all the way.

"You are very funny," she said slowly, finally realizing that I was serious. "And handsome, too. Emaciated, but certainly cute. Yet you have no idea what you've gotten yourself into. She eats boys like you for breakfast and forgets them by lunchtime."

"Always wanted to meet a woman who'd eat me for breakfast," I said.

"Still haven't. By the way, did you just call her a whore?"

"The greatest one this campus has ever seen!" she exclaimed. "At least no one else I know has ever been caught in a threesome. You're a good boy, I bet you had no idea ..."

I froze. The best picture of Martina I'd ever seen was a group shot of her theater class, in which she was flanked by two scoundrels who were touching her rather frivolously on either side. But I couldn't indulge in the memory before figuring out whether Diane was extrapolating the story from the very same source, or not.

"No, I didn't," I said with the greatest equanimity I could conjure. "Did you catch her yourself?"

"Bram did."

"Who?"

"Bram," she repeated disinterestedly. "In the lifeguard locker room."

"She wasn't a lifeguard," I said automatically.

Diane snorted.

"Who were the guys?"

"You're asking too many questions. Besides, why would you care?"

"I wanna fry their asses for not inviting me to join."

She laughed, rather disparagingly.

"Would you have?"

I laughed, rather enthusiastically.

"You *have* taken me for a good boy, after all!"

"You know," she said, riding the aftermath of her laughter. "In my whole life I have never heard any rumor about your sex life."

In her accent, this simple statement sounded like a death sentence.

"How about gossip?" I suggested, wanting to hear more.

"Not a chance."

"Makes me very proud of myself."

"It shouldn't," she said, suddenly leaning over. Her breath was hot and it smelled after the water she had just drunk. "Because it makes me feel that there was nothing to tell."

I recognized the look in her eyes: that of a cat who has forced a mouse into a corner. My eyes searched her face for any sign of respite, but it was nothing but a meticulously crafted mask. She waited for me to make an advance so she could make a fool of me before leaving, but I already knew it was over—there was no chance of recovery. Dissatisfied, she leaned back and, after a moment's silence, got up, relieving my feet of her pleasant pressure, softness and warmth. The decision seemed harsh, abrupt and hasty, but I knew that she must have planned it since before she'd even left the cliffs.

Diane was gone, but the taste of her presence lingered. Now I wanted a cigarette, which was a bad sign. Yet I didn't know why Diane's words had upset me. Not only had I heard rumors about Molly, I'd seen her libertine impulses myself, only regretting not being their object. And by the way, why had Diane not slept with me? I'd passed the screen; she hadn't gotten laid; she was drunk. Was she tired? She definitely hadn't been her brightest self, but she certainly could have prolonged her vigil by an orgasm or two. Or did she want to punish me for loving Molly? That would be so rude of her. How can you set out to punish someone for loving the acme of dramatic perfection? *I am so close*, I thought, clenching my fists and feeling feeble. Which meant: she needed to get here. As soon as possible. Before it would be too late to even hope.

The rest resembled a walk in a dream. I got up, fog, haze and hail in my head, collected my shoes and began to move. The distance seemed disproportionally greater, and the slurring time offered no help. *Dear me*, I thought, clinging to the slightest sound I could catch in the eternally lonesome corridor, but it was full of nothing except my own fantasies and lamps. I fell on the door to my room with the weight of my entire body, unsure whether I'd be able to open it otherwise. A strip of light showed me the way to my corner, and then I released the handle, and it was dark again.

I carefully put my shoes under my bed and then collapsed on it, barely aware of what I was doing. A lethargic snake, I slid out of my clothes, including my underwear, and threw them on top of the chest of drawers; then I slipped under the blanket and curled into a tight ball. Flashbacks of the day's events exploded before my eyelids, and the clear saltiness of defeat surrounded every one of them. *You've just jumped a mile to the right place without seeing*, I thought, pressing the tip of my tongue into the roof of my mouth and twitching. *And yet you're back to feeling like you're seventeen again.*

COHESION

IV

Awakening

I woke up a few hours later and stared at the ceiling for a while. I felt bad. Nausea assaulted me, not from the stomach but from the throat, and there were no objective reasons for it. My head was filled with the fog of a hangover, and my temples were squeezed by a very familiar pain that could result in a nosebleed after any inauspicious turn of events. My motivation was not zero so much as negative, but the worst was that I had no idea what to do.

After spending around ten minutes in this state without the slightest improvement, I forced myself to get up and hit the bathroom wearing only briefs and slippers. The corridor was remarkably quiet, but I bet there were already several well-rested good girls in the dayroom sucking on the piquant details of last night. *Should've brought them milk chocolate*, I thought on my way back, sensing that my excursion had slipped by unnoticed but not regretting not having worn briefs.

Vince's clock indifferently showed a quarter past eight. Last night's gals were unlikely to appear before noon, but I did not want to see them in any event. I sat on the bed and looked out the window. The branches of a linden tree hung profusely over it, but they couldn't obstruct the emerald grass below. Some types of grass look best under the clouds, and such was the kind growing here: it was wonderful to lounge on in the sun, but it ripened to its lushest shade just before the rain. In the past I'd known how to use it to determine whether I'd need an umbrella. Hell, that was a long time ago.

I heard a muffled murmur behind my back. Right, Vince. But who was with him? I was perplexed, realizing there was another body in his bed. Vince had paradoxical taste in women: he never slept with his own classmates. Who could he have gotten in trouble with? Surely not with a cook? I twisted my neck and squinted, trying to discern the woman's shape through the dusk in the room. Georgetta? Matilda? Antoinette? I couldn't see and didn't care to stand up. Having stared at the grass some more, I began to shiver from the cold and got under the blanket again.

There, memories assailed me. What had happened the night before had been a pure farce, yet it but served to stress the single important realization: that Martina had not come. That was followed by another realization: that if she wasn't already in the dayroom, she wouldn't be showing up later, either. The thought made we wince. I tried to come up with a reason for her to skip our reunion, an event coveted by every reasonable ACer. Did she have so little to brag about that she was afraid to appear a failure? Or did she have a conflict with something of such paramount importance that it outweighed the chance to remind our former scoundrels what worthless classmates they were? I may have just put some words in the wrong order, yet the first explanation had to be dismissed. Molly was, after all, a somewhat professional actress: she'd had to learn to maintain a cheerful facade and present herself from a favorable angle regardless of circumstances. But what about the second one? And did it involve a man? Not your another man, of course, but the one worth marrying, even if out of spite? It would be so her, too: to have a wedding on the reunion weekend, to emphasize how much higher he was in the hierarchy of her priorities ...

And then I screamed in my thoughts. Last night must have shattered me completely. Sure enough, three hours of sleep hadn't helped, but how could I have deteriorated into such a wreck?

"*You fucking wanker,*" I whispered, pressing my forehead into the pillow. "*Your girl hasn't made it, has she? Why don't you cry about it? Jump into the shower; that way no one will know why your eyes are so red. Give it an honest cry, like a five-year old who's let his favorite toy fall from the window and smash on the sidewalk. And, amidst all the drama, ask yourself the only question you should be asking: what exactly triggered the leap last night?*"

The thought was sobering. Despite the standstill, last night still had to be reckoned with, and the jump was only part of it. There were also a considerable number of people on campus whose idea of me had suffered a break in continuity and who had to return to their comfort zones. At my expense, of course. Well, whatever it took to take my mind off Molly: if she were to arrive, it would happen only when I was thinking about something other than her.

Then I considered showering again. That thought seemed the best I had had since waking up, even though I hate showering in the morning: it chills me, and today's weather wasn't enough to make up for it. Yet I had to escape this misery, and water could prove the very element capable of providing some assistance.

The price I'd paid for the reunion (two hundred and twenty-five pounds, if you were wondering) included two fresh towels of unequal size and equal whiteness but no other bathing paraphernalia, which was alright as I'd taken the first-class kit from the plane, which contained more liquid soap and shampoo than I'd need in a week. I removed the briefs again, wrapped the larger towel around my hips, and neared the mirror by the door to study the obscure reflection emerging from the shadowy air. I was haggard and disheveled, yet my eyes had the shine of someone who knew everything. I opened them wider and studied my pupils. I wanted the effect to temporarily go away until I could figure out what's what, but I was glad I had it. I looked over at Vince's bed once more but saw only the girl's dark hair flowing over the top of the blanket. As such, she could have been anyone except who I needed, so I quietly opened the door and left the room.

Moses in the Shower

The corridor remained pleasantly devoid of human noises, but I wasn't the only one reconsidering their personal cleanliness. I heard splashing coming from the shower area of the bathroom, which was filled with hot steam, and I was struck dumb when I identified the culprit as Moses. He looked like he'd had a rough night and was falling asleep again, standing with his eyes closed, his hands spiraling around a hairy chest that already had too much soap on it. He didn't notice me until I turned the valve next to his, stepping out of the stream to let it warm up. He slowly opened his eyes and, continuing the spiraling, asked hoarsely through the water and his pirate beard:

"What's up, Courage?"

I looked straight up at the ceiling.

"Not much. How about yourself?"

"Not too bad." He finally put the bar of soap aside. "Trying to wake up."

"Late night?"

"Pretty late. Was catching up with some people."

"Good for you. Me, I barely caught up with myself."

He coughed.

"They missed you at the cliffs, man," I continued, stepping into the stream. It was too hot, but there was no way to fix it other than walking around the wall and adjusting the master knob, which would also affect the temperature for Moses. Such was the challenge ten years ago; it remained the same, but I wasn't used to it anymore. "You know the girls: they want a sexy guy around to pretend the jittery feeling between their legs was because of the coffee they'd drunk at lunch."

"You went to the cliffs?"

Now it was my turn to close my eyes. I was surprised Moses ran the water so hot; but then again, when we'd met I'd also had no idea he'd have such an undeniable impact on my favorite women: I doubted Chloe would have returned to me had he come to the cliffs. I froze, now remembering the girls, the water itching its way down my back.

"Who did you go with?" Moses asked.

"Most of the Cliff Girls," I retorted, yawning. Water ran into my mouth and I spat violently, trying to get rid of the metallic taste it brought. "They haven't changed: posh, judgmental, stunning. Not one has gained weight. I think some may have lost some."

"I never knew you were a cliffs goer," Moses said with skepticism audible even through the running water.

"The cliffs is the only place around here where I feel like myself," I said, and those words were true. "Some of my most brilliant breakthroughs have happened there, but they've also witnessed some of my utmost gruesomeness. I remember this one time I was in love with Beatrice. It hit me harder than usual, so I went to the cliffs in the middle of the night with a kerosene lantern and a leather rope. Now, you may wonder why on earth I needed the lantern, but Vince had gotten it two or three nights before and ..."

"You were in love with Beatrice?" Moses asked incredulously.

"Like a madman without a chance of recovery," I said, turning around and facing him. "Frankly, though, was there a better girl on this campus in the two years we spent here? I've heard folks say Diane was peerless, and she's truly one of the fairest ladies you can hope to set eyes on, but if I may be as honest with you as one naked man with another on a Saturday morning, to my mind, Diane is too obsessive. I mean, she needs to be the one driving one hundred percent of the time, and I don't buy into that—even for all she has to offer. Now, Beatrice is a different case. A nutcase, some said, especially those who saw her French-kissing Rohatyn on stage in the assembly hall in front of a three-digit audience of close friends and enemies. But what Beatrice won me over with was that, while she is undoubtedly insane, she lets out her true self, which is priceless. And I'm not just talking about sex; no, I'm talking about group behavior, if you know what I mean."

"Not really," Moses said, frowning. There was no aggression in him; he was merely confused.

"I'm not surprised." I made the gesture of someone losing his patience, drops flying off my fingers and landing on the opposite wall in a line that stretched all the way up to the scabs of peeling paint on the ceiling. "I'm not making sense to myself either. I should've gotten wasted last night: I'd still be asleep now. Then I'd have woken up, stolen some of whatever Vince takes when his head is about to split, and three cups of Earl Grey later I'd have started thinking that last night had been great and tonight's gonna be even better."

Moses froze, water trickling down his short, wiry body. Suddenly I noticed a long red scratch running from the top of his right thigh down to the kneecap. It looked like it'd hurt like hell when he got it. It seemed to have come from a sharp dry tree branch, but what adventure for two would involve tree climbing?

"How did you get that?" I asked.

"You mean *that*?" He threw a quick look down. "Just caught myself a little, nothing special."

"More special than not having caught yourself at all. Where did it happen?" He didn't respond. "Definitely not on the cliffs, unless someone hammered a nail into them. But that's impossible: these people have no imagination." And then it dawned on me. "The estate shed!" He look puzzled, his rate of thinking lagging behind mine by an increasing margin. "I never understood why they wouldn't throw coat hangers on the very nails they use to hang coats on. But it had to have been quite a fall ..." I tried to remember what was above the plank that held the nails. "Good Lord, you went all the way to the roof!"

"I have no idea what you're talking about," he said gravely, and who could blame him? The problem was: he was lying.

"You don't have to be coy with me: I've confronted harder truths, also wearing as little as I am now," I assured him, switching focus to the stream on my face. "You did the girl. Good for you, because she was the one choosing. Thing is, man: I was never jealous of you and Beatrice, because you're a better option for her." The soap was making my left eye itch and I rubbed it gently. "Not because you're a better man, but because your values align with hers. Besides, a girl like Beatrice will always go for a guy like you to raise her status in the eyes of her competition. Our imperfect being demands validation, and sex is the kind of validation that most people dig."

"Sounds like you were having fun last night, after all," Moses said. His tone surprised me: I thought he'd resist.

"AC is a peculiar place: I've never managed to enjoy it sober. Which puts me at a disadvantage, because I don't drink." I looked straight into his eyes. "I'm actually glad you didn't go to the cliffs, but I'm unsure about Beatrice."

"Unsure?"

"If she had gone, I would have gone after her," I explained.

"Maybe you should have," he sneered. "I doubt you'd have gotten much out of it, though."

"Other than a scratch?" I wondered innocently.

He released the string holding the valve of his shower: you had to fix it that way, otherwise the water stopped every few seconds. The stream petered out. I let him walk out without another word. I suddenly felt flat. I'd always liked him, and he always disappointed me. His towel flashed from the edge of the wall as he dried his hair. Someone told me that having expectations of people is a sure way to be disappointed, but having no expectations is an even surer way to die bored.

Moses was gone. The bathroom door shut behind him with the very slam that had woken me up at night before I'd begun gluing bubble wrap to the jamb. I finally got used to the water, now indulging in its heat and thinking, and the new conclusions I came to were more optimistic. I realized that I'd done very well distracting myself from Martina last night, arriving at a state where everything was equally unimportant. As a result, the actual events that took place did not matter. I could have gone to bed before the cliffs or stayed in that lagoon, and it would all be the same because, if I'd survived, I would have woken up exactly like this: nauseous, exhausted, demotivated. Yet I had to drag myself out of this, even if by my hair, which hadn't gotten greasy enough since I'd last washed it and was now turning into a thick, heavy mass that was difficult to soap.

As I massaged my skull, my sporadic and incoherent thoughts began turning into a consistent flow. I saw the error I'd made in not having considered ending up in this situation. Granted, it was unlikely, yet it wasn't inconceivable, and the advantage of having a plan ready was that I'd have developed it from a stable state of mind, unperturbed by the heaviness crushing me now.

Then I remembered there were also women here. Those I'd had sex with last night didn't count because they'd probably try to trample upon me today, but there were others. I tried thinking of unobjectionable activities I could engage in with them, but I didn't want anything unobjectionable—not without Molly, anyway.

"*Hold on right there*," I whispered to myself, keeping my mouth closed to avoid getting water in it again. "*You're never closer to losing than when you've done everything right half way. What women? The only two left are Diane and Beatrice, and you can't even look at Diane. Had she lied? No, don't go there. And as for Beatrice, she's tricky because no one can predict her next move, not even she herself. Moses sure couldn't, although he's no expert on the female soul, either. Wait.*" I froze, the splash of water flooding my head. "*Were there really so few desirable women in your entire class?*"

I had an impulse to start pacing back and forth. What about Mallory? Gretchen? Esther? I realized how pointless it was to think of them, and the realization stuck as a silent reproach. I didn't even want to be here. With Martina taken out of the equation, I was left with only memories, but nostalgia had never been my cup of tea. I hadn't missed AC because I'd missed too much while being here, and now that I'd come back, the petty, ignominious part of me wanted to collect the debt with interest, which meant I had to keep myself in check: at whatever price.

I shut off the stream abruptly and squeezed the excess water from my hair, listening to the drops fall into the puddles on the floor. I was inextricably lost. I needed to withdraw and recuperate. This meant, above all, being completely alone. And that I could not allow myself—not yet.

I heard the door open. I'd left my towel on the radiator by the sinks; one look in that direction would have betrayed that someone was in the shower, but the heavy steps approached the toilets instead. Judging by the gait, it couldn't be Vince, and talking to any other man seemed wrong. So as soon as I heard the characteristic noise emerging from the direction of the cubicles, I wrapped the towel around my hips, droplets flying off my body as I hurried back to the room, shivering from the very post-shower cold I hated.

Vince Motherfuckers

I heard Vince's alarm clock from the corridor, but not until I opened the door did I fathom the true shrillness of the sound. Calling it obnoxious would be an understatement: it was the kind of strident shriek emitted by a fire alarm. Vince was clearly distraught, rubbing his eyes and uttering unintelligible phonemes while his blanket slowly slid to the floor, but the girl was gone.

"Turn that motherfucking thing off," he said as if addressing someone who'd murdered his cat. The thing must have been on for a while.

"It's your clock," I reminded him, shivering again.

"For fuck's sake!" He rolled in bed like he always did in the morning, resembling a giant newborn drowning in bedsheets. "I'm gonna shoot this one, too."

"Kill the fucker, will you," I said sharply, locating the fiendish device. "It's right by your left arm."

He opened his eyes, turned his head, saw it and clubbed it to death with his hand.

"I have good news," I said, using the smaller towel to dry my face. "The girl left without bumping into me."

"The girl?" he repeated, as if it were a word from a language he didn't speak. "What girl?"

"I didn't catch a good look; I only know who she wasn't. Not from our year, right?" I carefully inquired.

"Probably not." He moved his head absentmindedly from one side of the pillow to the other, likely wallowing in hazy recollections.

"Any idea where *that* straight shooter is?" I made a general gesture toward the third occupied corner.

"You mean Tiger? I don't have the slightest clue," he somberly declared. "The last I remember is Adeline and the pants …"

"Who was trying to get into whose?"

"… but that was before the scotch." His eyes were now fully open, his face assuming a look I knew better than to interrupt. "But after the tequila."

"Do you know if he's dating anyone these days?" I asked, drying my crotch with the larger towel without taking it off my hips.

"Why?"

"He never had a reason to turn women down in the past; I wonder if he does now."

"The women have amply rewarded him for his reasons, whatever they were or weren't," he said slowly in the absurd tone of mentorship that worked well with his accent. "What would you do in his shoes?"

"I'd have to try them on to know. But I don't want to: they'd be too tight. Do you really not remember who you brought here last night?"

"It was already morning. And you weren't here." His face lit up with another breakthrough. "Hey, I just realized something." He sat up in a single rapid motion that scared people who weren't used to it. The rest of his blanket made it to the floor at last. "I haven't seen you since we played Durak! Where were you, motherfuckers?"

"Depending on the exact time, I could have been on the cliffs or anywhere nearby," I said, relieved. For a moment I thought he knew more about my adventures than was good for him.

"You went to the cliffs last night?"

"Is that shocking?"

"Nothing is shocking in this place." He was pensive. "I just thought you'd have saved it for later."

"Friday night, Saturday night—what's the difference if everyone's trying to get laid anyway?"

"Some aren't just trying. Who did you go with?"

"Where, to the cliffs?"

"To the cliffs, to the cliffs, to the fucking clits!" He was angry, possibly remembering something he'd rather forget. "Where else?"

"The Cliff Girls." I gave him a look of a displeased teacher. "Who else?"

"The Cliff Girls?" Watching him struggle to bring his vision into focus, I was afraid to imagine how much he'd drunk the night before. "The Cliff Girls had an outing?"

"A little bash, like they used to."

"And how did you find out?"

"By stumbling upon them before they took off. I had something they didn't have but needed, so it was a naturally symbiotic affair."

"Didn't have but needed? You mean, a cock? Listen." He'd moved on to an entirely different subject. "Llantwit turned out a major bust. The guy I used to know got shipped a while ago, so I'm off to Bristol today. And Bristol is a place where treasures can be found."

"And lost," I reminded. Martina's suspected absence suddenly became slightly more tolerable. "What are we talking about?"

"At this point, anything. Is there something particular you want?"

"I suppose it wouldn't be a stretch to expect your Bristol fellow to have acid?"

"He ain't my fellah." He looked at me with reproach. "I just know someone who can help."

"And how many folks on campus know?"

"The two of us."

"That's a slim count," I remarked. "But I have a feeling that if folks around here learned what was going on they'd jump on board. The problem is, you have to know who they are before asking. When are you going?"

He gave the clock a long look.

"In a few hours. And I need to do something about this hangover before that. Do you know if there's breakfast?"

"Definitely not in the dayroom."

"Fuck the dayroom." He was spite itself. "Who was DJing last night? I hope the fucker gets crippled. Britney Spears, on a night like that?"

"What songs did they play?" I asked with avid interest.

"All the ones you've never heard. What about the dining hall? They've gotta have some food going."

"There's only one way to find out." I nodded. "And that's not through the top of my head."

I knew where things were going when he grabbed what looked like the alumni welcome booklet, two or three colorful slips of paper flying from its pages and hovering in the air for much longer than I expected.

"Okay, if the time's right ..." He said a minute later, frowning at the clock. "We have twenty-five minutes."

"When is lunch?"

"Twelve-thirty to one," he answered after another long look into the booklet.

"That's what it always was on Saturdays." I smiled. "Don't your countrymen know just how to uphold a tradition?"

"If it's a good tradition, yes. Will you wait for me while I shower?" he said in an almost humble voice. "I'm assuming it's not from a diner that you're returning, so we can go eat together."

A spark of nostalgia flickered before my inner eye. Vince was already on his feet, throwing his larger towel over his shoulders.

"Don't you move until I return, motherfucker. And think about that girl. I wanna know who she was."

"She may tell you herself later. Go, motherfuckers!" I added when he wouldn't budge. "We ain't got no time to waste."

The Saturnine Celibate

Vince didn't disappear until after he'd taken his medicine, and I politely waited to take off my towel until he'd gone. Then I unlocked my valise and pulled open the underwear compartment, the zip momentarily catching on a stray thread halfway in. Here we go.

Dear men, if you somehow make it to this part of my story, take this advice: when you run even the slightest chance of having sex with the same woman two nights in a row, make sure you change your underwear to a visibly different alternative. "Visibly different" is crucial, because putting on fresh underwear that looks the same won't help. Do you think the woman in question will study it to ascertain its cleanliness? No; they'll just assume it's the same pair.

I had learned my lesson a while ago, so what I had at my disposal now was a solid selection of cotton and nylon boxer briefs that could hold me up tight any way I wanted. But what color should I choose? Last night's cobalt was an automatic choice for the jeans, but Saturday called for something more reserved. After some consideration, I decided I could satisfy its requirements with a silvery gray T-shirt, a dark gray long-sleeved polo shirt and cream cotton pants, adding neutral black socks and dark purple sneakers. I pictured myself: the outfit seemed fine, nor did I want to spend too much time on it. Not before I saw Molly, anyway.

But then a most devastating epiphany hit me, cancelling the momentum I'd begun gathering after putting on the gray underwear, making me retreat under the blanket once again, the sheets readily absorbing water from those parts of my body I hadn't yet reached. The bed's cavity retained some of the warmth accumulated during the night, but instead of enjoying it, I put the pillow against the wall, leaned against it with my back and stared into the open valise. What I realized was that I'd gotten so lost in my nocturnal quests the night before that it wasn't before sunrise that I'd begun listening to Saturn, which meant I owed it a serious apology, and the most appropriate thing to do seemed to vow celibacy until sunrise on Sunday.

You want to be friends with the mysterious and powerful planet Saturn because it controls both time and death. And when time is on your side, doesn't life feel right? Yet Saturn demands particular behaviors from those seeking its favor, including patience, perseverance, modesty, and hard work. You'd do well to practice those virtues as a matter of course, but Saturday augments their importance to an extreme because that day belongs to Saturn from beginning to end.

Friday, on the other hand, belongs to Venus. Many people erroneously believe that Venus is responsible for sex; that, however, is in the realm of the Moon, while Venus supervises the social aspect of life—communication with others. Last night was a great example of what one should do on a Friday: dress beautifully, socialize, and flirt. And there was nothing wrong with taking the latter to an extreme, except for one thing. There are two ways to separate the dominions of the planets over the days of the week: one draws the line at midnight, while the other draws the line at sunrise. Since Saturn is the most powerful of the planets, I usually begin recognizing its power at midnight and consider it in charge until Sunday morning. But last night I failed to do so, frisking about in sensual affairs throughout the night and pursuing Diane near dawn. This recklessness meant that I had to do penance to counterbalance my guilt, and one of the things that Saturn most approves of is celibacy.

Celibacy, by the way, is almost always a good idea. It's like a ticket to impeccability: regardless of what you do, you can't be sexually reproached, which gives you an edge over most people. Have you ever worked with a fellow who didn't take up much space in your head? You'd never think about him when remembering your colleagues, but if you did remember, it would be with pity. Quiet voice, average looks, shy moves, never part of the social scene? You don't know a thing about his life but if you had to guess you'd say he isn't seeing anyone, and hasn't for a while, and won't be any time soon, unless it's an unattractive woman with low self-esteem and no clue about how to raise it with clothes, make-up and perfume. But what if you learned that, instead of putting himself at the disposal of the insatiable pornography industry, the guy abstains from sex altogether? What would you think then? A pious freak, a mommy's boy, a non-English patient? But what if the answer to all those is *no*? What if the guy practices celibacy not out of religious, health or self-image issues but because to him it's a currency with which he buys things so precious all the richest people in the world combined can't afford them?

We have a deep-seated subconscious fear of those who can control their sexuality in ways we can't. Why do we care when celebrities are embroiled in sex scandals? Because it erases the barrier between us and them. They may have better looks, more money, better luck—but hell, we're all human; we're all after the same thing. But if someone disregards sex, you know he's after something else. He could sit at the very next desk, doing the very same tasks you do—those that make the company owners rich and earn you little but an overdue promotion and a few extra bucks for many hours of additional work and stress—but on the inside, he is playing a game: one that, if won, will take him to divinity. I won't pretend to be that kind of guy, because my sex drive is akin to an exotic zoo of wild beasts that tear each other to shreds when their urges go unsated, but even a libertine like myself can master a modicum of discipline when he believes it's the optimal course of action.

Having made up my mind, I sighed regretfully, dried my hair with the hairdryer I'd brought from home, and dressed as planned. The look turned out just as I wanted: nothing special, yet elegant and clean. The bathroom door slammed several times in the meantime, but it was only after I'd hidden the pass in my pants' pocket that Vince stormed into the room.

"How much more time do you need?" I asked.

"Two minutes," he answered, and I remembered that he never dried his hair.

"Perfect," I said, involuntarily imitating his accent. "Meet me in the dayroom."

I saw no one in the corridor but heard voices and music coming from some of the rooms. Four steps later, I realized I was running, but I didn't slow down until I'd reached the door to the dayroom. It was closed, and that infuriated me. In the whole two years I'd spent here I'd seen it like this no more than a dozen times, at least half of those occurring between three and five in the morning when people were having sex there. Keeping it shut at this hour on this occasion spelled unallowable carelessness. The stone doorstop was nowhere in sight; it must have been moved inside. I stood still, ready to go but taking my time. Then I grabbed the handle, my knuckles turning white from the pressure.

"*Now you'll see her,*" I thought. "*Remember: no simpers, no ferreting for the best phrase. Relax and be yourself.*"

Then I muted the internal dialogue and flung open the door.

A flood of morning sunshine hit my eyes, but my pupils contracted quickly, allowing me to discern various bodies of various genders engaged in various activities. The kitchen lamps were on, projecting a reflection onto the glass wall opposite the door and exposing the only area that would otherwise have been hidden from me. Two more bodies filled that space, cooking something healthy, judging by the smell. I made a quick inventory of everyone present. Three men and six women, grouped into three pairs and a trio. The cooking couple had slept with itself. The ones at the table next to the fire exit would do so soon. The rest hadn't gotten laid in so long I was unsure why they'd even come here.

Martina wasn't there.

I took two steps forward and released the door. It closed behind me with a dampened thud. I looked around, but the stone wasn't there. Today was different, though: everyone in the room saw me. I made it to the center of the space and froze.

"Good morning, guys. Has anyone seen the stop-stone?" I said loudly.

No one answered.

I made a slow circle around the perimeter like a fighter aircraft searching for a target, but the stone was gone. Then I remembered breakfast. If she wasn't here, she might ... Not thinking another word, I walked out. I wanted to head straight to the castle, but I had to fetch Vince first. Fortunately, he was already on his way to me, kicking the corridor door open as if no one could be on the other side.

"I thought you said to meet you in the dayroom?" he said, looking like a movie gangster in his white dress shirt and pitch-black jeans.

"Fuck the dayroom," was my peremptory reply. "It's breakfast time."

Breakfast of Champions

You have to be careful about what you eat. Especially on Saturdays. Sometimes I fast on Saturdays, allowing myself no food or water. This results in higher clarity of perception and occasional breakthroughs, but today drinking was indispensable as dehydration could decrease my resilience against future onslaughts. I knew more was coming: it was as clear as the crunch of dry gravel under Vince's shoes.

"Okay, you gotta promise something, motherfuckers," he was saying in the meantime. "We're not gonna sit where you always used to …"

The phrase triggered a heated argument: Vince had touched a sore spot that had contributed to me falling short of my own expectations as a student. One of the things my classmates had censured me for (and perhaps the only one that did deserve their censure) was that I ate alone. As I eventually discovered, it was equivalent to shooting myself in the head, as this kind of behavior was considered appropriate only for losers; but unfortunately for my social standing, the habit was dictated by science.

It's a long-standing fact that talking during meals hampers the digestion. Remember my advice that attention is key? The rule holds in the context of gastronomy as well. While digestion does not require conscious effort, a distracting environment reduces its efficacy. And, given the inordinate amounts of energy my mind was burning to keep up with all the romantic tragedy, that was a luxury I couldn't afford.

I often wondered why girls put extra weight at AC while boys tended to lose a lot of it. Ten years later I still lacked an answer, but I didn't lose a single pound in four long and foul semesters here, even when I was suicidally depressed. Yes, I was: for the grand total of three months. It's when you wake up in the morning feeling fine, but only until the first conscious thought reminds you of where you stand with the girl you love. Then you collapse into an abyss, and for the next eighteen hours you suffer so much that you'd rather be dead, until you fall asleep again to repeat the cycle the next morning.

I didn't want to indulge, but as I entered the corridor leading into the dining hall, a cruel recollection hit me. It was here, by this very window, that Molly refused to be my date to the St. Valentine's Day ball. I stopped, looking at the sill cushions that were as soiled now as they had been then. Vince didn't know, marching toward his buddies who were waving at him, so nothing interrupted the resplendent apparition condensing before me. This wasn't a ghost, as the vision was a product of my memory which, despite not being photographic, could capture such moments in all their fullness, supplementing the imagery with the associated sounds, smells and feelings. The latter were akin to having been run through with a sword, yet the vision remained, quivering gently in the humming of the crowd feasting right around the corner from where I stood, hidden behind a concrete column.

She had been cruel to me so many times that I was prepared for anything, except for that tone, which I could have sworn was contrite. Her eyes shone apologetically as she spoke, slowly and softly, perfectly aware of my feelings and cautious not to bruise them with a careless word. She said how grateful she was for the beautiful card I'd made; she said how moved she was by the poem I'd written; she even said she was sorry and didn't say that she had already accepted an invitation from Ganymede! It was more than tact: she was exhibiting an aristocratic degree of magnanimity, and now I saw a beam of brilliant light burst from the top of her golden hair into Infinity, which, for its part, listened as attentively as if to an angelic tune. Yet, unrealistic as this was, I had to yank out the sword and seal the wound for good, so, employing all my concentration, I began moving my fallen assemblage point up.

See, episodes like this are not kept in our mind, if by the mind you mean the network of neurons within your skull; no, they are stored in positions of the assemblage point, which gives two advantages: one, the very exhaustive quality of the experience, the most asinine details included; and two, a much larger storage capacity, since the mind is like a USB drive while the assemblage point is a supercomputer. What followed that conversation was another month of suicidal depression as I fell to the Emotional level, so the remedy was simple: to move the memory higher, at least to the Mental one. In sorcery, the rule of thumb is that traumatic experiences of any caliber, no matter how atrocious, should never be forgotten, as that devalues them, leading to a most egregious injustice: instead of propelling you upward, your sufferings become meaningless.

The blood suddenly rushed to my head, leaving me dizzy. There were people at the other end of the corridor, and at least two more were approaching the buffet, but no one was close enough to witness my struggle. The picture from the past, now superimposed over the real-time one, became bright and acquired the dimensional depth of a vivid dream. The dizziness worsened, and I felt a pain in the crown of my head radiating to the forehead in an array of thin lines resembling the carcass of an umbrella. Then the vision grew so lucid I could compare it with reality, like photographs in an album. As it turned out, I'd been wrong about the cushions on the window sill: they were cleaner now, as was the stained glass itself, which must have been washed since then, but the walls had darkened, the marsh green of the stones showing more dusty grayness, with brownish spots that had to be organic.

Next, I experienced vertigo and sank down on the cushions, leaning with my back against the wall. It was cold, but it couldn't be any colder than February. Emotions sizzling inside like oil in a red-hot frying pan, I closed my eyes and viewed the memory as an impartial observer. The Mental keys I gathered in the next minute rotated around Martina's niceness, forcing me into a corner where I had to forgive her for the human attitude she'd showed. I had no logical reason to expect her favor; I had suspected something was up between her and Ganymede; I was late with my invitation, sending it the night before, while most students had made their arrangements way in advance. I was simply desperate as we were in our last semester, graduation day looming behind the final exams like a death sentence. And even if she had accepted, what good would have come of it if, at the end of that ball, she was bound to retire to the boys whose company seemed valuable enough to be taken all the way to the bedroom?

And then I knew the truth: not on the Mental level, but on the Causal one. The Causal level is what reduces long and involved chains of events to a single origin, like when you trace the success of a self-made billionaire to his decision to wake up at five o'clock every morning and take an ice-cold shower. The Mental level will fail to make this connection, but the Causal will see that these regular and sustained ablutions improved the man's health, discipline and fortitude, so that, whenever he found himself in a stressful and demanding situation that could go either way, he—unbeknownst to himself—came up with that extra modicum of strength needed to tip the scales in his favor. The example's simplistic, but my predicament was no harder because its root was not the kindness Molly had displayed; no, this was but a clue marking the event as one of critical significance. The crux of the issue was that, on that particular fourteenth of February, Martina had chosen Ganymede, a deceitful philander who enjoyed and abused forgiveness from everyone whose trust he betrayed. No man in AC was more different from me, and Molly's choice was a refined indication that my fate was to lose the women I loved not to *other men*, but to the worst men those women could choose. This made perfect sense if the reason behind it was to teach me a lesson. The cornerstone emotion I feel toward people is pity, and what could cause more of it than seeing my angels misused and mistreated by men unworthy of being their fettered slaves?

I bent my knees and let my body slide flat onto the cushion, now staring into the top of the window, silken strands of cobweb drifting lazily in its corners. What had just happened was a victory, but turning it into a triumph required climbing to the Buddhial level where I'd know not only *what* my fate was, but *why* it was so. This is what I'd done last night before the leap, and I didn't mind taking another one; yet I had to relax, extracting every drop of enjoyment from what I'd achieved before venturing any higher. The Causal root of many of my troubles was that I often neglected life's pleasures, impatient to get to the end. But, as Buddhists put it, *there is a road, and there are flowers by its side*, and there's no harm in appreciating those if you don't steer away from the final destination.

A group of middle-aged men passed by; they were gossiping about someone who wasn't present. Suddenly I felt thirsty, remembering that I hadn't drunk anything since yesterday. This explained the headache that didn't go away after I performed a reality check, so I hopped off the cushions and headed toward the buffet with the gait of someone who hadn't experienced a single heartbreak in his entire life. The immediacy of relief is a sure sign that you've done everything right; I only wished I hadn't carried this thorn for so long. No, not even that: I wished I'd known what to do with it as soon as it had gotten inside.

The buffet consisted of two sections: one for food, the other for drinks. Vince was still at the first, tray in hand, talking to boys I didn't know too well, so I went to the tea urn, grabbing two mugs on the way. They looked the same as they used to, but they had to be new: the rate at which dishes were broken here bespoke a place overpopulated with overprivileged brats. I filled two thirds of one mug and three quarters of the other with hot water and added equal amounts of cold water into each; then I noted that the cooler mug was in my right hand and walked into the dining hall. The castle dated to the fourteenth century, but none of its dungeons bore this historic honor with more dignity than the dining hall. Yet it wasn't the carved stones, or the window arches, or the wooden framework under the roof that I liked best. It was the long, charcoal tables made of such solid wood they gave the impression that they weighed more than any number of people who could sit at them, all their crap included.

"See the bunch over there?" Vince finally caught up with me, his buddies trailing obediently after him. His entire food selection consisted of coffee and broiled tomatoes with black pepper on top. I gulped involuntarily, lightheaded from the sight: these had always tasted sinfully good. "Let's crush that powwow."

He was referring to a group of our classmates that looked like a boy scout club in the field: there were no girls among them. This alone was reason enough for me to go elsewhere, but our reunion demanded its toll. At least they were giving off a positive vibe: the other parties were scattered, scared and small. This was strange: I thought there'd be more twenty-year alumni as this had to be their last chance to seduce an old favorite. Or was I underestimating modern pharma? One pill for the erection, one to help immature … I mean, premature ejaculation, and one to fall asleep. A sudden jolt of disgust electrified my torso, and a lump of nausea stuck in my throat. I took a sip of water from the right-hand mug; the temperature was close to ideal, and the lump's prickly edges began melting away.

"Courage, is that really you?" Luke said as I passed behind him to take a seat. "I thought you had a magnet up your ass that brought you to that far corner of the dining hall!"

See what I mean? If I meet these people in thirty years, having become all I set out to become, that will still be the thing they'll remember me by. And they'll gladly tell the tale in every interview with those assembling my biography. *So, what's the first thing that comes to mind when you think of Courage? Well, he was destined to do great things, but he was an asshole! How so? Well, he always ate alone!* What these people had never understood—and never would—was that I welcomed every one of them but refused to reach out first. My logic was simple: if they liked me, they would; and if they didn't, why would I care? The present situation was a great illustration. Not one among these boys was my friend or even a close acquaintance, but if they invited me I would gladly join them, bringing out my best self, being pleasant and affable, helping them overcome their own insecurities and fears and biases so that they'd shine like a handful of diamonds in the sun, like all human beings deserve to shine.

Naturally, they never invited me anywhere.

The conversation that had been underway carried on; this was another reason why I preferred eating alone. Meal chats perennially revolved around the topic of "*Did you guys see who pulled who last night?*", the word *pulled* here carrying the specific meaning *kissed vehemently in front of countless spectators while the object didn't object.* To me, this was as trite as a TV talk show, except deserving of more pity. *If you guys knew what happened here last night*, I thought, feeling a slight sting of regret where the nauseous lump had just been. *But even if you'd seen it, would you know?*

"Hey Courage, are you gonna meet with the community?" Nixon asked.

"Definitely," I said, having no idea what he meant. "Who do you think I am?"

"Hey Courage, what do you do for a living?" asked Bishop.

"Nothing dishonest, why?"

"How's America holding up with Trump?" added Clark.

"Not quite as you see on the news."

"Looks bad on the news," Gable remarked.

"Depends on who owns the channel."

"Hey Courage, how much are you gonna donate?" Darius chimed in. He was one of those who thought they could donate more than everyone else combined.

"A lot. But not money."

"What, then?" he asked with bewilderment in his otherwise empty eyes.

"Fame."

Soon I was left alone. Vince did all the talking, and I focused on my subtle bodies. The water was working: the headache subsided, and I was feeling generally better. I finished both cups quickly and was considering refilling them when I saw Kirk Rush, the Principal of AC, making his way to our table. He was one of the few faculty members who remained from ten years ago, and the interceding decade had left plenty of marks on the face below his now-uniformly-gray hair. His face was cleanly shaven and had a peculiar expression I didn't remember him having: that of an old man who no longer cares to conceal that he doesn't care. I hadn't spotted any other faculty in the dining hall, but his arrival seemed normal. What didn't was that he was walking like someone who doesn't want to show his nervousness, and that when our eyes met he looked away before looking back at me.

"Good morning, guys," he said as he approached the table. "How is your reunion going?"

Most of the boys pretended they hadn't heard him; some voiced the usual banalities expected in such situations.

"Excellently, Kirk," I said when they'd finished. "I wish I could hear the same from you, but I'm sure these reunions get repetitive after a while."

"You'd be surprised." His lips smiled a smile that didn't reach his eyes. "There are always new things to discover. I actually wanted to talk to you about one such thing. Do you think you could stop by my office after breakfast?"

Murky conjectures stirred inside me, but they were all amorphous.

"It's been a long time, Kirk." I yawned. "I don't remember where your office is, even if you still have the same one. But if you give me a minute to return these lovely items of crockery, I'd be happy to walk there with you."

"I can show you the way," he assured.

Show me the way to go home, I sang in my head, rising and picking up the mugs.

"Gentlemen, I wish you all a pleasant rest of your stay," I said warmly. Most of the boys pretended they hadn't heard me; some voiced the usual banalities expected in such situations. Vince was silent but he gave me a nod on my way out after the mugs had been deposited into the washing rack from which they were bound to depart as unwhitened as they'd left it last.

So much for the community. *Pleased to meet you. Hope you'll guess my name.*

Rush Hour

I suddenly remembered where Kirk's office was, but I let him walk us there without saying so. We talked about neutral things like his kids and my job (I told him I was an art director), and his voice was predominantly suave, but I'd have noticed the tension in it even if it were natural for the

Principal of AC to snatch an alumnus from breakfast for a private conversation. I was certain he wanted to talk about my adventures with the keys, but I knew neither how he'd spin it nor how he'd found out.

When we got to his office, he closed the door and invited me to take a seat in front of his table. I did, assuming the character of a loafer who is amused yet more eager to return to pastimes of his own choosing. Kirk, in turn, shifted to a more professional attitude as he sank into his armchair, his shoulders rising higher to his neck. So far, everything indicated that I needed to wait for his serve and return it in an addling yet unobjectionable way. It would buy me time: I had to be missing important information, playing to my disadvantage.

"Oh, well," he sighed, looking at my smiling countenance with the intensity of an amateur sleuth. "I've spent twenty-five years in this place, but I still seem unable to predict what may happen here the very next moment."

"That's why life is so amazing, Kirk: it always throws in a drop of chaos that compels you to evolve," I said, not losing my focus.

"Last night, for instance," he continued as if I hadn't spoken. "I was sure the alumni were busy drinking and catching up. Imagine my surprise when I learned that someone had used the cover of darkness to infiltrate the Visual Rescue department."

There it was: the piercing stare of the interrogator; coming from Kirk's eyes, it looked very amusing.

"I say!" I whistled. "But why would you be surprised?"

"Excuse me?"

"Well, from the AC folks, is it really astonishing?" I asked, suppressing scorn. "And what did they steal? The cameras, must be; the cameras and the equipment." Now I was pretending to be talking to myself. "What else? *Did they steal the leads*?" I fired, savoring the allusion, which was nevertheless destined to go unappreciated in this staid office that smelled like no one had ever had sex here.

"I can't talk about the details, I'm afraid. Not until after we've made a public announcement," Kirk said slowly.

"So they did steal the leads." I said in the tone of immutable finality. "When are you gonna announce?"

"Well, that's what we're trying to decide at the moment." Kirk looked away, nervously wiping the corners of his mouth with his fingers. "If we knew the whole truth, we could have disposed with the public part and kept it between ourselves, in the gentlemanly spirit of the reunion. But for that, you understand," he gave me a seemingly never-ending look, "we need to be sure that the truth is complete."

"Nine out of ten times I would have said *that's the smartest thing to do* here. But you know," I looked at him with reserved frustration. "I think there's something you aren't telling me."

"Well, that's why I wanted to talk to you in the first place. See ..."

"See, Kirk—and I'm being completely transparent with you," I said, throwing my right leg over the left, my head leaning on my palms, fingers interlaced behind my neck. Now I was acting like one of my former bosses, who thought that this pose and choice of words made him look cool. "The fact that you're telling me this means that you think I'm involved."

"The matter of fact is, and that's what I've been trying to tell you all along, that earlier this morning I had a conversation with a concerned alumnus who was ... ah ..."

"Concerned?" I suggested, feeling my feet get hot. This was an excellent sign.

"Worried about the VR department," Kirk said almost happily.

"Stated reason?"

"The alumnus claimed to have overheard a conversation during which some people had discussed the possibility of infiltrating the Visual Rescue."

"The possibility of infiltrating?" I couldn't believe my ears. "Were those his own words?"

"Well, I can't disclose the gender of the person ..."

"Is that really what he said? That he was considering the *possibility of infiltrating*?"

"I can't get into too much detail here ..."

"You already have. But don't you worry." Now I was confidence itself. "Whatever we've gotta do, we're gonna do. These bastards are all the same. They have a hundred million in a trust fund, yet they can't help stealing a fiver from their roommate's drawer. We're gonna nail him, Kirk: you and I."

"Nail who?" he queried suspiciously.

"The guy," I looked at him as if he were a child. "Do you think a girl is cut out for a job like that?"

"A job?"

"This infiltrating business. Have you already tried him?"

"Whom?" Kirk almost cried.

"The guy who brought you the clue!" I wanted Kirk to think that I was taking him for an idiot. "If he did it, he'd sure want the investigation to go the wrong way from the start, especially if he stole something. What plays to our advantage is that he'd have to keep the stolen stuff somewhere on the cliffs to pick it up before leaving. Not to mention the leads. But you know what, I'm not looking at it with a burglar's eyes. Did you notice?"

"Notice what?"

"That the burglar mindset is not how I saw it. That I was looking at the thing from a totally different perspective. Hey Kirk, is there something you're still keeping to yourself?" I added in a voice that he must have heard only in action movies. "Cause if so, now's the time to tell."

"No; I'm just listening."

"No; I'm talking about this Visual Rescue infiltration." I mimicked his voice so well that he flinched. "I think the term's dumb, and I hope you came up with it just to confuse me. But are you really not telling me that someone got murdered on this campus last night?"

"Courage, what are you talking about!" he exclaimed indignantly.

"What everything is pointing to," I said coldly. "A homicide happened here last night, didn't it? One of the bigger shots was found with a blade in his throat, so now you're afraid the survivors won't donate shit."

"Please stop it!" Kirk cried, making me pity him. I liked the guy. I'd never want him to be my father, but he meant well. "No one's hurt, thank God."

"Is that so?" I demanded, my apprehension deflating little by little. "You should still keep an eye on the guy. If he did it and expedited the discovery, he's nuts and will flip out, because he must have been sick for a while before this kleptomaniac outburst."

"We can do that," he said, unconcerned whether I believed him. "But let's not worry about the informant for a moment. Can you tell me what you yourself were up to last night?"

It was finally time to give him a very long look.

"I'm afraid I can't," I said at the end of it.

"And why is that?" For a split of the English second, he seemed taken aback.

"For the best of all reasons," I said with a smug smile. "It involves a lady. You understand."

"A lady?" he said a moment later, watching him intently. He wasn't trying to be polite, so I deduced a note of curiosity.

"I spent last night with a lady, and I can't reveal who she is, even if my alibi depended on it," I explained.

"But … why?" He looked like he actually didn't understand.

"Because I don't have her consent," I shrugged. "Look Kirk, these alcove romances, they're much harder on women if they go public. Or viral. Girls always risk more when they get into bed with us. And, since men in general don't give a fuck about the women they fuck, there has to be at least one who does: otherwise our universe would be unsustainable. I am that man."

"What if you had her consent?" he almost whispered.

"I wouldn't consider it appropriate to ask."

"So there's no way?"

"No," I said, suddenly sensing an opportunity. "But I can still tell you what I know about the VR."

"I'd certainly like to hear it," Kirk affirmed, his back straightening as he leaned toward me, his elbows resting on the table's top as he locked his palms together in front of him.

"*It's not something for nothing*, Kirk!" I said, silently rebuking myself for my excessive reliance on quotations. "If you want to know what I know, you need to tell me something."

"You know I'm within boundaries!" he exclaimed, dropping back into his armchair. I eyed him in silence. "Perhaps we can consider alternatives?" he added a moment later.

"If you agree, I'll go first and tell you everything I saw," I said implacably. "But I need your word first."

He vacillated.

"You're putting me in a very precarious position," he said.

"Kirk, do you really think so little of me?"

He looked away and scratched the back of his neck. Then he leaned forward again, his chin pressing into the finger lock he'd assembled anew. Then he let out the sigh of someone who's lost all hope.

"Okay," he said finally. "You have my word."

"Last night was a very peculiar night for me," I began, as if all the necessary preamble had already been given. "I went to the cliffs to take care of the memories that had been sitting in me like barbed hooks, and I was ready to do more than my best to extract them. After some preparations, I entered into a trance that took my perception outside my physical body, so I began seeing things." Kirk was listening to my every word, not showing the slightest sign of impatience. "It was like a motion picture played in my head, and it was a most eclectic series of scenes. In one of them I saw a man walking into the VR: straight through the door, as if it hadn't been locked. A few scenes later I saw him walking out: he looked the same, but his aura was brighter and slightly more golden around the edges. That's all," I concluded.

"Courage," Kirk said quietly a few seconds later. "I never doubted that you were a man of many talents. You displayed them profusely as a student, much to my and the other faculty members' delight, and it seems you've added even more facets to your astounding personality. But there's something I need to know."

He looked at me as if expecting my permission to ask.

"Anything you'd like, Kirk," I said with a charming smile.

"Did it seem to you that the man entering the VR looked like you?"

They say if God wants to punish a man, He takes away his wits. I say if God wants to punish a man, He takes away his imagination.

"Kirk," I said quietly. "Are you fucking kidding me?" He was silent.

"I'm telling you that I saw a man walk into the VR like in a fucking movie in the middle of my fucking head, and you ask me if I was that man?"

"But you could have seen his face, if the picture was clear!" he insisted.

"The picture was clear, alright. But I was after other things, and most of them weren't in the frame. Besides, I had no idea exactly what I was seeing. For all I knew I could be tripping balls, except I was sober. But this kind of thing happens to us in dreams all the time."

"Dreams?"

"I don't mean what we see when we're simply asleep: I'm talking about *dreaming*." I emphasized that word as if he could understand. "And, since I *dreamt* that whole thing, it had to have taken place in reality, in one form or another."

"So, was this whole story in fact you telling me that you fell asleep on the cliffs?"

"Of course I fell asleep on the cliffs," I said patiently. "How else would I have woken up in the lagoon?"

"Was the lady with you at the time?" he asked, as if trying the last resort.

"No; women don't stay with me that long: they use my body and then ditch me," I said in the tone of someone revealing an unflattering truth about himself.

"And yet you refuse to tell me who she is," he said disapprovingly.

"Kirk," I said in a tired voice. "Why do you think I came here?"

"Nostalgia? I don't know."

"Nostalgia my ass. I don't even know what that word means. I'm here because of a woman."

"The woman you were with last night during the supposed infiltration?"

"Supposed infiltration?" Suddenly I knew it all. "Did anyone break into the Visual fucking Rescue last night, or not?"

"We're assuming so," he said after a pause, avoiding my eyes. Checkmate; now I needed to get what I wanted.

"Kirk," I said in a tired voice. "I took you for real. I thought something was up, and I thought I could help by revealing a story that is painfully personal to me. Now I feel betrayed." I saw sorrow in his eyes; I didn't want to cause it, but I had to. "Do you know Martina Flawd?"

"Yes, of course." He nodded affirmatively.

"Have you spoken with her about this?"

"She isn't here. She cancelled her reservation a few weeks ago." Then he blinked twice, his eyebrows breaking in two barely noticeable creases. "Why do you ask?"

In boxing, they call it a *knockout*. In judo, they call it *ippon*. I never came up with a word for it, but if I had, it would be too foul to say.

"Because she'd know," I said, not recognizing my own voice. "Pleasure seeing you, Kirk." I got up and extended my hand over the table to shake his. He gave it automatically; it was dry and warm, and I made sure I didn't squeeze it too hard. "I hope nothing spoils your time here before you bid this place goodbye."

"Thank you. But I thought you wanted to ask me something?"

"Ask you?" I smiled, my head soaring high in the clouds as I enjoyed the panoramic view of the campus. "It's nothing to worry about. Anymore."

"By the way." He retrieved his hand gently. "It wasn't a guy."

"It wasn't?" my lips said as I kept smiling and soaring.

"No. That clue we got on you, it wasn't from a guy."

"It must have felt great: to get a clue on me. Wait—what?" It was like the fight hadn't stopped after the *ippon* and I'd gotten another kick in the head that made the panoramic view disappear at once. "The clue wasn't from a guy?"

"This remains between us," he reminded. "In the gentlemanly spirit of the reunion."

And then I began laughing—hysterically. It was as if a dam broke inside, letting out emotions that had been bottled up for too long. I laughed for maybe a minute, tears flooding my cheeks, while Kirk was studying me as concernedly as that girl must have looked when she'd talked to him. Except, for her, it was a carefully calculated act, whereas this man wished me well.

"Kirk, forget everything I just told you," I said at last, wiping my eyes with the tissue he handed me. "It's junk."

"Why?" he said as if my words baffled him even more than my laughter had.

"All I said was about a guy. These stratagems, hypotheses, and seemingly sound logical constructions are only worth anything when you're up against a man. Against a woman, they crumble and collapse under their own weight while she doesn't even notice. I don't know how they do it, Kirk," I added, seeing incredulity in his eyes. "The power is theirs from birth; it's like our ability to remember sports scores. Except much more useful."

Infinite Improbability

I left Kirk's office on autopilot, not a single thought interrupting my inner silence. I had no interest in guessing who'd snitched: I knew the girl had done it to hurt me, and without good reason. Gretchen was the only one who had a somewhat acceptable reason (I was undeservedly rude to her once), but she also had dignity. No; this was a continuation of the game that had always flourished here, the one where the players cut each other's throats simply because they could, simply to feel powerful and to derive a sick pleasure from watching the blood flow with impunity. But if I'd never cared about it before, why would I now?

I exited the castle through the assembly hall and descended to the second of the four lawn terraces running down to the lifeguard quarters. There I sat on the corner bench where no one could see me and stared at my hands for a very long time, begging them to change shape. They didn't. Then I began poking my left palm with my right index finger; it didn't go through either. Then I started punching the bench: gently and at regular intervals. Then I realized I was crying and stopped the checks: I never cried in dreams.

If this is reality now, you should have known it was a possibility when you were getting ready, I thought, trying to get a grip. Yet another thing I should've known. Another Causal cornerstone, my believing I should have verbed so many nouns. Why, though? Who said I wasn't supposed to be taking the world as it unfolded, not worrying about theoretical variants or, God forbid, trying to take them all into account? But of course, I had to: how else would I do everything I could?

I inhaled deeply and looked at the ocean. Most of it was obstructed by the landscape, but there was a visible strip wide enough to reflect the sun's lazy shimmer. What a mesmeric view it was, specs of light glimmering like the scales of a phenomenal fish on a thick off-white line hanging in the aquamarine sky. I remembered that, for a true sorcerer, a view like this was enough to start perceiving energy as it flows. I maintained the view until my eyes hurt, deep bluish furrows persisting when I looked away as some of the photoreceptors in my retina were burned out by the blinding brilliance, but ordinary reality did linger.

Recognizing my shortcomings, albeit momentarily, gave me some relief: it was slight yet perceptible, and even the bench didn't seem as hard anymore. It wasn't the one I'd carved during the long and cold estate service hours when, fighting the depression exacerbated by the taunting of my fellow students and the faculty, I worked on what I wanted to become the best bench on campus. We weren't allowed to use nails, employing only axes, wedges, bores, planes, chisels and wooden mallets, and in the end my creation was no better than the bench I was sitting on now, but by the time it was complete I had received a full scholarship from the American university I wanted to attend, so all the AC pain became worth it. I suddenly felt the urge to find my bench: it was good enough to be displayed as a proud example of how seriously AC students took the idea of environmental sustainability. But that was another stratagem of my mind, which was trying to distract me from the need to accept, fully and unconditionally, that my rendezvous with Martina had to be postponed.

I reached into my back pocket and felt the pass. I had had it for three years, learning marvelous things in anticipation of the moment when I'd return it, but now was the time to acknowledge that the true reason why I'd wanted to see her was because I'd thought that—finally—I had enough power to make her like me. Having sex with Molly (or any woman) was never an issue: it was that I felt I deserved to be liked by any woman I liked. And hell, I didn't even ask for too much: there were only a dozen AC girls I liked, three of those plain and two flat-chested. So, what's a fair proportion of one dozen? One half? One third? A quarter? Let's make it one sixth: pretty measly but still viable, wouldn't you say?

My number was zero.

I put my right ankle on my left thigh and leaned back, supporting my body with my hands wrapped around the knee. You can be unhappy in love once, twice or thrice; but when you've come up short twelve times in a row, you can rest assured probability has nothing to do with it. Yet here I was, lamenting the dire injustice I'd suffered instead of learning another invaluable lesson. The Mental would have gotten stuck on the rules of attraction; the Emotional would have collapsed into endless self-pity. But how would the Causal play it?

I rubbed my face violently with my palms, wiping the rest of the tears away. I had an annoying sensation: that of not being able to find the answer despite having more than I needed to do so. Something had to be wrong with my choice of women … or was I a wizard who could destroy any woman's attraction to me?

As the thought crossed my mind, my soles abruptly felt as though they were on fire. I yanked off my sneakers and socks, inserted the latter into the former, and placed my feet on top. Then I straightened my back, closed my eyes and went through the same routine as when warming up on the plane, paying attention to my entire physical body at once. The body is a superb sensor that always knows whether we are right or wrong; we're only oblivious to its wisdom because we're perennially focused on the internal monologue, that heinous fiend responsible for all human misery. But these flames were too obvious to ignore; now the challenge was to tune the burning to the silent thinking.

The epiphany I was after didn't come for so long that I gave up hope, grew despondent, nearly yelled in furious impotence and then almost fell asleep. Each time I was about to surrender I recalled the same image: that of me sitting on the wall of the watchtower at three thirty in the morning after that St. Valentine's Ball. The agony I'd felt then was beyond reckoning; in fact, I'd fervently wished my consciousness would shut off by itself, causing me to plummet twenty yards to the ground and die. It was the acme of my weakness, the pinnacle of my shame, and now it served as an implacable motive to prove I was better than that.

I did.

It came in the form of a soft melody ringing not even in my head but in the area just above it, which I still perceived as a part of myself. At first I was afraid some alumni had spotted me and decided to pull a prank, but then I realized the melody was cognizant of bestowing its heavenly presence upon me. And when it ceased, dissipating seamlessly into the dimension it had come from, be it parallel or perpendicular, my body had learned a profound truth, even though I didn't yet have the words to express it to my stupid mind.

"*You fucking wanker*," I muttered in a whisper that wouldn't have been audible even to someone sitting next to me. "*You've been given the opportunity of a lifetime, a chance a true sorcerer would kill for, and all you do is juggle statistics? You're toying with the idea of leaving, aren't you? You're considering dumping your impeccability down the drain on the basis of someone else's words? Someone who could be mistaken or even have deliberately lied to you once you made yourself available? But it's not even that. You forget again that, as long as there is a cubic millimeter of chance, you have to act as if it were all you needed, because if you can't turn that cubic millimeter into Infinity, why would Infinity even notice you?*"

The next instant brought utter sobriety. I was so alert I could distinguish individual bees buzzing around the rose buds on the opposite side of the terrace by focusing my attention on them. If I'd been in a dream, I could have maintained it for hours. Or until I found and isolated a scout. But my true self wasn't done with its revelations yet.

"In your fit of infantilism you are forgetting that Infinity is impersonal. It stabs you where it hurts simply to find out what you're really worth: a squadron moves only as fast as its slowest ship, and a chain is only as strong as its weakest link. And by doing so, Infinity is showing that it hasn't given up on you yet, and that if you follow its command you'll be rewarded in ways your linear mind cannot even comprehend."

My linear mind was a miscreant in its own right: it's what brought me to the watchtower that Valentine's night. And it had taken over again, the internal monologue flooding my brain and breaking into several imaginary conversations with Martina, Kirk, Vince, Lady 2-7 and Emmanuelle's mother. Repelling the onslaught of prolix thoughts that surfaced like sparks from a fire into which logs were being thrown, I scanned my surroundings. I felt as if I had fallen from an immeasurable height; and yet I fully belonged to this place. As such, it was mine to use in any way I deemed appropriate, and I intended to do just that. I knew that my time on the bench was up, but as I put the socks and sneakers back on my cold feet, I hung on to the blissful feeling blossoming in my throat: that of carrying a golden key to myself that, sooner or later, had to fall into my open hand.

Press on Molly

I avoided everyone who knew me, giving the friendliest smiles and hellos to everyone who didn't, and by the time I reached Sunley I had a plan. The deep introspective plunge I'd just emerged from called for a change of focus, so I decided to expose myself to the public by sitting in the dayroom and working on this novel. This seemed safe: I'd be left alone, yet the presence of others would be distracting enough to give me a break. Besides, I felt inspired and invigorated, my early morning gloom and post-breakfast despondency yielding to a self-sufficient detachment; not using this state for creativity would be criminal simply because it was bound not to last long.

With my laptop's battery half full, I dragged the charger along. It took me a few moments to settle on the most propitious spot: I wanted to sit alone on a sofa facing the center of the room without being blinded by the sunlight or having it flood my screen. In the end I settled for second best, as no such place was available. I could have created one by moving the sofa currently occupied by Selma, who was perusing *The Times* with the look of someone enjoying herself blue, but talking to her was never a good idea—she was the kind of argumentative maniac who could turn a *hi* into a charge of sexism. She was also the ubiquitous intermediary linking the good girls with the bad, all of whom hated her: the bad girls because she was smarter than a dozen academicians, and the good girls because that never proved an obstacle to her sexual involvements with the most desirable men on campus.

I rearranged the sofa cushions and stretched myself out comfortably, anticipating an even more pleasant stretch of productivity. Apart from Selma, the population of the dayroom consisted of Fury and Brooke, who were sharing a bowl of spaghetti drowning in tomato sauce, and Esther, who was whispering something to Adeline: her pants were on, and Tiger wasn't around. *Everyone's probably meeting the community*, I thought, suppressing a lighthearted chuckle. Beguiling passages were burning inside my head, and I was so impatient I didn't wait for the old file to load, opening a new one. But my happiness was short-lived. Before I could lose myself in the first paragraph, Selma exclaimed:

"Oh! My! God!"

If you've ever dealt with people, you probably know that this phrase can be pronounced in a million ways, all equally useless. But this tone wasn't quite like any other I'd ever heard: it got my attention.

"What's that?" Adeline demanded with open hostility, reluctantly taking her blue eyes off Esther's cleavage.

"Guys, you're never gonna believe this!" Selma continued, addressing all the girls in the room with an urgency exceeding even my own curiosity. "There's an article about Martina in *The Times*!"

Had a grenade exploded in the room, decorating it with the brains and viscera of my beautiful neighbors, I would have been less shocked. The elaborate phrases that had been aggregating in my mind a moment ago were wiped out, and I was back to inner silence. Except this time it was accompanied by a profound foreboding.

"She committed mass murder with an ax?" Esther supposed. She could have meant *ex* here.

"She made it on Broadway big time!" Selma's eyes were back to the news. "She starred in what they call *the most expected play of the summer*!"

"What play?" Fury inquired, a severed line of spaghetti falling from her mouth back into the bowl.

"It's called *Skinny Love*. Apparently, it's about a prostitute!" Selma revealed jubilantly.

"Flawd played a whore?" Brooke giggled, showing her yellow teeth. "That's surprising!"

"Let me take a look," Adeline said, dropping onto the sofa next to Selma.

"Here." She solicitously pointed into the newspaper with her finger, which was adorned with several scabs of torn skin. "*While the other defunct creatures of the era …*"

"I can read, thank you." Adeline dismissed Selma like someone who had an old grudge that she wasn't prepared to forgive even for this discovery. "That's gotta be a mistake."

"Well, how many Martina Flawds are out there?" Selma asked

meekly: this meant she was preparing to make Adeline look foolish. "And how many of them did their masters' at Oxford?"

This almost made me choke. A master's at Oxford? I had no clue!

"The play failed!" Adeline declared to Esther a few seconds later in a savage tone. "Most of the audience left before it was over!"

"*Make it fifteen percent*," I thought through the vertigo that clouded my vision. "*If it were most,* The Times *would have reported that no one had stayed*."

"D'you mind if I finish the sauce?" Fury asked.

"Go ahead, I'm full." Brooke covered her half-open mouth, letting out a burp.

"That must be so discouraging!" Adeline continued. "To be on stage and see people leave."

"*Most of the time you don't see shit because of the spotlights*," I thought, wondering why she was happier than Selma. "*That's why the audience has to boo*."

"I wonder why she kept it a secret," Esther said. "Neither Chloe nor Gina knew."

"I know why," Adeline said with ultimate conviction. "The bitch is just too good to talk to little people like us."

"Still, it's a big deal." Fury said pensively, now wiping the corners of her mouth. "I don't know anyone else who's performed on Broadway. Do you guys?"

"Dear, don't you get it?" Selma exclaimed, annoyed with Adeline for taking the role she must have envisaged for herself. "Princesses expect to be ..."

"She probably thought we'd see the pictures on Facebook. I wonder if she's gonna post any now," Esther interrupted with a cannibalistic smile.

"I'm sure she will. That's Broadway. That's where she always saw herself," Adeline reminded. "I just don't understand why she didn't organize some stupid group to invite all of her friends to come to the show."

"She did think she belonged there," Selma said, regrouping and reminiscing. "Remember her complaining there were no good plays with teenagers in lead roles?"

"Don't you guys find it ironic that Flawd played a whore?" Brooke said with a grin. With her slouched back against the edge of the table and her feet up on the bench in front of her crotch, she resembled a venomous insect. "I wonder why she sucked."

"What do you mean?" Fury asked confusedly, as if unsure of what sense of *suck* Brooke had intended.

"Cause being a whore is what she does best," Brooke readily clarified.

The conversation continued for another couple of minutes, the three other girls ridiculing Molly and Fury being impressed with her achievement. Much as she tried, Selma couldn't fit in: everything she said was too cerebral. She channeled her frustration into the nastiness of her remarks at first, but then she wearied and left, tossing the newspaper onto the table between the sofas—so close to me I could grab it without compromising my semi-recumbent position. But I didn't until Adeline and Esther got into a catty quarrel over something that stemmed from them insisting on what an ungrateful twat Molly was. At that point more people appeared, and as Brooke began divulging the news, I extracted the necessary page, folded it to completely conceal it behind my laptop screen, tossed the rest of *The Times* stealthily onto the sofa where Selma had sat, and began the dive.

I must admit: I love reading English reviews of works I did not create: it's both humbling and instructive, as most critics' command of the language exceeds mine. I never rush through a review, taking slow and deliberate glances at each sentence and savoring particularly masterful grammar. Does it make your heart melt when you see gems like *aleatory* and *parvenu* in perfect context? And how about a cascade of synonyms to hammer home the point while avoiding repetition? As for the review itself, it displayed just about every property of a sadistic laceration, the author making an exhaustive list of the subject's flaws before dissecting them one by one to expose the canker. In the first two paragraphs there were three words I didn't know, one of which I'd never seen, and yet it was clear that no critic would allow herself such acerbity had the play not deserved it, at least in part. But alas, part was enough, since my darling strove only for unconditional love. To shine and rule, to be the center of social gravity, to sail beyond reproach: this, I'm sure, was the goal she'd set for herself before setting her foot on stage. And if she'd fallen short, it was nobody's fault but hers.

Two paragraphs later, the number of words I needed to look up had grown to five, but I'd also acquired a fair grasp of the plot. Many critics take the approach of diligently narrating the story; usually it helps neither those who have seen the creation nor those who haven't, but this time I didn't complain. The author didn't spare the spite even when it would have been better, stylistically, to do so—yet her caustic remarks couldn't conceal that the story itself (that of a young woman from a mainly rural district of a mainly rural state who had come to Los Angeles to become a porn star) was not bad.

The critic's main—and personal—issue was that the heroine did not have a greater aspiration. She wasn't another lost starlet who'd come to LA to conquer Hollywood and turned to pornography rather than waitressing: no, starring in adult movies was all she wanted. This provided a segue into a plethora of moral issues, mercilessly exploited by the critic. She did a terrific job of compiling a text that would appeal equally to the hypocritical bigot and the pseudo-intellectual, compelling the reader to turn into either or both of these, if only to obviate the need to argue against the review's seemingly irrefutable stand. As such, she epitomized the very parochial priggishness that has robbed some great people of happiness by putting a moral premium on even that freedom of sexual expression that diminishes no one's quality of life. The more I considered it, the more I respected the playwright, who had the courage to approach such a controversial topic from one of the few angles from which it ought to be approached. But the question of morality is much more often that of faith than of best judgment, and once that faith is inculcated, it takes more than a heavy blow to break through to the truth buried underneath.

I knew exactly why I'd begun pondering morality: the next paragraph dealt with Martina personally, and I was simply afraid. The text was building upon itself, so by now any reasonable reader would have grown indignant and begun demanding a beheading, a curiously popular source of satisfaction among zealous moralists. Yet I couldn't help wondering how exactly it would be done. I paused momentarily, opening the fold that covered the end of the text and catching a whiff of lead in the air; I had always been amazed by the delivery of fresh papers, which seemed to appear in the dayroom like an email set to auto send … *Nah*, I thought. *You never guess these things right anyway*. A self-deprecating smile broke out on my face and I nodded slightly, as if agreeing with someone. And so I read on.

"Amidst the phantoms of adolescent satyriasis hardly suitable for an author in his early thirties, there was an etiolated chance of redemption embodied in Skinny Love herself: a chance dismissed by the female lead with the disdain of a brothel owner who knows better than to disappoint her patrons. While it is true that Ms. Flawd was burdened with a task taxing even for a talented actress, her failure to produce a convincing performance was as devoid of grace as her heroine's motives. Of all the options open to her, it was grotesque that Ms. Flawd elected this, falling into a farrago of farce and the Kafkaesque and flaunting a stupefying knack for shielding sham emotions with counterfeit confidence. Her ability to imitate the fiasco of a sinful soul who takes a fallacy for a phallus is nonetheless praiseworthy, but her readiness to intimate approval of the heroine forces her into a raunchy corner where nothing but lechery may survive. The only fortunate thing for Ms. Flawd is that she never returns to stage after the fourth act, a cunning move on the playwright's part possibly intended to give the heroine the upper hand in the bout for atonement she so desperately needs; yet, much like everything else in this tortuous story, it

comes as a hint too unsure of itself to be taken seriously."

The rest focused on Martina's male counterpart, but I wouldn't have been interested even if they'd had real sex on stage, assuming she'd slept with him anyway. I got up and walked to the bookcase by the entrance where the *Oxford Dictionary of English*, a hard-cover volume printed some fifteen years ago, was located. It was this very tome that had enabled me to breeze through the long and pointless Sunday meetings full of tales of unsanctioned night riding and accusations of indecency that our house parent poured over us after some or all of the usual suspects were once again caught partaking in illegal and otherwise prohibited activities. Three or four times he'd forced me to return the book, making me drag through the wretched tedium along with the others (some of whom were as innocent as I), but most of the time he turned a blind eye on me, probably respecting my passion for knowledge.

All those memories, condensed to a single spark, flashed before my eyes as I opened the dictionary and, leaving its hefty body on the shelf, began to browse. The words I was after were *farrago* and *etiolated*; I was reasonably sure I'd figured out the former, but the latter left me perplexed. Having enlarged my vocabulary (I'd been right about *farrago*), I closed the book, noting a deep scratch on its front cover that had not been there ten years ago, and returned to my laptop.

To say that I was furious would be an understatement: my head was boiling with rage. Blood pulsated in my temples as if driven by a steam pump, and the only thing counterbalancing that sensation was a thin layer of sweat enveloping my chest. I knew this state too well to expect anything good from it, so I kept still. Alas, in accordance with some law of nature, a noisy group entered the room, turning the space into a raucous cage in which every sound rivaled that of a fork screeching on a porcelain plate. I had to retreat at once, and I knew where: Diane had already solved the problem for me.

At Bram's

I took the review page with me and destroyed it in the bathroom, washing my hands afterwards. I expected to find someone in my room, but it was empty. I made sure my valise was locked; then, yielding to a strange impulse, I exited through the window and made a wide circle around the backyard where four or five bodies were bathing in the sun.

The sight of Gina rubbing sunscreen into Rohatyn's naked back momentarily mesmerized me; I shifted to peripheral vision, hoping for a surge of energy, but none came. I dropped my pace to a lazy saunter and faked a smile for the benefit of whomever would see it. All the vigor and inspiration from the bench session became but recollections having no effect on my emotional state, as if I'd gathered them from a book I hadn't written myself. But now I was ready for that personal redemption the critic had mentioned, and I intended to use my chance against all odds.

In a place like AC, there must be at least two people whom you trust: a girl and a guy. You tell them the same thing, hear two diametrically opposed opinions, and build your course of action somewhere in between. I never had the girl, but Bram was a trump of a guy. A language teacher, he was feared for his uncanny ability to see through hypocrisy and treat people accordingly; naturally, he became my best friend. Our interaction took place on a different cognitive level: he understood me without words. He was something like a jaded version of myself, a cynical rendition of my character taken to a comfortable compromise allowing one to function in the everyday world without giving up too many of his desires. He was also married, although I was never sure whether that gave him an edge or dulled the one he had.

Ten years ago, he was a house parent, terrorizing his pupils with his sharp wit and sardonic humor; he also let them drink and fuck as much as they liked. By now he must have grown tired and quit, so I had to find out where he lived, which couldn't be harder than asking the family that had taken his place. I observed the building intently, each step bringing memories that I methodically suffocated in order of appearance. I used to wish that I lived in this house: five of those twelve desirable girls did. Now I was happy I hadn't: I couldn't even remember all of those girls.

The bell of the house parents' apartment was out of order, so I knocked—gently but firmly. I heard steps immediately, but they were rushing away. Different steps followed, and when the door opened with a forceful push, I froze, astounded.

"Bram?" I asked, blinking inanely.

"Insurance agents are not welcome here!" he cried in German. He had grown much older than I'd thought he would, and yet in spirit he was probably younger than I.

"I didn't think you still were a house parent," I said, nervously shifting from one foot to another. "I was expecting someone who'd have no idea where you were."

"Sounds like you owe me for the time and effort saved," he grinned. "Come in."

I stepped forward and gave him a warm hug. He accepted it with the air of someone who deems the ritual excessive, but we both knew it was a show.

"What would you like—wine or whiskey?" Bram asked nonchalantly, extracting himself from my arms and walking toward the minibar. It held no wine, as far as I could tell, but the selection of liquor was impressive.

"Sparkling water," I said, checking out the room. It was empty except for the two of us, but I knew at least one person was listening. I hoped it was one of Bram's daughters. "Your space doesn't feel like I remember."

"Tell me about it," he said, filling two tall, fragile wine glasses with seltzer. "When you have three women in your family ..." He stopped and gave me a long look. "Do you need a special invitation to sit down?"

"I'm a man of good manners," I said with dignity. "And you're a host I respect."

"Then do me a favor: take a seat in that green armchair by the coffee table. And make yourself comfortable in it.

I did; the armchair was remarkably comfortable.

"No trays for you, sir." He handed me one of the glasses. "Can I get you anything to eat?"

"Thank you, but I've had an excellent breakfast recently," I assured.

I drank greedily while Bram dragged an old black rocking chair from the corner and put it on an old oriental carpet in the middle of the room, facing me. He sank into it, stretching his legs forward and crossing them at the ankles. Then he picked up his glass.

"My wife doesn't like this chair," he said jovially, observing me like someone who hasn't made up his mind. "She urges me to throw it out every time she rearranges this room. I have no hand in that either, by the way." He took a long sip from his glass and made a smacking sound with his tongue. "Nice! This is the bubbliest one I've had in a while. I try a new brand every so often," he added almost apologetically. I still didn't know why he was giving me all this theater.

"Try mixing it with juice," I said, studying him attentively. He couldn't have been over fifty-five, but his hair was mostly gray, as was his stubble. But his eyes shone so bright it seemed they would glow in the dark. "Half-half. Just pour the seltzer first, otherwise they don't mix well."

"I used to do that when I was your age. Helped me fight hangovers." He was rocking in his chair, looking somewhere beyond me. "So. How have you been?"

I told him: it took me no more than five minutes, and he had only two questions.

"What about you?" I then asked.

He told me: it took him one minute, and I had no questions at all.

"I'm glad to hear that," I said. "Any big plans for the future?"

"Nothing bigger than getting the hell out of this place!" he laughed. "Which is the same plan I've always had. How about you?"

"Plenty." I paused, staring at my fingernails. "I'm trying to advance to the next evolutionary level, but the past is not letting me."

"Ditch it, then," he said disinterestedly.

"I can't." I shook my head. "I have to draw the right conclusions first."

"Do it, then," he said in the same tone. "Why haven't you yet?"

I thought silently, but every answer that came to mind seemed an acknowledgement of my own weakness. Bram was in no rush, watching me like an actor in the spotlight and drinking his seltzer. Then I gave up.

"Bram, I need to ask you a question," I said. "And it's pretty fucked up, because I know I shouldn't be asking you this question, because asking this question means indulging in the shit that I specifically forbade myself to indulge in. But I'm afraid I have no other option, by virtue of not wanting to have any other option, because I have this one available, and of all the people I ever met on this campus, you're the one I trust the most."

"Such an honor!" he said in German, laughing. "But at least now I know you didn't stop by just to be polite. Go on."

"Last night I heard a very unflattering rumor concerning a lady who happens to play an important role in my life, much to my dismay. At times … At times like this," I continued as I saw a perspicacious spark in his eyes. "When my most cherished hopes come to a screeching halt, leaving me despondent …"

"Just fire," he said in English, his voice instantly stripped of all playfulness. His eyes became cold and sharp; all his affability was gone; he suddenly had the forbidding demeanor of a military judge.

"Okay," I said, stepping off the edge of a precipice. "Have you ever caught Martina Flawd having sex with two guys at the same time?"

"I have," he replied immediately, not a single muscle twitching on his face. "Twice."

He looked at me for what seemed an eternity but couldn't have been more than three seconds, and then he began to laugh. The laughter wasn't quite like anything else I'd ever heard. It was akin to the roar of a facetious bear, which was surprising to begin with but even more so coming from Bram, who was rather slight in build. He was making so much noise I expected the alumni to bang on the door, and just as I thought he'd run out of breath, he started howling.

"Courage," he said a full two minutes later, wiping off his tears with a blue pocket handkerchief. "You are the dumbest smart guy I've ever met."

"Better than the smartest dumbass," I grumbled, waiting for relief. "Listen, you don't need to humor me. If you have, it's all right: she was a big girl, and I am a big boy, so it's not that big of a deal. I'm not gonna kill myself over it, it's just important to me to know the truth."

"You're anything but a big boy," he said sternly, but then another fit of laughter convulsed him. "By the way, who told you this crap?"

I vacillated, looking at him with a silent plea, which he ignored.

"Diane," I admitted at last.

"Who else?" he scoffed. "Do you know why it's so disgusting for a grownup to live on this campus? You can't hide from teenage love affairs. Somehow the drama will always seep through to your own kitchen."

"The two of them fell for the same guy?" I asked cautiously.

"You know nothing about it?" He blinked in astonishment. "Tell me: just how do you manage to be so unaware of the things that are so important to you?"

"I haven't figured that out yet," I confessed.

"When I realized that you had the hots for Molly, I was actually happy. I thought she'd teach you something important." He looked as if waiting for me to ask what that was. I did. "That life is not what you think it is, no matter what you think it is."

I liked this convoluted thought, but I couldn't fully appreciate it: I was too preoccupied with the fact that I still felt the same. There was no relief, nor release, nor recovery. And definitely no personal redemption either.

"Naturally, you were too stubborn to learn that lesson," Bram went on. "But I thought you knew about the nuisance she got herself into with Rohatyn."

"They fucked?" I asked indifferently. It was impossible to find an attractive girl on this campus who hadn't been nailed by that guy. "Wait. They fucked while he was dating Diane?"

"Quite so. And apparently Diane was the first to find out. Chances are, only the three of them know what happened, but I wouldn't be surprised if Diane still hates Molly's guts."

"So trivial," I remarked with sudden annoyance.

"What did you expect, a carnival of originality?"

"The carnal evil of the carnivorous," I mocked him, forcing myself to at least smile and not succeeding.

"Women aren't wired the way men are," Bram said after a pause. "Theirs is the most practical approach to life. You still write?"

I nodded.

"Why?"

"Because I like it."

"Bogus!" he cried, visibly enjoying my discomfort. "You write because you're good at it. But what happens when you bring your poem to the girl you love? She doesn't see it the way you do, does she? Otherwise she would've jumped in bed with you before finishing the first stanza!"

"You think I'm poking fun at you, but I used to be in the same boat," he continued, placing the empty glass on the nearby coffee table. "I wrote for women. And they laughed at me. It took me years to realize that a woman perceives not a piece of writing but the advantage she can extract from it. When you dedicate a poem to her, it immediately boosts her self-esteem. Then she calculates how many people she can boast about it to without compromising her reputation. Although, surely, she counts on you telling everyone: that way she remains on her high horse at your expense. But the value she can extract from your poem depends on your personal value. If you're a popular guy, the poem could be an utter blather and she'll still be yours, shoes and hat. But if you have no social weight, your poem could beat the complete works of Shakespeare without earning a smile from her. You see what I'm getting at?"

"Yes, but I don't see why you're getting at it."

"Because you look like you're about to die."

I knew what he meant. The brooding introspection that was burgeoning between my temples had always found its clearest expression on my face. I was surprised Bram had misread it, but perhaps he was just proving his point.

"There is a time and a place for everything," he went on. "If you came here not to cut the past loose but to chase after it, you're setting yourself up for a pretty awkward bummer. In fact, you got lucky dodging one already. What if Diane had named someone else instead of me?"

"That's precisely what got me," I said, amazed at how distant my own voice sounded. "I couldn't take it that you knew something like that and didn't tell me."

"Didn't tell you?" His eyes rounded in genuine amazement. "Are you serious? Suppose I did catch her: you really think I would tell you?"

"Not directly, of course. But as a veiled joke or a shady reference. You would have probably alluded to it in a deliberately low-key style, just to watch me freak out."

"And what would I have done when I saw you had no clue?" he asked with avid curiosity.

I thought for a moment.

"You got me there. I don't know."

He didn't laugh this time but became pensive, rocking in his chair and looking over my head.

"Listen," he said finally. "You wasted two years on this campus. Wasting any more isn't prudent. In fact, it's stupid. I don't believe you don't have anything better to do now than to ruminate over that girl. Is she even here?" I was mournfully silent. "There we go!" he exclaimed. "If she rattled you to pieces without being here, imagine what would have happened had she come!"

"I don't want to: she always gets the better of my imagination. But you're right: there's plenty to do here, and not enough time. Bram, thank you," I said, standing up, glass in hand. "You've helped me tremendously."

"Not at all. People can only help ourselves. Give me that glass, will you?" he teased. "Listen, you better take care of yourself. Get drunk, get laid, get laid with someone else: that's what reunions are for. Don't fight the flow, and by all means don't concoct the impossible, even if only as a whim in your own head."

"That's the best advice I've heard," I said seriously. "You always save your silver bullet till the end."

"To shoot myself with." He laughed, but this time only briefly. "Get out of here, Courage. The longer you stay, the more I'll miss you."

"Unlikely!" I laughed, shaking his hand. It was the kind of handshake whose strength surprises both parties. "You don't miss anyone, let alone men."

He didn't reply, his eyes still shining with the same brilliance that used to mesmerize me in class. It was the shine of someone who knows better than to replicate the mistakes of others but isn't detached enough to avoid making some terrible ones of his own. And I was afraid that, as our eyes met, he was thinking the same about me.

All the Pain that I Do

I left Bram's apartment and began walking toward the estate shed, a wooden shack in the northern corner of the campus hidden behind by an ash grove. I was in poor shape, but the fog in my head began coalescing into some recognizable shapes. Now the whole story appeared so far-fetched I couldn't believe I'd believed Diane. To have slept with two guys at once did seem like Molly, but to be caught didn't. Was it that yearbook photo that had made me so gullible? And was that also what had sent Diane down the gossiping slope? It was, after all, a remarkable shot that would have been a favorite in a contest for the lewdest image, no matter what nudity it went up against.

The funny thing is: there was nothing overtly inappropriate in the picture. Everyone was dressed, fully and neatly, and no obscene gesture was permitted. All in all, it was a becoming snapshot of a group of classmates pretending to have more fun than was truly the case. Yet the expression on Martina's face spelled unadulterated lust. It was something impossible to appreciate without seeing, but I'll say this much: with her arms thrown over the two handsome lads flanking her, she looked like they were inside her.

It started in her eyes, semi-closed and introspective yet piercing the viewer with uncontested arrogance; it continued along her nose, its tip pointing upward as her nostrils opened just a tad wider to let out a quick breath; it lingered on her lips, which were fixed in that infamous *I know you want me, and I despise you for that* smile; it slid through her neck, twisted slightly to insinuate sexual tension on either side; it bounced between her shoulders, unsure of which one should drop its dress strap first; it hovered over her chest, glowing in the pale amber of oblique sunbeams falling from behind the camera's insatiable eye; and it settled around her breasts, aroused under the lime-green cotton to the point at which perfection is stripped from its verbal prison and becomes one all-encompassing, immutable state.

I shut my eyes, restoring the image. Was there another woman who could look so haughty? So undeniably, irrefutably vain? I knew then beyond a shadow of a doubt that my depraved darling had had sex with several guys simultaneously—and on more than one occasion, too. It must have been something she was curious to try and then liked so much there was no point in stopping. I bet there were times when I'd seen her in the morning after another threesome and, inspired by the healthy roses in her cheeks, taken my poetic license to new heights, depicting her as a paragon of purity anew.

The realization made me sick. I had no problem with Martina's promiscuity: my assumptions were what disgusted me. Somehow I had always combined my monstrous sex drive with a view of Molly as a chaste angel. Did I love her too much to accept her basic instinct? Of course not; it was that very instinct that saved her in my heart on the rights of a sexual match: someone I could be myself with, knowing she'd both appreciate it and feed me a few brilliant ideas.

I gulped thirstily. I felt like I was being watched by a female stranger whose impressions were being registered within my own consciousness. I looked around, but nothing betrayed surveillance. I considered probing the landscape with my ethereal body, but I lacked the energy; besides, for someone seeking to satisfy their voyeurism, I had to be a very boring sight.

I slowly approached the shed. It had been recently painted, and the door was locked. I momentarily regretted having left the pin in the pocket of my jeans, but there was no reason to get inside: it was used mainly for tool storage, although some adventurers did employ it for other purposes. I took a long look at the set of nails I suspected of causing Moses's injury and then took a few steps back to examine the roof. There was some dry foliage at the top.

I circled the shed, touching the walls and trying to discern an alien sound through the chirping of the birds; then I sat on the bench by the door. The sporadic thoughts in my head were all musical, and I began humming one of the tunes. A pair of thrushes frolicked in the air, chasing one another in a series of loops and freezing at the apices before free-falling; after a minute of watching them I got very tired. I lowered my head, covering my face with my hands, but instead of respite there came a picture of me in the khaki-green army uniform I used to wear during estate service. It was an eerily clear image of me on the verge of eighteen, with a winsome smile and a profound sadness in the eyes that were yet to witness more pain than I cared to remember, but the emotion that reigned in me as I observed my younger self shimmering in the golden halo of his best intentions was a unnerving lack of compassion.

And then came a devastating blow. Without any obvious segue or warning, I recalled the one and only other time I'd met a girl like Martina. The resemblance was alarming; I was on a train coming home at an unusually early hour, but the sweet anticipation of lucidity was dashed against the immutability of at least a dozen posters, newspapers and other text and number strings I studied as part of an extensive reality check. In the end, I had no choice but to sit down next to her and strike up a conversation. And then I saw that the similarity between Molly and her went no deeper than appearance.

The girl was nice.

She showed none of the arrogance, none of the self-importance, and none of the superiority complex; in fact, she was as friendly to me as I was to her. It moved me so profoundly that I committed an unforgivable blunder. The day before I'd heard a song that had rendered me smolten, if you'll alloy me this mixture of *molten* and *smitten*. And as soon as I got off the train I texted a link to that song to the number she'd given me. I knew it was real: her phone had rung when I'd called.

She never responded: not to that, nor the two other texts I sent. A few weeks later I left her a voicemail narrating an incredible episode that had happened to me that night: the very night America trumped Clinton. I knew the damage was irreparable, but I wanted to share the magic, even if she didn't believe a word of it. She must have blocked my number: that's what all girls do after meeting a guy who'd give up his life for them, if only to compensate for the mistreatment they'd suffered from the guys they keep on speed dial.

The flurry of thought growing more beautiful, I felt the earth's energy rush into my spine through the bench; I grabbed its sides and flexed my neck muscles, forcing the current higher into my throat and head. With my eyes closed, I was waiting for the sensation of waking up in zero gravity. It never came, but instead the juxtaposition of the girl on the train and Martina took over my mind as two flows of light, the silvery-blue and the fiery-red, amalgamating into a yellowish-green stripe along the middle where they gingerly touched, as though cognizant of each other's lethality. It wasn't a battle of strength but rather a controlled experiment run by something infinitely greater than me, much as a renowned chemist might combine two precious substances his lowly assistant had obtained at risk of both his life and his sanity. No conscious thought disturbed me as I watched this dance, the fiery flow repeatedly lunging and the silvery one parrying effortlessly but not advancing itself. When the strip had widened to about a quarter of my visual field, it turned translucent, revealing a thick darkness smeared with nebulous, stellar clusters; and as I zoomed into it, the flows fluttering and fluorescing on the periphery, I saw the simple answer to what had seemed the greatest predicament of my life.

Who first said that we love not people but the illusions of them we create? Tell him I said *hi*, because the Causal cornerstone of my ruinous romanticism was that I had attributed to the women I loved qualities they couldn't have. And the inimitable Martina Flawd perfectly summarized the disparate fragments of my past since, had I had the courage to step closer and see her for what she was, I'd have realized that I kept her made-up image mothballed because of the only thing I knew about her for a fact: she was the most accomplished whore I'd ever met.

I opened my eyes and returned to the world as if I'd never left it. It was a strange, unfamiliar feeling: as if all the blanks had been filled with the same word, and that word was God's. The bench squeaked under me, and I wasn't even surprised to realize it was the one I'd crafted myself. I bounded to my feet and studied it. The soil of years had penetrated deep into the seat, and the feet were worn down, but the thing retained enough of my soul to elevate the sitter to the minimal altitude required to secure an epiphany.

I squatted in front of the bench and put my hands over it as though it were a furnace. Subtle waves radiated from it, reminding me of the wavelength I'd picked up from a beautiful woman I bumped into on my way to work one morning: the morning when I didn't make it to work until the next day. My thoughts made a somersault through Manhattan and returned to the origin. I realized, angrily, that I didn't even know the source of Martina's parents' wealth. Her train doppelganger flashed before me; that girl had been penniless, burdened with student loans, and had been dating the same guy for two and a half years. And how long had Molly's longest relationship lasted? A fortnight?

I gave the bench a couple of affectionate slaps, and it didn't wobble. I smiled at the thought of how similar we were: nothing ostentatious, perhaps even a bit austere, yet eternally prepared to command a surprise. A squirrel rustled through the fallen leaves and froze between two specks of sunlight penetrating the trees' thick foliage, its tiny, obsidian eye sparkling with reproach. *Had you had the courage*, I thought, *you'd have at least seen her act*. The dull sorrow of having forfeited a beautiful opportunity filled my sinuses, feeling just like when self-pity would assault me after yet another failed attempt at romance.

I rose to my feet in one quick motion, the startled squirrel disappearing into the shrubbery. I felt exhausted, but I couldn't quit—my task remained incomplete. I gave the bench a final glance and bid it a silent farewell; then I turned around and walked away. Each step soaked my marrow with the foreboding of menace, and deep inside the snakes' nest of my deepest anxieties was disturbed. I thought I saw a black shadow rise up behind me, but when I turned with a speed that dizzied me, there was nothing but the languid serenity of trimmed nature reluctant to induce any respectable attack.

Was I really as bad as I felt in moments of weakness? And what did it mean, to be bad? To genuinely wish that something bad would happen? To put one's own interest above that of the rest, even if that meant causing the rest disproportionate pain? To hate God? The last thought seemed close, but there was a gap as I imagined the distance between myself and the power that had created the laws I lived by, without hope of justice—at least in a human sense—which nullified an awfully important part of the equation. God may manipulate me however He wants; but does He still get to feel all the pain that I do?

Catharsis

The Shed was built at the edge of a valley the size of a football field. On the opposite side, hidden in another grove, was the watchtower that had played such a crucial role in my spiritual excavations. It had been around for centuries, and approaching it was prohibited. The authorities feared it would collapse onto an oblivious student, jeopardizing that year's fundraising, but I wouldn't be surprised to discover the thing in the same shape if I stopped by in a thousand years. Although I hoped to have better things to do then than to come back here. This place was too safe, too pampered, too ready to pander to one's sexual desires, and I was fed up with its quasi-amorous spectrum of hackneyed lust. It would have been better to be stranded on an island of cannibals or to face a maniac capable of walking through walls. I imagined fighting him with a medieval blade. No; a maniac wouldn't do without the cannibals, and even they might not distract me from the hell my assemblage point had just reached.

Thoughts besieged me like an avalanche as I paced through the woods, unsure of where to go but knowing I wouldn't miss. My associative thinking being grounded as much in emotion as it was in events, I alternated between recollections of a drunken neighbor kicking his small child for a minor infraction, a romantically hapless coworker sending herself flowers for her birthday, and the denouement of *Donnie Darko*, all of which had left me similarly disconsolate. This gift is a blessing for a writer as it allows for the piecing together of hundreds of scenes in one seamless streak, but its real-life implications are such that, instead of one enemy at a time, you have to deal with a whole legion sharing the most unexpected commonalities.

By the time I reached the foot of the watchtower I was shattered to the point of abandoning thoughts before completing them. I also recalled, quite malapropos, an episode from my first year at AC when Vince had had friends over and we'd all come here to smoke weed. I didn't, because my first adventures with cannabis had nearly ended in my death—but perhaps I should have, as my desire for one of those friends might have subsided. It was an unusual experience: I recognized that the girl was not attractive, yet my pants were practically on fire. The memory of that night came to me in a single chunk, complete and ready for consumption, and it felt like I relived it fully in just a few seconds. After my companions were sufficiently high, we went to the bar and played a few rounds of Durak while drinking. I was waiting for the right moment to talk to the girl, who refused to acknowledge my presence, but then it was all over—on her way to the bathroom, she picked up a stranger who joined her inside.

My fists clenched as the memory of the sight replayed in my mind, rendered in such minute detail that it went beyond the torturous. I could describe it in a few sentences, bringing up the subtlest clues to evoke in every sense a vicarious witness, but if I were to boil this and a dozen other such episodes down to their irreducible residue, I'd be left with the same verdict: I'd only ever fallen in love with women who deserved to be loved the least. It was as if I'd existed in a parallel universe which I'd tried to tie to the one which my body inhabited, unaware that that was as impossible as it was for those women to not take advantage of me.

The watchtower suddenly emerged from the surrounding forest; a grove of ash stood around it, but even the tallest of the trees fell yards short of its top. I jiggled the wooden ladder leading to the first floor; it was as rickety as ever, even though it was probably a newer one. I'd never ordinarily have considered using it, but I had no choice. The entrance yawned a good five feet above my head, and even a champion of pull-ups would have struggled to leverage the narrow ledge under it, which was the only available purchase.

I carefully set my foot on the first step; there was a series of ominous cracks, but nothing broke. I shifted some of my weight onto my hands and proceeded. Two steps later, the ladder shifted off-center. I froze, expecting to fall, but the thing held. Conscious of every part of my body, I continued moving, and a few seconds later I reached the top of the base.

Without a pause, I entered the tower's stairwell. In it, dusk and mustiness reigned. The campus lore claimed that the stairwell was home to a colony of bats, but I'd never seen one myself. Yet, as I began to ascend, a feeling of disgust gripped my throat and upper stomach, and soon I was practically suffocating. At first, I kept going as if nothing were out of the ordinary, but with each step the grip of the feeling became more merciless, until I was compelled to stop and lean on the wall.

I wasn't sure what was happening, but it felt as if the morbidity of my thoughts had finally found their reflection in my physical state. I gasped for air, sweating profusely and struggling to remain erect as my body begged to collapse. I was sick, unexpectedly and inexplicably, and I was certain that not eating since the day before played no more than a trivial part in my condition.

Still leaning on the wall, now supporting my weight with both hands, I continued upward. I felt increasingly wretched but clung to the amusing notion of how metaphorical all this was. I barely had enough strength to move, but had I been able to focus on the vibrations the edifice had collected over its centuries of existence, I'd probably have recognized some of my own at the morose end of the spectrum.

The stairwell curling into an ever-tighter spiral and my legs flagging, I finally stumbled, stretching out across the stairs but hurting only my pride. Tempting as it was, crawling was out of the question, so I waited for the next wave of nausea to subside and got back to my feet. I did not recall the way up ever being so arduous, and when the stagnant air was finally pierced by oblique beams of sunshine, my eyes squinted, refusing to believe what they saw.

As elated as a child who has found a jar full of cookies, I smiled and looked up. The cloudless blotch of noble ultramarine sky that hung over me formed such a dramatic contrast to everything else in my frame of reference that I froze, mesmerized, the iron grip on my throat turning into an evil necessity. As if on cue, my spirit soared; and when I realized that

I could unleash any emotion, without the slightest chance of being observed by another human, I pushed myself clear of the wall, stood up straight, and yelled like I never had before.

Ricocheting off the stone surfaces around me, the stream of my voice became an almost visible axis rooted in the center of the earth and extending into infinity. When I finally ran out of breath, my throat ached and scratched, but instead of coughing I took a gulp of air and yelled again, this time tilting my head back and splitting into two parts: one crumbling under the mounting sickness and the other sloughing off the first part. The axis persisted and intensified, and thrust outward by its momentous, resonant trembling I yelled again, the sickness jerking inside like a pike on a fishing line before coming to a single focal point that lay outside all of my energy fields.

It wasn't like I ran the last few steps to the top of the watchtower; rather, it seemed like the ultramarine blotch fell upon me at once, bringing the parapet of the observation deck to my chest. Then a powerful spasm reverberated through my throat and in a series of violent convulsions I threw up, tears streaming down my cheeks. And the only conscious decision on my part during all this was an unyielding resolve to not let a single drop of my inner contents land on the walls: a task I tackled with great success.

When I was done, I lay motionless for some time. My mouth tasted hideous, and I coughed countless times, but otherwise I was better. Soon I was well enough to rise and survey my surroundings. Planted fields in the distance, the cliffs and the ocean, the patches of campus, the sky and the sun … I tried to identify the sentiments the picturesque view evoked but couldn't reach the answer through the metamorphosis that was taking place within.

The illusions of the past shattered on the dry and dusty asphalt of objectivity, and, perhaps for the first time, I allowed Martina no excuses. And yet she was only an illustration. My life was a ridiculous roundelay of errors caused by my attempts to solve a nonexistent problem: that of not getting what I wanted from the women I loved. But as I wiped my mouth with the back of my hand, observing the distant figures approaching Sunley without any curiosity as to who they were, I was indifferent to the point of being unsure whose life I was contemplating. If God had offered me the chance to spend eternity in this state, my visceral impulse would have been to accept, although I'd still have liked to know what my alternatives were.

There had to be a universal law defining power as self-sufficiency, in which case I was more powerful than ever. Think of the self-proclaimed gurus who spit truisms as though they were maxims, their eyes glazing over with self-appreciation. They will reveal tremendous truths, telling you that money is not a goal but a means, that we cannot change the world but only our attitude, and—worst of all—that happiness lies within. Have you ever wondered why such statements resonate so deeply within us without making us change? I hadn't, until I learned that understanding was not a question of information but of energy.

"*Take you, for instance,*" I thought. "*One of the greatest egomaniacs who's ever lived, you've walked away from copious opportunities to be attain perfection—not because you lacked the discipline to stay put, but because you were ignorant of the status quo. As a result, you now have to face the challenge of forgetting Martina. Now, how does it make you feel?*"

I laughed out loud and spat all the way down to the ground.

"*Good. You were getting hung up on the penultimate step, thinking the problem was you never learning what Molly really was. Who cares? The real problem is: your imagination is outrageous. Normally, the issue with those who raise the bar too high is that they themselves are nowhere near that level. But you raise the bar until it doesn't even matter where you are because it's impossible to find you a human match anyway. Do you realize that what you want from a woman is, in effect, to be a goddess?*"

Something incredible was happening to me. I sensed, with unprecedented clarity, the ultimate impossibility of encountering a suitable woman, and the realization was liberating, as if a long, fruitless path had finally come to an end. I smiled to myself, thinking of the fields I could shift the freed resources to. Dreaming was one option. Bending reality was another. No reward, you say? This spirit alone is worth everything because, even if you are erased, Infinity will still have to reckon with what you were as a creator when it turned all the odds against you.

"*Your fault lay in believing that you'd reached a threshold beyond which everything falls in place. While such thresholds do exist, your opinion on whether you've crossed one doesn't count because it's biased. So, instead of waiting for the status quo to conform to your ideals on its own, take Martina for what she is, an anchor sunk deep into seabed sludge, cut her loose and get to the surface, because there is no point in growing wings if your lungs don't have a drop of air in them.*"

My descent was anything but laborious. Instead of using the ladder, I sat on the edge of the wall, brought my legs as low as possible while leaning on my hands, and hopped off, landing softly on the ground. The sunlight breaking through the maze of foliage drew an intricate pattern around me, and I observe it in admiration until the sun moved and broke it up.

It was much easier to find the campus walking from the watchtower than vice versa, so in a few minutes I was traversing the lifeguard quarters, the outdoor pool shining coldly and the monstrous oak overseeing it from the pine garden swaying solemnly in the breeze. Unwilling to be visible, I took a right at the end of the lifeboat pathway, now moving along the bottom of the cliffs and searching for a suitable spot. The shore was all stones and boulders, the spaces between full of tidal water, and soon I discovered what I sought.

A party of seagulls sauntering nearby took off with vexed cries, brushing heavily through the air, but the waves were so gentle they didn't make much noise. Squatting next to a large rock, I washed my hands, scooped up some water and brought it to my mouth, but as soon as the water hit my taste buds I began coughing compulsively in disgust. Then I spat, the residual saltiness intensifying my thirst, but grabbed several more handfuls, swishing the water around my mouth until my teeth hurt.

When I was done, an unanticipated thought possessed me. I had never climbed to the west of the campus and, judging from a distance, there wouldn't be any soil to spoil my first attempt. Ridding my hands of droplets in a series of shakes, I slowly approached the cliff. It was noticeably slanted, offering all sorts of cracks and holes to exploit, and, not thinking twice, I let my body take charge. I ascended in a straight line, even though it would have been easier to zigzag, and when I'd covered the last stretch it still proved not hard enough.

I was right about the soil: at the top, there was none.

But there was Beatrice.

Beatrice

"Courage? What are you doing here?" she asked, as if she'd been prepared to see me all along.

"You know what? I'm getting tired of hearing that question." I landed on the grass next to her as if she were my old lover, skipping only the part where my arm goes around her shoulders. "Why don't you say something like *Oh my God Courage so good to see you I've been missing you awfully all these years how've you been?*"

"It's not every day that I see a guy scale a pretty high cliff to get up to me," she said, probably taking her remark for a paragon of plausibility.

"It's not every day that I scale a pretty high cliff to discover a girl of your value sitting at the top all alone," I returned.

"A girl of my value? What do you mean?"

"The social value: a convenient label that quickly tells you who's who," I said, as if explaining that two plus two equals four. "People are measured on a scale from One to Nine, and on that scale, you are a Seven Minus."

"Who's a Nine?" she asked with a tinge of surprise.

"A true ruler of the physical world. People like the Rothschilds, the Rockefellers, or the Queen of England. The Eights are billionaires and leaders like Bill Gates and Bill Clinton. The Sevens are mostly the cream of pop culture and sport: Taylor Swift, Johnny Depp, Lionel Messi, and so forth; high-profile multimillionaires also fall into this category."

"Why are there no Tens?"

"The Tens would include Jesus Christ, Buddha and the Prophet Muhammad, but such folks are transcendental."

She laughed like the pampered child she'd always been.

"Courage, how do you come up with these crazy ideas?"

"This one isn't mine. In fact, I paid money for it. But it was a good deal."

"I don't like being a minus," she complained.

"Then start singing."

"I have no voice," she said, as if revealing a dark secret. "What's your number?"

"Well, that question is secondary to a much more pertinent one. Namely: what is a Seven Minus girl with your looks doing at the top of the Atlantic cliffs all by herself while there are dozens of men nearby who'd throw me right off this cliff to take my place?"

She gave me a long, pensive stare that aroused me more than anything had since I first set foot on campus last night. Beatrice was what I call *sexually excellent*: the kind of girl who'd hit on a guy first, drag him to bed and make sure he gets the sex of his life. As such, she had been immaculate with me: she hadn't dragged me anywhere. I had never loved her, but I desired her anyway: for her stupefying appearance, and for one unique gift that I had never seen replicated even in movies. Regardless of what she wore, Beatrice looked naked in it.

Nevertheless, her knee-high black dress was gorgeous: it alone increased the appeal of any woman wearing it by a power of ten, but she also wore a string of coral-colored beads with it; and, owing to the length of the string, it went quite a long way. The image was already so potent that the red hairpin at the crown of her head was but the cherry on top of the icing of her meticulous makeup. Had she been carrying it since last night? *She hasn't slept at all*, I warned myself. *Be careful.*

"You go first," she said at last.

"OK," I shrugged, a smile of indifference touching the corners of my lips. "I've just undergone a profound catharsis that liberated me from a load of unreasonable shit that plagued me over the last decade, which culminated in a violent seizure with subsequent puking, so I wanted to wash my mouth with seawater, which isn't too much better than vomit around here. Once I was done, I remembered that I used to climb these cliffs with the ease of a wild jaguar and felt the urge to prove to myself that the whole business was, in fact, a piece of cake. So, here I am. Your turn," I concluded, the corners of my lips curving upward.

"Something tells me you didn't have much company while doing all of this," she said slyly, and it felt as though a vicious elf had just struck a match inside my briefs.

"None since I left Bram's house," I retorted bravely, wondering what the fire extinguisher might look like under the circumstances. "Why, are you waiting for someone?"

"No, I'm hiding from everybody. But you can stay, if you want."

"First, I need to know something." I'd seen too many flukes like this to be serious about it yet. "Why did you come here specifically? Of all the places you could have chosen instead?"

"I just did."

"Have you ever been here before?"

"Many times, when we were kids."

"Alone, I mean."

"Probably not."

"I should tell you about this place, then. It favors those who like seclusion. *Seclusion* means being alone," I added, my eyes sliding up and down her body. The shoulder straps of her dress were begging for an opportunity to fly off.

"Well, seclusion is exactly what I wanted. Maybe I should tell you," she added with a note of doubt as I kept watching her. She was unbearable, her face as strong a magnet as her body. "Or maybe not. Do you ever get the feeling that, whatever you do, it doesn't matter?"

"I live in it."

"Then what stops you from jumping from these cliffs right now?"

"I just came from down there. But, to answer your question: curiosity. Since I know it doesn't matter whether I jump or not, I might as well not jump and see what happens."

"It seems to take a lot of energy." She turned her head away, now facing the ocean and squinting to protect her eyes from the shimmering glare on the water; yet her attention was mine. "I envy ghosts: they don't have bodies."

"I bet a lot of ghosts would love to have yours," I said matter-of-factly. "But for most people, the body is the source of utmost pleasure. Although they pay the price. They're perennially grounded by their animalistic drives. Imagine: you're having sex, and the physicality of it is the only thing you can perceive."

"I'm not sure I know what you mean."

"I know you don't, but neither do I," I confessed. "Hard as I try, I can't conceive of sex where the physical comes before the psychological. There were numerous occasions in my life when the story of getting in bed with the woman was the most exciting part of the sex. And yet, for most people sex is all about the rubbing, and even their orgasm is not that different from the relief of taking a piss."

"Why are you telling me this?" she asked, amazement ringing through her Southern accent.

"Because you're not telling me what happened between you and Moses last night," I explained.

She blinked three of four times. Then she made up her mind.

"How did you know?"

"I noticed."

"Very observant." She bit her lip. "I thought no one saw."

"I didn't. But that was a giveaway in itself. You guys can't simultaneously disappear from a reunion like this without raising a red flag. By the way, how did he get that scratch? Did he fall from the roof of the estate service shed?"

She gave me a penetrating look.

"Courage, what do you do for a living?"

"Various things, why?"

"You talk like a detective." I sustained an interrogatory pause. "No, he didn't fall. I pushed him. And I don't regret it. Do you have a lighter?"

"Only matches," I said, watching her produce a pack of cigarettes from a pocket I didn't even realized her dress had.

"You want one?" She put one in her mouth, its long, slim tail hanging a great deal below her otherwise impeccable lip line.

"Yes, but I don't smoke. Today." I drew my hands close to her face. No recoil. I struck a match, watching her pucker her lips in advance. Then she took a long, greedy drag.

"I'm confused by men who don't smoke but have matches." Beatrice said, exhaling; she held the cigarette between her knuckles, dropping the hand at the wrist like a noir star. I automatically scanned her ethereal Body, but I could have saved the trouble: the amount of sexual energy she generated was practically visible to the naked eye.

"Some men begin smoking just to find a match," I said.

"Remember when you sold us cigarettes?" Now she was looking at me as if measuring me in some way. "Yours were the best, and they cost the same."

"My fondest memories of this place," I said sincerely.

She took another drag, flicking the ash with a nonchalant move of her thin fingers.

"I thought everyone's best memories from here were about sex."

Nothing worth saying came to mind. Now that the nicotine started working on her I saw she was nervous. And then I realized four things. One, that I was a celibate for the next seventeen hours or so. Two, that I wished that wasn't the case. Three, that Beatrice's ethereal body was making an unequivocal advance towards mine. And four ... but let me explain the third first.

Sexual contact between physical bodies is always the lagging result of a connection established between the higher subtle bodies. Depending on the habitual position of the assemblage point, the initial contact can either be very high, up to the buddhial body, because in the atmanic one there is no more difference between the male and the female. People who talk about pure love mean a connection of the mental bodies; sexual encounters, as you're aware by now, are guided by the ethereal body. So right now this noble part of Beatrice clung to mine, much as mine had clung to Lady 2-7's. The main difference was that I engaged the mental body and its beautiful ideas as well, while Beatrice ignored that possibility, inviting me no higher than the Emotional and not emphasizing that level too much either. Put simply, she was horny and wanted to fuck. See, it doesn't take being a sorcerer to use the subtle bodies; yet a sorcerer does it consciously. But there was also the fourth thing. What was it? Oh, I remember. That of all the women within reach, it was Beatrice whom I desired the most.

"I wanna ask you something." She tilted her head back, exhaling the smoke toward the lazy sun. A dozen possible responses flashed in my head as I remained silent. "May I?"

"Yes," I said.

"How does it feel for a man to have sex with someone he doesn't love?"

"Depends on the man." She was finally getting to it. "Some despise themselves if they do it once. Others die of old age not having loved once, and all they feel is pride. But it's still harder to have loved a dozen times without ever having had sex with a woman you loved."

"Is that your case?"

"No. I went up to thirteen."

We were silent again. I thought she'd follow up with a question, but then I realized she wasn't thinking about what I'd said.

"Do you know what it feels like for a woman?" she asked finally.

"No. But I know what it feels like to you."

She turned away for a moment.

"You wanna know why I came here?" she asked. "I came because I realized that everything I thought about the man I loved was wrong. Is it too much to expect from a man," she continued, fully aware of how irresistible she was blowing out the smoke with her eyes squinted, "to expect that he'll be manly?"

"I see …" I chuckled in a way that worried me: I did that only when I had an unbeatable hand.

"No, you don't," she snapped before restoring her look of seduction. The line of ash was about to drop right onto her dress.

"What did you expect? That those fairy tales the media show you will come true? Dear, it's time you knew: a person pretending to be happy in love is lying ninety-nine percent of the time."

"Are you saying there are no good men?" she said defiantly.

"There are plenty, and you've snubbed all those who've crossed your path," I chuckled again. "A good man is undesirable to women as everyone takes advantage of him. A desirable man, on the other hand, takes advantage of people himself. Especially of women."

"You're such a cynic," she scoffed. "No wonder. To love so many times, and …" She stopped, fishing for the right thought.

"Yes?" I inquired, genuinely interested in her choice of words.

"And to not fuck even one of them!" she declared.

"You should have said *to not have fucked*," I sighed, disappointed. "But we were talking about you."

And there it was: the brisk, sharp move of her hand that drew the line under all that happened between us. It started from the elbow, accelerating through the wrist and culminating at the tips of her fingernails, which flashed dangerously close to my eyes as she threw the cigarette toward the edge of the cliff. I watched it become a gray dot in the air, resembling a fly soaring in search of some unseemly sustenance, and my only thought was: did she have enough to put it over the edge? And as the fly, the dot, the butt and everything else it could become in the eyes of the beholder, even if for a moment, reached the apogee of its flight and started its descent I yelled as if the sound could prolong its hyperbolic flight and carry it into eternity. But alas, this transient toy of Beatrice, still burning over the heady sweetness of her lips imprinted on the tarred filter, landed in the dust as quietly as a solitary soul, seeking solace, yet missing the boat to paradise by less than half a foot.

I thought she'd complain, or taunt me, or cover her ears, or do some other inane thing an ordinary woman would do in her place, but she only stared, her emerald eyes mesmerizing me as I bathed in a feeling of unadulterated loneliness.

"Courage," she said quietly. "Are you insane?"

"Why?"

She batted her long black eyelashes a few times, as if unable to fathom me.

"Because you are alone with a pretty girl who likes you, and you have not even kissed her yet," she said.

The surest way to never sleep with a beautiful woman is to miss the first time, I thought. It was preposterous, to wish for all women to be like that, but I still wished they were. I wanted Beatrice madly, but I couldn't take her. See how sorcery screws you? If you make good on your vows you'll be rewarded amply, but the trick is to be consistent in the face of hardship and not grow despondent when the reward that is already overdue doesn't come.

"What? The? Hell?" I suddenly heard. Beatrice's intonation was superlative, but I couldn't figure what she meant. Until I realized I was crying.

"I'm crying," I confessed guilelessly.

"I see that. Why?"

"Got emotional." I was telling the truth.

"You look like you're about to die."

"Do I?"

"I hope not. Is it because of me?"

"No."

Silence followed.

"What hurts you so much, Courage?" I heard after a while.

"Nothing, anymore."

"You shouldn't lie to me, after all. I may hurt you."

A joint cracked in my body as a gentle reminder to stretch: it'd been a while since I'd done it last, and the grass at the edge of the cliff wasn't too lush.

"Please don't," I said.

"You came here because of a woman." It was a statement. "And now you're wishing she was here instead of me."

In her Southern accent, this sentence acquired perfect piquancy.

"I heard that one should never wish to be somewhere else: a warrior because no situation is better or worse than any other, and an ordinary man because he never knows where he will find his death," I said.

"Are you a warrior or an ordinary man?"

"I'm neither. But I'm surprised you should ask."

"I don't know you," she reminded. "You've always been a slippery one."

"You mean elusive?"

"No, not illusory. But no one could say they knew you."

"What do you want to know?"

"I want to know," she began in a tone that could only be described as sultry. "What do you want me to do?"

"To be happy," I said honestly.

"No," she shook her head as if I'd said something idiotic. "I mean, what do you want me to do *for you*?"

The question more than puzzled me: it brought my thoughts to a dead end. I observed a moment of inner silence. Then I realized she was serious.

"To be happy," I repeated.

"I'll let you do anything you want; how about that?" Beatrice continued, looking me in the eyes with fierce intensity. "I'm very kinky, and if I don't make the man come twice I don't count it as sex."

"That makes you an excellent lay," I said didactically, suddenly sensing great danger. "And on top of that, you're smoking hot. But, much as I'd love to take advantage of this, I'd already made up my mind. I won't have sex with anyone until sunrise on Sunday."

"You've always been a good boy, Courage," she continued, and her tone made me shiver. "I bet you've never come inside a woman. Or have you, naughty boy? You can come inside me, too. What do you like better: to come into the pussy, or to come into the ass? Will you come inside my ass, please?" she said imploringly. "I will lick off every drop of cum that clings to your dick and swallow it."

"This dirty talk coming from you ..." I rasped, trying to rearrange my thinking. Her voice crawled inside my consciousness, igniting every cell responsible for arousal. "It's beyond fabulous."

"But that's what I want to do!" she exclaimed, jumping to her feet with grace a panther could envy. "I wanna be a bitch you use as you like. Don't you want to use this body of mine? Come on; take a peek." She threw her head back and bent down, pulling her dress above her hips. "You like it?"

She wasn't wearing any underwear.

This was getting serious. Beatrice wasn't the sanest person who'd ever walked the campus, and it seemed that she'd been through some trauma recently; but I was more worried about myself. I was dying to have her, and it was only the saturnine discipline that kept me where I was. I knew I had to bring out more than I'd woken up with today to resist that berserk madness that made the entire area between my legs one scorching reminder that I hadn't ejaculated in exactly forty days and forty nights.

"Beatrice," I said, staring into the middle of her forehead when she straightened up and faced me, her legs wide apart, her dress up, her left hand playing with herself and the right behind her back. "You are breathtakingly gorgeous. In fact, I keep crying as I speak because I cannot regard you without awe: both for your beauty and for your daring. It's impossible to express in words how much I want to have sex with you, doing a lot more than you mentioned because, let's face it, you have no idea who you're dealing with. But I'm under an obligation that prohibits me from doing so until tomorrow morning. Thus, my answer to you has to be a respectful *no*."

"You fucking wanker!" she shrilled, and the next thing I saw was a stone hurled at me.

I tried to dodge it but couldn't, the memory of the stone launching from Beatrice's hand (as well as the puzzlement as to when she'd picked it up) lingering in my head just a little too long; then there was a sharp pain, black spots, a muffed thump.

I was unconscious for only a second, yet Beatrice could have finished me off if she'd wanted to because, for that second, I was nothing but a helpless target. But when I lifted my head, I saw her slim silhouette scurrying away, her dress assuming its place along the contours of her body, and a thin line of milky smoke coming from one of the nearby fields. Had I offended her? That would be sad. I still wasn't sure why it was not okay for a man to reject a woman. Even Beatrice could have a sexually unlicky … I mean, unlucky day. Could Molly? I paused for a moment that felt long. God. That girl had one hell of an ass!

That What I Am

I sat on the ground and rubbed where it hurt; I had a slight scratch, a rivulet of blood trickling down under my hair, but nothing serious. Angry as she was, Beatrice could throw stones with only so much force, and I'd dodged pretty well, except for the miscalculation. Or had I wanted to be caught in the head? No, rather: had I wanted to bet my head to prove that I could dodge the stone that way? In retrospect, it seemed more reasonable to have fallen flat onto the ground or to have rolled to either side, although if I hadn't done that fast enough she'd have gotten a piece of my body which had soft spots. Still, risking the head? But then again, hadn't I been so sure I'd dodge it?

I got up and began moving toward campus along the cliff edge, and the further I got from Beatrice's spot, the less I thought about her, instead rewinding the events of the previous night, which had suddenly acquired a new perspective. The topic that consumed my attention was the Cliff Girls outing. Yesterday I'd believed it was my debonair persona that had procured the invitation, but now I saw that all Diane had wanted was to punish me for the way I handled her during that initial exchange. The invitation that had purportedly originated from below had to have been passed down by Diane herself: she must have thought I had no chance against the impact of their collective beauty. Why are they always so oblivious? But she wouldn't do this just for me. She'd also have wanted to throw her girls into the fire, if only for the smell of it. Which meant she knew that someone in the clique was wet for me. That, of course, was sheer treasure, because a Cliff Girl who slept with me would immediately fall into the abyss of contempt. But Diane was upset thinking it was Bridgette; did she have someone else in mind, and was that Gina? If so, the poor thing had better not tell anyone about Visual Rescue. I had a feeling she could, but who would listen? Except for Diane?

I slowed down, ruminating. Could the world really be so fucked up? And me, too, as part of that world? For myself, I could answer for sure, but Diane remained. I was recollecting snippets of her as I remembered them by the fire. Was she attractive? Why would a polite answer be expected to that question? But the real question was: was she more attractive than the rest of the Cliff Girls combined? And she, among them all, had had my trust! Blind trust, I should say. And for what reason? Why would I ever have expected her to like me? Not sexually, of course, but as a person. Studying the world through that girl's eyes, how did I look? And would anyone know it but she?

I call this subjective objectivity: it's when a beam of light is caught in your glasses where it is invisible to the rest of the world but more real to you than anything else you see. I almost stopped, yet willed myself to keep going, now considering our early morning exchange and trying to come up with a justification for it. *Okay, let's say that she had the right to lie about Molly. For whatever reason. For you not needing that information anyway, for instance. Does that change anything? Because, in any feasible hypothetical scenario, you remain nothing short of a bloody bastard. You do end up a bastard often, have you noticed? And is it ever for a good reason? Except it also doesn't matter if you are ready to die knowing that your reason is best.*

I wasn't ready to die, at least not until I jotted down a few thoughts, which I did as soon as I reached my room. It took a while, going over and editing the same paragraphs multiple times, but no satisfaction was to be had. On the contrary, I had to deal with a very annoying notion, suspecting that the words I'd just poured out were to be deleted from the final draft as unnecessary and distracting. I read the excerpt once more; I liked its playful assertiveness and surreptitious humor, but the sensitive subject matter compelled the reader to take sides, which is usually a hindrance in a love story. So, having reduced the new text to the lowest possible point size, I held the laptop across my chest like a shield and walked to the dayroom.

This time, it reminded me of what it used to be on Saturdays back in the day: bright, quiet, and largely empty. Aside from a group of married good girls on the couches by the bookcase, the only party present was one eating sushi for lunch at the table nearest the glass wall. It was an elitist kind of lunch. Presiding over the table with her back toward the door was Selma, with Gina and Chloe flanking her and facing Fury and Nicolette, respectively. Thalia and Evangeline occupied the right-hand extremity of the table, and on the left end sat Moses and Bartholomew, whose presence was as surprising as it was unpleasant. They were engaged in a sluggish conversation about politics, the only person interested in it being Selma; the rest, vexed to various degrees, couldn't wait for an opportunity to talk about something else.

It'd be a shame to let them down.

"How are you guys doing?" I said, approaching the table.

I was ignored by everyone, although some wouldn't have done it without the pressure of the others. Those who ignored me willingly each did it in his or her own quaint way, some freezing for a split second, some adding an unnecessary move, some suddenly putting an excessive focus on what they were doing. They all thought they did a good job, though.

"That's a lot of ginger," I said in a pleasantly genuine tone when my eyes landed on the box full of pickled root: it was so huge it could have been in the dining hall at dinner time. "Who got all this?"

"Diane," Fury said through a roll. "Help yourself; I'm sure she won't mind."

"Thanks, I'm on a diet today," I chuckled, circumventing the table and sitting down between her and Nicolette: into a space that had to have been Diane's. The bench was too far from the glass wall for to lean on the latter, so I straightened my back and prepared to work.

"You shouldn't be," Evangeline said disapprovingly as I opened my laptop. "You're already skinny as fuck."

"I hoped you'd say *as love*," I said, my fingers dancing over the keyboard in an unstoppable foxtrot as I was empowered by an idea of how I could capture every word without repeating the predictable beats.

FURY. What are you typing?
ME. A novel.
CHLOE. Poetry doesn't work anymore?

[*Pause, keys clicking.*]

NICOLETTE. What's it about?

ME. Sex and love.

The girls fidget in their seats.

BARTHOLOMEW. What hasn't been written about that!
ME. I haven't read it all to know.
THALIA. Well, what makes your novel different?
ME. You'll have to read it to find out.
SELMA. Is anyone we know in that novel?
ME. One second. [*Pause, keys clicking.*] Everybody present.

The girls exchange worried looks. Evangeline gets up, approaches me and tries to see the screen, leaning over Nicolette's shoulder.

EVANGELINE. Show me!
ME. No.
GINA. That's unfair.

[*Pause, the clicking stops.*]

GINA. You can't just write about us without us knowing.

[*The clicking resumes*]

ME. I just told you.
THALIA. She means without us knowing what you're writing.
ME. Yes, I can.
BARTHOLOMEW. You aren't typing up this conversation, are you?
ME. You'll find out when the book is published.
MOSES. Any chance it will be?
ME. Why wouldn't it?
SELMA. Cause most books aren't.
THALIA. I'd rather watch a movie than read a book.
NICOLETTE. Me too.
ME. Would you guys be able to star in a story about yourselves?
CHLOE. Why wouldn't we?
ME. Cause most people aren't.

I saw what was happening, which gave me the kicks of a poker pro who's just got a sure tell on the largest stack. The party had turned into a single organism, the previously disparate players ganging up on me like the good jackals they were. From now on, it was but a matter of time before they would bite, and I couldn't wait to find out who'd be the bravest. I quickly counted their noses; excluding Fury and Moses, there were seven.

I chuckled again.

Did they really think it was enough to take me down?

They kept talking, taking turns at taking stabs at me, and I felt sadness aggregate behind my eyes. How could I help them if even Chloe and Gina were treating me as a foe? Yet they had no choice. For them to be on my side now meant acknowledging that they'd been wrong in the past. And how often do people admit their mistakes, especially in matters of intrigue? No, it was simpler to wait for me to show the first vulnerability and then to sink their teeth into it, inviting everyone around to follow suit until I was trampled upon and thrown into the ocean with a stone tied around my neck. Such had been my lot from birth: to snatch what was mine by right in bloody and unequal fights, and I would be a darn fool to complain about it. None of the heights I'd already attained and had yet to attain before leaving this world for good could be surmounted without this pressure. And since I had no power to either change these people or to show them how much more rewarding their lives might be were they to change their cannibalistic stratagems, I could only thank them for their ruthlessness because, regardless of whether they tried to cut my throat or ignored my existence entirely, they compelled me to evolve.

Suddenly I had another moment of internal vision akin to what I'd experienced on the cliffs before leaping, except with my eyes open. I saw myself as a fiery angel in the middle of scorched battlefield. My body was roughly its own size, but my wings were immense, stretching out wide and blazing with brilliant whiteness. I was being assaulted by a legion of dark shapes, and there was a sword protruding from the right-hand side of my chest, but I couldn't die yet as I was covering for the retreat of my army. They were fleeing, quivering souls that seemed almost transparent, and the thought of improving their chances brought me a euphoria the threat of death could not annul.

Then my perception shifted as I saw the commander of the dark force; a furious beast, he turned crimson with rage scolding his generals for failing to vanquish me despite my mortal wound. Next, I was on board a plane, the crew struggling to calm the fear-crazed passengers as I remained motionless in my seat, trying to get the situation under control with pure cognition. Images flashed faster, ranging from a tribal sacrifice in a lush green jungle to a futuristic city on a planet with two suns, but the leitmotif was the same: the endless pity for the poor souls who knew no better than lowly egoism, and the obsessive urge to show them that everyone in the universe has a shot at matching Infinity. The pictures faded and merged into a single rotating spiral, its origin lying in blackness condensed to a quantum inside a whole. And as I came close to diving into its fathomless, static cosmos, I understood that vehemence was contagious, and knew what my next novel would be about.

The arms of the spiral were still visible in the dayroom when Bridgette, her hair and clothes unusually disheveled, stormed in. She noticed neither the good girls nor the few other couples who had appeared in the meantime, heading straight for the final table. Her breaths were rapid and forceful; she looked like she'd just seen a malevolent phantom.

"Guys!" she said in a voice that trembled with confusion, impatience and fear.

I was the only one who paid any attention: the rest acted as if she wasn't there.

"Guys, goddamn it!" Bridgette yelled then in a voice that sent a chill down my spine, smashing her miniature fist against the tabletop.

Silence followed. Everyone stared at her. My heart was racing, but I slowed my pulse in time to withstand the blow that nonetheless moved me to within an inch of my death: the ultimate region where everything one did or didn't do truly counted.

"Guys!" Bridgette whispered, gulping. "She's here. Martina. Flawd."

V

Sweet, Vicious, Badass

No one visibly reacted to these words, but no one struggled with it more than I.

God, how hard it became! My body turned into a single electric current, my throat desiccated, my eyes liquified. The previous interpretation of reality, whatever it had been, was gone. I forgot not only what I had been thinking about but whether I had thought at all. Fairy tale, myth, phantasmagoria: everything blew up into a mottled mixture, threatening to transmogrify into the grotesque.

And then it did.

When Martina entered the dayroom, I thought I would die. Not faint. Not go crazy. Die. It had nothing to do with the past: had I seen her then for the very first time, I'd still have fallen for that ferocious flair, whoever'd showed it. But then again, who else could? In her crimson cardigan, white dress shirt, dark-blue pants and violet heels she defined the whore of a princess undecided as to whether she should castrate all these men and burn all these women immediately, or have an orgy with the lot of them first. I was literally spellbound but then, as if emerging from the normally inaccessible corners of my perception, a vague notion came to the rescue; and just before she came close enough to make not noticing her preposterous, I looked in her eyes. There it was again, the cognitive split, and from some higher level I realized that everything I had done before she appeared was irrelevant because I hadn't loved anybody. Now I did. Better still: I loved her.

She spared me the first trial by ignoring me completely, and I couldn't have been more thankful: I simply could not speak. There was a glass half full of water before me, and I told myself not to drink from it under any circumstances. Then I carefully looked around without turning my head.

The clique was weak and uncertain: without Diane present, the girls tended to adore Molly. With Diane, they let the two decide who'd drive the chariot. There'd be sporadic attempts by Chloe, Fury and even Nicolette to take over, but those were one-offs that neither lasted long nor ended well. But more importantly, I was growing progressively more aware of my boner which, in turn, was growing progressively larger.

God, why did it have to be so hard when it was already unbearable? Even Selma could finish me off right now, and I didn't want to do anything about it as my genitals, lower back and sternum coagulated into a single fucking pyre. *This is what the inside of a nuclear reactor must be like*, I thought. Then my chest responded to the unsustainable pressure from below, loosing an arrow of fruity nectar into my throat, causing a buzz in my temples that was disorienting but nevertheless pleasant. Had the buzz stopped? I wasn't sure, but the crown of my head now demanded an egress into Infinity. I saw a magenta oval pulsate around it for a heartbeat or two, and then my mind opened like a tin can. Everything fell into place, although I wasn't sure how exactly; I clung to this holy state with all I had, but my concentration was rapidly waning. My infernal angel, despite taking me to these tremendous heights, also absorbed all of my attention, draining me of energy.

"So good to see you, honey!" Chloe lied excitedly in the meantime as Molly exchanged cheek kisses with her. "We thought you wouldn't come! What kept you so long?"

"A most brutal conflict," she said, almost, but not quite, apologetically. "Two of the things I couldn't wait for had to happen on the same day. Where does this lovely necklace come from? It looks like it cost an old man's fortune."

"Anything serious?" someone asked. I tried remembering who'd read the news with Selma this morning, running scenarios of how things could go wrong from here. The possibilities were too numerous, and I instantly stopped.

"Not serious at all, as it turned out, which is not to say that I don't mind." Martina took a step back, putting the table fully into her field of vision. "But I'm here at last. It would have been tragic to miss your pretty faces!"

"Why are you doing such a poor job of staying in touch!" Nicolette exclaimed. "I've been in New York twice in the last two years, and I could've seen you!"

"Why didn't you call? I do poorly figuring out where my friends are by the pictures they post."

"If I still had your phone number ..."

"Try Twitter," she said, as if talking about something utterly unimportant. "I keep my profile real. It was hacked recently, but I got it back."

"You were hacked?"

"Alas. Not pleasant, and a great deal of loose ends to tie up."

"Would you like some sushi?" Fury inquired. "We have plenty left."

"That's a lot of ginger," Martina observed, advancing and sliding between Chloe and Evangeline. She was now within arm's reach, with her left side to me, and it was so bright I nearly cried. "I would have tried it, but I overate last night: so badly that I shouldn't be eating again. Ever."

Have some ginger, I thought. *It'll whet your appetite for other things, too.*

"So," she continued in a perfectly ambiguous tone. "Since I've missed last night's party, will you reveal what happened?"

"Oh, we had a grand night!" Chloe exclaimed, a beatific smile widening on her face. Did she actually fancy Molly? "The welcome dinner was so very nice, and then we went to Sosh …"

Martina's face assumed a knowing look. Now she resembled a character from some of my poems. Which weren't even about her … I think.

"I bet that's when it all started."

"No, before that." Fury hated beating around the bush. "Some peeps had already got wasted at Marcross. Most made it through dinner, though."

"I'm sure everyone was fine. Moses, what have you been up to?"

"Not much," Moses was taken by surprise. I had no idea they had a history. "Just chilling. Missed the cliffs, though."

I didn't believe my ears.

Next, I made a blunder that went unpunished: I gave him a penetrating look. I wanted to see if he realized anything, ready to spin him one way or the other, depending on how the rest of the conversation would go. He'd inflicted the curse upon himself, and if I had to sacrifice him for Beatrice's sake, I'd do it without thinking twice.

"The Cliffs!" Molly said, as if announcing the arrival of a rich uncle whose will could be changed at very short notice. "That's something I wouldn't miss for the world. Now I need to know everything. But first of all, I need to know why Moses didn't come."

"I didn't know about it, all right," he said a few seconds later when even Nicolette knew it was his turn to speak. "No one told me."

"We couldn't find you, man!" Bridgette said, perhaps too hastily. "Both you and Rohatyn, you guys just disappeared."

"And I bet you guys didn't disappear together." Molly looked like she was about to start her famous deduction game. She had always been eerily good at that. "Let me think. Who did go to the cliffs in the end?"

A pause followed.

"A lot of those people must be sitting at this very table," she went on.

"Bridgette, dear, tell me: did you go?"

"Sure I did. I got the drunk bitches together in the first place."

"Oh, you weren't drunk!" Gina protested.

"And I was sober," Nicolette added.

"So." Martina had to be solving for Rohatyn. "Fury, Diane, Chloe plus the three of you." She held a pause. "So? Are you telling me last night's outing was all gals?"

"Courage, why are you silent all of a sudden?" Gina demanded. "You aren't even taking notes anymore."

"Courage went with us," Nicolette revealed apologetically when I didn't speak.

Something changed in the vibe Martina was giving me, but she still denied me the first look.

"Ladies, your resourcefulness never ceases to amaze me," she said softly. "So, who does that leave for Moses and Rohatyn?" She was watching Moses; he had a clear look of *what the heck is going on?* "Did Beatrice come?" she asked almost as an afterthought, but I knew that every syllable of that phrase was as weighted as a gemstone.

"I saw her briefly last night," Fury said, possibly mistaking the topic for a safe one. She always underestimated the cruelty of her friends.

"That takes care of Rohatyn," Martina said with a foxy smile, inflecting the intonation upward and staring at Moses intently. He took that well, as in: he didn't melt into a lukewarm puddle. "But whom did you show the constellations through your telescope last night?"

"Is it that important?"

No, the guy was not up to the task. I saw that he'd always wanted Molly, but something had always told him it was a bad idea. He'd listened, and now he regretted it. They say a man should grow wiser with time, but how many men don't regret not having slept with a desirable woman?

"Who said important?" I remembered the name of a show—*Sweet Vicious*. I'd never seen a second of it, but it must have been invented to describe this precise tone of voice. "We're only reconstructing last night, one piece at a time. And yours is completely missing."

Something was strange; something was terribly, horribly strange about all that was unfolding. I felt my heart slow down, and then it must have stopped as no more blood rang in my temples. *I'm a slave*, I thought. *And my master is a harsh one. Does it even matter what I do if this woman means so much to me? Doesn't doing something per se already profane the sanctity of the feeling? And what's the point of having this feeling in a world where it is rebuffed? To serve as an illustration? But people should know what's possible without me needing to suffer. Which means I need it myself. But for what? To redeem the sins of the past, or to temper myself for the future?* From every conceivable viewpoint, it had to be both. But what had I done to be brought to such extremes, except for discovering that there is no point living in the middle where your life becomes only a lullaby?

And then it came—the one and only thing that could be my salvation, because nothing else would drag me out of that saccharine death I was dying. It was Vince who walked into the room like it wasn't there before realizing, one, that it was, and two, that most of its populace expected socially acceptable behavior from him. Then he saw me and relaxed. I never understood why he liked me until I figured out that no one else ever advised him on what courses of action were best avoided. Like sending that suicidal letter to the girl he loved. I knew the price: all of my suicidal letters did reach their addressees.

Vince walked to the table looking at no one but Martina, and I read in his eyes more than I'd ever known about him.

"Hello Molly," he began in the tone of someone who knows he has only one shot. "You remind me of a joke. A guy walks into a bar and sees a horse …"

"You remind me of how I got through an audition last year," she said, mimicking his accent to unnerving perfection. "The director told me I'd have the part if I could make his horse laugh. I took it to the bathroom, and it laughed hysterically. When we returned, the director said he'd star me if I made his horse cry. I took it to the bathroom again, and it cried like a baby."

Deadly silence followed. I had not heard the joke, but Vince wouldn't bite.

"You are a weird woman," he said matter-of-factly, his voice resembling that of a child who's just confirmed that Santa doesn't exist. "But your dick can't be that huge. I'm off," he added, talking to me. "I thought you might want to wish me well."

Without a word, I rose from my seat, leaving the laptop where it was, and turned my head as if to avoid a sunbeam, catching a glimpse of …

"I need money," I heard next. The voice belonged to Vince, and we were back in our room.

"Who doesn't?" I nodded, unsure of too many things. "How much?"

It finally made sense. I had no memory of getting to the room, which still bore no traces of Tiger except for his suitcase, and my body felt like an oil well on fire. My hands were mine, but I didn't trust them anymore, prepared to run the only reality check that had never failed me.

I already had a plan of what to do when I got the proof. The character playing Martina was, of course, a scout: a guest from another universe capable of taking me there. It was surprising that she hadn't followed us into the room, but I knew she'd be where I left her, feeding off my dreaming attention and showing me anything I needed to give more of it …

A chill of impatience ran over my skin as I touched the light switch.

Here we go, I thought, flicking it.

The light obediently turned on.

"... and others," Vince was saying in the meantime. "It used to be fifteen for ecs and twenty for ax, but that was a long time ago."

I flicked the switch again. The light went out.

"Can you do me a favor?" I rasped.

"What?"

"Can you slap me in the face?"

He obliged me without question.

"I should have done that last night," he said didactically.

"How the fuck did we get here?" I yelled, rubbing my cheek. "I don't recall walking."

"Shit, man." He gave me a look of understanding. "You're underway already. What did you take?"

"The baddest of all. OK." I got a grip and took out the roll. Reality be it. "I'll give you a hundred, and you'll get all the acid it buys."

"Sounds like we'll end up with a lot of acid," he chuckled. "I recall you having rolls like that when you sold us cigarettes."

"Those were made of twenties."

"And I gave you a lot of them." He looked like he wanted to nudge me but changed his mind.

"Very few. You'd always show up with a fiver."

"Well, I bet you always had enough change. What was that tube-thing you kept the coins in?"

"It was either from medicine or vitamins. Remember how I pissed off Gretchen by giving her seventeen one-pound coins for change on her twenty?"

"No, but I hope she was pissed." He told me something about Gretchen I'd never have imagined. "Can you imagine?"

"No." I handed him the bills. I liked how he took them: like they were just paper. "But if we do end up with a lot of acid, who'd you feed it to?"

He named a few names.

"No," I interrupted impatiently. "I mean the girls."

He named a few more names; Martina's wasn't one.

"Sounds like a party. Provided we get the stuff."

"That's what I'm gonna find out soon. Wanna join me?"

"I can't: I have an affair to attend to."

"My friend, your parlance is full of Americanisms," he said jovially. "What kinda 'fair?"

"A hopeless one, of course," I grumbled. "When will you get back?"

"Shouldn't taek longah thanah couple 'ours. Will you kindly stop fucking around with the light switch?"

"That's too early," I said, stopping.

"Not if we wait till dusk. By the way, what's up with Molly?"

I didn't like the words that made up that question. I didn't like the tone in which it was asked, either. And, above all, I didn't like the fact that all I wanted was for Vince to go on.

"What's up with her?" I asked with a nonchalance that cost a monumental effort to affect.

"Her eyes." He looked at me as if I were a child. "They're like amber."

I felt the ground slip from under my feet but somehow didn't fall.

"You think she's on something?"

"Dunno. But she's weird. Like you."

"She's always been weird. How did you like her … oh, you weren't there. Cool, we're all big boys, aren't we?" I gave him an inquisitive look; he didn't object. "Cocaine is a no. Also, for us tonight. Definitely not acid. Meth is doubtful, so is ecs. I mean, really: what's left?"

"I wouldn't dismiss acid so hastily. You never know what it'll do to a human being. I mean, *human* doesn't apply to Molly, but she is a *being*, after all."

"Why don't *you* like her?" I said with annoyance.

"She got the two of us into bed and then called it quits as soon as I took my pants off," he said with the most honesty I'd ever seen from him. "Did I never tell you about that?"

"No, and don't—I'll give you this one anyway." I looked at him, a smile in my eyes. "That *is* a good reason."

"Okay; I'd better get moving." He threw a final glance around, trying to see if he'd forgotten anything. "Be a good boy, alright Motherfuckers?"

I started undressing myself before the door hit the jamb. Vince had a habit of coming back within seconds, but I urgently had to return to the dayroom, and before I did, I had to change. I also had to calm the fuck down. The thought of a lone Martina being circled by those piranhas made me sick, so the shirt and the pants flew onto the bed in a single motion, and I was already putting on new pants. The best dress pants I'd ever had, they were softer than pajamas and a pure white. Then there was a heavenly blue T-shirt, fitting me tightly and handsomely, and a thin, dark-blue pullover, pure wool and more pleasant to the touch than anyone's cashmere. My socks remained black and I didn't change my underwear, but the shoes had to be the very pair that had abandoned me on the cliffs.

For some reason, this didn't seem like a bad idea; besides, I hoped any magic that had gotten inside them remained. I glanced at the mirror briefly: not to give myself any extra polish but to spot any obvious irregularities, like the placement of the pullover's neck over the T-shirt. The next thought was a single perspective of the corridor terminating in the now-open dayroom door; then I returned to the scene.

Two Queens

During my absence, the balance of power had shifted. Martina had kept her seat, but most of those present now formed a menacing semicircle around her. All the spots I could take would reinforce the pressure—all but one, which was also the only one I wanted: that next to her. But it wasn't time yet; besides, I wanted to see how she was doing without me. So, invisible as I was once again, I approached the table by the kitchen wall, some fifteen feet from the action and, having made myself comfortable on it, watched and listened.

"… had a performance last night?" the serpentine Selma was saying in the meantime. I froze, trying to catch every move and every gesture, every smile and every look: anything that could tell what these people were thinking and feeling behind the lies they voiced.

"You call that a performance?" Molly dismissed her without thinking twice. "I call it a mess. Broadway and 46th, full house, all coughing and whispering like at a preview. The light guy got the colors wrong for the last act; too bad at that point it didn't matter. The male lead broke his leg dodging a half-eaten apple. Should've kicked it on the fly. Except he'd've missed, fallen, and broken his leg anyway."

She didn't allow even a gentle chuckle, and, in my head, I applauded: I knew how hard this stunt must have been for her.

"What was the play about?" Selma insisted.

"The same thing every play is about nowadays. Sex." This word pierced the air like a bullet. "If you knew how sex-deprived modern playwrights are, you wouldn't even be laughing," she continued, despite no one showing any inclination to do so. "Women included. They must think the easiest way to get laid is to make up a man. Too bad they don't get to cast for the parts, unless they become directors. In which case it's even worse."

"So, how did it go?" asked a now-confused Selma. "The play?"

"The play?" Martina gave her a look she'd give a street beggar. "It was a flop."

"A flop?" Chloe cried.

"A huge one."

"A huge flop?" Gina couldn't believe it either. Neither of the two faked.

"The greatest one I've ever seen."

"But why?" Selma ventured. "Was it because of the sex?"

"Of course not."

Martina gave her a perfunctory look and leaned backwards, slightly arching her back and crossing her legs in that very way that had always hit me below the belt. She was clearly taking a pause, everyone growing impatient in his or her expectations, but I didn't care about the silence because no sound that could be begotten in this room at this minute could have beaten the sight of her legs. They went beyond elegant: they were sublime. They could have awoken every basic instinct in a centenarian even if they'd been covered by something modest; wrapped in these infernally tight pants, they were utterly seductive. I remembered Lady 2-7; it was as if she'd been Martina's top apprentice for years but, boy, when it comes to the legs, it really pays to be the mistress. Fearing the loss of my mind, I checked out the other girls. They were attractive—some were even hot—but their sum total had just lost to a single uncontrived, insouciant movement of Martina's.

She took a deep breath, and, just as there were perhaps only a few seconds left before she'd speak, poor Selma, her body leaning forward and her jaws tight, lost the last of her patience and demanded:

"So, why was it a flop?"

Martina didn't take the phrase into consideration, simply continuing with her own momentum; and when, two seconds later, it was time, she said:

"Because I didn't pull it off."

She didn't add anything, and it was so perfect that I thought of *Black Swan*. The gauntlet was thrown in everyone's face, and it was impossible to either pick it up or think of a way around it. Now she could pause for as long as she wished, commanding the pressure and threatening to put it all on whoever spoke. It was awfully tempting to chime in, but my perfectionism demanded a better setup still. Fortunately, I didn't have to wait long for escalation: the pause was still uninterrupted when Diane walked in.

She noticed Molly instantly, even before setting eyes on her. It looked like a slight jolt went through Diane's body, eventually turning her head in the right direction. And when her mind caught up, she did a poor job of masking herself, not even thinking that anyone could be watching her as closely as I was.

"My good fucking lord!" Diane exhaled, staring at Martina and displaying a mere fraction of the emotions I was hiding within. "Look who's made it to our orgy at last!"

"Is that what you've been up to?" Molly recognized Diane's attitude instantly, politely, reservedly, and with a devilish grin. "It's good to see you, dear. Why don't you come to NYC more often?"

"You sure had something that kept you in New York City last night," Diane said, like only very few English people can do it, disrespecting every syllable of that name. "Good job not letting us down: must have cost you."

"What's cost when it comes to things money can't buy?"

I had never seen Diane and Martina pitted against each other like this, and the spectacle was rather unnerving. Diane was in rough shape, struggling to conceal her emotions; she was also afraid and had no idea what to do next, tarrying by the couches. But then Selma came to the rescue.

"We should be grateful that Molly made it," she said, sham deference in her eyes. "She's a famous actress now. She starred in a Broadway play last night."

"Last night?" Diane's eyebrows went up so high that they disappeared under her fringe.

"You don't know about it?" Selma continued. "It's all over *The Times*."

A second later Diane was already by the press table, browsing the periodical with a fervor she could barely contain.

"The arts section," Selma prompted.

"We were just talking about it," Evangeline said. "Turns out, it wasn't exactly a hit, was it?"

"The critics called it a fiasco," Selma confirmed.

"It's not here." Diane's eyes flashed with anger as she flipped through the pages.

"Are you sure?"

"It's still amazing," Fury said to Molly. "I'm very happy for you. And the next time everything will be great."

"I can't find it." Diane dropped the newspaper back on the coffee table and sat on the couch with the majestic air of a queen expecting her court to gather around her. "What a shame. I *so* regret having missed it. Any chance it will happen again?"

"The play's on tonight," Molly assured her. "Same place. If you hurry, you may still make it on time."

"Wouldn't be worth it, with you staying behind."

"You just want to keep an eye on me, don't you?"

"Was it really that bad?" Diane frowned at her girls, none of whom had budged. "It had to have been, for you to flee from the next performance. Darling, I don't even know if I should admire or pity you!"

"Somehow both of those feel wrong coming from you."

"Let that not be a reason to question their candor. Or to deny a toast. I see you're not a particularly huge fan of sushi; but, with all this exciting news, I do hope you'll be kind enough to accept a drink?"

"Not until I'm sure I know what I'd like it to be. And, judging by the sun's location, it may be a few more hours before I can decide on that."

"I don't quite recall the sun's ever being an obstacle to your drinking. I'd say you're getting older, except that it only would be a guess."

"A guess worth its weight in gold, if by older you mean more prudent. Although, when it comes to guessing, few can boast having that much weight."

"You certainly can't, although a few more ounces would be in order. This acting business seems to have trimmed you even more. Well, what won't we do for the immortal art?"

"Lose face, for one."

"That can hardly be a concern for someone wearing a mask. And this one must be your unfortunate character's. See, I would have called you miss Pink Flawd, had your eyes not been so elegantly amber."

"My dear Diane," my dear said amiably. "We all know how remarkable you are at assuming the most unlikely social roles, but that of arbiter elegantiarum has never been within your reach."

"For someone who thinks in roles, you aren't playing yours too well. But then again, we all know which role is the only one you excel at."

"Will you enlighten me?"

"That of a whore."

And then Martina laughed. It was most sonorous laughter that rang like a silver bell, pressing an almost palpable sweetness onto my palate. What would I not give to listen to it in private, slowly stroking her velvet wrist with my fingertips? It was the winsome laugh of a soul blissfully oblivious to the avaricious expectations of the public; but did it not befit this personification of royal éclat? Some folks think you need a princess to make it count; yet the best queens are taken from the aristocracy.

"Darling, of all the people I knew in this place, you're the only one who can state that with any authority," she finally said, still smiling. "No one else here knows what that word even means."

Diane froze, distressed and waiting for the coterie to act. The latter, however, was silent, knowing that whoever spoke was bound to become a target, and lacking both the guts to withstand the pressure and the curiosity to try. I had plenty—both guts and curiosity—but there was no point in wasting the first phrase in a decade on such a trifle as a queenly clash.

Ways Out

Suddenly there was noise behind the glass wall; then the back door opened, letting in Rohatyn, Sabrina and Brooke, who had been sunbathing with the bare minimum of clothes. I added the newly arrived girls to the aggregate sexual appeal, but the status quo was maintained: beside Martina, they looked like a disheveled troupe from a country fair in need of a shower. She recognized their appearance by a slight turn of the head, a mysterious smile on her lips, but no one could know what she had on her mind.

"What have you guys been up to?" Rohatyn asked in his usual manner, addressing not so much the people but rather the table they were sitting at. He looked red and hot, and smelled like a mixture of sweat and the scents of most of the girls present.

"Not much," Chloe sighed, looking at him languidly. "How about you?"

"Brooke just had an idea," Rohatyn continued, still oblivious to Martina but staring at Diane with that idiotic expression that makes women wetly fond of a man they're already attracted to. "Why don't we all go to ..."

Hell, I thought and stopped listening, peripherally observing the body language of everyone present. Rohatyn wanted Diane. Chloe was giving him nervous appreciation; Bridgette, Sabrina and Bartholomew were all displaying similar forms of affection; and Moses had finally chilled out. Brooke wanted to go to the bathroom; Selma was hunkering down like a vulture; and Diane couldn't decide whether exiting on this segue would save her. And Molly ... I turned my head imperceptibly to fit an extra inch of her into my field of vision. She was calm, as if watching the scene from her living room couch, removed by miles, years, and a great deal of sophisticated electronic equipment.

"That's a great idea!" Chloe exclaimed, throwing around a pleading look. "Are you guys going now?" she added; and then Rohatyn realized that I was not the only person in the room who questioned his right to be there.

"Good morning, beautiful!" he said with the kind of guffaw you'd expect from a gelding. "I hope your alarm clock works better next time."

"Molly's just arrived!" Nicolette announced fawningly, shifting her eyes between the two as if unsure whose favor she wanted more.

Martina looked into him with the expression of someone who knows she'll not be able to hide her superiority but will nevertheless try.

"What?" Rohatyn asked dejectedly, missing only a pouty lip to become a thirty-year-old replica of a three-year-old boy. He was instantly drawn to Martina, forgetting the other girls, including Diane; but even if their trio had ever had any constructive potential, that time was long gone.

"She's trying to wrap her mind around a little term I introduced a moment ago," Diane said, measuring Rohatyn. "Turns out our own Molly doesn't know what a whore is."

"Well, that's easy!" Rohatyn exclaimed excitedly. "A whore is someone who works in a bordello!"

"Or has the mind of one," Diane continued, smiling at him benevolently. "And isn't ashamed to show it to the right audience. Like that made of old playmates who're too precious to just forget."

I studied Diane, thoughts twisting in my head. She was standing before the man who'd cheated on her and the woman he cheated on her with, and she was making an alliance with that very man as if none of it had happened. A perfect response to the need of the moment, some might say, an example of flexibility, the clever use of a prop; but I could practically see her count out a chunk of her human value in exchange for … I vacillated, unsure of what she was trying to gain. The satisfaction of walking over an enemy? The restoration of her status in the eyes of significant witnesses? A stroked ego? I sighed. All of it seemed cheap.

And then I knew I'd given this room too much leeway, the current stalemate being a consequence of freedom of will exercised by those who'd never fought for it. If you take pleasure for granted and have the luck to back you up, life becomes a stroll in the park, but when the sun rises to illuminate your trail, you see that you've been walking in circles. And that was a luxury I couldn't afford. So, looking inside myself as if surrounded by mirrors, I left the kitchen table and returned to the seat I'd previously occupied, casually brushing the laptop's touchpad to restore a familiar black-and-white maze on the screen. And, with Martina sitting to my left, sylphlike and deadly as a white chess queen, I couldn't wait for the pieces cluttering the board to realize how superfluous they were in this grandmaster game in which they'd be sacrificed before they knew it.

"My dear Diane," Martina said. "Much as I appreciate your admiration of my persona, there are areas in which your supremacy is quite impossible to destroy. Being unmatched your whole life must have proven lonely, so you've created a rival out of thin air. I'm flattered—truly flattered—that you've chosen me, but I would never compare, even if I cared to try."

Diane was about to speak when Rohatyn said something silly, and the next thing we all knew, Beatrice arrived.

Her gait was completely feline: in the animal game, she was an obvious panther. But as I watched her cross the room, I wondered if she had any motives other than the animalistic. *Is she on something?* I thought, entertaining a vision of Vince feeding her cocaine off a long plastic knife. I burned the image, but the thought didn't sit right with me. That entire time on the cliffs I'd had adamant certainty that I'd survive anything. I should have known better then, and now I had to know best.

"How's your head, baby?" she asked me when she reached the center of the room, acting as if we'd bumped into each other in a haberdashery an hour ago. "You should make use of a little ice."

Few things are more detestable to me in civilized socializing than the conscious disregard of an innocent speaker, and doing that to Beatrice after she'd showed her worth was particularly painful, but I could only give her a fleeting smile before returning to my screen. Something was happening to me: I saw white threads pierce the air and disappear inside my head, except that seeing them had nothing to do with the eyes; and, in this light, the scene unfolding in the dayroom acquired the properties of a movie. It was one hell of a clusterfuck, but boy, did it have inherent beauty. This boring, untidy space was more electrified than any royal party had ever been. We were exotic fish in an aquarium, its walls magnifying and distorting our colors and shapes and, unwilling to resist an imperative impulse, I swung forward and began to type, struggling to feel the right path among all the terrific possibilities and somehow capturing the spirit, even if in incomplete sentences, abrupt phrases and standalone words. The room was an arena, an episodic cross-section of reality containing nothing but the germane; and if we all had to die here now, lives away from what we had yet to accomplish, our demise would have to be reckoned with by Infinity as a clear diamond shining in a pile of soot.

"You guys look like ghosts," Beatrice declared, now standing by the table and helping herself to the ginger; it was the same color as her lips. "And I thought I was the only one who went through the night."

"You couldn't sleep?" Selma asked solicitously, and I almost saw her nose transform into a hooked beak.

"Not with all this high-school drama around!" Beatrice scoffed, her clavicle jerking up as she caught a piece falling from her mouth. "It's really remarkable how little responsibility men take," she went on, making a sucking sound with her tongue. "Even for themselves."

"Men don't take responsibility?" Gina asked bluntly, throwing a stealthy look at me.

"Not at all!" Beatrice assured, making a move with her left shoulder, behind which Moses sat. "Blabbermouths," she added cutely. "All talk." She picked up another piece of ginger from the tray and bit into it. And then she raised her eyes, and I realized that she meant me.

"What about women?" Moses asked, audibly frustrated. "Or do they think they can just do whatever they want, and it'll be fine?"

"A real man does have a woman like that," Beatrice told me, ignoring Moses. "The woman he forgives for anything. The one he accepts with all of her flaws and imperfections. That one-and-only one he carries in his heart wherever he goes. Wouldn't it be something, to meet a woman like that?"

"You got the steps in the wrong order," Molly said suddenly, and I shivered. "First, there comes something, and then he knows that she is the one."

I heard her voice as if through a layer of running water, reality warping around the now-visible curve of time. Diane and Rohatyn flirting for Molly's sake, Chloe eyeing them, Gina perplexed as to my status; Nicolette envying; Selma regretting; Fury getting hungry again ... Soon they all blended into a striking kaleidoscope that took me back to my early childhood, and when I reached the perspective's endpoint, it was but Molly and me alone.

I exhaled and stared into the laptop screen, looking peripherally. The most reasonable assumption was that I'd just shifted dreams, carrying the scout along, but the letters held stubbornly and—worse yet—they made sense. In the end, I had no choice but to shut my stalwart companion, take another careful breath, and turn to face my uncovered fate.

Vince was right: her pupils held a shine, and it made me viscerally afraid. As she kept looking, I felt her stare pass effortlessly into my head and ignite the deeper layers of my consciousness, some of which had been so hidden I'd never known they were mine.

It was time to be impeccable.

""Go toss the crutches; we're almost done!" That's what they say every single Thursday," I said, feeling the pass resonate in my pocket to the sound of my voice.

"Today's Saturday," she said.

"Is that when you started getting ready for this reunion?"

She kept looking at me with the exact same expression as after "Saturday".

"You didn't fly here from Rome?"

Her face didn't change again, but this time something felt wrong.

"Too bad you had to miss last night. It was a lot of fun. You would have liked it."

"You stayed up late?"

"Till dawn."

"How was it?"

"Shabby."

"You look like you went through the night with a bag of flour on your shoulders."

"You look rested. As if you slept until you entered the dayroom."

"I got wasted last night. Two bottles of wine and a pizza."

"We had vodka and cognac."

"I drank vodka with coke once. Couldn't stop puking. Puked seven or eight times, twice after I thought I had nothing left inside."

I understood her. Completely.

"We didn't have coke. Vince showed some class, though. Did you know he could drink vodka from the bottle for seven seconds straight?"

"I'm surprised he stops so soon. Why are you friends with that clown?"

"Because he's a badass. And he's funny more often than not. He stops because the rules don't require him to go on."

"What rules?"

"Those of *Seven Seconds*," I said, as if it were the most obvious thing in the world. "It's a game where you have to gulp vodka from the bottle. For seven seconds in a row."

"Why would anyone want to play that game?"

"Because they are badass." I repeated the *most obvious thing in the world* gambit.

"Did you play? Wait, you don't count. You'd only do it to impress somebody."

"Who? It's pointless to try impressing anyone but you. You're the only one who doesn't get impressed."

"How about Brooke? Have you heard anything decent from her?"

"I might. Have you?"

"I never spoke with the bitch."

"I don't blame you. She's rather scrawny."

"Not when she goes vegan. Then she's just green."

Our eyes remained locked throughout the exchange. I had no clue what she was thinking but, breaking away from the amber radiance, I saw us in a cabin in the mountains, flames from the fireplace lighting the wall in a series of concentric circles of slightly varying shades. We were about to begin a slow dance, with my hand gradually …

"I wish you'd seen Fury by the fire last night," I interrupted myself. "She looked like she and the flames were one. Except she was brighter."

"Right. How did you end up on the cliffs?"

"I had to bury the past."

"I mean: how did you hook up with the Cliff Girls?

"Curiosity, mostly. As well as some emotions that would lose a great deal of value if they became public."

"You've always made your emotions public."

"Not those that counted most! You know that."

"Do I?"

"Which reminds me." I was looking at her as if pretending to cover a slip of the tongue. "I need to talk to you."

"You are."

"Not like this." I shook my head. "In private."

She looked around.

"We're alone."

"It's the dayroom. I think Sunley's east end will do better."

"East end?"

"Yes. Take a right at the building's exit and walk to the end."

She was now carefully considering her options.

"Why?"

"Are you afraid of me?"

"Are you afraid of kittens?"

"Then meet me at the east end in fifteen minutes," I said, getting up and collecting my laptop.

"Do you think I have nothing better to do?"

I was already at the door when she spoke, but I turned around and smiled.

Then I left the dayroom as if it were an abandoned ship.

Games of Evasion

There was a fresh draft in the hallway, which meant that the entrance door and at least one of the windows were open. It brought memories of a beautiful moment when a Southern-born classmate of mine saw snow for the first time in her life and asked me if I was doing so, too. It would have been much more beautiful had I slept with the girl, though. I paused before the stairs, wondering if my heart had already stopped, but it was simply beating so fast that the individual beats blended together. No pain had ensued yet, but I still opened the door cautiously to minimize any impact on the chest.

In the corridor, there was no one but Diane. She shouldn't have been there either. There were so many other things she could be doing that, at first, I couldn't come up with an excuse for her being in my way. She seemed to be waiting for someone, a hurt animal looking for a lair to settle down in and lick her wounds. And then I remembered that Rohatyn was staying in the room next to mine.

"Hey Diane," I said, stopping in front of her. "What's your favorite Pink Floyd song?"

"What?" She looked me up and down.

I smiled, remembering that the dumbest thing one can do is confront a human being directly. Then I went ahead and did just that.

"Why did you lie to me?"

"Lie to you?" She was Miss Innocence. "When?"

"Last night. Or, rather, early this morning."

"Last night? Don't be preposterous. I wouldn't have had a chance even if I wanted to."

"How about the talk in the dayroom?"

"What talk? Are you drunk?"

"The talk we had at about half past four when you came to the kitchen for a drink," I patiently explained.

She blinked a few times, as if in silent disbelief. Then she laughed.

"You must have dreamt it. I went to bed long before that."

I gave her a penetrating look. She stared right back, a challenge in her eyes. Either she was a better actress than Molly, or she had no idea. I kept looking, and the corners of her mouth moved, her face assuming the expression of a countess looking at a serf who had failed to do what she'd asked of him. And then I suddenly knew.

"So, you wouldn't remember even if we had had sex?" I asked.

"What?" Now she was masquerading her concern with indignation. "Where is this coming from?"

"In other words." I was not letting her eyes go; she kept it up for a while, but my stare was too sterile to grab onto anything, so she looked away. "You have no memory of what happened between us in the dayroom before dawn this morning?"

"I wasn't with you in the dayroom this morning." She was adamant. Thoughts were running in my head without me thinking; then I made up my mind.

"You were. And you lied to me. And it was a bad lie."

She seemed taken aback for a second.

"Well, what did I say?"

"Why talk about it if you don't even remember it happened?" I snapped. "I wonder how many men have had sex with you like that."

"Why are you bringing up sex again?" she snapped. "Who do you think I am?"

"A sleepwalker. And a sexy one." I smiled, stepping into her personal space; she didn't lean away, didn't even become tense. The heat of her body enveloped my skin; I was fully within her ethereal bubble, and it felt like lying naked in bed with her. Our past molded into cubistic, lopsided shapes that condensed around my eyes into a vivid, colorful sequence, but it was still not enough to disabuse me of my pity for her. Was it related to birth, a peculiar malady making its way into noble families? Or perhaps running in a family for generations and marking only its most distinguished members? Those who knew where to hit their enemies best.

"Look," I said firmly. "I'm sure it was nothing personal: just a tribute to the upbringing, a little exercise in keeping things under your thumb. And, of all people, I'm very forgiving of what one does when asleep. But if you lied about Molly like that …"

"Oh, so, this is about her?" Diane interrupted, a furious furrow crossing her forehead.

"… it could only be because you wanted to hurt her. And that's a shame. Have you ever had a relationship with a man that would compare to being friends with her? It would have been so much fun."

"This is just great," she said as if not having heard anything after *Molly*. "You know what? I don't care if you made it all up or not. And I don't care what I told you last night. Whatever it was, it had to have been right, otherwise I wouldn't have done it. Now, do me a favor …"

"You haven't answered my question," I said charmingly.

"What question?"

"Your favorite Pink Floyd song."

"Go to hell. Do they have a song called that?"

"No." I said, walking around her, her ethereal body ripping off mine like a Band-Aid. Then I pushed open the door and entered my room. It remained empty, which was the best piece of news I could have asked for.

I put the laptop away, sank down on the bed and glanced at my watch; I had about ten minutes. Would she show up? I was ready for her not being there, acting as if nothing had happened when we met later and expecting me to bring up the subject. But before I went to the east end to make sure, there was nothing to do. I was too destabilized to act, so I lay on my back, staring into the gray ceiling tiles and counting on a zephyr of inspiration to touch me at the right time.

A couple of minutes later I felt a strange tickling around my eyebrows, and then I shook from a powerful jolt that uncorked my bottled-up emotions all at once. I wanted it to be over. Everything: my trip, my love, my need to remain in the physical body. The knowledge of the gap between me as I was and me as I wanted to be hit me, horrifying in its abysmal vastness and tantalizing in its taunting realism. It felt like I was at the nadir of my AC times again: morose, exhausted, drenched of the will to live, and starving for a love that shone like a distant beacon on a dark horizon, a phantom reminder of something greater than the quagmire of my lower self.

Being so close, a bare breath away from touching it, how did I dare to sink into weakness, and so soon after the watchtower epiphanies, too? Did Diane provoke it? This idea seemed a comic relief to a preposterous drama, and I began laughing hysterically, eventually bursting into tears. After a while I scratched my head violently, the pain sharpening the sensitivity of my mood but doing nothing to sober me up. And then I glanced at the watch again. It was time to go.

I wiped my eyes against the pillowcase and got up, dizzy as

menacing dark circles spun before my eyes. I waited for this to pass, locked my laptop away and listened for objectionable sounds from the corridor before leaving. I saw people in the dayroom hall, but they ignored me, to our mutual satisfaction.

I exited the house slowly, vacillating on the porch and scanning the area for any witnesses; when none were revealed, I took a right and followed the wall. The gravel produced a soothing crunch under my feet, and the birds chirping in the air made me feel at home. I stopped at the final turn, listening so attentively that it hurt my ears; there was nothing but the idyllic countryside afternoon, so I took a deep breath and entered the east end.

She wasn't there.

I checked my watch again; it was time, so I had to decide how long I'd give her before going back. Five minutes was the start, but I didn't want to go beyond ten because staying here was inconvenient. Located in what looked like a tiny ravine, the spot was secluded and visible only from a few points, all of which should have been inaccessible to the alumni, but offered nothing to do. The smokers used to bring chairs here, but either my entire class had quit, or they hadn't found the damn chairs. I took another deep breath, locked my hands together and stretched up, relaxing my neck muscles and closing my eyes; I remained in this pose for a moment, increasing the tension to a painful degree before letting it go and opening my eyes …

She stood right in front of me.

I look at her, puzzled and completely disregarding the fact that nobody had ever crept on me like that, even from behind. It was undeniably Martina, but her clothes had completely changed. Perhaps I gave them too brief a description in the dayroom, but it hardly mattered: she wasn't wearing any of those items anymore.

This time, she was emerald around her pearl dress shirt, its wide embroidered collar encroaching on the lapels of a malachite vest. Within the latter, marvels lay. I had a fleeting vision of the two of us on the balcony of a penthouse, me holding her by the waist, her pressed into the railing. *Is it even possible to desire a woman so much?* I thought. *Shouldn't there be natural laws preventing this kind of madness?* It didn't feel human anymore: it felt beyond. As a countermeasure, I looked down. Her pants were dark green and seemed sturdy, yet they shone like only silk could. The thin laces of knee-high boots formed at least a dozen tight crosses on the light-brown leather, and the seams running along the sole gave a strong impression of durability, but boy, the boots did a very poor job of concealing the svelteness of her ankles and calves. Fox-hunting was one appropriate purpose for this attire, yet the most startling was the attitude she assumed in it, stretching the fabric along all the right corners and curves. With her knees slightly bent and her legs set apart, torso straight and arms akimbo, chin high and eyes shining, she really was ready to go a long way.

"Good thing you're already here," I said, as if she'd had to wait for me. "I need to talk to you."

"You are."

"Not like that." I vacillated, taking a deep breath. "I need to meet some expectations."

"Courage meeting expectations; that's new!" she laughed, but not like she had in the dayroom: this was just between the two of us. "Are you actually meeting any?"

"I don't think so. But neither have I been myself yet."

"You'd better start, then."

"Okay. Let's go hit the cliffs."

She changed immediately. The alteration was so imperceptible it would have slipped by those relying on straightforward sight but, with peripheral vision, I caught a change of coloration around the contours of her body … which in this case is a euphemism for saying that her aura became a brilliant red. I had no idea that was possible and moved my eyes around, gliding cautiously over her chin, and lips, and nose, and back to her lips again as they parted to allow her tongue to emerge in a teasing moisturizing gesture, and finally looked at her directly, trying to ignore the earthquake in my chest, stomach, and crotch. There could be no mistake, neither for a fool, nor for a poet: hers were the eyes of a lioness ready to sink her fangs into her prey.

"Why would I do that?"

All right, I thought. *Time to bring out the one hundred and eleven percent.*

"I have a gift for you."

"A gift?"

"Yes, but not like they mean it in German. In German, *Gift* means poison. What I have, however, is a different kind of gift. I'd call it a present, but it's not. It's a *gift*, if you know the difference."

She was silent, watching the sunlit grass in Sunley's backyard. I heard voices mumbling unintelligible nonsense from behind the edge of the house, but I couldn't tell if she either saw or were seen by the interlocutors.

"It's been ten years, hasn't it?" she said at last, softly.

"We never were on the cliffs together."

"I'm talking about you wanting to take me there."

"Make it twelve."

"No. I met you in August, and we're still in July."

“Eleven years and eleven months, then,” I concluded, shifting from foot to foot to shake off a sudden chill. She remained unfazed, but the fright I felt was sufficient for both of us.

“Why the cliffs?” she continued, ignoring the trickery of the numbers despite being the one who’d brought it up. “What’s wrong with this place? At least we’re already here: no need to walk.”

“The campus is host to many disturbing vibrations, with plenty of new ones coming soon. We need a sanctuary.”

“We do?” She almost laughed but didn’t, as if choosing to save it for a better occasion. “Do you think I came here for that?”

“I hear you, but I wouldn’t be so sure. This place still has a lot of you. What did you come here for, by the way?”

“This place never had anything of mine.”

“Then it’s about time to start leaving an imprint. Or do you think some people might mind? Like Diane?”

“I don’t think Diane matters.” She gave me a lingering look. “I’m still unpersuaded.”

“About?”

“Going to the cliffs. 'Cause I’m gonna bet you want me to go alone. Am I right, or are you making a play here?”

“I *am* making a play,” I said with the polite dignity of a born writer. “But what did you expect? That I’d be inviting you on behalf of the Cliff Girls?”

She paused again, this time looking at the clouds; her chin was so high up that it almost pointed into my forehead.

“This gift. Where is it?”

“In my pocket.”

“And what is it?”

“It’s a physical object.”

“That’s a start.”

“I can tell you more.”

“Entertain me.”

“It’s a piece of paper.”

“A piece of paper?”

“Yes, a piece of paper.”

“Just a piece of paper, this thing?”

“Yes.”

“This thing you want me to go to the cliffs with you for?”

“It’s a piece of paper. Not a ring.”

“A ring?”

“No, it’s not a ring.”

“Not a ring?”

“No. It’s a piece of paper.”

"And for that piece of paper …"
"I shouldn't have brought up the ring."
"Why did you bring up the ring?"
"Yeah, I brought up the ring, but I shouldn't have."
"Why did you do it?"
"What, bring up the ring?"
"Yes."
"I didn't bring up the ring. I mean, I didn't bring it. I just said it, 'cause …"
"Yes?"
"'Cause I thought …"
"Yes?"
"That's what you were thinking."
"What *I* was thinking?"
"Yeah, that's what I thought."
"So, you thought that I was thinking …"
"Yeah, and that's why I said it."
"Because you thought?"
"That that's what you're thinking."
"That that's what *I* was thinking?"
"Yeah, but it's not that. And I shouldn't have brought the ring."
"So, you brought it?"
"What did I say?"
"What did you say?"
"About the cliffs?"
"No, about the ring."
"You mean the piece of paper? ..."

Five minutes later, on our way to the cliffs, walking as jubilantly as two runaway kids, she was still unpersuaded:

"You have to understand. It's not a ring."
"Course not."
"That thing I said about the ring; it's only a piece of paper."
"Yeah, that's what you said."
"I just thought we should get it straight."
"You think I'm stupid?"
"'Cause I thought you could be thinking that I have an engagement ring for you."
"An engagement ring?"
"Yeah, an engagement ring you'd throw back in my face."
"Is that what you have?"
"Is that why you're coming?"
"Is that why you think I'm coming?"
"What do you think?"

Masks and Masculinity

I spent so much narrative on these cliffs that you may be thinking that this darn AC place is all cliffs; but actually, the cliffs consisted of two distinct parts. One ran toward the east, parallel to the campus, ending at the fringe of the woods. That was where the Cliff Girls had gone the night before, and behind that was where I'd woken up in the lagoon. The other part stretched to the west, from the lifeguard quarters to the lighthouse, a mysterious edifice remaining completely functional despite its old age. It inspired such awe in me that I'd never come close to it, and only once had I gone beyond it on a thrilling motorboat ride. The ride culminated in ringing a sonorous rescue bell and throwing the first-year students into the water; I was a first-year student, and the water was freezing, causing me a prolonged illness, so I had no faith in West Wales. But the stretch of cliffs between the campus and the lighthouse was ideal. It offered picturesque views, and it was from here that, while seeing none of the campus, you could feel the presence of something momentous. Here I took my friends for pleasant strolls during the daytime, here I came alone at night when things were not going my way, and here I was finally taking my darling who had to wait for her turn of the wheel of fortune for such a long time.

They say good things are worth waiting for, but a huge part of me vehemently disagreed. I'm impatient to begin with, and when gratification is delayed by a decade, I go wild. That's what happened to me as soon as we hit the road. Every so often I shook with fury as the sleazy beast of self-pity licked my solar plexus with its serpentine tongue, reminding of all the wonders I could have had over these years but didn't: wonders I'd never regain. The empty space inside me demanded blood and satisfaction, and, observing its pitch-black event horizon, thoughts and feelings distorting into hideous shapes along its edge, I knew I had to find endless stores of self-irony to counterbalance its inhuman, predatory pull.

"All right; let's say I'm wrong," I was saying in the meantime. "But are you certain that right now you're not finding yourself in a dream?"

"One hundred percent."

"That's too bad. Gotta go up to one hundred and eleven."

She gave me a strange look. It was northern this time: the good old Viking times, with long winter nights by the open fire and jangling necklaces on top.

"You still haven't told me where we're going."

"That's still undecided. I'll let the path take us where it runs. But we are going toward the lighthouse."

"Lighthouse so important?"

"Undeniably, especially in view of some recent developments."

"Developments? The thing hasn't changed for ages."

"That's debatable. But it reminds me of something. Why are you rude to me?"

"I'd better start excusing myself after every sentence."

"Better before. I'm serious."

"You think I'm rude to you?"

"To everyone. But to me you're rude in a very particular way."

"Like how?"

"You know, I was consumed by happiness when I learned the word *thoroughfare*," I continued, as if we'd been talking about it all along. "Even though I couldn't forgive myself for not having known it for so long. It is as if a chunk of my soul finds its place whenever I hear that word. Thoroughfare. Does it strike you as anything remarkable?"

"The word, or the way you're talking about it?"

"See?" I exclaimed jubilantly. "You never try to outwit anyone but me!"

"Is it because you're trying to outwit me and get beaten?"

"Trying to outwit you?" I almost didn't understand what the phrase meant. Then I realized: she was only teasing. "All right." I waved my hand, disposing with the levity. "We ought to talk about something before we get to the right place."

"I thought you didn't know where we were going."

"I don't. But when you get to the right place, you know it."

"So, we're going to the lighthouse, along the cliffs, while you're looking for that place?"

"Looking is not the right word. And not me. Both of us."

"Oh, really? I'm also gonna be looking? Great."

"Looking is not the right word. But there's nothing impossible about it. In fact, you've already done it countless times."

"What is it you've got?" she said tiredly. "Just give it to me here. There's no one around; no one will see."

"You already know that it's a piece of paper. Telling you more would be underestimating you."

Suddenly she stopped. I stopped too, looking at her.

"You wouldn't drag me here for a postcard, would you?"

"You think I wouldn't?" I was furious, letting some of the internal pressure out. "You really think I would not?"

"Why, to make a fool of yourself?"

"Why of myself?" I kept walking. She followed. "Of you."

"I'd like to see you try. You can only be one way with me, sweetheart: all for nothing. I remember your eyes then; you have the same eyes now."

“And you don’t,” I said resolutely, as if voicing a thought that knew it had a right to be there and moved ahead to take its place. She didn’t so much as look at me, likely thinking it was an act.

“Those folks in the dayroom,” she continued nonchalantly. “Tears and rain. Do you realize that they’re all still exactly the same?”

“I’d be more surprised if they weren’t.”

“Aren’t people supposed to change?” she continued, visibly indifferent to my opinions.

“Depends on who you ask. Some believe human consciousness is compelled to grow only in life-or-death situations.”

“What?”

“You want an example of a life-or-death situation?”

“No, I want an answer to my question.”

“The ability to change over short periods of time is a gift, and it is distributed sparingly.”

“Too bad you didn’t catch any either. You’re as disappointing as ever.”

“I can’t be. Not to someone who has no hopes for me, anyway.”

“You’re right: there is absolutely nothing to expect from you. Other than a love poem in a foreign language. Not that writing in English would help, but at least there’d be fewer surprised people.”

“Am I hearing this from someone who lives to flabbergast?”

“It’s different. You aren’t flabbergasting. You’re just …” she looked away at the ocean, and just as I thought she’d moved on, she said:

“Fine.”

“Thanks. And you?” I was finally beginning to feel something. “Please, keep going: I want to learn more about myself.”

“Then start talking to people.”

“Is that why you do it? Can’t be: you always hear the same thing. Men want to impress you with flatteries; women want to ruin you with lies. I’m so glad the two of us were never friends,” I exhaled suddenly, unsure of where the emotion came from but willing to ride it. “Every time I saw you with your coterie I thought: here is a bunch of divas who have no clue they’d have so much more fun if they stopped pretending and enjoyed what they already are! If you ever get a chance to read Thackeray’s *Vanity Fair*, don’t,” I concluded. “You’ll hate your friends even more than you already do.”

“The book’s been on my nightstand since last Christmas.”

“Pass or not, but I owed you one.”

“You still do. When are you going to give it to me?”

“When we reach the right place, like I told you. Do you ever get that feeling, by the way? That of being in the right place at the right time?”

"Always."

"Then tell me when it leaves you: it will mean we've arrived."

We walked in silence, and as I tried silencing the internal monologue her presence was growing more and more powerful, absorbing my attention to the point where the rest of the world blended into a single indefinite blob.

"I am definitely not going all the way to the lighthouse," she peevishly announced. "I'm already bored with this walk."

"You sound disappointed. Why; did you think I'd dance around you like a monkey?"

"You mean, like you always used to?"

"Is that what you thought I did?"

"That's what you did. That's what all insecure boys do. They come to you shaking and trembling, thinking them not peeing their pants is enough of a reason to hit on you …"

"And the worst part is that they have the audacity to expect you'll like them back!"

"Why do you guys not learn?" I bet she rolled her eyes as she said it, but I didn't turn to look. "I mean, is it really that difficult, to hit on a girl properly?"

"It's a mystery—for all the good boys, anyway. That's what makes them good. They would have eventually solved it, but they don't practice enough."

"They should."

"They would, but the bad girls hurt them too much. By the way, how do you turn men down?"

"I pretend I'm an apricot."

"You'd make a spoiled one. But I know …" My mind went blank, dissolving between the iridescence of the sky and the chalky dust on the road. "You stare, silent and cocksure, until he runs out of lines. And then you just leave, and he is so stifled that he can't even chase you."

She revealed nothing at all.

"That wouldn't have worked on me, though. Wanna know what I'd do?"

"Keep that revelation to yourself."

"*You want a revelation, you want to get it right, but it's a conversation I just can't have tonight*," I sang quietly.

"Tell me something: has there ever been a woman in your life who appreciated you reciting poetry at her?"

"Truth or dare?"

"Really? Not one?"

"Truth or dare?"

"Then why do you keep doing it?"

"Because it's worth it! Don't you see?" I was incensed. "It's all about capturing a beautiful feeling accessible only under rare circumstances. And you know exactly what it means, to say to a needy man who's plagued you with his nonsense that whatever he wants to whine about is a conversation you *just can't have tonight*. Can't, because it requires too much energy, which every ghoul has been sucking out of you the entire day, leaving you an empty shell wanting nothing but to come home to her loving man who understands what kind of crap she has to put up with! And honestly, you wouldn't even mind humoring that bastard of yours, no matter how exhausted you were, had he approached you with the tiniest modicum of compassion as opposed to throwing himself at you like he were the only thing in the universe that matters."

"I understand that very well," she said coldly. "What I don't understand is how it's relevant."

I scoffed.

"Then no wonder you don't understand how hard it is for a good guy to hit on a girl he likes."

"Then why is it, for some men? Some men are just on; you need a much better reason to reject a man like that. And you usually don't have one."

"You still do, out of bad habit. But it doesn't matter because those men don't put the emphasis on anyone in particular. When a man like that hits on a woman, she's the tenth one he's approached this month. Four burned him on the spot, three gave him false contacts, two dropped out in the middle of the first date. The last one slept with him, running another one-in-ten chance of becoming his stopgap girlfriend. Do you know what he does next? Sifts through ten more women before the month is over."

"We aren't talking about the same kind of man."

"Then you're talking about a man who doesn't exist. Men's and women's fantasies, although inherently different, are remarkably similar in their lack of verisimilitude. Take you, for instance ..."

"Why me?"

"'Cause you're right here. Besides, you are what ninety-nine percent of straight men are after ninety-nine percent of the time. What's your type, anyway?"

"Your opposite."

"A dumbass? I think that, choosing between a Hollywood star and a tycoon, you'd go for the latter. But you'd still expect him to have Hollywood looks. You want a trophy: someone who will solve your problems, give you the ultimate confidence boost, and be remarkable."

"Like I said: your opposite."

"There we go!"

"Where exactly?"

“You just showed me your trump card.”

“It must have fallen under the table while I wasn’t looking.”

“No, you flashed it before my nose, thinking I wouldn’t see.”

“How silly of me. What suit was it?”

“The one I wore when I invited you to the graduation ball. And the ironic part is: I was coming home after a card game.”

“You have an immoderate memory for insignificant details.”

“When the exasperation is there. You were dressed up, too.”

“I actually remember. They put code locks on all the houses; but Sunley’s was already broken …”

“We disabled it, so that fair young ladies wouldn’t struggle to get in through the windows.”

“It was so ridiculous of you: to ask me out like that.”

“It was perfect. It was me snatching my cubic centimeter of chance, for a change. We were alone, both looking sharp, both high on emotions. I was one of my best selves: confident, jocular, earnest. And you … well, you were the only thing you can be.”

“At least you didn’t faint like you did when I didn’t go to the St. Valentine’s Day ball with you.”

“It felt easier: I knew we’d both be going to the States. I just didn’t want to wait. But then again, nothing disciplines a man more than the need to make a particular woman fall for him.”

“This is impossible!”

“It only requires a bit of imagination.”

“Have you ever managed?”

“Yes, although it took a long time.”

“How long?”

“Ten years.”

“Tragic. Although for you getting one woman per decade is not too bad for the average.”

“Doesn’t make your math any better. Of all the men worth being hit on by, how many did actually hit on you?”

“Every one of them.”

“Then you may marry a man of your liking within a decade. It doesn’t matter who you go for: they’re all the same. The only difference is: most are cowards, and the rest are fools.”

“At least they aren’t both, like you.”

“I’m not a man of your liking, remember?”

“You *are* a coward who’s afraid of women. And a fool who believes that he can hide that.”

I saw an array of wrinkles gather around the corners of her otherwise flawless mouth, and I didn’t know even what the expression was intended to show, let alone what it hid. A sobering gust of cool wind reached under my clothes, and I surrendered to its caresses with the abandon of a true warrior, allowing my self-pity to squeeze through the pores of my skin. Then I took a deep breath and closed my eyes, prepared to wake up in the place I had been accustomed to call home, but as I looked again nothing had altered, except that her wrinkles had disappeared and her face had returned to the same expression I could watch forever, oblivious to the flow of time.

The Stage of Life

"You know, if we were characters in a book, our readers would hate us so much they'd quit long before the ending."

"Your readers."

"And what about your viewers? Do you think they'd watch the blade fall?"

"You know about it?"

"I was in the dayroom."

"I'm glad everybody knew. Spared me the need to improvise."

"Who cares? The fact is: they wrote it. The critics. It was another round of GRE vocabulary, but their friendliest term was *frigid*."

"So undeservedly!"

"I agree."

"You haven't seen the play."

"I know you. And you were nowhere near your best. Seriously: the critics aside, what does Miss Flawless think of her performance?"

"Don't call me that."

"You weren't thrilled either?"

"It was a difficult role. There were scenes where I had to be my opposite, but just as it was time to revert, I'd get so into it I couldn't be genuine. And I can't act myself, if you know what I mean, which you probably don't. But the worst was that I had to exit at the end of the fourth act. The stupidest heroine I've ever played!"

"I see the frustration. Don't see a problem."

"How would you? It takes being an actor to know."

"Or a playwright. But regardless, what you just said isn't true."

"What exactly?"

"All of it. Where do I even start? How about: there couldn't be a single moment in that entire play when you were anything but yourself."

"That's the most unveiled veiled insult I've ever heard."

"I'm not talking about your sexuality. Yet. But here's another lie: you don't *act* yourself, you simply *live*, as if the stage were your private parlor. Which leads me to believe that you flubbed the role precisely because you were yourself. Not a provincial girl on a quest to conquer L.A., but a haughty aristocrat who thinks that what she doesn't like shouldn't even exist."

"Is that what you've been taking me for all these years?"

"Most of the time it wouldn't be a deal-breaker, but the play's subject matter was too sensitive. See, the hope a man cherishes when watching something is that the actress could be his. It's that "girl next door" thing that means a magazine with Jennifer Aniston on the cover sells twice as many copies. No matter how stunning she is, she looks like she could be anyone's neighbor. But your Skinny Love could not. And when a man sees a stunning woman he knows he can't have, he grows despondent."

"I believe you: you have a lot of experience with that."

"Thanks to you, but did it give you an advantage to put every man in my shoes? Now, what exactly was your problem with exiting at the end of the fourth act?"

"And you call yourself a playwright? Isn't it obvious that you have to give your best outside the climax?"

"Sounds like you. But it seems you didn't get the play at all. After all. What's it about?"

"You really think you know the answer?"

"I know I do. And I know you don't, because you don't know why Skinny disappears before the fifth act."

"And why is that?"

"Because the play is about what everyone thinks should *not* happen. Skinny should *not* turn down the acceptance offer from the great college in the first act. She should *not* bribe the sheriff for the fake ID in the second. And when, in the third, we learn that she came to LA to become an adult actress, the audience should jump up and scream: *NO!* But when we find out that porn is all she actually wants, things can only go downhill. That moment, which I bet is in the middle of the third act, that's the climax. And Skinny is right there: shining in all her beauty, which is to be profoundly profaned soon. Soon, because we're already halfway through, and the girl hasn't gotten banged once. So, at the end of the third act, she loses her virginity to the stranger in the hotel ..."

"Fascinating."

"Cruel, if you ask me. The fourth act confirms the trajectory, culminating in the scene that reveals the scenario of the film Skinny is to star in if she aces the audition ..."

"Casting. I meant: stop."

"Which, of course, she does. But that scenario is the only piece of raw meat the audience will get."

"Seriously?"

"It's like a scary movie that becomes much scarier when you don't show the monster, except this one is about both the monster and the beauty. So, when the Dildo Studio doors close behind her, that's it: the transformation. The turning point when Skinny loses her human form and becomes a dream. Now, even if the fifth act ended with a messenger telling us that she'd suffered a violent death that had nothing to do with her personally, like being shot during a robbery at a candy store, it wouldn't change anything. A true heroine is someone who influences events without being present. But, since the vehicle of the play is sex, it's all about the aftertaste. And if it was bitter, it means the audience disliked not Skinny, but you."

"Well, well, well. Same as always; you surprise me still. To dissect a play on the basis of its synopsis in front of the lead actress, being so sure … That's just shameless."

"That's just a taste of what creativity has for breakfast. What's shameless is that everyone else starves."

"That's one thing I've never understood about you. Why do you celebrate your life as if it were the most remarkable thing?"

"Because I've never encountered anything more remarkable. This is what ordinary people don't get about creativity: it's not measured like money, power, or love. It's an opportunity to be God."

"Did you just call me ordinary?"

"Your whole life is a testimony."

"You don't know anything about my life, thank God."

"What's there to know? It's simple. Why does a story captivate us? Allow us to live a life in two hours? Because it's saturated with life—like life itself can never be. A play is quintessential life; life stripped off everything that dilutes its purity, which is why the play is the antipode of life. Life is a travesty, so a surrogate is needed. A drug we can shoot straight into the heart. And, since that drug doesn't occur naturally, it must be synthesized: from the souls of the few condemned to relish both the greatest pleasures and the greatest pains. Their lot is to dwell in a trap, capped at the top by Infinity and at the bottom by the mundane, craving the magic dose that will release them. But then there are moments. Moments of retaliation when you level the playing field and become not individual people but the source that made them itself. And it is but there, on the ghostly frontier that perennially coexists with us without becoming visible until we know where to look, that you can take a deep breath and admit, if only to yourself, that that moment was, in fact, worth living."

"OK, I get it. I really do. You are the textbook definition. But these things you cling to, what you call art ..."

"Creativity."

"They're simply a coping mechanism—an antidote to the painful fact that you can't get what you want. So, in reality, it's only an attempt to escape ... well, reality."

"Escape reality? Are you serious? Reality is a woman: she never turns one loose. But, if you must insist on psychiatric terms: anything that anybody does willingly is a means to cope with life's ugly mien. You're laughing? Look at yourself. The most desirable woman since the invention of sex, you still can't have enough unless the house is full. Why? Because deep down you know that, no matter what you do, your life will never match the worst of your favorite plays for more than an instant, after which there'll be the same gray fog. Life is mostly noise that doesn't matter. But on stage, everything counts. The trick is to live the same way: then life becomes the only stage you'll ever need."

Pride and Prejudice

I paused and took a deep breath. I almost got carried away but didn't. And she was beyond reproach: an impenetrable façade of beauty not giving an inch even as an afterthought.

"I know this about you because, if we set aside the obvious differences, the only real one between us is that my responsibility is greater," I said, studying her masquerade with admiration. "As an actress, you dance to the playwright's will, without any guarantee that he wished you well. But I, as a playwright, must handle all the pressure of free will, judging myself through the eye of God, making sure that I create a totality, and blessing my muse with the best intentions I could possibly gather for her imperative part."

"I would never take part in a play you wrote," she said as gently as one could expect from the mask she wore.

"What if you didn't know it was mine? What if you read the script and got it all, as if it was all about you? What if the director fell in love with you and handed you the main part, which you knew nobody else could pull off? And what if, on the day of the first rehearsal, you found out the irreversible truth? Would you give it all up?"

"Well, judging by the extent of your success, I don't have to worry. Seriously: you must have been writing for years now; why haven't I heard about you yet? Do you use a pseudonym?"

"Pseudonym? Me?"

"Just to prove the point."

"Are you sure you'd be able to take a book I wrote without catching a fever? In any case, it won't happen until you feel so complacent that you stop fighting for more. Then one night you'll have a friend over, another actress with uncertain prospects and two bottles of wine, and a few glasses later you'll both feel you don't need anything except for your cat and that new TV show with those dubious acting choices. The nth episode will be over, and you'll have to disturb the cat to fetch the other bottle; and, screwing the opener into the cork through the foil, you friend will mention a novel she recently read. She'll begin recounting the plot, and you'll lose interest instantly; but, guided by subconscious civility, you'll ask who wrote the book, and she'll tell you, adding that it must be a pseudonym since no modern writer will have the courage to have such a ludicrous name."

I turned and looked at her; she wasn't listening, staring at the waves. But, as I watched the peach glimmer on her cheek, I grew aware of something that was going on parallel to our talk. It was a sensation of great urgency, and also that of removing the last piece that stood in the way of the crucial, so that nothing could interrupt its flow.

Suddenly I was ill at ease. The pause hung heavily on my ears, and desperation scratched its claws against my innocent soul. I thought of all the things I could be doing now, and none of them seemed even remotely comparable to the spellbinding beauty of walking with Martina. There we were, two people who lived and breathed magic, but never had I felt more acutely the invisible wall separating us. My thoughts, verbal and visual, ran with astronomical speed, yet their entire kaleidoscope fell short of the single plot unfolding with each step we took. I was suffocating, perceiving myself as a little boy playing with pebbles on the shore of the prehistoric ocean, knowing there'd be no other being to match him for the next seventy million years, and getting nothing but indifference in response to his accusatory cry.

"Why do I feel so lonely walking with you?" she said at last, turning to me. "Like you aren't there when you're silent, and even further away when you speak?"

I didn't reply, looking away. The claw turned into a scalpel, and its slow, lacerating slide brought cold shivers to my skin. Blood rushed to my head, and I felt exhausted like a wanderer who's gone ninety-nine percent of the way and is afraid that the rest won't make any difference. My thoughts became a mess and my feelings entangled into a knot as I groped for the missing key, grabbing nothing but dust and cobwebs from the corners of dead ends. But no matter how much suffering one has to endure in the synopsis, there is always but one way to finish a masterpiece right.

"If I'm wrong, then what is it that you like about acting?" I said firmly, ready to burn the last bridge. "You've always dreamt of being an actress, but why? You still can't answer that question, can you?"

"I know exactly why."

"I'm all ears," I said sincerely, but she didn't speak. "You're so accustomed to taking every whim of yours with such royal seriousness that you've never bothered to examine even your greatest passion! But what about the questions they ask in theater school? Would you still be an actress if you knew you'd never be famous? Would you still be an actress if you knew you'd never be rich?"

"Why?"

"Why are you not answering? Because if you can't, you've gotta be the kind of cunt who is after the admiration only."

"What did you just say?"

"Doesn't it puzzle you that you know so little about yourself? You spend your life concerning yourself only with yourself, and yet you still haven't arrived at an understanding of what you are because, every time you try to pin it down, the answer ends up being a petty attention whore."

She stared at me in silence: no smile, no scorn.

"How dare you insult me, you squirt?" she said quietly, a pale shadow crossing her face. She was so good that I couldn't figure out what her predominant emotion was: fury or fear. "You, a pitiful scribbler with delusions of grandeur? You have nothing valuable to offer, your castles are built of smoke, and your love is perverted beyond repair, yet you keep thinking that's everybody else's fault and that everybody around you must change to suit you, starting with the women you want to fuck!"

She stopped, looking at me scathingly; I shook, paralyzed by an epiphany of undetermined origins. She was expecting a riposte, but I had to regroup. It was around two in the afternoon on the north shore of the Bristol Channel, and we stood in the middle of a narrow country road, about half a mile from the lighthouse. No other person was visible either on the road or in the nearby fields which, kissed by the listless air, glowed with the brisk salad of a major golf tournament. The languid sun trundled slowly above the flaccid sea, and but a few feathery clouds disturbed the otherwise pristine azure sky.

"*Goddamn it*," I thought. "*Ever since you took off, you haven't paid attention to anything other than this woman. She addicted you again, without you even knowing: how insidious, and how like her. Like her? Love her!*"

And there it was, right where I'd thought it would be, before forgetting about it. On top of the stone wall separating one field from the next sat a raven of such blackness that in the sunlight he seemed to give forth a shade of red. He croaked once, and I began counting, muting the internal dialogue and probing the crown of my head for any promising sensations. The raven kept croaking, and on the twelfth caw he took off in a single powerful motion, heading due west along the whispering shore.

I waited for the beautiful bird to dissolve into the sky and turned to Martina. It was like diving into a pool of warm, soft, liquid, transparent amber honey. I tasted it gladly; it was sweeter than dreams.

"Did you hear what I just said?"

"Here it is. The right place," I whispered.

"Oh, really? And how did you know?"

"I didn't. You did. It was the first time that you said *fuck*."

Gift of Power

"Oh, ain't that one fucking great piece of news!"

"Forget all that," I said in an alien tone. "It's not important."

"Really? Cause it seemed to matter a hell of a lot just a moment ago."

"We didn't have cohesion then," I explained. "Now we do."

"Are you gonna give me what you have or not?"

"Yes. But I have to ask you something first. What do you think about when you hear the word *sorcery*?"

"Like I'm standing at the top of a pretty high cliff, wasting my time."

"False. You think of *Aladdin's* Jafar," I said calmly, letting my words sink into her. "You gave yourself away in a conversation I overheard," I went on. "It was about green tea with jasmine, and you alluded to the cartoon. You must have liked it because of the colors. Remember the rubies in the Cave of Wonders? They used to drive me mad as a kid."

"Three things," she said gruffly after a pause. "One: your memory is uncanny. Two: you are demented. Three: where is my gift?"

"In my pocket."

"Then why don't you give it to me?"

"Because that would be equivalent to stealing from you."

"Stealing?" she repeated in mock disbelief.

"Everything in this world has three layers," I said. "Two of them are the actual and the metaphorical. The actual is what things are, and it's sterile. Within it, a spade and digging a hole in the ground remain merely an object and an act. The metaphorical level is concerned with situational meanings. It is when you use a spade to dig a hole in the ground to hide treasure, having killed the pirate whom they'd belonged to with that very spade."

She was silent, waiting for me to be done.

"Care to know what the third level is?"

A few seconds passed; she could have been employing a theatrical technique, as she looked impermeable.

"All right, don't tell me I didn't ask," I said in a tone of utter resignation. "Here it is."

And then I produced the pass and handed it to her.

She snatched it from me like a hawk, but when she realized what it was, her movements slowed, as if her body was underwater. I saw her eyes dart across the slip, and every second made her more worried. Then she made up her mind, tilted her head, and pierced me with her stare.

"What is this?"

"The boarding pass you left on a plane three years ago," I reminded her. "In Rome."

"Rome?"

"A most remarkable city. We may go there one day, if I don't grow tired of you." I checked her out; she was uniformly stunning. "Which is unlikely, after all."

"How the hell did you get hold of this?"

"By reaching into the pocket of the seat in front of me."

"It doesn't make any sense," she shook her head violently. I was prepared to give her all the time she needed. "For you to have this ..." she looked at me as if uncertain of whether she should continue. "You had to ..." I was silent, waiting for her to do the math herself. "You had to have been in the same seat!"

"Incredible, isn't it? Of all the cities on Earth, of all the planes, and of all the seats, we had to end up in the same one, one after another." The nostalgia in my voice must have seemed out of place, but I wasn't feigning it. "What were you doing in Rome, by the way?"

"That's none of your business."

"Even after this?"

"After what?"

"After this little conundrum you're trying to brazen your way through."

"I see no conundrum here."

"That's what you're hoping to not see. But it's there. Because, against all odds, it had to be me."

She deliberated for a while, acting as if I weren't there.

"What am I supposed to do with it?" she said finally.

"Whatever you want. It's yours."

She wavered.

"I've already tried to get rid of it once."

"You didn't. You dismissed it as a trifle unworthy of your attention. But trifles can be transfer stations of power; this was a case of that."

"It's just a boarding pass."

"Are you playing the fool, or taking me for one? Of course not. You've always taken me for a maniac."

She let out a deep sigh, turning to the ocean. The tide was still low, the white wave crests crashing on the shore so far away it was hard to believe they would ever make it to these cliffs. But we both knew that within a few hours the ocean would be splashing less than ten yards underneath.

"This is sick," she said, looking me in the eyes again. "I feel like I'm about to throw up."

"Don't hold it in. Your energy body has just gotten a tremendous jolt; your whole system needs a reset."

"Look." She was struggling to speak. "Can you just leave me?"

"Of course," I said, not moving and thinking how hard it would be to carry her back to campus should she faint.

She paused for another minute, as if thinking about something totally unrelated.

"What do you want from me?" she demanded finally.

"A most trying question," I admitted. "Not because I can't answer it: I'm afraid you won't understand."

"You think you're a connoisseur of human nature?"

"Wanna test me?"

"Not at all."

"By the way." Inspiration exploded in my solar plexus. "What do you want? Let me rephrase that," I added a second later when the explosion ascended into my lungs. "What is it that you want the most?"

"It doesn't concern you in the least."

"Then it must be a platitude. But you really have no idea what you can achieve. That's a common human fallacy." I sighed. "And it's also what I want from you. To see it."

"Are you saying you know more about me than I know about myself?"

"Can you really not allow for that possibility? Why, you're only a model, a combination of the desires you seek to satisfy. Yours are insanely twisted, true, but not unique. What changes is the decor: people, places, parlance. But reality always takes place on the inside."

"Are you saying my life doesn't matter?"

"No more than that of any other human being. Which is why I want you to become ..." I checked her out again; I loved her still. "A goddess."

“You’re mad,” she said with joyful conviction.

“You only say that when you have nothing to say.”

“It’s a fact.”

“Like this one?” I pointed at the boarding pass she was still holding.

“Look,” she paused, expecting me to continue. “I agree it’s a strange coincidence. Yes, goddamn it,” she added resolutely, annoyed by my silence. “This is the strangest coincidence I’ve ever seen. But it’s still only a coincidence. Nothing more.” I remained silent. “You think there’s some meaning behind it, but only because that’s what you want to believe. You simply got caught in a loop, back then, twelve years ago, and still can’t jump off the track.”

“I didn’t make this choice,” I shrugged, vague thoughts stirring in my head. “Wait a minute. I know what your problem is. You think I love you like any other man would.”

Her face remained completely unchanged.

“I know; it’s the most reasonable assumption,” I nodded. “Besides, you’re used to men seeing you only as a cunt. I’m not impotent,” I added to save her from at least one barren idea. “It doesn’t matter what you ultimately want: the basic instinct is there. I, too, wanted a match: a woman I could treat as an equal. And what did I get instead?” I looked at her with suspicion. “Do you understand that your only real forte is how well you fuck?”

“One more word and I’ll hit you.”

I smiled.

“You know what makes us akin? Petulance. We both go crazy when things don’t go our way. The difference is: I recognize it as a flaw. Are you going to hit me or what?

She looked at me with hatred but didn’t move.

“Good girl. You’d have missed anyway.”

“Never hit a madman.”

“Are you back to having nothing to say?”

“You proved it. You said you didn’t make this choice. Who did, then?”

“The force whose tune we all dance to,” I replied meekly.

“The force whose tune we all dance to?” she repeated tauntingly. “And what would that be? Gravity?”

“I don’t really know,” I confessed, appreciating her irony. “Some call it Infinity. I do, too, but like I said: I don’t know. Maybe “chance” will work better?”

“Well, you’ve wasted yours,” she said with an intonation I hadn’t yet heard that night. “And I pity you. I always have. You walked this campus for two years, so scrawny and lonely, and every time I saw you I wanted to give you a handkerchief in case you started crying and had to wipe your nose on your sleeve. You’re an orphan, aren’t you? The boy who didn’t know where the campus post office was 'cause he never got a parcel. Your distorted sense of reality must have made you the target of every bully. I always knew you weren't sane, but …" she paused for a moment and then continued, to my amazement. "I guess I respected you, after all. You didn't have a chance in hell here. And you almost made it, but not quite." Her voice grew ever more melodious; she sounded like she was reciting a lullaby. "You should have lived only in the now, but perhaps the past was too grave. You may have had *idée fixes* before; then I became another one. I must remind you of someone who played an important role in your life; perhaps a nurse at the orphanage or a woman you saw momentarily in the street and got all worked up about. And then your mind deviated. You knew education was your only chance and spent all your time studying, but you went too far. An *idée fixe* is far more dangerous if it has an intellectual spin. And then this pass …" Her voice was filled with a hopelessness I never expected. "Perhaps it was the price of having been here. That was the worst part: getting a proof of his interpretation of reality is a curse for a paranoiac. I don't know if you have enough in you to overcome your condition," she concluded in her normal voice. "Personally, I don't think so. But what the hell do I know?"

It was my time to take a pause. It was deliberate and long.

"The handkerchief's tops, even if it's a lie," I finally exhaled. "What depth. Talk about master's at Oxford. It's funny: you do remind me of someone important, but you'd be really surprised if you knew who."

"I don't care."

"I know. It's because you think this is the end. That you'll leave this place, go back to your life and not see me again. At least not until the next reunion."

"That's the plan. The best I can do for you is recommend a specialist. I actually have one in mind: a friend of mine, an excellent …"

I was prepared to listen to her for as long as I had to, but, amazing me once again, she stopped right away, as if she'd remembered something, and gave me a puzzled look.

"Strange, isn't it?" I said, eyeing her and feeling my ethereal body thicken. "Like you know it's pointless to say anything. And what's that tickling in the pit of your stomach? Watch it closely: it's the deeper part of you getting hooked. Don't fight it: you're simply learning to appreciate what you truly are."

"What are you talking about?" she whispered, and for the first time in my life I heard fear in her voice.

"You're very brave," I said reassuringly. "You went to the cliffs with a man you consider a lunatic, and you've held yourself together. Today, curiosity brought you treasures. It was left up to you until the end. But this time, not even knowing it, I made the safest bet. You're not like me at all." I paused, smiling. "You snatch every one of your chances."

"Are you hypnotizing me?" She suddenly coughed.

"All this is out of my reach. But when I returned this to you," I pointed at the pass, "I did something on all three of the levels I mentioned. On the actual level, I gave you a piece of paper: that's where you tried to ground yourself with reason. On the metaphorical level, I proved that there was a connection between us. And on the supernatural level, I completed a cycle of power. When the pass reached your hands, my part was done. So now it's all up to only you."

"And … now what?"

"You will be introduced to the world of lucid dreaming." I hesitated for a moment. "I was not doing you justice when I said the only thing you're good at is sex. Because, my dear, on top of being a natural whore, you're also a natural dreamer."

She gave me a completely blank look, and I felt the acute nausea that was overtaking her as she said:

"A dreamer?"

"A dreamer is someone who uses dreams to travel to realities that are inaccessible to the physical body," I explained. "Real places where you live just as you do in the ordinary world. And die, too, if you aren't careful. And, if I understand anything about you at all, when it comes to dreaming, you're like a born tennis champion who's never held a racket in her hands. But now that she's grabbed it, she's going to hit a few balls."

"How do you know?" She looked better, but very pale in the face.

"It's in your eyes. The eyes are the dreamer's sword. A double-edged one, of course. Soon you'll know. By the way, have you ever dreamed about me?"

"Are you crazy?"

"Vivid images, breathtaking scenarios, occasional clarity," I nodded. "It's all useless. Those are mere dreams; they have no value. Dreaming is something else. By the way, have you ever dreamed about me?"

"Of course not!" she exclaimed, and then she realized. It was going have to be very close.

"Perfect! I was afraid you did. When that happens, remember that you're having a dream," I said, snapping my fingers in front of her nose.

"Dream on," she said with annoyance, slowly coming back to her senses. "Although, to be fair, you might be right, actually. I won't be surprised if after all this you do pop up in my dream. And I bet it's going to be a fucking nightmare."

"That wouldn't be a good sign," I said, somewhat deflated. "Better if we have a nonchalant exchange. But you have to know that you're asleep. Without control, dreams are useless."

"Control? Of dreams?"

"It means that you're aware that you're having a dream, and you don't let the dream change unless you change it deliberately."

"Impossible."

"It's not that hard, and for you it's peanuts. You have a gift some would die or kill for."

"I still don't see it. What's your final proof?"

"C'mon: you're nuts, yet you're successfully functional. A vital characteristic of a dreamer is controlled insanity, something you've practiced your whole life."

She looked at me as if considering punching me.

"I just paid you a compliment," I said, just in case. Why; you thought you're normal?"

She remained silent for a moment, and then she laughed.

"You're damn right, Courage! I gotta be crazy to have come here with you and listened to all this. But guess what: I'm leaving, and you're not following me. I want to be completely alone. Do you hear?"

I stared at her, and she didn't look away. A seagull's cry came from above and seemed to drown in the distant whisper of the rising waves. Tall, attractive, proud: she was a worthy challenge indeed; but I still didn't know whether I had to win, lose or immortalize her.

"You haven't decided about the pass," I said.

"I have." She tore it in half, dropping the pieces on the ground. "The cycle's complete."

"When the wind picks it up, it can fly anywhere."

"Whatever you want to do, do it yourself."

She turned around and began walking toward the castle, her gait utterly resolute. She thought she was leaving me behind like a captain marooning a mutinous sailor, and I thought only of how sharp her silhouette looked against the reddening sky. No other woman gave me the sense of being in a movie, and sometimes she made me forget everything and dissolve: into her and into the reality condensed by her presence to a liquid state.

1/2

As soon as she disappeared, I turned to what was left of the pass.

The pieces were lying just where she'd dropped them, but it took me an effort not to leap on them. Losing the halves now would have been unforgivable, and if they were blown off the cliffs I would have jumped after them without thinking.

My first impulse was to burn them, but now that they were in my hands, there was no point in hurrying. Unconcerned with the rest of the world, I sat on the ground and began the inspection. The rip followed the crease that had formed as I'd folded the pass to fit it into my pocket, but only for nine tenths of the way. At the border of the last tenth, it took a sharp turn, gliding almost perpendicular to the edge and forming what looked like a thin, long tongue on one of the halves and a mirror deficiency on the other.

I studied the tongued half first. With all the numbers, it was undoubtedly mine; it was also this part that my eyes had landed on when I'd snatched it on the plane. The other bore Martina's name. *Is it the end?* I thought, detaching my stare from the pieces yet failing to see anything but the unfolding of my own meditation. *It will be, if you burn them. Once and for all. Now, isn't that what you want?*

I automatically reached for the matches and counted them. One had lit my cigarette of nostalgia; three had gone to the fire; another one had honored Beatrice. I considered incinerating the rest at once, but it struck me as cheaply melodramatic; besides, burning both halves in one go was a move too rich in unnecessary connotations.

I covered my eyes and rewound what had just happened. Her departure felt belated. Or did it have to feel that way after it'd been so long? I didn't want to end everything this way, but she'd left me no choice. Or had she? I looked at the ocean. For the first time today, it had crept close enough to shore to make its movements noticeable even to a poor observer like me.

The simple solution that had formed in my mind called for destroying only one of the halves, but what would I do with the other? Returning it to Martina was out of the question, as was hanging onto it. No, the story had to end here, and the responsibility was, once again, all mine.

Okay, listen, I thought, watching a blissful cloud lose the shape of an old man's face. *It's still Saturday, and you have plenty of matches left. Start with your half, see how it goes, and then ...* The cloud turned into an elephant, its slim trunk pointing straight ahead. I nodded, not so much agreeing as acquiescing to the plan that was only a palliative.

I hid Martina's half in my pocket and lit one of the matches, the flame expanding with an aggressive hiss before dwindling to a docile blob. I tilted the match so that the blob had some wood to creep up onto and brought the tongue of my half towards it. The paper didn't want to catch, but little by little the yellow droplet became a healthy oblong and broke into several squiggly prongs, each shivering and enveloping the stub until it became but one disintegrating backdrop.

I waited as long as I could before letting go, and when it fell I folded my palms over it, greedily absorbing every calorie of the heat. The black symbols were quickly buried under the blacker wave, and soon the stub had turned into a torn and twisted phantom with no more power in it than there was in the dust on which it lay. I tried to assess my feelings, but they'd all been wiped out by the gust of wind that had stirred the ashes a moment ago and was still visible in the shaking of a distant tree. *Feelings—is that the crux of it?* I thought, staring at the hoary flakes dancing in the air with unsurpassable abandon. *Or is it still thoughts?*

The road back was fast, the other half of the pass scorching my haunch like fire; at some point it became so unbearable that I had to temporarily take it out. It was fine. I was crossing the cow field then, and suddenly the idea of walking through that Sunley corridor became anathema. Surrendering to the spur of the moment, I hopped over the fence as if it was topped with lilies instead of barbed wire and, the soles of my shoes sinking into the moist earth, made a wide semicircle around the dorm's west end, emerging in the backyard behind the house parent's quarters. I had no idea who held the post these days, but even if I'd been spotted, no one interfered with my convoluted route.

My room's window was open wide enough for me to fit through the gap without necessitating any acrobatic feats, and I would have laughed when I discovered the place empty yet again had I not been afraid to jinx it. Tiger's bed showed signs of someone's presence: I glanced at it out of the corner of my eye while pacing from his corner to the empty one: the stretch was the longest straight line in the room. Seventeen or so turns later, the burning in my rear subsided, but the dilemma remained.

I kept pacing. I've done it, right? I delivered, she did what she wanted, and now I had to let go. Completely, as if none of this had ever happened, except perhaps in a dream that grows more fragmented as you try to recall it. Besides, the celibacy wouldn't be over until tomorrow morning, and by then it would already be too late, unless I wanted to marry her. It's only 3.00 p.m. … "What the hell?" I whispered, staring at the clock; then it made sense. "Three o'clock. You can use this time, whatever you have before Vince comes back—or Tiger appears—to get some sleep. Now, the question is: what time will the sun rise tomorrow?"

"*You aren't actually thinking about it, are you?*" I thought, and, to my horror, it wasn't the voice of the devil's advocate.

"No, not actually."

"*Not actually?*"

"No."

"*But you are thinking about it?*"

"About staying behind?"

"*Yes.*"

"About staying behind and dropping acid?"

"*Yes.*"

"Hell yeah, I'm thinking about it."

"*About staying behind and dropping acid?*"

"Well, I do have a loose end here."

"*Like what, for example? Like, what would be an example of a loose end at this point?*"

"Like that one with Molly."

"*A loose end you have here with Molly?*"

"Yes."

"*Now that you've cut off the one that was twelve years long?*"

"You know what I'm talking about."

"*What are you talking about?*"

"That loose end …"

"*Which one?*"

"That loose end of never having fucked her?"

"*Oh,* that *loose end?*"

"Yeah, that one."

"*Of never have fucked?*"

"Not once."

"*Tough luck. But how about that time?*"

"What time?"

"*That time. That one and only time.*"

"Oh, you mean *that* time ..."

"*What else?*"

"Well, that time doesn't count."

"*No? Why?*"

"No. Because it was a dream."

"*Except it wasn't a dream.*"

"It wasn't real either."

"*Did it feel real to you?*"

"It sure did."

"*Then what the fuck are we talking about?*"

I stopped pacing and sat on my bed, staring out the window. My alter ego was right: I'd just completed a decade-long circle, and I was failing to be impeccable. In this game, love was not the goal but the fuel, and if I had to burn it all out, I might as well do it with dignity.

"OK," I said reluctantly. "Let's get something straight. Namely: that doing, or not doing this, is not a matter of acid."

"*Of course not.*"

"It's a matter of spirit."

"*What else?*"

"Because I have turned down acid before."

"*Remarkable.*"

"And women."

"*But never the spirit?*"

"Hell, no."

"*Few men can say that about themselves.*"

"I'm happy to be among them."

"*Even fewer with a straight face.*"

"So, I've made up my mind."

"*Care to speak?*"

I assumed a serious sitting position.

"This whole thing has been out of hand ever since it began, and there is no reason to believe that anything has changed. Which means that I have no idea what will happen when the acid arrives. For all I know, the spirits roaming this place may possess these folks, turning everyone into Beatrice."

"*That would be a sight.*"

"Except Molly would be there as well."

"*Leading the possessed.*"

"So, if I stay, I will necessarily have to take part in it."

"*Why, because you're the one who woke up the spirits with the jiggling of your balls?*"

"Will you shut up for a moment, you fucking bitch-ass hoe? I'm trying to have a civilized conversation here!"

"*I thought you're coming up with an excuse to stay.*"

"No, I can't. It would be improper; things can go wrong; innocent people may die for no reason."

"*Is that your final call?*"

It was not.

Long Gomukhasana

I approached the mirror and looked at myself. Then I emitted a violent cry and slapped my cheek. *Is that where you're really at?* I thought, shivering. It felt incredible, like I wasn't supposed to have gotten this far and survived. *How is this not a dream?* I did the hand routine, flicked the light switch, remembered how and where I'd last woken up. *And what happened next?* I winced at the idea of reconstructing my entire day, but there was a surer way to ascertain the truth. It would take ten minutes, but even if someone walked into the room and caught me red-handed, they'd dismiss it following a quick and plausible explanation. No need to initiate them into the intricacies of the Long Gomukhasana … unless they already know.

The Long Gomukhasana is a variation of a yoga pose for the Swadhisthana chakra. The Buddhist monk I learned it from prescribed eight alternations, four on each side, each thirty seconds in duration. He assured the effect would be obvious if I practiced the pose at least twice a day for at least half a year. The deal seemed fair, but I was impatient so, instead of thirty seconds, I stayed put for a whole minute, thus creating not only a workout for my ethereal body (controlled by the Swadhisthana chakra), but also an opportunity to test reality by both physical and digital means.

It's funny, I thought, folding the blanket and stretching it out on the floor from the window to the door. *You used to dread these ten minutes, and now you can't take enough delight in the fact that you won't have to make up your mind for at least that long. Why; are you* that *afraid to give in?*

There was nothing to prop up my cell phone with, so I used the shirt I'd worn the night before. I decided not to cheat by arranging my legs and arms in advance but didn't start the phone's stopwatch until I was ready. The pants were too tight across my inner thighs, but boy, did they feel smooth. I found the balance point instantly, stretched my back and checked the time. Seven seconds and change. I inhaled, simultaneously adjusting the feeling. It was at nine seconds when I allowed myself to begin.

If you are mathematically inclined, the crux of this should already be clear. To cram eight one-minute alternations into ten minutes, you have only two minutes for everything else—everything else being seven transitions and the initial setup. This means that those cannot take more than fifteen seconds on average. I wouldn't be surprised if some yoga adepts can make the transition in under three seconds, but I also knew that the transition was the only time to rest. And when your legs have been falling asleep for a minute, you want to transition slowly, choosing the new position carefully to minimize the next minute's discomfort. Even without indulging, an overly careful transition could take half a minute. But if patience is an asset for a warrior on the path of knowledge, discipline must be his weapon.

There it was, one-nine: transition time. The six seconds I had salvaged could be used at any point, but my plan was to keep adding to the surplus and have enough at the end to do it my way. I left the pose effortlessly, uncertain if I'd gotten anything useful out of the last minute. I did play it safe finding the balance, ending up in a suboptimal position to avoid wasting time, and, when I froze, it was already one-twenty-three.

That was slow. A fourteen-second transition is what I expect on a very tired and rainy morning when I woke up in the middle of a sleep cycle having had much fewer cycles than I'd have liked. Yet the position was not too bad. It may take some time to develop the feeling and improve hip and knee dexterity, but sooner or later you start to feel the right way. So, each time you need to return to that feeling, evaluate your success by scanning the area at the base of your stomach. It is where Swadhisthana is reached from, and it is also where it manifests itself the most obviously. I bet you already know what to do with it: internalize the feeling until it becomes as natural as feeling your hands.

Two-thirty-six, left leg, right elbow, thirteen seconds.

Feelings again … but a chakra is, in effect, a feeling. And if the feeling is strong enough, it becomes manageable and reliable; then it's only a matter of how you'll use it. Swadhisthana, for one, is not all about sex: the entire knowledge of the animal world is stored there as well. Imagine wearing on demand the character of a lion, a tiger, or a bear. Our universe is not so much complex as entangled: perhaps this is why we appeared in it in the first place? Or perhaps not in the first? I wonder what it feels like, to be the oldest civilization in the universe. Or is that civilization already extinct? Which does say something about the universe.

Three-forty-nine, right leg, left elbow, thirteen seconds again.

By the way: what I'm doing now isn't right: you shouldn't think about anything during Gomukhasana. During Gomukhasana, you ought to focus exclusively on your ethereal body. But if you're anything like me, you can snatch a sandwich from both tables, getting the physical boost while the higher emanations work on the problems occupying your mind. A lot of prestigious gurus would disavow this move and, frankly, I'd agree with the spirit of their disavowals … except none of those gurus had ever been cornered by Molly, and I'd very much like them to have been before taking their opinion for truth.

Five hundred, left leg, right elbow, eleven seconds.

This is what I was talking about: eleven seconds is a much brisker transition; too bad it hasn't changed a thing. Why did I burn the first half so hurriedly, so compulsively? Was it because I knew there was neither a way back, nor a way forward? Or did I believe it was over once the stub had been torn? No, I'd dragged the thing through so much doubt and sex that I'd sought a quick release; which, naturally, wasn't there. Yet, it had been on me when I woke up in the lagoon, and I still had no clue if I'd have been able to pull that stunt if it had not been …

Six-twelve, right leg, left elbow, twelve seconds, why was it slower?

I could keep going in circles, but Martina remained: in all her short-sighted folly. This never-have-fucked business is surely noble and nice, but if she chose to walk away from a story like this, there truly was nothing left to do. It is undeniably sad that the woman you loved for so many years turned you down at the final showdown, but you have your own agenda requiring, among other things, that you don't waste time. Besides, suppose you do stay and get her excited; then what? You can't back out of your celibacy vow, and at a reunion, sleeping with someone after dawn on Sunday makes sense only if you are going to propose to her right after.

Seven-twenty-four, left leg, right elbow, twelve seconds.

Why wouldn't you marry her, by the way? This beast of elegance, this siren of style? Is it because she's slept with dozens of men whom you wouldn't say "hello" to even knowing them: not out of spite, but because they were unworthy? But why do you not hold that against her otherwise? What is it that always made you forgive her? You say she's unique? Not in the sense you'd say that about anyone: no, talking about her, you imply the sublime. But what if you're wrong? Did you ever allow this possibility?

It was eight-twenty-four, and this was finally time to transition my way: slowly, deliberately, using as many of the saved seconds as needed to fold my legs and lock arms in a perfect balance where my Swadhisthana chakra was held like a bright orange flower in the careful palms of a devoted lover. I knew that shutting the internal monologue off was impossible but still tried, quitting only when I felt pain in my skull; but by that time, I already knew that I had to leave, leave immediately and definitely: leave this place, these people, and even Martina to whatever had to happen, because my part was done. I had come here to repay past debts, but I could also collect a bonus, concluding not only a twelve-year-old story of unrequited love, but also the obsession that had fed it all along.

I considered this realization as if holding it aloft with tweezers before a magnifying glass, marveling at its austere beauty. It was a consummate solution: all I had to do was to execute. But instead of the surge I normally got at the end of Gomukhasana, I felt hollowness, and when the glossy face of the cell phone showed 10:00, I rose up, fell onto my bed, buried my face in the pillow and mooed like a cow at a slaughterhouse: desperately, repeatedly, and through a stream of hot, suffocating tears.

I was shattered and torn, reality resembling the work of a lazy apprentice who'd slapped together some slabs without bothering to align the sides or clean the seams. It wouldn't have been so humiliating, but the apprentice was me: an alien soul in a typical universe that judged by the cover and killed on a whim. And yet, shining through the abysmal depth of my self-pity, there was reason to be content: the reason I clung to as the rest of me was sliding down.

It's easy to be God, to need no external element to attain completeness, but where's the honor in achieving optimal results by using optimal tools in optimal circumstances? Now, how about breaking into God's while being a man, an imperfection plagued by animalistic drives that keep him caged without his knowledge? Except, unlike the others, I knew. And when the best one decided against her lot, choosing instead to not matter, it was my solemn, though anguished, duty to let her have it the way she chose.

I got up in one motion, opened my valise and threw all my stuff in, saving the laptop for the end; it took me at least three minutes as I packed the shoes into separate bags. When I was done, I observed the room with the nicety of a surgeon about to begin an abstruse procedure that would either cure or kill. Then I extracted Martina's half of the stub and held it against a sunbeam; it rendered the paper near transparent, and yet it wouldn't ignite and burn. Cold on the inside, devoid of reason, I drew out the matches and tore one off. But just as I was about to strike it, I raised my eyes to the only door; there'd been no movement, nor sound, nor shadow; and yet there stood my Martina Flawd.

The Woman I Loved the Most

I could have sworn she hadn't been there a moment ago. But she was now: in a sleeveless red evening dress that covered almost none of her legs and only as much of her breasts to fit the last tier of judgement before it defaults to *lewd*.

It was Martina, and yet it wasn't. And yet it was, and the thought of it drove me nuts. What I felt toward her was so much stronger than love, or lust, or desire; it went beyond obsession, even monomania, attaining the level of pure chaos. A man dying of thirst in the middle of a desert does not crave water as much as I craved her. It was completely inhuman, and the only feeling I had besides that was fear.

It was not the kind of fear that stuns the heart during a horror movie as a ghoulish apparition coincides with a shrill in the background. No, the fear I felt of Martina was a fear I'd felt only once before—when, just before coming to AC, I dreamt of meeting the Devil itself. And yet, under the ice-cold terror pouring over my skin, I was burning, a streak of sweat slowly sliding down my right temple.

"You know," she said, closing her eyelids and beginning a series of slow steps toward me. "You may be thinking that I came here to have sex with you. Nothing can be further from the truth!" she exclaimed, her eyes piercing me like a lance. She paused and gave me a sly look. Then she puckered her lips, mocking disappointment. "I thought that would make you laugh. But you're positively no fun! How do I cheer you up?" Now she was near me, and I could feel the heat of her body as if it were real. "Are you not the kind of guy who can make a girl laugh?"

She laughed. That dulcet laughter was what a movie director would want for a fairy. But it only twisted my fear into another coil.

"I was thinking," she continued languidly, inflecting the penultimate syllable with that very anodyne haughtiness that made my ears ring, this time adding a winsome note to it. "My little boy has changed a little on the surface. But, deep down, he's his same old self. So, something must be missing from that puzzle he brought me."

I gulped, and my desiccated throat hurt as if it was being sandpapered.

"By the way," she continued, the tip of her tongue making two barely noticeable glides over her lips. "It was very kind of you. Bringing me the pass. Chivalrous. Knightly. You know ..." Her face assumed a perfectly reminiscent look no actress could have portrayed better. "The reason I never liked you was because you pretended like it was all about me. But let's master some courage, shall we, and admit one inconvenient truth." She paused, staring into me. "Everything you ever did was, in fact, for yourself."

Exactly the opposite, I thought, but my frozen lips couldn't part even to let me exhale, let alone speak.

She laughed—at me.

"Silly boy!" she said cheerfully, grabbing me by the cheek. "You think I can't read your mind?"

My reaction bordered on fainting. With all the tropes in my arsenal, I can't quite explain how afraid I became. *Mortally* is perhaps it, because there was no difference between this and any other touch I had ever received in the everyday world.

"Martina ..." I whispered, considering whether it would be proper to drown in the wave of beastly melancholy that engulfed me. And perhaps I would have died, had I not wished to prolong the torture.

"Keep talking. Why did you stop?" She said quietly in a raspy voice. "No? You're such a bastard," she continued, bringing her lips closer and stroking my neck under the chin. "Such a hopeless, absolute bastard. Show me your hands!"

"Take a look at yours," I parried, somehow.

A second passed. Then another. Then a third.

And then I saw she didn't know what I meant.

At first, I felt relief. Then disbelief. Then elation. Next, panic began to let go of my spinal cord, a tickling warmth spreading from each vertebra. She was looking at me inquisitively, unaware of my transformation, like a character in a dream would. Suddenly I became angry. I thought of the last few years of my life: struggle, study, discipline, practice, and only a smattering of results ... and all it had taken for her to arrive at the top was a single episode of profound stress. Except, superb as she was, I had to take care of her.

"Okay," I said, openly hiding the pass and the matches in my pocket. She didn't see it. It was going to be a difficult role, but at least my faculty of speech had been restored. "I'm a bastard. I'm not, but I wish you'd always thought so." I paused, scanning her from head to toe. "Are you sure everything's fine?"

"Why?" she demanded, astonishing me again: blissful, she had still sensed a shift. Now the question was whether she had enough cohesion to continue the ride after the revelation.

"Okay, we're gonna do this very, very carefully," I went on in a whisper, eyeing every cubic millimeter of her. "Not one false move may be allowed. It'll be like sex with a virgin princess, except a million times lighter; like dancing on rose petals, like listening to the stars. Let's start with the dayroom … Actually, let's not. Tell me: weren't you afraid to go to the cliffs with me?"

"I was, the entire time," she said sharply.

"Bogus," I said, smiling. "You had no weapon on you. Not even a scarf. So, you went, and then, on the cliffs, you ran away. But now you're in my room. So." I gave her a long look, feeling like I was drinking her beauty. "What happened?"

"I was afraid you'd misinterpret my being here," she sighed.

"There's no misinterpretation." I shook my head. "You came because you wanted to, because you always do only what you want."

"So, what's your explanation?" she said, charmingly and daringly.

"Simple. You couldn't have enough of the maniac."

She paused, then smiled.

"You're a cheater. And you have something that's mine. And I want it back."

"What will you do then? Say 'thank you', and leave?"

"I wasn't going to thank you."

"Stop taking yourself so seriously!" I cried, secretly wishing she'd gone for the *leave*. "Imagine what it would be like—to be utterly impersonal."

"I think I ought to have it," she said in the tone of a detective who is exposing a criminal.

"No, you don't think you ought to have it; you think you are obliged to. And, behind this illusion lies your self-importance." I sighed.

"And behind this masquerade lies yours," she said with an unrelenting stare. "You were hiding one thing from me when I came, and now you're hiding three. Is that what you call being utterly impersonal?"

That shook the rest of the fear off me. I smiled involuntarily. I just couldn't keep doing this to her anymore.

"You whore, you have no idea what's going on, do you?" I asked.

She stared at me, a silent question in her eyes. She was alert and, for once, attentive; but it didn't even occur to her to get insulted.

"By the way," I kept smiling, "isn't it tiresome to change clothes every hour? You must have come here with a large suitcase. Where did you leave it?"

She blinked a few times.

"And how was your flight, honey: not too long, I hope?" I continued as her forehead furrowed. "Mine flew by in no time at all, although I admit I didn't have to rush to the airport straight from the theater after a very …"

"Stop," she commanded. "What are you getting at?"

"Many things." I chuckled against my will. "The most important being that, what you're taking for yourself right now is not really you. Because right now, your so-called real you is lying in your NYC apartment, and when you wake up there, you'll vanish from here at once."

She laughed. I gave her time. She needed very little.

"So, you aren't real?" she asked then. "And none of this is? Will you kindly evaporate?"

"Not quite." I shook my head. "So far, every reality check I've run proves that this," I waved my hand around, "is ordinary reality. Which you infiltrated with your so-called dreaming body." An arctic chill ran down my spine as I spoke, comprehending the implications of this simple phrase. "Which is rather remarkable for someone with no proven track-record in sorcery."

I was prepared for a long barrage, for mistrust, arrogance, and the foolishness of a mortal who's trying to prove to God that He doesn't exist, but Martina had smothered them all by herself. She studied the room like a crime scene, nothing escaping her amber eyes that were now glowing brighter. But, as far as I could tell, she was merely curious.

"Don't try to do anything bizarre, like walking through the walls, or through me," I implored. "That may result in severe damage to the walls—or to me. I'm not afraid to die. Anymore. Anyway. But the two of us can do a lot more if we're both alive."

"I knew something was off," she said, feeling her dress. "None of these clothes are mine. And I'm not wearing panties either. What's the time?"

I thought of Vince's clock, but she was already looking at it.

"Five hours less," I reminded. "Do you often sleep that late?"

"I had a late night last night," she said distractedly, rubbing her hands together.

"What did you do?"

She vacillated.

"I ran away from the theater. I was so sick I couldn't remember where to go". Her voice sounded as if she were recalling a forgotten script. "Then I caught a cab and crossed the bridge. I stopped at the store and bought wine. Then I got home ..."

"What was the latest time you remember seeing on the clock?"

She closed her eyes. I thought that was the end and felt a sting of reproach for wasting her last seconds; otherwise I was calm, prepared to face the empty room with integrity and grace. But she looked at me again, and the bright amber in her eyes made mine water.

"Three forty-six," she said in a tone of adamant certitude.

"I was already awake," I said, calculating her sleep cycles. "Is this your first time?" She wasn't listening, touching the door and the walls. "Just don't look at yourself in the mirror," I warned. "You never know how that may go."

She turned around and stared back at me, an introspective look on her face.

"How did you know?"

"You took too many shortcuts. I should have figured it sooner. But you look exactly like yourself."

"You haven't seen me years."

"Well, I guess you look exactly like I expected you to."

"Great." She was displeased. "Will I do it again?"

"I don't know. This whole time was a brilliant fluke, and a brilliant illustration. Why do you not believe me when I tell you something about you!" I said bitterly.

"I needed a proof. But how do I go again? You need another boarding pass?"

"You're unlikely to repeat this without an emotional quake. Last night's fiasco, along with the regret of missing the party, dislodged your assemblage point. It's what arranges perception into a coherent flow." She knew. "But then again, calling from one end isn't enough: someone on the other end still has to pick up. Push and pull, ebb and flow ..."

"So, you're actually as sick as you appear? Or are you even sicker? Why are you doing all this? What for? What are you trying to get?" she fired, as if unsure whether I was hearing any of it, sparks of brilliance falling from her eyes.

"Whatever I ask for," I smiled. "I would tell you, but I'm afraid you'll never forget."

"So grave? You're definitely corrupted."

"Only by impossible influences."

"You have to tell me."

"No reason as such. Plus, the sentimentality."

"You're intolerable. But it doesn't make sense. Wasn't it all about me?"

"It's not about either of us. But to answer your question: by carrying it through. I took the pass as magic and didn't waver. The rest was up to imagination. Mine isn't modest."

"So. What did you gain?"

"Other than you standing before me in your morning glory?" I chuckled, scanning her waist. Her dreaming body was a superb replica of its physical counterpart: it transmitted all of the sexual appeal. It suddenly occurred to me that I had no idea what would happen if I had sex with her right then.

"Don't even think about it," she said, yanking me out of my thoughts as if by pouring ice-cold water down my spine. "You will drop dead."

"You really think so? Makes me more curious to try."

"You can barely look me in the eyes: you think you'll survive the shock? You must have been reckless recently."

"I was."

"How foolish of you. But when did you ever choose your women wisely?"

"I never made a mistake." I neared her. She was right: my skin was numb, and my forehead tickled; but boy, did I feel a flame inside! She stood still, as if daring me. "Not once."

"Let's not make this the first time," she replied, and I heard a brass note of medieval Catholicism. "I don't want your dead body here. Not because of the body, but because of the here. Besides, you haven't deserved it. I'm in my dreaming body, all right. Where's yours?"

The next movement was brisk: I encased her in my arms but felt only a body. Her body. The rest was like waking up from a nightmare: I expected anything but that.

"I never wanted to die in this place." I said in the tone of someone who'd gained his life back a moment ago. "I hate it too much. I'd love to do you, darling, but I can't: I'm a celibate until the sun rises tomorrow."

"Will you take your hands off me, then?"

"How does it feel?" Taking my hands off her was the last thing on my mind, so I slid one under her gown. "Real?"

"I'm not sure," she said, closing her eyes, relaxing and taking a deep breath. "But it feels great. I mean, I can feel everything you're doing."

“And how does it make you feel?”

“Like you’re gonna stop at some point to maintain your celibacy.”

“You sneering? You really think it was a bad idea?”

“It’s too old-schoolish. Pinch me right there. Again, and hard.”

“It works.” An image of Beatrice flashed before my eyes: she was fully dressed. “I’m not sure if you’d even be here if it wasn’t for that.”

“Oh, oh, so this is all your triumph? A little higher. Yes, yes. And I’m not even asking why you’d want to put a geas like that on yourself …”

“How do you know what a geas is?” I asked.

A moment of silence followed.

“Looks like I have to stop,” I whispered, continuing.

“I so don’t want you to,” she whispered, twitching lightly. “But I think that would be best.”

“The best would be not to lose control when you wake up.”

“How am I gonna explain this?” she said like a child, keeping her eyes closed and wrapping her arms around my neck.

“That’s the beauty: you don’t have to. Except to yourself.”

“Don’t try to fool me. You think I don’t know what’s going on?”

“I think you haven’t got the slightest clue. Which is amazing, because you are manipulating the thing masterfully.”

“I’m losing control,” she said, yawning. “And you’re wasting my time. Why wouldn’t you tell me? Because you’d rather not lie?”

I looked at her lovingly. She’d always suspected me of base motives when I had none. I still didn’t.

“At first, I thought it was some place you wanted to visit,” she continued, and I saw that she was truly fighting for herself. I almost expected her to turn into a hologram, yet my eyes wouldn’t register any change. “Something that meant more to you than anyone could imagine. But then you changed your mind.” She opened her eyes abruptly: they weren’t human anymore. “You think you’re gonna win? I mean, everything?”

“It’s up for grabs, just like anything else. How did you know about the place?”

She shivered, and I let her go. She took a step away and stared at me blankly. Then a shadow of remorse crossed her face.

“Sometimes I know things I know I shouldn’t know,” she said. “It scares me.”

“Knowledge about all you need is permanently stored within you; you access it little by little. But why the scare? It’s pure gold.”

“It makes me doubt what I am.”

“It’s about time. You can’t spend your whole life without questioning it, otherwise it’d be a waste of a life. You’ve kept yours unquestioned for too long.”

"And how do you know?"

"Because you haven't made it to the club yet: no yacht, no Oscar; not even a man. See, if you choose to play by the rules of society, nothing else matters. It's whatever it says, whenever it says, and whoever it says. And if it says that bananas are swell at midnight you must agree, or you'll be eaten alive by the laws of a vibrant democracy."

"Do you think I agree?"

"I know that you don't, at least some of the time. But when that happens, you get hurt. Which is a reason to ask yourself why: you should be able to dodge little fractures. But the clock is ticking, and time won't wait. If you're serious about achieving something non-trivial, a breakthrough must happen soon. Sure, you can be a director at any age, but getting the first lead role as a forty-year-old actress seems like charity anyway."

"This was my first lead role," she said sadly. "See what happened?"

"You'll get another. It's okay to flub the first try if you don't do the same on the second and it doesn't take too long between the two. But to get it right that second time, you have to learn every lesson from the first."

"How do you learn from a fiasco?"

"You break it down, study the parts that went wrong, and make sure you don't include them again."

"Speaking of parts." Even with her eyes being two sources of light, I still read reproach on her face. "Are you going to give me mine?"

"So, you knew all along?" I smiled, taking her half from the pocket and handing it to her.

"No. But I kept an eye on you." She said, accepting it. "What was that flower pose you were sitting in?"

"It's supposed to look like a cow's head." I wasn't surprised anymore. "It's called Gomukhasana."

"Go where?" She glanced at the pass. "I need a pen."

"*Go* means cow. *Muk* is head. *Hasana* is position," I said with a smile that I hoped she'd take for mischievous. "Will a pencil do?"

"Yes," she said, and I produced one from my valise. She took it, scribbled something on the pass and put it on my chest of drawers along with the pencil. "Hey Daniel." She smiled, looking terrifying yet beautiful. "Can you do something for me?"

"Like what?"

"Call me when you get back to New York?"

"Why?" I blinked, knowing she was seeing me through.

"How else would I know that this wasn't a dream?"

A pink halo began shimmering around her, filling me with a profound calm that reduced all my desires to mere apparitions that could either stay or go without making a difference. It lasted for a few moments, Martina's shining not letting my eyes go, until I regarded her not as the most precious sliver of the universe but as a part of myself. And then I remembered.

"Remember this date," I said, inhaling deeply through my nose and prepared to die, or live, or neither.

"Why?" I heard as if I were waking up.

"You may have to reference it in the future." Her eyes became nothing, and I smiled. "*It's time, my duchess: go, have your fun. And, by the way: have a happy birthday.*"

A sudden dry draft rushed in, fatiguing me. I blinked for what seemed a tenth of a second, but when I looked again, Martina was gone.

I waited for a while to make sure.

When I was certain, I looked at my hands.

Then I rubbed them against each other.

They were immutably mine.

My legs soft as cotton, I approached the chest of drawers, which loomed like a sleeping predator. Martina's half of the pass lay where she'd left it, and I trembled as I took it, unsure of what I feared more: that there'd be something written on it, or that there wouldn't be. It was just as I'd remembered, her name printed in bluish blackness; but now next to it there was also a string of digits written by hand.

I looked at the number for less than a moment, and, sooner than I took my eyes off it, I knew it was enough. I'd never seen it before, but it was hewn on the insides of my eyelids and glared distinctly whenever they shut.

Then I knew what I had to do. I pierced the pass on the pencil like a piece of barbecue meat; then I found the match I'd torn off and struck it. I burned the pass to ashes, and when the last of the flames had turned into smoke, the fire alarm above my head went off, screaming as unbearably as it always had. There was an immediate ruckus in the corridor, shouts of vexation, a nervous racket, and several doors slamming in their frames.

With the flakes of ash still clinging to the pencil, I approached the window and shook them off. Then I hid the pencil in my pocket, my head exploding from the sound of the alarm, carried the valise over the sill and followed it, instantly feeling better. Then I walked away across the empty backyard, the wheels of the valise sinking into the grass but moving nevertheless.

Memories of the details that had seemed insignificant were already coming at me.

I chuckled, thinking of everything that might or might not happen now.

Should I honor her request, or should I leave her stranded?

It was going to be one hell of a tough call.

June 2010–June 2nd, 2018